This is a work of fiction. Any references to historical events, real people, or real places are used fictitiously. Other names, places, and events are products of the author's imagination, and any resemblance to actual events or places or persons, are not to be construed as real. Any resemblance to actual persons, living or dead, is entirely coincidental.

MAIDEN'S GRAVE. Copyright © 2020 by Kevan T. Hunt.

FIRST EDITION 2020 published by Local Pocket Guides, Inc.

Printed in the United States of America

Cover designed by Brittany Williams

For author and ordering information visit
www.kevanthuntnovels.com and www.localpocketguides.com.

ISBN: 978-1-886403-64-2

Acknowledgments

There are few more beautiful or inspirational locations on the planet than the California foothills and the high country of the Sierra Nevada Mountains. I will be forever grateful for the opportunity to live, work and write in one of the most scenic, natural, and peaceful settings anywhere.

My deepest thanks to my critical readers Tory Spence, Marv Hampton, Anne Platt, Terri Lobdell, Lisa Hunt, Kate Dowden, and Meredith Davies Hadaway, all of whom gave me valuable help, feedback, support, and encouragement along the way. My thanks to Thomas Cahill, Hollis Hunt, and Alden Spence for technical and creative support. I am especially grateful to my husband Michael who always seems to find a way to make dreams come true.

This book is dedicated to the memory of my mother.

MAIDEN'S GRAVE

By

Kevan T. Hunt

Darkness is the great canvas against which
beauty becomes visible.

John O'Donohue

Prologue

Selena sat on a small camp chair pulled up to a plastic foldable picnic table. A scattering of young Hispanic kids and dreadlocked vagrant hippies hunched over bunches of branches cutting small leaves with tiny, sharp scissors. Selena's best friend Alex had talked her into trimming to make some extra money. It wasn't going well. Day after day for hours at a stretch, Selena's back ached and her hands burned from the open blisters on her fingers. There were only a few weeks in October to mid-November when the work would be there, Alex had told her. But it was hard, meticulous work using tiny scissors to cut the leaves, exposing the flowering bud and crystals. Her fingers turned black and sticky, and the tips cracked from constant cleaning with rubbing alcohol. Whenever she was finished and had filled a plastic bag of green, fulsome and spicy smelling buds, Selena would reach for the drying rack where bunches of plants had been hung upside down for curing and grab another bunch to start trimming again. There were few breaks. There was no real toilet, only a trench dug in the woods from which a nasty smelling brew of urine and feces swilled and made Selena gag every time she had to visit the area to squat and do her business. Empty bottles of chemicals and trash were strewn around several rusting trailers. At night, she and the other workers collapsed in sleeping bags on the floor and bunks of fusty trailers until dawn roused them from fitful sleep to start all over again. Never again, Selena promised herself. She hadn't showered in days. A few hundred bucks could not possibly entice her to continue. She would have run away except she was slated to do this for at least a week during early October, and Otis Seaver loomed large and imposing in his blue work shirt and cowboy boots, rodeo buckle gleaming in the lamplight, holstered pistol at his side. Alex sensed her thoughts and desire to escape.

"He'll shoot you as soon as look at you and bury your body in the woods. Don't fuck with him, Selena. We'll be done in a week, and once he pays you, you never have to see that cocksucker ever again."

She had nodded understanding, too exhausted to argue. The other workers talked of going north and trimming for other growers, with Oregon and Washington being the holy grail for trimmers. They said they could make thousands of dollars in a season and then head off to Tahiti or Thailand or the Yucatan and spend the winter surfing. But this backwoods redneck grower was mean and cheap. Just a brief waystation along the secondary roads north. No one planned to stick around for long. It had gotten frosty at night, and Selena's hands felt stiff and her fingers cramped up with the cold.

"Fuck, Alex. I can't move my damned fingers."

"I'll get him to plug in the heater later," Alex whispered in return, their voices muffled by the hum of the generator right outside their tent. "He's okay once you get to know him."

Otis hefted his bulk around the tables to glower at his workers so that they didn't accidentally slip some buds in their jackets. She had been watching him for a few days. The night before, after the others had headed off to their trailers to eat gas station fried chicken, she had followed quietly in the dark as he climbed into his larger, more comfortable and well-appointed double-wide and opened a cabinet in which there was a locked metal box. He had pulled keys out of his jacket pocket opening the box, then quickly stuffed what looked like wads of cash inside then shut and lock the box. That's where you keep the cash, you fat bastard, she thought to herself. The keys went back into Otis Seaver's sagging jacket pocket. He moved away from the cabinet and hung the jacket up on a peg by the trailer door. Selena watched and waited. You never knew when a chance might present itself that might change your whole world.

2

1.

Sidney's running shoes pounded the crumbling asphalt road winding through green foothills dotted with grazing black cattle. Behind barbed wire strands, the spring calves scampered as she ran by, David Bowie's "Rebel, Rebel" thumping through her earbuds. She kept a close eye on the uneven stone walls lining the road. Jack had warned her to beware of baby rattlers emerging from the stacked rocks to bask on the warm tar. After a three-mile loop, a quick shower at the gym and a drive-through stop for a latte, she headed into town for breakfast. There were few breakfast places in the old Gold Rush town of Jackson, California, fifty miles east of Sacramento, population 4,200, and Rosie's was where everyone gathered for coffee and gossip.

"Our coffee not good enough for 'ya?" Hello, My Name Is Anne, demanded bluntly, her heavily mascaraed gaze resting on the tall Starbuck's latte container next to Sidney's water glass. Sidney's usual waitress prominently displayed her name tag over a huge breast taut with red polyester and she now planted herself next to Sidney's table, right hand on her ample waist, left hand hovering with a pot of steaming Farmer's coffee. Sidney had learned many weeks before that a lone young female was an oddity in a country coffee shop, where the waitresses' good-humored bantering was reserved for male customers of any age and variety: singles, pairs, or in groups. She turned heads just walking in, feeling out of place and conspicuous. Sidney stared at the offending Starbuck's container.

"When you serve better coffee, I'll be happy to drink it," she responded flatly and just as directly. Anne shrugged and wheeled around, apron flowing.

"You'll want yer usual, I guess," she shot back, not waiting for a response. That was progress, Sidney thought, I've been acknowledged. Granted, she had never yet varied from her order of hot oatmeal, brown sugar, raisins, nonfat milk, and wheat toast without butter. Since nothing she ate was slathered in grease, her usual must be pretty unusual for Rosie's Country Café. Sidney turned to reading the local newspaper quietly, hoping the county's daily gazette would reveal something enlightening about the local happenings, but so far, stories of highway accidents, bake sales, spaghetti dinners, and the performance of the high school's basketball team hadn't been particularly illuminating. When her breakfast arrived, she looked up briefly and made a point of thanking Anne, who nodded unsmilingly. Behind Anne's shoulder, Sidney spotted her boss walking towards her, his thick, muscular torso weaving through the crowded tables, stopping here and there to slap shoulders and beam his irrepressible bonhomie as he flashed a big grin, lighting up the room.

Sidney reflected on how handsome Jack McGlynn was even in his late sixties. His year-around tan glowed with his love of all things outdoors and his passion for hiking the Sierras, the deeper into the wilderness the better. Her godfather made his way through the morning breakfast crowd of farmers, local businessmen, retirees, and ranchers. Sidney admired Jack's skill with people, a talent that she regretted not having. It was that gift that had brought him as a young district attorney to the State Assembly in Sacramento, from which he had launched his national political career, serving eight terms in Congress, until new district lines had been drawn, essentially leaving him without a viable base from which to run. Jack blamed the Tea Party Republicans who had done him in for his more moderate views, especially his support for strong environmental legislation that many in his party opposed as being anti-business. He was a maverick that people loved, but the party leaders feared because his positions couldn't be either predicted or controlled.

Halfway to Sidney's table, Jack stood with his leather collar still upturned against the early morning chill, his attention entirely focused on the elderly couple who had interrupted their meal to command his views on some issue of importance to them. The large, bespectacled lady had a hold of Jack's leather jacket at the sleeve, but Sidney noted that Jack never once looked anxious to make his escape. His early-morning wake-up call had announced that he was driving to Jackson to meet with her on a pressing client matter, but at the moment he gave no sign that he had anything more important to do than to listen to his former constituents and assure them of his continuing interest in their affairs. Once he broke free, Jack slid opposite her in the small booth and waved down her waitress. Sidney couldn't help but be irritated by Anne's sudden change in attitude in seeing Jack. The surliness disappeared, the penciled eyebrows arched even higher, and her heavily rouged cheeks lifted when parted by her broadly smiling lips. Without glancing once at Sidney, Anne took Jack's order as if scrambled easy were the most thrilling words she had ever heard.

"Right away, Jack," she trilled, as Jack turned his attention to Sidney, unaware of his effect on their waitress.

"Funny. She had a personality transplant the minute you walked in the door," Sidney said.

"Now, Sidney, you know how people are. Just give 'em a little bit of the right attention and even the meanest old barncat'll be licking cream out of the palm of your hand."

"Your hand, maybe. And you sound like a total hick, Uncle Jack."

"I am a hick, nowadays. Proud to be. You've got the right stuff, Sid. You'll decide when you want to use it." Jack smiled up at Anne the moment she put down a cup of steaming, if inferior coffee right in front of him, shooting Sidney a challenging look. Watching Jack shovel his eggs, bacon and home fries with obvious relish, Sidney's irritation was suddenly overcome with the warmth that she felt for her godfather. By some rare stroke of discernment, her parents had honored Jack McGlynn at her christening, and it was a responsibility that Jack had assumed during Sidney's entire life. If it were not for Jack, Sidney doubted that anyone would have employed her, especially after her father's very public fall from grace.

"I got a call late last night from an old friend and client," Jack began, stirring two heaping teaspoons of sugar into his coffee, and pouring in enough cream to raise the entire level of liquid to the very brim.

"Maudey Hill has been a client of mine since just after I graduated law school. Of course, she was my father's client first and then mine when Dad passed away."

Sidney knew the story. Old Joe McGlynn, as he was called, was a county district attorney, then a well-known local lawyer, until a fatal heart attack at a relatively young age pried his son Jack away from his promising career as a young associate at Thayer, Snow and Marcus, one of the most prestigious firms in San Francisco, forcing him back to the hills of Jackson to take over his father's local practice. At the time, Jack keenly resented this intrusion, but stayed on, long after he finished winding up Old Joe's affairs. At first, he had assumed that small-town law practice would be temporary. For at least a year, he had longed for his 28th story view of the Bay Bridge and the elegance of his firm's walnut-paneled lobby, the weightiness of big-time litigation, the multiple millions of dollars at stake, and the calls from important corporate general counsel asking him for advice. For a while, he couldn't wait to get out of Jackson and get back to circles of power and influence in San Francisco. But something happened to him during that small-town year. He started to enjoy being recognized as Old Joe's son, having people stop him in the street, engage him in conversation and care what he had to say. He was invited to local Rotary and Chamber meetings; small farmers and business owners called for advice, and pretty soon, he had a thriving practice. More importantly, he was happy. In San Francisco, even brilliant young associates were fungible commodities in a world where corporations and their executives didn't care about their outside counsel other than to judge their win-loss records and blame everything on the lawyers when things didn't go their way. Sidney had learned all about that the hard way. Jack had felt respected in Jackson, and people came to him because they actually liked and trusted him. His wife had not felt the same way. She had taken their two small children back to her family in San Diego's ritzy La Jolla enclave and waited for Jack to come to his senses. He never did. After a few years, influential friends of Old Joe got together and decided that Jack should run for State Assembly. Jack won on the Republican ticket, replacing the representative whose term limits had expired. One of those friends backing Jack had been Hans Hill, the grandson of the founder of the Hill Ranch, and founder of Quarry Hill Vineyard. Jack's years of legal work for the ranch and the winery had not made Jack rich, but it had made him very comfortable. It was Hans Hill's widow, Maude, who had called Jack at home late the previous night.

"She asked for you," Jack said, frowning at Sidney in mock disapproval. "After thirty years, I guess she wants a sweet young face around and not this old codger. Guess I'm too old and grizzled now for Maudey."

Sidney felt that beneath Jack's bluster, he really was pleased. She remembered when Jack had brought her to see the winery and meet Mrs. Hill the previous fall, before she had left San Francisco, when the vineyard leaves were turning russet brown and the warm, golden hills surrounding the winery waited for the autumn rains to end the long summer drought. Sidney had found Mrs. Hill to be direct and charming, with a youthful sweetness that seemed somehow incompatible with her piercing appraisal of her.

"You're Adam Dietrich's daughter," she had remarked suddenly during lunch out on the wisteria covered flagstone patio. "I'm sorry about your father."

Sidney had been taken aback by the sudden mention of her father, whose very public arrest for fraud; his subsequent trial and ten-year prison sentence had crushed the life out of them both. She sat mutely, her senses aware of the gentle warmth of the autumn sun, the leaves of giant oaks rustling in the slight breeze, and the silence at the linen-covered patio table.

"You're a brave girl," Mrs. Hill whispered, laying a light, cool hand on Sidney's own, as if words alone could not express fully the depth of her sympathy. Her touch jolted Sidney to life and she looked down at the thin, sun-mottled skin, strong, work-worn fingers, and ropey veins that enveloped her own hand in an intimate clasp. Mrs. Hill withdrew after a quick squeeze and changed the subject as quickly as she had raised it. Sidney was so accustomed to her own stoicism that any demonstration of tenderness could undo her completely, and she blinked back tears. At the time, Sidney might have concluded that her effect on Mrs. Hill had been minimal, except for the mention of her father. Now, she was quite curious as to why, many months later, Mrs. Hill might ask for her help.

As if reading Sidney's mind, Jack said, "I really don't know any more than what I just told you. She's mighty cagey with me all of a sudden. Maybe she wants to talk to a woman." Jack shrugged at the incomprehensibility of his elderly client.

"When does she want to see me?" Sidney asked, ignoring the comment.

"Just as soon as breakfast is over. It's about a half-hour to the ranch, I mean, the winery."

"I remember how to get there." She didn't want him thinking that she would get lost searching for the place.

"Good. Now just keep me company while I sweet-talk Anne here into giving me some ham with these home fries. Just exactly what my doctor didn't order."

Jack waved his hand and looked around to catch the waitress's eye. By all accounts, Jack should have died after his massive heart attack five years before, but there was something too strong-willed and irrepressible about Jack McGlynn. Weak heart or not, he had an iron constitution, and still thought of himself as the twenty-two-year-old Marine who could backpack twenty miles a day carrying seventy-five pounds on his shoulders. Sidney had no doubt that he could still do it in a pinch, heart attack or no heart attack. After Jack had tucked into his ham and eggs, home fries and coffee, he dropped a twenty-dollar bill on the table and said a quick goodbye to Sidney. She knew it would take him another fifteen minutes of glad-handing to get out the door, and she was eager to be off. This was the first of Jack's clients who had specifically asked for her, and she didn't want to keep Mrs. Hill waiting any longer. As she exited the crowded coffee shop, she was aware of eyes shifting to stare. Her lithe, athletic, figure and glossy chestnut hair would have attracted hardly a glance in San Francisco, where there was a surplus of young women who looked much like her. Here, she was an oddity and felt out of place wherever she was.

With a wave from the cafe door that Jack barely perceived, Sidney clomped down the uneven sidewalks that lined the old gold-mining town's streets and jumped into her Subaru Outback. She had plenty of lined legal tablets and pens stuffed in her satchel in case her iPad didn't work at the vineyard, and so armed, she drove from the picturesque country stores of Jackson's typically named Main Street and headed southwest on Highway 88. Just past town, she slowed down for the orange and white road kill truck that had stopped to pick up a deer carcass. From the gory mess smeared all over the road, she wondered whether a fast-moving automobile had even bothered to slow down. A dark-haired teenager, most likely just out of high school, was dragging the carcass by the leg toward the back of the truck, where the remains of other roadkill were piled high, enveloped in sheets of black gardening plastic. That's another thing I'll never get used to out here she thought grimly, swerving around him to get by.

2.

Ten-year-old Matt Dunleavy dragged a heavy shovel in one hand, bending over to pick up stray pieces of logging detritus with throbbing fingers raw and stinging from the cold. Cut cables, frayed and rusting at the ends, littered the woods. He struggled to pick up the cables, not so much because they were heavy, but because they were unwieldy and stiff, clinging to whatever brush or rocks they wound themselves around. They snagged his jacket and jeans as he pulled to unwind them and haul them away from the clearing. He stepped gingerly in his father's muddied footsteps behind the logging truck belching thick diesel fumes, his father's stride stretching Matt's much shorter legs awkwardly. His father called to him, and Matt dropped the cable and walked toward him.

"It's an old mine," his father whispered and pointed with evident glee to what looked like a badger's hole in the hillside, partly obscured with dead oak leaves and a twisting branch of madrone growing straight out of the side of the mountain.

"Take a look," his father said. Matt walked toward the hole and froze, the unmistakable warnings of a dozen rattlesnakes piercing his ears. He looked around wildly, suddenly ringed by rattlesnakes slithering from the oak leaves, coiling up and waiting to strike, their black eyes glittering and hard. Warning rattles grew louder as their heads swayed towards him, fangs bared. He jerked away, trying to run, but he couldn't. His father's laughter stung him like a whip.

The dream went dark as Matt woke up to the jarring noise of his phone jangling repeatedly from the downstairs kitchen wall. Groggy and irritated, he stumbled out of bed and clambered heavily downstairs in the dark to pick up the receiver. The same terrifying dream had repeated itself countless times when he was an Amador County Sheriff. First the rattlesnakes: a memory that had haunted him since childhood, when frozen with fear he had been surrounded by them, having disturbed their winter nest near the mouth of an old gold mine. Then the sting of his father's betrayal in leading him there. He thought the dream would go away, once he resigned his job. The nightmare persisted. Each time, he struggled to awaken even as darkness weighed him down.

"Matt!" He heard Bud O'Connell's deep voice straining over the maddening crackling of Bud's poor cell phone transmission. Matt refused to own a cell phone anymore. They were damned worthless in the mountains. No coverage. Now that he was no longer Sheriff, he didn't want one going off and scaring the bejesus out of him when he was just trying to get a cup of coffee at Rosie's, or out riding Sage, or doing any of the other things he wanted to do in peace and quiet. Cell phones were for the frantic, rushed pace of the Bay Area. He'd had enough of that to last a lifetime.

"Matt!" He was fully awake now, recognizing Bud's deep bark piercing his nighttime confusion.

"Can you hear me?"

"Yeah, Bud. What is it?"

"We're mounting up, meeting at the meadow in front of the Rangers' station in an hour. We've got a missing teenage girl. Her car was found in that ditch by the side of the road near Misery Creek. You know that bend where Bob Murphy's always sliding into a hole whenever we get a freezing rain."

"Who's the girl?" Matt asked, fully alert. He knew just about everyone in Amador County, population just over 35,000, and it was likely that he'd know someone local who might be missing.

"A Mexican girl from that vineyard south of Jackson. The old Hill Ranch. I've got a picture from the family."

Matt knew the place all too well. The Hill ranch had been transformed practically overnight from a sprawling cattle ranch into Quarry Hill Winery, another one of the boutique Sierra Foothill wineries that dotted Amador County's premier wine country. The Shenandoah Valley, near the tiny old mining town of Plymouth, was just beginning to win gold medals for its rich, fruity old vine Zinfandel and deeply complex Barbera. If they weren't careful, Matt thought, the country feel of family-owned wineries operated from old stone mining shacks and ranch houses would evolve into the Napa Valley, a magnet for mobs of urban tourists, where the countryside had largely disappeared, covered by strip malls, motels and huge, modern factory wineries owned by international liquor conglomerates and celebrity dilettantes.

As an Amador County native, Matt was used to visiting hundred-year-old cellars that might have been transported stone by stone from crumbling Tuscan farms. The original Italian settlers in Amador had planted vines right after the Gold Rush and had produced small quantities of hearty reds for generations. Just within the last couple of decades, visitors who were looking for a more authentic and rustic experience than Napa had discovered full-bodied reds that the golden Sierra Foothills produced. Matt recalled Quarry Hill's own colorful but tasteful label, with a painting of the original stone mansion back when Henry Hill's grandfather had become wealthy on Sierra silver, gold, and timber. Matt shook his head. He couldn't place any Mexicans who might work at the vineyard. Most of them came and went seasonally, delivered by trucks from Central Valley farms as far away as Fresno to work for a few days or a few weeks, only to move on to another crop's planting or harvesting season. Matt reflected that it had been a very long time since he had stopped by the winery. Not since he and Sarah had split.

"I'll see 'ya at the Ranger Station," Bud signed off without waiting for any confirmation. Matt hung up the receiver, fully awake now, the early morning call filling him with a familiar bitterness of something gone wrong with someone at fault. His anger had poisoned work in law enforcement for him. The senselessness and stupidity of criminal behavior had left him permanently disgusted with most of humanity. He breathed in, reminding himself he wasn't Sheriff anymore, and that this was just a routine search and rescue, or so he hoped.

It was still dark out, but the moon was full, lighting his path to the barn. In early April the contradictory threat of either another snowfall or a premature heat wave changed daily and kept everyone guessing. Snow had fallen in the high country during a late winter storm just the previous week. If it all melted off in the warmth of the day, valuable evidence might be destroyed. Before the light of dawn this morning, Matt would have guessed another snowfall, the way the air was so cold and still with the heaviness of an impending front moving southeast over the Sierras toward them through the Carson's Pass.

Sage hung his head out of the stall window, his ears twitching, curious as to why Matt was here to see him so early. His white blaze caught the moonlight and looked as if someone had streaked his face crookedly with a whitewashed paintbrush from the middle of his ears to his nose. Matt ran his hand gently over Sage's head and neck, hoping that he would stay calm for the work ahead.

"Easy, boy," he crooned. "It's just me." He went past Sage's window and around to the front through the doorway of the barn, clicking on the light and opening the tack room door. Matt pulled Sage's blanket, bridle, and saddle from the pegs off the wall and draped them over his arms. He strode heavily down the concrete aisle, boot nails scraping rhythmically, until he reached the stall.

Matt rode Sage to the Ranger's Station as light started to brush the foothills from the eastern valleys, quietly winding its way through the thick pine forests. He shone a flashlight just ahead, so they could see their way through manzanita-choked deer trails. After about an hour, they finally cut through to the paved streets of a small one-acre lot subdivision that fronted Highway 88 and emerged in the glare of the rising sun breaking over the crest of the eastern mountains. Once he reached the road to the Ranger's Station, Matt could tell that he was one of the last to arrive. Horse trailers and pick-up trucks lined the narrow drive, and a small posse of Sheriffs' patrol cars pointed nose first at the side of the road, illuminating the ditch with their headlights. That must be where the girl's car is, Matt reflected and reined Sage well away from the scene to keep him steady. He could see an early model two-door, well-used red Honda

Accord resting in the culvert as if it were hiding from the big cars passing behind it on the highway. As the official Mounted Search and Rescue liaison with the Sheriff's Department, Bud O'Connell was reviewing the scene on the road, getting a lengthy briefing from Sheriff Dom Colangelo. Matt noted as he passed behind Colangelo that more of Dom's waist was hanging over his belt buckle every year. Instead of reining Sage in to address either Bud or Colangelo, Matt looked around for the mounted patrol, the volunteer rescue team that was the closest thing Matt had left to family. He had known Bud and many of the rest of them since Kindergarten at Buckhorn Elementary and had ridden in the mounted patrol since he was a young teenager. He spotted them encircled together, idling with their horses, waiting for instructions. Matt wedged Sage into the circle and dismounted, rubbing his leather gloves together and tipping the brim of his Stetson up off his forehead. The grouped horses' breath chuffed like steam in the thick air around them, creating the illusion of warmth in the bitter cold. The sun hadn't warmed the frosty pines yet, and most of the men wore thickly lined Carhartt canvas jackets. They stomped their boots to keep the feeling in their toes, and to dispel the nervous energy that hung around them whenever they began a search. Nodding in unison to Matt, they murmured his name in quiet greeting, waiting patiently in an eerie silence where every little noise felt like an alarm had sounded.

Bud O'Connell strode up to the group. A huge man, he stood half a head taller than Matt, who was an inch over six feet. They all looked up to Bud, literally and figuratively. A thick-haired, hard-drinking power company lineman, Bud knew every inch of Amador County. He had personally hooked up power to every cabin, outhouse and fishing shack west of Blue Mountain for the last twenty years. A tender husband and father, despite his tough exterior, Bud had almost lost his mind when his fourteen-year-old son was killed in an ATV rollover five years before. Every man on the search and rescue team had taken turns night after night for weeks, watching Bud drink all night long, sobbing uncontrollably and threatening to shoot himself for having bought the cursed machine that had taken his son's life. After many months, Bud had come through, but the spark of life was extinguished in his wife Molly, who had taken to her bed, speechless and sedated for months on end, and whom no one ever saw anymore.

Matt understood what they had gone through, maybe, a little. He had fallen into a similar self-destructive pit when Sarah had left him a couple of years before, and it was Bud who had helped him through it, by calling him for every emergency, then dragging him along on training exercises, pack excursions into the high country and medical certification classes; any damned thing to keep him within the circle of human company. Bud gained renewed purpose in keeping Matt away from Jack Daniel's and the temptations posed by Matt's fine Western rifle and pistol collection that he and Bud put to good use by destroying countless inanimate cans and bottles. Bud had been determined to save Matt from himself, something he had been unable to do for his son or his wife. For the most part, Matt reflected, watching his friend approach firmly and steadily, they had helped each other, although life for each of them had changed irrevocably. Bud addressed his team.

"You've seen the car. We don't know if just the girl was in it, or someone else. It's being dusted for prints. Right now, this is a missing person's search of this entire mountainside, in case she's lost. Here's the topo map, if you need it, but a lot of you know the terrain." Bud unfolded the green U.S. Geological Service topographical map of the northeastern portion of Amador County.

"There's a couple of fire trails and logging roads in here," he gestured, "They all kinda run in the same northeastern direction. The girl and her car were reported missing by her family yesterday, so she could be pretty far off the road and into the woods by now. Everything west of the highway is National Forest. Except for some snowmobile trails and fishing cabins near the creeks and lakes, there's nothing out there."

Bill Gibbons cleared his throat to ask a question and Bud paused to let him speak.

"So how come no one thinks she ditched her car after it broke down, and then just hitched a ride down the highway? She could be in Jackson in some garage waiting for a ride back."

Bud paused, glancing around him, and his voice was lower when he answered.

"Now, you know I'm not supposed to pass on any confidential police information." He looked at Matt for approval. "But nothing's wrong with that car. It didn't break down. And she disappeared from her parents' house at Quarry Hill without a word to anyone. Left with no warning at all."

The same way Sarah had left, Matt thought. Only he knew where she'd gone. The regional wine buyer had stopped at Quarry Hill Winery all summer long, during a particularly hot and oppressive heat wave two years before. Sarah had managed the sales for the winery. She had yammered on about the "VP of Marketing" for the regional buying consortium, but Matt had only half-listened. He had been deeply enmeshed in his job as County Sheriff, preoccupied by the occasional pot farm and methamphetamine lab bust, the wife-beatings, DUI's, knifings, shootings, and miscellaneous accidental deaths. The one that haunted him the most that summer was a 12-year-old Boy Scout, who had been fishing downriver from the Tiger Creek power plant spillway. He'd been horsing around with his friends and had fallen into the current. Matt had found the body downriver, caught in a culvert, mangled from the rocks. He couldn't shake the distraught parents' grief and he'd started drinking maybe one beer more than usual, and then a couple more than usual, then close to a six-pack every night and when that wasn't enough, he'd hit the Jack pretty hard.

Matt had thought that it was the heat, or work at the winery making Sarah short-tempered and wound tight all summer. Later, he acknowledged that it was the unbearable tension of being married to him. By fall she was gone. By the following spring, there was a new wine buyer for the region, and a new sales manager for the winery, and Matt's life had crumpled in on him. Matt and Bud both knew that the temptations of ending life by suicide was very real in the mountains. Just the previous spring, an old man who lived by Tiger Creek had been found by a nosy real estate agent, a week or more after shooting himself in his junkyard of a front lawn. The hysterical woman said that he had been sprawled face-up, buck naked except for the .38 in his hand, his eyes staring straight up at the sky. There was no note and no one ever found out why he had done it, except that he was completely alone, living in a rusted trailer amid scattered car and machinery parts, without a damned reason in the world to get up in the morning.

"Anyway," Bud said, "I've got a snapshot of the girl from her high school yearbook. One for each of you." Bud handed several 3x5 snapshots around and Matt tucked his into his front shirt pocket after a brief glance. Bud flattened the topo maps on the hood of a truck and they all crowded around, mapping out the routes each pair would take. Bud had assigned Matt to team up with Glenn Lucas, a recent refugee from the Silicon Valley, who had earned a comfortable early buy-out after years of selling software and consulting services. After building the biggest house in the county, Glenn had bought two fine quarter horses and had built a beautiful cedar barn to house them. Bill Gibbons had told Matt with undisguised awe that the barn even had its own bathroom. Glenn's first activity as a new county resident was to volunteer immediately for search and rescue. That raised some eyebrows at the Buckhorn Bar, and there were a lot of jokes about how the trails around here didn't provide private restrooms and the fire lookout towers didn't serve cappuccino. Despite the jokes, Bud and some other volunteers took Glenn out and tested him on several trail rides. Glenn had kept up and then some. A taciturn, graying man with round eyeglasses and a worn cowboy hat, Glenn didn't say much, but he looked fit and packed a .45 in his saddlebag. Finally, the volunteers had wormed out of Glenn that he had spent his childhood on his dad's ranch in Montana cutting calves, so he was all right with them, even with that big house and fancy barn.

Matt was glad to be paired with Glenn, even if Glenn didn't know the back trails the way Matt did. Glenn's senses were sharp, he was sober, and he didn't talk much. Matt reflected that in a rescue, something could be missed very quickly if your entire focus wasn't on the search. A hiker or camper could be injured and unable to talk or signal just four feet off the trail. One missed cue could sentence someone to death. This morning, Glenn's long face was drawn and grayer than usual. Matt remembered that Glenn and his wife had a daughter in college, probably not much older than the missing teenager. They spoke quietly together about the route they'd take and examined the USGS topo map. Matt was quite sure that if the girl was lost, she'd try to stay within sight of the highway. Neither of them expected any trace of her to be found deep within the woods.

They looked up from the map suddenly as Bud strode into the group's center with Elden Harper, the best Mi-Wuk tracker in the County, and Matt's second cousin on his grandmother's side. Matt glanced to see if Elden's old white Ford pickup still sported a decal of a fierce cartoon Indian raising a tomahawk with the written warning, "Indian Attitude. White boys back off!" It did. But Elden wasn't a threat to anyone. Matt appraised his cousin quietly and with affection. Elden was a short, stout, dark-skinned Mi-Wuk with long, black hair held back in a loose ponytail who spoke so quietly that he could barely be heard and avoided eye contact from under the brim of a worn Giants' cap. He had grown up on a poor scratch of red dirt ten miles outside of Jackson, along with a dozen other Indian kids in an unheated trailer, lacking electricity. Just fifteen years before, the local hunting and fishing guide and occasional handyman had been elected vice-president of his tribe when his mother Loretta was elected tribal leader. Loretta had set up a bingo hall in an old Quonset hut right in the middle of a patch of red dirt and scrub oaks. Within five years, Loretta and her extended family had ushered in a new era of prosperity for their Jackson band of Mi-

Wuks, when construction finished on the tribe's new Indian gaming casino and resort hotel, right on land where Elden had played in the dirt with his brothers, sisters and cousins, careful not to be bitten by rattlesnakes lurking in the dead grass. The small tribe and its members became rich beyond anyone's imaginings. Although previously marginalized by the whites they had lived among all their lives, Elden directed the tribe's charitable foundation that contributed to the poor rural county's social services and had personally donated a fine Logan horse trailer to the search and rescue. Matt watched as Elden examined the abandoned car and the dead vegetation all around, walking away from the Honda in several directions. His examination had taken a full fifteen minutes, and he had already filled the Sheriff in on his conclusions. He was not a man of many words, and the team had to strain to hear him.

"Hey boys," he greeted them softly. "So, there was two of 'em. Man and a woman, I guess, from the size of their shoes. She walked ahead of him. Her prints are close together and scuffed; maybe she's struggling. Three or four hours ago, hard to tell. There was a light frost during the night. I lost them in the blackberry bushes at the edge of the creek. They may have waded up the creek or crossed over somewhere else. They're headed northeast through the woods."

"Thanks, Elden," Bud nodded.

Elden looked up at the group and found Matt's eyes. "Hey, cuz," he greeted him quietly.

"Hey, cuz," Matt nodded back. Everyone born in the county was related in one way or another, but very few were Mi-Wuk tribal members as Matt was, by virtue of being one-quarter Mi-Wuk.

Bud divided up the topo map grids among the teams, and Matt was glad that he and Glenn had received the assignment to follow a trail parallel to Highway 88 northeast for a five-mile distance, close to the road. It was a rise of over one thousand feet in elevation, and they would hit more patches of snow. Tracks might be easier to spot in snow, Matt thought, still convinced that these two would not have strayed that far into the woods. If she's unwilling, he'll want to stay close to the highway to make an easier escape. In unspoken unison, he and Glenn mounted and clucked their horses forward as they began their ascent. In a few minutes, they were clear of other people, vehicles and noise. The land northeast of the Ranger Station was part of the vast and dense El Dorado National Forest, and there were very few rest areas, gas stations, and stores along the way. They rode at the very edge of wilderness, beyond which stretched millions of uninhabited acres all the way to the Oregon border.

After a few minutes, they easily found an old deer trail that paralleled the highway. Matt and Glenn rode on through the trees, invisible to distant passing motorists whipping by on the straightaway in excess of seventy miles per hour as they hurried to reach the gambling casinos at Lake Tahoe's South Shore. Wilderness frightened most people, Matt had concluded. They didn't mind looking at cold, windswept vistas from the safety of a heated car, but most of them never stopped, even at the highway turnouts created at heavy taxpayer expense. The day was warming up, but it was still cold in the tall pine forest that shaded the trail. Matt and Glenn didn't speak. Their eyes glanced right and left, sweeping methodically, looking for footprints, broken branches, personal items; anything that could connect them to the missing girl. If she were being restrained, they didn't want even a whisper between them to alert her captor. They kept the horses quiet, circling around branches that might snap if stepped on, choosing the softer paths strewn with pine needles or broken up by patches of snow. Matt had strapped on his .45 shoulder harness before they had mounted, as soon as they had heard Elden announce that they were looking for a man as well as the missing girl. The .45 was fully loaded, with the safety off, resting in a stiff leather holster above Matt's left hip.

At the top of the ridge, they broke through the woods at about the 7,000-foot elevation. The sun sparkled off the snow-capped crests of mountaintops, and granite peaks glowed burnished with gold. Immense valleys opened up below them among scattered pine forests and huge, granite boulders. There wasn't a building, telephone pole, shack or sign of another human being for miles around them. Retreating snowcaps rested in the pockets and crevices between mountain peaks, where the sun's warming rays couldn't quite penetrate the shadows. The view was one of the most breathtaking in all the northern Sierras and the unbroken magnificence of virgin wilderness always made Matt humble and grateful that he was alive and could still absorb such beauty. Distracted only momentarily by the view, the searchers recovered their concentration and continued to inspect the ground.

Matt's heart suddenly quickened when he spotted long dirt streaks just ahead among the otherwise undisturbed pine needles. He motioned to Glenn to stop behind him. Matt dismounted and knelt to examine the tracks, while Glenn's eyes scanned the immediate area for any signs of life. They didn't speak. Matt could see imprints of a man's large feet shuffling alongside the two parallel furrows. The markings disappeared at the top of a knoll straight ahead in the center of a clearing. Matt knew the place. It was the Maiden's Grave historic marker. There, legend told, the body of a lone young woman named Rachel had been buried. She was a member of an 1849 wagon train from Iowa, just after the start of the gold rush, when pioneers set sail from the East Coast around the tip of South America and disembarked at San Francisco, making the dangerous Sierra crossing bound for Utah on the Mormon Emigrant Trail. The wagon train had been about to reach the Carson's Pass to descend along the eastern side of the Sierras, but she had died before reaching her destination. Her grave had been marked and had become a highway turnout that no one ever used. Instead, people stopped on the opposite side of the highway to take pictures of the Desolation Wilderness peaks to the northwest, never noticing the unknown young woman's grave, to which their backs were turned, just a hundred feet off the highway. This place had always saddened Matt, commemorating as it did failed hopes and premature death.

Now, he looked at the knoll ahead with a sudden, cold premonition.

Matt rose from his crouch and caught Glenn's eyes, each communicating the same chilling thought. He brought her here. It's where we'll find her. Glenn dismounted quietly. They both allowed their horses' reins to drop, ground-tying them so that they wouldn't wander away. They took off their Stetsons, resting them on their saddle horns, opened their jackets and pulled their weapons from their holsters simultaneously. It was unspoken that Matt, who had been a trained law enforcement officer and the former county Sheriff, would proceed first. Glenn followed stealthily. Matt crouched low, to avoid being seen over the knoll, moving awkwardly in a half crouch over bent knees until he reached a thick sugar pine tree. He stopped there. Glenn had followed and was now hidden behind another pine, just ten feet behind Matt. Matt's head moved just an inch so that he could clearly see the rocky knoll in full view. The grave marker was just twenty feet ahead of them, and on top of the exposed dirt mound surrounded by melting snow lay the body of a girl. He could see the top of her head nearest to him, and her sneaker-encased feet pointing to the scenic vista across the highway. Her dark hair was parted in the middle and loose strands of it stirred in the morning breeze. He couldn't see her face, but he knew what he would find.

Matt turned around and got Glenn's attention, motioning that he would circle the area. Glenn understood from Matt's signal that he was to stay put and cover Matt from behind. As soon as Matt darted from the tree around the knoll, Glenn thudded against the same pine Matt had been leaning against. Then Glenn saw her too, and a sick, sinking feeling grabbed his gut. A few minutes later, Matt strode into plain view from around the other side of the knoll, coming full circle back to Glenn.

"There's no one around," he said. "He's long gone."

They both emerged from the pines and carefully approached the girl. She had been laid out ceremoniously, with purple wildflowers entwining her fingers. Her eyelids had been purposefully closed, Matt knew, otherwise she would be staring, unseeing. Matt approached and felt her neck for a pulse, knowing that there would be none. A thin baling wire was still embedded in the skin around her throat and blood had crusted around the wound. She had been garroted, and her lips parted to reveal her swollen tongue. From farther away, she looked as if she had fallen asleep on the knoll, her dark hair arranged around her shoulders, and her body stretched out straight. He noticed that her fingernails had been elaborately done, with the sparkly little stripes and decals that young girls seemed to like, and her hands rested on her chest, surrounded by a dozen deep purple wildflowers. Matt guessed that the girl had been deliberately posed so that she would be found like this. She had been lovely, he thought, his heart heavy. Her photograph, still in his breast pocket, had revealed intense dark eyes and long, raven hair parted in the middle and fastened with a large clip at her neck. In the school photo her smile was full, and her expression mischievous, as if she were flirting with the photographer. She'd had a strong life force, Matt thought. It must have taken a tremendous strength to wrestle her uphill and strangle her like that. Grim-faced, he walked over to Glenn and they both turned to find their horses. Matt pulled the two-way radio out of his saddlebag and asked Glenn if he could watch the crime scene to make sure that a stray tourist didn't stumble into it looking for a pioneer memorial. Glenn's face was haggard. He nodded without speaking. The radio crackled loudly, and Matt asked for Bud, waiting for Bud's voice to come through.

"Are you somewhere we can talk? No civilians around?" Matt asked pointedly. News of the body would hit the volunteers hard, Matt knew, and he didn't want to risk even the slightest chance that the girl's parents might be close by and listening.

"Go ahead. All clear," Bud barked back.

"There's a body here at the 7,000-foot turnoff to the Maiden's Grave marker on Highway 88. It's a young female. Looks like a homicide. Area clear. We'll hold our ground until the Sheriff gets here."

"Roger, Matt. Sorry, man. Helluva thing. I'll tell Dom. They'll be up with everything they need. Over and out."

Matt released the talk button and turned to look again at the young girl as the breeze stirred across the open knoll. In the quiet stillness of mid-morning, with the sound of an occasional car speeding by in the distance, it felt like any ordinary trail ride, as if they were just stopping to let the horses relax. Matt's gaze swept the endless horizon, taking in nature's transcendent beauty. He then dropped his eyes, staring at the sickening reality that had brought them to this desolate spot. It was at that moment that it struck him that he had forgotten to ask anyone for her name.

3.

Sidney almost missed the sharp right-angle turnoff from State Highway 88 onto the Alexander Valley Road heading east into the rolling hills, pastures, and vineyards of the Amador County wine country. She winced as an FM country station blared a twangy, overheated guitar solo interspersed with the song's endlessly repeated refrain, "I'm gittin' drunk on the plaaaane…"

"Shut the hell up. Just freakin' pass out already." She jabbed her finger at the "off" button. "That's better." Sidney passed a tranquil pond where a few black cattle slaked their thirst, their hooves sunken in the mud. Well-grazed horses dotted the landscape, swishing away flies with their tails, their chestnut coats glistening in the sun. Magpies scattered from the single-lane road as she drove, fluttering toward the safety of nearby oak branches.

Her mind drifted to the time just months before when she had abruptly left San Francisco. There wasn't a day since that she hadn't yearned to go back. So much noise, she recalled fondly: so many buses, cable cars, streetcars, ambulances, and crowds of people. Sidney yearned for her Marina District flat: a 1930's Spanish art deco apartment in a four-story building framed by elegantly swirled white columns and a red tiled roof that was right across the street from the little house where Joe DiMaggio had brought Marilyn Monroe home after their frenzied wedding on the steps of Saints Peter and Paul. The place had not worked out for Marilyn and Joe. It was perfect for me, Sidney thought. It had taken her years to get into that building: potted palms lined the lobby with its rich, patterned carpet, and antique lead-paned mirrors softly dispersed the light, so that whenever she came home, Sidney's eyes were always drawn to the delicate scallop shell patterns in the white stucco ceiling. Recessed alcoves embraced white plaster vases overflowing with fresh flowers. She had loved the herringbone hardwood floors, the deep, wide seat in the bay window stuffed with pillows, and especially the partial view of the southern end of the Golden Gate Bridge. Slaving all hours and weekends for a corporate law firm had a few perks, at least, even if she didn't have a much time to enjoy them.

Sidney missed Italian bakery hot cross buns on Chestnut Street, the ambling shoppers, lovers and friends parading by, the intensity of the lean and sun-bronzed runners breaking free from the lethargy of the sidewalk crowds as they sprinted toward the Marina Green, pounding out their energy in a loop to the Golden Gate Bridge and back. Most of all, she railed silently against the crappy coffee absentmindedly served by Anne, her morning waitress at Rosie's Country Café. Tears of self-pity welled up. Oh, no, she thought, here it comes. She slowed the car down and pulled over on the side of the road, breathing deeply.

"God, Sidney. Pull yourself together," she scolded. She sniffed and wiped her eyes with the cuff of her sweater, pulling the visor down and looking at herself critically. Honey-colored hair cut shoulder length framed a thin, oval face. Wispy bangs brushed her eyebrows. Her light hazel eyes were huge from having lost weight and were ringed darkly from lack of sleep. I look like hell, she thought. Her harsh and clinical self-examination stopped her tears. She looked like what she was: a deeply unhappy woman barely over thirty. She tried a smile in the mirror to see what the effect would be. Totally fake.

"Snap out of it," she muttered.

She knew her momentary attack of painful nostalgia had much to do with missing Paul, or at the very least, the place Paul had occupied in her life. For months, she had vague and anxious dreams that Paul had married someone else. Upon awakening most mornings, the reality hit her. He had done just that. He didn't waste any time replacing you, she reminded herself. She was sure that the other woman was already in the picture before they had even broken up.

"Bastard. Rot in hell." She liked the sound of the curse so much, she repeated it loudly. "Rot in hell!"

Calmer now, she started the car again and pulled out, having checked the rear-view mirror. Hers was the only car on the road, she marveled. As much as she missed the city's frantic energy, she felt peaceful when she drove through the valleys and pine forests of the Sierra foothills. It still felt odd living here, she thought. It was if she were on some kind of extended vacation. In reality, it felt more like an exile. She still had not put down roots or made friends. There was no way she would have stayed in the county for very long unless she had been fired.

Naturally, it had happened in a most genteel way after her father's arrest and conviction. Nothing as crass as being physically booted right through the double-paneled mahogany doors of her law firm; just an ever-so-polite but icy cold discussion as to what would be best for the firm and its clients. Her professional execution had been well-planned. The senior partner had shaken his head, full of phony regret. Other clients would not understand, he had said, why the daughter of a convicted criminal was still with the firm, when the firm had been publicly embarrassed by the discovery of their own client's fraudulent transactions. Sidney's cheeks flamed scarlet and her hands shook with suppressed anger. She pressed back what she wanted to say but couldn't. Fucking son of a bitch. She had been the one duty-bound to report the suspected fraud and then compelled to cooperate in sending her own father to prison. Wasn't that punishment enough? But there was no point. She shook her head, nodded grimly, said she understood, and hurriedly packed up her personal belongings in a moving box conveniently produced for the occasion. Her assistant was coming out of the elevator as Sidney entered it. Just a few years younger than Sidney herself, Karin had burst into tears when she saw the box Sidney was carrying.

"It's okay, Karin. I'm moving on," Sidney said firmly, trying to console her assistant at the same time she willed the elevator doors to close on the image of the tearful girl waving a sad goodbye. Sidney had watched her reflection in the polished brass doors all the way down to the garage level, as if she were watching a movie, feeling completely numb. Five years of Sidney's life and she had almost become the youngest partner ever at Ware, Lyman, and Cohen. She had never said goodbye to any of the associates she had worked with, argued with and competed with to see who could stay the latest and come in the earliest, and win the approving notice of the important partners. After she walked out, Sidney had screened her calls. She never spoke to any of them again, comforting herself with the knowledge that at least her relationship with Paul was secure. But that illusion crashed and burned quickly.

Paul had announced that he thought they should "see other people." Sidney had been stunned, but not really surprised. She had sensed for some time that her father's downfall had been too much of an embarrassment for Paul. The newspapers were full of the fraud, conducted on a massive scale for years, and hidden from investors who had railed bitterly and publicly. It was clear to Sidney that her own career reversal was one burden too many on her relationship. Paul couldn't handle her tears, her days of depression. Their parting had been abrupt. He said he was sorry, but that he needed 'time to think.' She couldn't believe that Paul could use such a hackneyed phrase. His excuses had been so trite she almost laughed.

"I need to clear my head. With everything going on, I just need some time," he explained as he packed up everything he owned from her apartment and didn't return that night or on any other night. The days turned into weeks and then, she ran into Paul and a tall, attractive blonde at the flower shop on Chestnut Street, right next to Bechelli's, their favorite place for breakfast. She recognized her immediately as a local newscaster from a prominent family. The perfect trophy wife for social-climbing Paul. She avoided his apologetic calls, knowing that Paul would go to great lengths to avoid being the bad guy. It was his reputation that he wanted to maintain and not her feelings. For days, Sidney had lain in bed in the fetal position. Her father was in prison, her mother was long dead, she'd been fired from her job and her fiancé had abandoned her. She wondered if there was any reason why she should want to continue to live on this earth. She occupied her thoughts by imagining all the creative ways that she could escape. Canada. Australia. Overdosing on Norco. Except she didn't have any Norco. She Googled the cost of living in Portugal, France, and Spain. But the cost of living anywhere still assumed a steady income. After her six-month severance was exhausted, there would be no income.

One day she woke up and announced to no one in particular: "That's enough." Sidney gave her landlord notice, packed up the Subaru, gave everything away that she couldn't sell on the sidewalk, and headed for the mountains. She stayed in a quaint and charmingly appointed Sutter Creek bed and breakfast inn by herself for three days before she called her godfather, Jack McGlynn.

"Where the hell have you been, Sidney?" he had growled at her. "I've been trying to get ahold of you. I have a job for you."

*****

Around the next turn, vineyards covered the gently rolling landscape cross-hatched with acres of vines, their tendrils clinging around wire supports strung between wooden stakes. Quarry Hill suddenly loomed like a medieval castle, emerging in the distance from the hilly vineyards. An enormous fieldstone and wrought iron gate announced rather than marked the entry etched with the winery's name in huge carved letters. Impressive, Sidney thought, as she turned into a wide gravel road marked "Private" that wound for a half-mile to the main house. The final approach was shaded by ancient leafy oak branches that sheltered a century-old stone-carved bridge arching over a creek. She gently drove over the stone pavers and then turned into the sweeping gravel drive, tires crunching noisily.

Sidney slowed her approach and gazed quietly at the house, studying its features, which were more dramatic than she had remembered even months before. Unlike so many pretentiously huge Napa Valley faux chateaux, the Quarry Hill house was the genuine article, a late medieval manor brought stone by stone from the Loire Valley. A gray-green patina of more than four hundred years gave depth and character to the stone and wood beam edifice, which was more roughly massive than elegant. The stones were all different sizes, as were the windows, framed by ancient wood. A medieval coat of arms crowned the twin carved oak doors, and two stone turrets stood like sentries at either end of the slate roof. Attic windows were etched in leaded glass, and the entire facade was solid but asymmetrical. Sidney guessed that over the centuries, pieces of the castle had been added on by different generations, giving it a slightly eclectic, uneven look. She marveled at the sheer arrogance of anyone dismantling a monument of European history and bringing it over to the New World piece by piece, reassembling its grandeur with admirable similitude.

As she emerged from the car with her view still fixed on the manor house, Sidney almost overlooked the thin, crouching figure of a woman among the rose bushes to the left of the ornately carved front door. The woman's back was to her, but Sidney could see a large flat-brimmed straw hat and a long cotton shirt underneath a red quilted vest. A print calico skirt almost brushed the ground. Sidney approached her to the side, not wanting to frighten her. Maude Hill's penetrating blue eyes glanced at her from under the straw brim, and recognizing Sidney, she handed her a rough woven basket overflowing with rose prunings.

"If I don't keep up with the garden, it soon overwhelms me," she announced. She kept on clipping furiously as Sidney stood and held the basket. "Right now, Carmelo is in a terrible tizzy, poor dear. I don't hold out much hope that the garden will get any attention today. One must do what one can."

Sidney stood quietly holding the basket, somewhat puzzled. After several minutes of clipping, Sidney found her voice.

"Jack told me that you might need my services with regard to a legal matter, but he didn't say what it was."

"No, he didn't, because I didn't tell him. My dear, I've known Jack a very long time, as did my husband. I'm afraid that if I discussed this very personal matter with him, he might try to dissuade me. I don't want to be dissuaded," she said emphatically, decapitating a deep red rose with a quick snap of her fingers and dropping the flower petals into Sidney's outstretched basket.

"I work for Jack, Mrs. Hill, and you're his client. I take my direction from him."

"Yes, I know, but I want you to take care of this matter for me. In this, I am your client. Once he finds out what I need, he'll leave you to it, I'm quite sure."

"I'm happy to help, Mrs. Hill. What do you need for me to do?" Sidney asked politely. She recognized her elderly client's reluctance and decided that patience, rather than assertiveness, was her best approach. Mrs. Hill silently rubbed the tip of her nose with the back of a tightly gloved hand, her trowel clutched in her fingers, as specks of dirt fell on the yoke of her blouse. She appeared suddenly lost in thought, and then just as suddenly, she turned back to Sidney.

"Miss Dietrich," responded Mrs. Hill directly. "I am dying." Sidney's eyes widened, but she said nothing in response.

"Not now, not immediately." Mrs. Hill's startlingly clear blue eyes searched Sidney's and the corners of her mouth lifted in amusement. "You don't know me well enough for my impending death to perturb you. I'm old, and my time has come. It won't be above six months. Maybe a year. I don't feel ill at the moment. But that day will come."

Mrs. Hill turned her back to Sidney and stooped to the ground, pulling up a thistle weed growing among the roses, giving it a sudden, strong jerk that pulled it up by the roots in the loose, moistened soil.

"Damned thing. If I didn't have my gloves on, it would cut my hands to ribbons." As she rose again, she reached for the basket and took it out of Sidney's hands. "Come inside. We'll have lunch."

Dutifully, Sidney followed Maude's thin, wiry form. Despite the wisps of white hair escaping the straw hat, and deep furrows of weather-worn skin, Maude Hill possessed the energy of someone decades younger. They went around to the back of the house, into a side door. This was clearly the "mud" room, where assorted dirty boots, gloves, gardening hats, and other outdoor paraphernalia were haphazardly stacked up on wooden benches or hung on pegs in the wood-paneled entry.

"I'm sorry to take you in this way, Miss Dietrich. It's not very grand, is it? But then again, I hardly ever use the formal entry anymore. This is more convenient," she said, holding onto the doorjamb to pry off her muck boots by the heel, pried against the toe of the other boot. Sidney wondered if she should offer to pull her client's boots off for her but was too embarrassed to ask. Mrs. Hill's woolen-clad feet searched for worn out house clogs and slipped them on.

"Follow me," she motioned to Sidney as she tossed her gardening hat onto a stack of others, similarly frayed. The front hallway flooded the interior with light, casting shadows on the stone floor. Here and there were scattered haphazardly what Sidney assumed were hand-woven Persian rugs. They passed by expansive, high-ceilinged formal living and dining rooms that could easily have accommodated cocktail parties attended by half the citizens of Jackson, had they ever been invited. Clusters of conversational seating areas with rich wood furniture and classically patterned upholstery, an ebony grand piano in one corner and polished tables with multiple silver-framed photographs furnished the room. Sidney's eye was caught by splashes of bold colors filling the expanse of wall space. Surprisingly modern portraits and plein air landscapes of the California countryside added life to the elegant, but otherwise monochromatic space. Mrs. Hill turned back suddenly.

"Those were my brother's paintings. Joshua Morgan: you may have heard of him. He was a very accomplished artist. If he had lived longer... well, I'm very pleased to have inherited so many of his works and I hear that they're quite sought after."

Sidney said nothing but was determined to study the many striking paintings more closely when she had an opportunity. After what seemed like several minutes, they ended their sojourn down the great hallway passing underneath its narrow, vaulted ceiling supported by rough-hewn wooden beams. Sidney half expected a pack of slavering wolfhounds to show up any second. Mrs. Hill opened a side door as they reached a dead-end marked by a massive sideboard table. Ignoring the kitchen, which was occupied with at least two very busy uniformed women, they entered a screened-in patio with flooring dotted with colorful inlaid Spanish tile. A small round table was draped in blue linen, and matching napkins with polished silver rings framed two brightly decorated Italian plates. Thick crackled blue glass goblets completed the setting.

Mrs. Hill crooked her finger, motioning Sidney to take the wrought iron chair facing the garden. When they were seated, a middle-aged woman appeared, bearing a platter of steaming slices of medium cooked roast beef, new potatoes, peas, and carrots. Sidney was surprised at the heavy fare offered and suddenly felt ravenous. Christmas dinner for lunch, she thought. Mrs. Hill tucked in and served herself quite a field hand's portion. The serving rituals lasted a good deal of time, and Sidney found her impatience growing. After slathering butter on her roll and taking at least several more bites of roast beef, Mrs. Hill paused and took a sip of ice water.

"I know you must be quite anxious to be off, but this is a story that is difficult for me to tell, and I don't intend to have to tell it more than once. My family has been marked by truly unfortunate events, tragedies, really." Sidney was attentive but unsure whether she should stop chewing or continue eating. Mrs. Hill wasn't looking at Sidney at all, but at a point just over her shoulder.

"I have two children. Grace is now fifty and Jeremy is thirty-five. I was married twice. Grace's father died in a boating accident during a sailing regatta on San Francisco Bay. I met my second husband, Hans, when I was taking a tour of lumber property that had belonged to Grace's father. Hans Hill was riding along the boundary fence on horseback, making plans to plant another vineyard. We nodded to each other and he tipped his hat to me. I was planning to sell the property, as my husband hadn't provided well for Gracie and me. I asked our agent if he could inquire as to whether the adjoining property owner wanted to buy. The message came back to me several days later that he did but wanted to meet with me personally. I was rather annoyed that Gracie and I would have to be dragged back from town just to sell lumber land, but Hans was very gracious. We rode on horseback all over the vineyards, and he told me of his dream to found a world-renown winery. He never bought the lumber land. He said that it was Gracie's and mine to keep. We were married just six months later."

Mrs. Hill paused suddenly, lost in thought. Sidney could tell that the years fast-forwarded by in her mind. Her eyes were half-closed, as if she were sleepy from the heavy meal. She reached out for her water glass with a hand that shook slightly as she sipped.

"We had Jeremy quite late. He was a surprise. Gracie was delighted and was as nurturing and caring of Jeremy as if she were his own mother. They were always very close; closer to each other than either one ever was to me. Maybe Hans and I were too much in love, too wrapped up with each other to give the children more of our time and attention. You had to have known him. He was a powerful man with endless energy. It had nothing to do with money, really, but coupled with the Hill family fortune, well, there were very few men in the state who could compete with him." Her pale blue eyes glimmered with tears.

"When did your husband die?" Sidney asked gently.

"Ten years ago, but it seems as if no time has gone by at all. Jeremy was only twenty-five. Gracie was already forty and we despaired of her ever marrying. She had only gone away from home briefly, to Mills College, and then returned to live with us.

She never seemed interested in marriage. And then, there was the accident."

"What accident?" Sidney prompted.

"They had both been invited to a party for young people. I felt as if Gracie was too old to be asked, but she was always popular with Jeremy's friends, and I also knew that she would keep an eye out for Jeremy. There was too much drinking and drugs among the young people. I was always quite nervous for Jeremy's safety. Gracie was so much older and protective. They spent the weekend at the home of Bob Cleary, one of the founders of Sun Meadows Ski Resort. It was their son Tad's twenty-first birthday. On the way home, Jeremy fell asleep at the wheel, dozing off for a few seconds. His car plowed into a huge granite boulder. Jeremy was thrown clear, but Gracie was crushed. She never walked again."

"I'm sorry," Sidney said, not knowing what else to say. Mrs. Hill shook her head slightly, her face framed with wisps of white hair.

"Not a word of reproach. She never blamed Jeremy. She suffered, of course. You can't imagine the rounds of hospitals, surgeries, and physical therapists; but never a word of complaint. I think that the accident drew them even closer. Then two years later, my brother Joshua died. So brilliant. So promising. They said that he committed suicide in his apartment in San Francisco, but I don't believe it. I never have."

"Mrs. Hill," Sidney interjected softly, not wanting to offend her elderly client. "What is it that I can do to help you?" Mrs. Hill's sharp eyes suddenly focused on the present.

"Well, Miss Dietrich. Before I die, I need to know what happened to my brother. It wouldn't do to leave things as they are. And I need for you to find out without anyone knowing that I have very limited time. Of course, my time would be limited anyway. I'm well over eighty, but this. Well."

"You have two living children, correct?" Mrs. Hill nodded in response. "But why don't you ask them to look into your brother's death?" Mrs. Hill shook her head.

"No, my dear. They have accepted his suicide, but I have not. There may be a great deal more that needs investigation that the police ignored. Ruling his death a suicide was too convenient."

"Do you have reason to believe that the police didn't do an adequate job?"

"Well, I firmly believe that Joshua did not kill himself – he never would have. His life was so full, and he was just on the edge of realizing his ambitions. That's why I need you, to find out for me."

"There are many very competent private investigators, Mrs. Hill…," Sidney was immediately interrupted.

"No. I don't want them. I want you. You have certain sympathy about you. You're a good listener and a critical one. I noted that when I first met you. I would appreciate your looking into this for me, at your usual rates, of course, with expenses." She didn't wait for disagreement. "If I were you, I'd start with Gracie. She knows more about Joshua than even I do. Joshua was very close to Gracie and Jeremy. My focus was on my husband. Not that I regret it," she paused. "Perhaps I was a better wife than a mother."

"Is your daughter here today?" Sidney asked, pausing to dab her lips with her napkin.

"She's at physical therapy. Frankly, I wanted us to meet first. She doesn't know about my health and I don't want her to know yet. I think that you could tell both Grace and Jeremy that I just want to make sure that all loose ends are tied," she nodded, looking off through the screen to the gardens outside.

"May I come to see Grace tomorrow?" Sidney asked, rising from her chair and placing her napkin next to the blue water goblet.

"Certainly, my dear. Tomorrow morning after breakfast would be fine. Grace is usually in the garden then. We'll be here. You can find your way out now, can't you? I'm growing quite tired."

Mrs. Hill's head reclined on the back of her chair, and she fell fast asleep. The woman who had served them emerged from the kitchen. She had a small pillow in one hand and a tray in the other.

Sidney walked back through the long hallway with floor to ceiling windows that let in the light from the afternoon sun. As she passed the cavernous living room, splashes of vivid color from Joshua Morgan's paintings again caught her eye. Looking around and finding no one, she walked into the living room and surveyed the dark-paneled walls, where a jumble of paintings hung from one end of the room to the other, creating a crowded gallery. Several stunning views of the Quarry Hill vineyards and house were interspersed with scenes of valleys combed in deep emerald green and blue hues, the red earth slashed in rows like scars below a deep blue horizon. Skies were streaked with lavenders, pinks, reds, and yellows as bright as Carnaval costumes. Sidney could sense manic energy in the painter, as if he were besting nature in imposing his own more intense vision. Next to the vineyard scenes hung a portrait of a man slouching at a wooden table behind a vase of unruly flowers, spilling their color all over the foreground of the painting. The seated man seemed solitary and shrunken behind the flowers, with an elongated face and thatch of pale blonde hair. His blue eyes afforded his drawn face a splash of color but somehow didn't add any warmth. At the bottom right above the gold-carved frame, was scrawled a blotch of red lettering: "Joshua by Himself." Sidney wondered at the dual meaning of the signature, both as self-portrait and as a commentary on loneliness. Another portrait next to it reminded Sidney of a Mary Cassatt, with a mother seated at a dressing table looking in her mirror as her small, dark-haired daughter stood behind her, holding blonde tresses in her hands while she lovingly brushed her mother's hair. Lettering underneath announced "Maude and Grace" as the painting's delicately rendered subjects. It was a lovely domestic scene, and Sidney stood for a long moment, admiring its poignancy. Joshua Morgan had indeed been an impressive artist.

Feeling as if she had been prying, Sidney made her exit through the mudroom entry quickly and found her car, her mind racing over her morning with Mrs. Hill. As her tires crunched slowly down the gravel driveway, she glanced back at the house through the rearview mirror. Far down the road, away from the vineyard, she passed by the same herd of cattle, now clustered in mud beneath sheltering oak trees. She considered that she had never done this kind of investigative legwork before and didn't want to do it now. Seeing the inner workings of other people's unhappiness was unsettling. It's hard enough, she thought, dealing with my own.

*****

Sidney arrived back at the Law Offices of Jack McGlynn above the Pioneer Hotel, an old stagecoach hostel that still looked exactly like photographs from over one hundred years before. The second floor housed a small suite of offices for Jack, his long-suffering secretary Marjorie Valovich, as well as an occasional part-time office clerk. Sidney was the latest addition and only other lawyer. On occasion, a hotel guest would barge in on them, lost while wandering down the second-floor hallway, but for the most part, their office worked independently of the hotel with its rowdy basement biker bar and occasional saloon band. The upstairs had reputedly housed a brothel in the old days, and according to Jack, many prominent locals had begun life as the offspring of brothel owners.

Marjorie was waiting phone in hand for Sidney as she walked through the old wooden door. Marjorie looked exactly like the middle-aged smoker she was, with graying hair flared on either side of her head in a layered cut from twenty years before, owl-shaped glasses framing nearsighted eyes, and thin lips creased with deep lines from years of puffing on any number of coffin nails. Even though there was no smoking allowed in the old firetrap of a building, Marjorie would sneak cigarettes on her breaks on the narrow metal fire escape perched above the rear parking lot, throwing the butts into the channel that guided a small branch of Jackson Creek through the downtown. Musty cigarette odor clung to her patterned, multicolored polyester dresses. At times, Sidney could hardly stand to be close to her, but Marjorie's fierce loyalty to Jack matched her own, and they understood and appreciated that about each other.

"Mrs. Hill," Marjorie rasped, handing the receiver to Sidney. Sidney took the call, surprised to be hearing again from her new client so soon.

"Sidney, dear," Mrs. Hill's voice was thin and strained. "Please come back rather early tomorrow. There may be some unpleasantness about Carmelo's daughter, Selena. She's been missing, and I don't know what to do. The police just called, and they'll be by first thing. I'm sure they'll want to ask a lot of questions. I want you there, so we don't appear unhelpful."

"I'll be there, Mrs. Hill. Please don't talk to anyone until I get there tomorrow, all right? No one should talk to the police without my being there. Can you promise me that?"

"Of course. We await your instructions in the morning." Sidney handed the receiver back to Marjorie.

"Cops," Marjorie sniffed. "I don't like cops."

"Especially when they come around our clients," Sidney agreed. "Marjorie. Find Jack for me, please. I'll need his advice before I go back to Mrs. Hill's in the morning."

"Sure," Marjorie nodded. "He's at Rotary. You'd think he was still running for office. Doesn't ever miss a meeting."

"I know. He's still up to his ears in it all. I imagine that he does a lot of good around here."

"Yeah, sure thing. But the good old boys still control everything. Full of "inis" and "viches.""

"What?" Sidney asked, uncomprehending. Marjorie shook her head.

"Italians and Serbians. From the old mining days. Names that end in "ini" or "vich" like mine. I married a "vich" God help me. Valovich. The "inis" are like Giannini, get it? Like I said, the county's run mostly by inis and viches."

"Oh," Sidney smiled. At first, she had been put off by Marjorie's blunt manner, but as the weeks had turned into months, Sidney found that Marjorie was an indispensable guide to local lore and personalities in a world virtually closed to outsiders. Like Sidney's new environment, Marjorie took a little getting used to.

"Thanks, Marj. Just let Jack know I need him, okay?"

"Rightio. Just as soon as he's done glad-handing per usual."

Sidney closed the door to her office. Jesus, she thought, as she sat down heavily in her leather armchair: I don't know a damned thing about helping a client navigate through a police interview. Years of big city corporate law practice had left Sidney with little practical knowledge. She sighed, painfully aware that without Jack she'd be clueless and alone, facing a shark pool full of inis and viches.

4.

Matt scanned the road without really seeing anything, lost in thought. He replayed the Sheriff's first press conference, if you could call it that, the morning following discovery of the body. Two young male reporters from the Amador Daily Dispatch and Upcountry News were joined by a woman from the Stockton Recorder hurrying into the Sheriff's office, late from backed-up traffic on Highway 99. The reporter from the Sacramento Bee simply called in. This was too small-time for them: murders happened every day in Sacramento. It would only bear a small column in the back pages of the Bee. Even so, Dom Colangelo made a lengthy statement as if the room were full.

"At 7:00 a.m. yesterday morning, two search and rescue volunteers came upon the body of a young girl, near the historic marker off Highway 88. She had been the victim of a violent crime. Her name is being withheld pending family notification and positive identification. The investigation will be led by former Sheriff Matt Dunleavy. Matt has been appointed as a Special Deputy, and he's agreed to give this case his complete attention."

After the usual questions that Colangelo avoided concerning motive, suspects and evidence, Matt was asked to address the reporters. As the former Sheriff, he was used to briefings and avoided answering questions even more adeptly than Colangelo, while still giving reporters something to quote. Colangelo had sidled over to Matt after the body was found and had asked him to take on the case. That way, Colangelo could appear as if he had appointed someone competent to head up the investigation, while having a handy scapegoat in case they failed to make sufficient progress or something else went awry. Matt was tempted to turn him down but walking away from the murder of a young girl was not something that Matt was constitutionally capable of doing. Colangelo promised a generous per diem plus expenses, as well as free rein in the investigation. They walked out of the briefing together to the Sheriffs' fenced-in parking lot.

"By the way, Matt. When we opened the trunk of the girl's car, we found something pretty interesting."

Matt waited for the Sheriff to disclose what that was. Colangelo shifted his weight from one foot to the other.

"Cash. A lot of it. It was in a school backpack. You'll want to see it. It's been booked into evidence."

"How much?"

"They're counting it now, but it looks like more than twenty thousand. Lots of different denominations. Not yer clean bank notes, know what I mean?"

Matt did. Meth houses and pot farms were full of the stuff. He wondered what the girl had been up to. Maybe it had gotten her killed.

Matt and Dom left in a patrol car, heading to the Quarry Hill Vineyard, where the girl's parents waited for word of their missing daughter. The drive took too long for them to dispense with polite conversation.

"Is old Mrs. Hill still alive?" Matt asked, knowing the answer full well. He was trying to draw Dom into sharing his views of the winery and its occupants.

"Sure. I hear she's still active in managing the place, but her son is taking it over more and more. Didn't you and he go to high school together?"

Matt nodded. It had been several years since Matt had seen Jeremy Hill. Matt remembered Jeremy's wispy blonde hair and liquid blue eyes. Girls seemed to melt around him, whether due to his looks or money, Matt could never determine. When Sarah grew so distant and cold, he had even suspected that Jeremy was the cause. One night, he had a drunken confrontation with Jeremy that he'd just as soon forget. But it had been over two years now, and he had apologized. Jeremy had accepted in that laconic way of his, as if nothing in life registered too deeply.

"Funny family, the Hills. Guess that's what money does," Dom mused.

"I don't know," Matt answered distractedly. "There are

plenty of screwed up people without any money."

"Yeah, that's true, too. But what about that sister?"

Matt thought about Grace Hill sentenced to life in a wheelchair. "Pretty sad," he commented.

They were fairly quiet the rest of the trip. Each pondered having to tell the Mexican family that lived on the Hill property that their missing daughter had been found. There was no easy way to break the hearts of a crime victim's relatives, who had been so desperate for any hope.

"We need to narrow the field of boyfriends pretty quickly. And figure out where the hell that much cash came from," Dom instructed Matt quite unnecessarily. "No matter how upset the parents are, we need to make sure we've got a pretty complete list in our hands by the time we leave. Some of the other help might have information, too. We'll have to deal with everyone there."

Matt nodded but said nothing, trying to be patient. He knew Dom was nervous and that his seeming condescension was just a way of staying in control and assuaging his own anxiety. Matt was convinced that as soon as the investigation was underway, Colangelo would lose interest and leave Matt to his own devices. The Sheriff's cruiser pulled off the highway, through the winery's well-marked public road fifty yards or so past the private entrance to the main house, which sat imposing and brooding even in the glare of the morning sun. The public road was meant for employees, deliveries, and tourists eager to taste the winery's award-winning releases. Matt reflected on the hundreds of times he must have driven up the same long driveway to the vineyard warehouse and winery tasting room where Sarah had worked for all the years of their marriage. He was surprised that the destruction of both his career and his marriage now seemed so distant, almost as if it had happened to someone else. He was sober now, so the violence of his emotions was no longer fueled by alcohol. It was as if the events of two years ago had paled in his memory. They took a private lane from the tasting room parking lot to the main house that was just wide enough for a narrow sedan or a couple of golf carts.

As they drove around the circular gravel driveway, they spotted Mrs. Hill weeding the garden under the immense front windows of the house. She looked at the Sheriff's patrol car from under her battered straw hat and stood up, frowning at them. The two men emerged from the patrol car and walked slowly toward her, approaching her almost reluctantly. She pulled off her gloves, dropping them in her gardening basket by her feet.

"Oh, it's you, Matt," she said, suddenly recognizing him. She should have known the Sheriff, but Matt was placed in the awkward role of introducing him to Mrs. Hill, who had known Matt since he had been in her son's high school class. Colangelo was several years older and unknown to her.

"I'm sorry. I was just surprised to see you. I was expecting someone else. Are you here about poor Carmelo's daughter? Has she been found yet?" she asked anxiously.

"I wonder if you could direct us to the family, Mrs. Hill. We need to speak with them first," Colangelo requested. "We'll also need to speak to you and your son this morning if you all could stick around."

"Why, certainly, officer."

"Sheriff, ma'am."

"Matt, you know where Carmelo and his wife live don't you? You can take the Sheriff there, only please don't upset them." Matt knew that there would be no way possible to honor her request.

"We'll try not to, ma'am."

Matt led Colangelo around the side porch of the house, past the fieldstone terrace off the cavernous dining room and around the geometrically shaped and colorfully tiled swimming pool. The landscaping was more traditionally English than new California, with large azaleas displayed against the terrace and pathways lined with short boxwood bushes and bay laurel trees. The entire garden required an immense underground network of irrigation pipes, hoses and sprinkler heads, all hidden from view. Beyond the whimsically designed octagonal guest house, the manicured feel of the overly green and flowered grounds gave way to wild grasses and tangled blackberry vines. At the edges of the garden, the hardened gold dust paths became red dirt, and scrub oaks lent whatever small shade there was from the increasingly warm morning sun.

Panting now, Colangelo asked, "How far is it?"

"We're there," Matt responded, as they rounded some bushes that looked suspiciously like poison oak. Colangelo looked up and saw a modest single-story manufactured house in a clearing, kept neat and clean with a small patch of grass surrounding the wooden porch and wire link fencing around the perimeter. A child of about four saw them coming and leaped off his tricycle, screaming "Mama! Mama!" for his mother. Suddenly, a man in work clothes emerged from the house, as his wife peered from behind the screen door, the child clutching her apron, as he looked out wide-eyed from behind her skirt. The man was a short, stocky Mexican of strongly indigenous descent, his hair black and thick although approaching middle age. He wore a worn but clean t-shirt that stretched tightly over a barrel chest. His dark eyes scanned their faces as he approached hurriedly, as if to get as far away from the house as possible to shield his wife and child.

"Mr. Rodriguez? I'm Dom Colangelo, Sheriff of Amador County. We're here about your daughter," the Sheriff said, taking off his Stetson and holding it in his hands.

Matt stared down at the man's look of complete comprehension, his eyes glittering with tears, his grief carving deep lines around his mouth as he fought for control.

"Selena is dead," he said flatly, turning to glance at his wife, "Or you would bring her home by now."

Matt nodded briefly, acknowledging the man's dread. Behind the screen door, the woman let out a piercing scream and fled back into the house, the child looking after her, bewildered.

"I'm really sorry," Colangelo said, clearly meaning it. "We need to ask you and your wife some questions."

"Please. Come back later. Let me go to her."

Matt nodded, an uncomfortable swelling sensation in his throat threatening to block any words. The man's dignity touched him deeply, and he needed to collect himself almost as much as the grieving father in order to proceed.

"We'll be back in twenty minutes. We'll ask some questions at the house first." Rodriguez nodded and hurried back through the screen door, picking up his youngest in his arms. Matt and the Sheriff turned and went back the way they came. The wails from the bungalow increasing in pitch and intensity as the mother's worst fears were confirmed. They walked back silently, each subdued by the weight of the family's grief. As they rounded the house past the swimming pool, Jeremy Hill came down the patio steps to meet them, his hand outstretched to Matt in greeting. Jeremy wore faded jeans and a light blue polo shirt. He looked younger than thirty-five, with long strands of blonde hair brushing his forehead, the color of his shirt intensifying the blueness of his eyes. Matt approached and held out his hand. They shook quickly, and Matt introduced the Sheriff.

"Matt here is in charge of this investigation, and I'm assigning a couple of my deputies to report to him. We just delivered the news of the daughter's death to Rodriguez and his wife. We'll be going back there in a few minutes. In the meantime, is there somewhere we can talk?"

For a moment, Matt detected alarm in Jeremy's eyes, but a controlled mask descended quickly on his features, and he looked grim but calm. Jeremy showed them up the patio steps to a wrought iron garden table with four chairs, placed in the shade of the overhanging porch. Once they were seated, a large Slavic-looking woman with a broad middle and high cheekbones appeared at the French doors and asked if they wanted anything.

"Iced tea? Anna, could you bring some, please?" Jeremy asked as the men nodded assent. A pitcher with glasses appeared quickly and Anna poured, while Colangelo and Matt observed Jeremy Hill silently. Matt knew that Colangelo expected him to cover the basics.

"You manage the winery now, Jeremy?"

He nodded, his blonde eyelashes blinking as if the sun's glare was too strong for his pale blue eyes.

"I've technically been in charge for the last five years. My mother is very much retired now."

"How long has the Rodriguez family lived here?"

Jeremy took a sip of iced tea.

"I'd say for about ten years. First, Carmelo came to work the vineyards, and then it became apparent that he was very skilled with all sorts of plants, as well as landscaping. After a couple of years, his family joined him. I think Selena was about eight or nine when they moved into the gardener's house."

"Did you know the family well?"

"I know Carmelo because I have direct dealings with him, but we respect the family's privacy. We don't go over to the house or visit, or anything social in that way."

"Who're 'we'?" Matt asked.

"My mother and I, and I suppose my father when he was alive. My sister is in a wheelchair and never goes anywhere on the property that is not wheelchair accessible. My mother would go over to Carmelo's at Easter and Christmas with food and gifts, but that's about it."

"Would you see the family's comings and goings, such as trips to the grocery store or taking kids to school?"

"Not really. There's a back gate that's an entry and exit used by Carmelo and other workers. It doesn't go by the house. It leads to a road that runs along the western edge of the vineyard. It's also used by water trucks and farm vehicles."

"How well did you know the girl, Selena Rodriguez?" Matt focused on Jeremy noting that he seemed oddly detached, lacking even a mild expression of concern. But Jeremy had always been somewhat listless in demeanor, even when Matt had confronted Jeremy over Sarah while angry, drunk and potentially violent. Matt wondered if there was anything that could get a rise out of Jeremy Hill.

"Selena lived here for ten years since she was a little girl. I knew her, of course. This is a busy place, Matt. People in and out all the time. It's hard to keep track of what's going on with all the workers here, and their families. You'd know that."

Matt wondered if the remark was a veiled reference to the smooth and well-dressed regional wine broker who had waltzed off with Sarah. He decided to ignore it.

"Anything you can tell us about Selena and her friends or boyfriends, likes or dislikes, activities and interests would be a help."

Suddenly, the French doors leading to the patio swung fully open, and a thin young woman with light shoulder-length hair strode right up to the table, staring straight at Matt, eyes glittering with challenge. She wore a casual lavender knit top and form-hugging black slacks, but her face was set for serious business. Matt looked up at her, unable to place her, startled at the interruption.

"Isn't that a question better put to the girl's family and friends? Why are you interrogating Mr. Hill? He doesn't need to answer any questions," she stated firmly. Dom Colangelo was the first to recover from the assault.

"Now, Miss, we're here on a murder investigation and you are interfering with Sheriff's business. I suggest you go somewhere else until we're finished with Mr. Hill," Dom was on his feet, staring down the girl from across the table. She looked up, meeting his eyes unwaveringly.

"I think not. I'm one of the Hill family's attorneys. I work for Jack McGlynn."

"Is this lady your attorney, Jeremy?" Matt asked him, not acknowledging the girl. Jeremy Hill shrugged and looked up at Sidney's tight-lipped expression.

"I guess so."

"Sidney Dietrich," she said firmly while thrusting her hand out to shake the Sheriff's hand.

"Dom Colangelo. Sheriff," he introduced himself, his huge hand swallowing hers like a bear's paw.

"And you?" her eyes landed on Matt, who unfolded from the

wrought iron chair and stretched himself slowly up to his full height of well over six feet. He looked down on her and extended his hand.

"Matt Dunleavy, Special Deputy on assignment for the Sheriff's Office. I'll be in charge of the investigation on this case."

"What case?" Sidney asked pointedly, her eyes narrowing. She looked Matt over, trying to take his measure. He wasn't in any uniform. He was tall and angular, wearing jeans, a light blue collared shirt, and dusty tooled leather cowboy boots. His lean face looked tanned from the outdoors, and his thick dark hair was rumpled and in need of a trim. Inquisitive brown eyes appeared to be appraising her. She was waiting for an answer.

"There's been a suspicious death. It hasn't been ruled a homicide yet, pending the Coroner's verdict. A young girl's body was found up Highway 88. She was the daughter of a caretaker here. She was only nineteen years old. As her father's employer, I'm sure your client here is willing to help in any way he can." His quiet but pointed description of the young girl's death took Sidney slightly aback, but she hoped she didn't show it.

"Of course, I am," Jeremy said, impatiently, "But I'm afraid I don't have any information that could be remotely helpful. I'll certainly make any of our employees available for questioning and cooperate in any way possible."

Sidney interjected quickly. "Do you have any additional questions for Mr. Hill? He's quite busy, I'm sure you understand. He has a winery to manage. Mrs. Hill has asked me to be your primary contact here in setting up any interviews you'd like."

"Well, of course, we need to talk to the family, and we'd like to take a look at the girl's room. At this point, the caretaker's house should be vacated, so we can get forensics in there. Is there anywhere else that the family can stay in the meanwhile?"

"Why, do you think anything happened here? As you said, the body was found up the highway."

"Yes, Miss. But there may be some evidence in this young girl's house or room that may lead us to her murderer. If you don't have a problem, that is. We can get Judge Carlson to issue a search warrant, if you want," Sheriff Dom was polite but insistent.

"I'd like a moment to speak with my client, please," Sidney asked, willing Jeremy Hill bodily out of his chair. Reluctantly, he rose and stepped inside the dining room with her. She took his elbow and steered him well into the room, their backs to the French doors.

"What's with her?" Dom shook his head in the direction of the dining room, where he could see Jeremy Hill and the young female attorney whispering. "I've never seen her before. I heard Jack got himself some big city lawyer to help him out, but he should know that's not how we do things here." Dom rubbed his forehead nervously where the band of his Stetson usually left a wide red ring. "What's she doing here anyhow? Is she Jeremy's girlfriend?"

"I don't think so," Matt responded carefully. "Jeremy was just as surprised to see her as we were." Matt fully expected Miss Dietrich to return and allow the search. As anticipated, they returned to the patio, and Jeremy gave them full consent to search the girl's home if the parents consented as well.

"Can we use a room away from the girl's house to conduct interviews? Someplace quiet and private, with maybe a pitcher of water, glasses, and Kleenex available," Matt requested.

"Sure," Jeremy said cooperatively, eager to be dismissed. "There's my father's old study on the first floor. It's perfect. It's away from the girl's house and private. There's a separate entrance and a bathroom. There's a phone there too if you need it. You can use it as long as you like. You can even have a key to the door for a few days so that you don't even need to come in the house. Let me know if you need anything else."

"Thanks," Dom said politely. Matt said nothing, looking at Jeremy. Uncomfortable under such scrutiny, Jeremy turned to go.

"Well, uh, if that's all, I've got work to do. You understand. If there's anything you need, let Miss... Dietrich know." Jeremy went back into house through the French doors and disappeared in the cavernous dining room. Matt turned to Sidney.

"Miss Dietrich? We'd like to see the family. Just the parents, maybe the father first. Can you show us to the study?"

Sidney looked at him and stared for a moment. She didn't know how to get around that one. She'd only been in the home the day before and had no idea where the study was.

"Mr...."

"Dunleavy. Matt Dunleavy," he said and waited.

"I don't know where that room is, and I actually don't know the girl's father. We've never met." Matt could tell that she almost would rather have died than to admit ignorance.

"Well, you're not going to be much help then, now are you?" Matt smiled, not unkindly. Sidney was mortified.

"I'll get what you need. Just please stay here," she said coldly and marched through the dining room doors. In just a minute, Sidney had Anna in tow ready to usher the Sheriff and Dunleavy through the house. She recovered her control of the situation, something she would gladly fight the Sheriff and his know-it-all sidekick to retain.

5.

Once Anna had shown Matt and Dom into the first-floor study, Dom called his office and excused himself from any further questioning. Matt knew that the interview with the grief-stricken parents would be difficult, but now that the interrogation didn't involve Jeremy Hill or Mrs. Hill, Dom really had little use for the proceedings. Over his cellphone, Dom summoned Sheriff's Deputy Tom Nelson, who had taken Matt's statement on having found the body and said his goodbyes. Matt would get a ride back to Jackson with Tom, whenever they were finished at the winery. Sidney Dietrich had been dispatched to usher in the parents. Matt had no doubt that she would use the opportunity to find out what she could in her aggressive defense of any member of the Hill family.

Matt passed the time perusing the study that had belonged to Hans Hill. It reflected the life and tastes of a very wealthy and powerful man of an earlier era. The desk was a massive Victorian piece of solid walnut, carved with ornate designs, the surface inset with a leather gold-tooled desk blotter. The hand-woven rug was patterned with a rich oriental design, and the paintings were late nineteenth-century Western landscapes, including a particularly romantic view of the falls at Yosemite, with billowing pink and lavender clouds filling the sky. Leather bound classics lined the bookshelves, the titles revealing a taste for the adventure tales of Jack London, Rudyard Kipling, and Robert Louis Stevenson. Photographs encased in heavy silver frames lined the polished reading tables on either side of twin leather armchairs. Matt picked up several black and white photographs featuring Hans Hill on horseback, Hans skiing, Hans crouched down holding Jeremy as a blonde toddler with a young and beautiful Maude, her golden hair swept up into a fashionable chignon. Hans was also displayed with a variety of political figures, including former Governors Pat Brown and Ronald Reagan. There were no photographs of Grace, Maude

Hill's daughter from her first marriage.

Matt suddenly remembered his and Jeremy's senior year in high school, when the class party had been held at the Hill's ranch before it was a winery. Matt had wandered dripping wet from the swimming pool, wrapped in a towel, looking for a bathroom, and had mistakenly opened the door to the study. Hans Hill was standing at his desk, barking into the phone about buying some AT&T stock, and Matt had hurriedly closed the door. Matt's vivid impression was of a tall, blonde, weathered Scandinavian man of great energy and authority, his eyebrows scowling, and face lined from constant exposure to the outdoors.

In sharp contrast, Matt's father was a former merchant seaman in love with his Seagram's V.O. and little else. With his drinking problem and a nasty temper, Matt's father, Ron Dunleavy, had moved to the Sierra Foothills from San Francisco as a favor to Matt's mother whose family lived and worked on a sheep ranch outside Sutter Creek. Matt's father had tried to work as a machinist, but work was often hard to find and easily lost when he failed to show up after a bender. Matt's mother supplemented their income with cleaning jobs in the antique and sundry shops of downtown Sutter Creek and Jackson. Matt's family life was defined by his father's alcoholic binges and his mother's worry and disappointed expectations. Matt had escaped into athletics at Argonaut High School and had become quarterback and star of the football team. He was welcomed into the homes of affluent ranchers and business owners, but he had never reciprocated by inviting any of his friends to his home. He had been deeply ashamed of their poverty and his father's unpredictable and violent rages.

All through high school, Jeremy Hill hosted pool parties every weekend during the summer and the Hills' octagonal guesthouse was famous for welcoming hard-core partiers, who were served far more than just a few beers. Quite a few of the local boys had tried cocaine for the first time with Jeremy Hill and when their own strained financial resources couldn't afford them unlimited access to coke, they turned to a cheaper and much more readily available supply of crystal meth. Jeremy also had sole use of the family's alpine home in Sun Meadows, right at the foot of the ski lifts. Many of the more willing local girls had spent time there with Jeremy, as well as the hard-core partying crowd. Matt had avoided most of the parties, as they were all too close a reminder of everything that was out of control at home.

"Can we get you anything, Matt?" Startled, Matt turned around from his reveries and found Mrs. Hill standing calmly in the doorway. In the photographs, she had been a middle-aged beauty, with coiled blond hair twisted up and wearing long, colorfully printed kaftans. Twenty-five years later, she was more sharp-boned as her skin had thinned, and whereas she had once been tall and regal, she was now stooped and white-haired. Still, there were faint traces of the beauty she had once been in her high forehead and cheekbones, and especially in her piercing sky-blue eyes. Matt strode toward her and held out his hand. She grasped his in both of hers.

"I am so glad to see you. You've changed, Matt. You're a very handsome man now, not that wiry teenager you were when you went off to Stanford. We were all very proud of you, you know."

"Thank you, ma'am," he nodded. He was surprised at how strongly she clasped his hand.

"I never thought you'd ever come back to us. I thought Stanford would be your key to a new and successful life."

Matt shrugged. "There are different definitions of success, ma'am. I could be wrong, but I don't know if the Stanford red-hots are really all that happy driving Teslas and yakking all day into their earpieces. I do know it wasn't the life for me. I like it here. I like being home."

He wasn't stung by her comment. Everybody wondered what had happened when he came back after Stanford and went through the County's training program to become a Sheriff's Deputy. A Comparative Literature major in his undergraduate studies, he had dropped out of the MBA program after less than a year. The truth was, he had hated interning in a start-up company, where he had found himself immersed in the frantic, anxious energy swirling around eager young MBA's, palpably desperate for the quick hit of big money that going public or being bought out by Google or Microsoft would surely bring. Considering other alternatives like real estate or investment banking just promised another version of the same thing: being hemmed into an office sweating under the artificial pressure exerted by driven executives with a rapacious greed for money. Matt had a yearning for home, for the mountains, pine-scented air, and the way billions of visible stars looked in the night sky, as if he could reach out and trail his fingers in the Milky Way. Mrs. Hill patted his hand reassuringly.

"I know you do. I wish more of our young people could find employment here. Maybe they would stay and raise families. You must have felt very fortunate when the Jackson Casino became so successful."

"Yes, ma'am. My grandmother was very lucky to have had such a smart sister. I don't take it for granted."

Unlike Jeremy Hill, not everyone had a stone manor house and hundreds of acres of vineyards to provide ready employment, Matt thought, but his own grandmother had the debatable good fortune to be full Mi-Wuk and related to the clan that started the county's first Indian gambling casino. His grandmother's sister, his great-aunt Loretta, had founded a bingo hall on tribal property thirty years previously, and the proceeds had been re-invested to build the huge Jackson Casino and Resort Hotel on two hundred acres of otherwise fairly useless red dirt covered by scraggly oaks and manzanita bushes. Since the first profitable years of the tribal casino's operation, Matt's mother, Peggy, never had to clean stores or houses ever again and she never had to do without. For all their early years of poverty, Peggy's retirement had been comfortably provided for by the tribe. The tribe had paid for Matt's expenses at Stanford that were not covered by his football scholarship and since college, Matt had received a generous allowance by virtue of his tribal membership.

"I know that you and Jeremy haven't always gotten along, Matt. But I want you to know that I'm grateful for any help you can give us during this very sad time and I'm sure that Jeremy feels the same."

"I'll do what I can."

Matt was fond of Mrs. Hill, but he couldn't make any promises. She deserved better in a son. Matt motioned to one of the leather armchairs. Mrs. Hill sat down wearily, pulling her patterned skirt to one side as she leaned toward him attentively. Matt took the heavy carved desk chair and turned it so that they faced one another. When he sat down, their knees were almost touching.

"Uh, let me ask you, ma'am. Your lawyer isn't here, so do you feel comfortable answering a few questions?" Matt heavily emphasized the word "lawyer," drawling it out into multiple syllables, calling to mind Sidney's small, combative personality.

"Of course, Matt, anything I can do to help. What a tragedy for poor Carmelo and his wife. We're all so upset." Matt wanted to retort that Jeremy had not appeared all that upset but kept silent.

"Yes, ma'am. Do you know any of the girl's friends or acquaintances?"

"No, I'm afraid not. I think she had a beau, but I'm not sure how I know that. Maybe someone mentioned it to me. I can't say I took any special interest in the young woman." Matt wondered how a child could grow up for ten years just yards away from the stone house without anyone taking any notice.

"Was she close to anyone on the ranch? Was anyone friendly with her outside her own family?" There was no point pulling out his notepad and jotting anything down, Matt thought. This conversation was turning into a time-waster. Mrs. Hill shook her head, clasping her veined hands together nervously.

"I am so sorry, Matt. I don't know anything that could be of help to you. I just didn't know the girl at all well, and I don't really know anything about her."

Sidney Dietrich suddenly appeared at the door, her hazel eyes glittering.

"Sheriff, I assumed you would know that no conversation would take place with any member of the Hill family outside of my presence." Matt stood up, turning the brim of his hat around in his hands.

"I'm not the Sheriff. I'm a special deputy. You can call me Matt, and Mrs. Hill specifically told me that she didn't require your presence. I'm an old family friend."

Maude turned and looked at Sidney guiltily.

"Oh, dear. I've upset my lawyer. I'm so terribly sorry, but you see, I've known Matt for almost his entire life, and I have nothing to hide from him."

Instead of mollifying Sidney, Mrs. Hill's apology had the opposite effect. She was clearly furious, her cheeks flushed. She had been home-towned by Dunleavy and they both knew it.

"Well, if you don't have anything further for Mrs. Hill, I'll bring in the parents. I don't need to tell you how upset they are," Sidney retorted brusquely. "By the way, another deputy just arrived. He's parking his cruiser now. I'll show him in. Let me know if you need anything else." Without waiting for a response, she turned to usher in the dead girl's parents. Matt turned to Mrs. Hill.

"Ma'am. Is there any money or cash missing from the winery that you're aware of?"

"No. I don't think so. But you would have to ask Jeremy."

"It's been a pleasure, ma'am," he said, shaking her hand.

"Oh, Matt," she said despairingly, clutching his sleeve. "Why do these horrible things have to happen? I've lived too long. Far too long."

As she turned to leave, the grief-stricken parents waited quietly in the shadows of the hallway. Seeing them, Mrs. Hill reached out to embrace each one in turn, an act of spontaneous kindness that caused the girl's mother to sob uncontrollably, half leaning on her husband's arm for support. Matt waited, braced to face the survivors of the most devastating loss imaginable. He had no answer for Mrs. Hill as to why. No one ever did.

6.

"Well, at least we have a name," Deputy Sheriff Tom Nelson confirmed as he drove Matt back from the winery to the Sheriff's office on Court Street in downtown Jackson. Matt was silent, reflecting on the interview that had taken just forty minutes and a toll on his emotions. The mother, Gloria, did not speak a word of English and sat through the proceedings with red-rimmed eyes and a catatonic expression, her fingers working their way through a strand of rosary beads. The father, Carmelo, had suffered through a hundred carefully-phrased questions with quiet dignity, but was able to give very little information. They had no idea whatsoever as to why their daughter would have been in possession of more than $20,000 in cash stuffed in a backpack. When Matt showed the mother a digital photo on Tom Nelson's phone of the "Dora the Explorer" backpack locked in the evidence closet, she had burst into tears. It was Selena's no doubt. The little gnome keychain attached to the zipper had been Selena's in the fifth grade.

Selena's parents described her as a normal, happy girl a year out of high school, who wasn't ever in any trouble. She was well-liked in school, got good grades, and was taking classes at American River, a nearby community college. They had drawn a blank with the parents, except for the name of a boy that Selena had dated her senior year, and who her father described as a "good kid" but "kinda jealous that Selena was going to college and not spending more time with him." The boy's name was Alejandro Almazan and he worked in the kitchen at the St. George Hotel in Volcano. They called him Alex.

"Yeah," Matt acknowledged, "We have a name." He didn't feel particularly hopeful. Even if this was a jealous-boyfriend scenario and they could close the case quickly, it wouldn't bring the raven-haired young girl back to life or bring any real comfort to her shattered parents.

After checking in at the Sheriff's Department next to the brand-new red-brick County Administration building on Court Street, Matt and Tom got back in the cruiser and headed out to the little Gold Rush town of Volcano, a favorite out-of-the-way tourist destination for those looking for the authentic Gold Country. Winding roads followed the natural contours of Sutter Creek past picturesque pastures that had been cleared long ago for cattle and horses. Ancient barns had a dilapidated but charming quality that was reflected in paintings that graced many of the area's art galleries.

Volcano consisted of: a one-block Main Street a few side streets with a seasonal outdoor theater, an ancient General Store, a fragrant bakery occupying the old assay office, the old and reportedly haunted St. George Hotel locally called "the George," the equally old Union Inn where vigilante justice had been quickly dispensed with the first hanging trial in the new territory, various whitewashed cottages sporting authentic tin corrugated roofs from mining days, and the old town cemeteries that dated from the first prospectors in 1848, very few of whom ever lived to see old age. The town's permanent population at the height of the Gold Rush had numbered perhaps twenty thousand, but in current times numbered barely more than a hundred. There were more live animals and cemetery residents than people. The town was named after the geologic depression in which it found itself, allegedly in a dormant volcano, but that was just a popular myth. It was cold and wet in the winter as a result of being situated at the bottom of a giant rock bowl intersected by a creek that had been overgrown with madrone, oaks, and thickly tangled blackberry vines. The sun's warmth never quite reached down to the bottom of the hollow during winter. Volcano was at its best at this time in early spring, when daffodils bloomed, wildflowers carpeted the pastures, and everything was still lush and green from the winter rains.

The Sheriff's cruiser made a final turn into the town, and the three-story balconied façade of the George loomed up quickly in front of them. The George showed its age but exuded antique charm like everything else in Volcano. Its balcony railings were slightly askew, as were its chimneys. Fortunately, Matt thought, they weren't in San Francisco where one good earthquake would have brought the whole building tumbling down long ago. They drove past the old wooden plank exterior of the adjoining Whiskey Flat Saloon. Tom cast an inquisitive glance at Matt, who looked back and shrugged.

"Yeah, I know. Don't worry. I haven't been back since... Well, since."

Tom had been the deputy on call the night that Matt had been unceremoniously tossed from the Saloon and had flipped his Jeep around the curve leading out of town. After checking Matt for any injuries, Tom had called the tow truck, had driven Matt home in the cruiser and tucked him into bed to sleep it off. Tom had never said a word to anyone, and Matt had been grateful enough to try and clean up his act. He owed him one.

Matt and Tom both knew Bob and Shirley Granby, the affable new owners of the George, as did everyone in the county. It was a second career for the Granbys as they were refugees from the San Francisco Bay Area. They relished being both bar and innkeepers and would mingle with the raucous crowd in the Saloon every Wednesday during Locals Night; when music, generous shots of liquor, and reasonable prices would bring patrons from all over the county to their original, rough, and wood-hewed low ceilings and miners' barstools for a meal and lively company. Everyone ended up at the George on Wednesday nights sooner or later, except for down and out locals who had a little discretionary money to spend. There were plenty of biker bars and pool halls up and down Highway 88 that catered to a less affluent crowd.

Matt and Tom entered the hotel lobby to find the Granbys since it was early in the day and the Saloon was locked up and empty. The lobby's wallpaper, period piece lithographs, and Victorian furnishings enhanced the antique feel of the place. A kid like Alejandro Almazan would be working in the back kitchen, Matt knew. Bob Granby was hovering in the entryway confirming a dinner reservation by phone. Gray-haired and portly with a white mustache, Bob was energy in motion when he was trying to manage the kitchen and the hotel. His eyes brightened immediately when he spotted Matt, but then crinkled with concern when he noticed Tom in his Sheriff's uniform. He motioned them over as he finished his call, jotting down a name and time on the reservations list. When he cradled the receiver, the phone immediately rang again. Bob rolled his eyes skyward, and engaged in another reservations wrangle, keeping the men waiting.

"Stay here and explain what we're doing," Matt suggested. "I'll duck in the kitchen and see if our boy's there."

After a delay of a minute or so, and almost simultaneously, Bob finished his call and Matt emerged from the kitchen.

"Find what you're looking for?" Bob queried Matt, as he emerged quickly from the culinary chaos. Matt motioned Bob out through the rear screen door and onto the porch, overlooking a lovingly tended garden bordering the creek. Bob waited expectantly. The three of them stood close together, as if Bob recognized that they had something of a confidential nature to disclose.

"Alejandro Almazan," Matt said quietly, and then waited for a reply.

"Good kid. Hard worker. Always on time. Never a problem. Why do you ask?"

"Just wondered where he might be found. He may know something in a missing person's case."

"Oh," Bob said, frowning. "Well, actually, he called in sick today. It's not like him. And it's Wednesday night, too. We're going to be busy."

Tom pulled a card out of his front shirt pocket.

"My number's on the card. Can you give us a call when he comes around again? Appreciate it, Bob."

"Sure, thing." Bob glanced at Tom's card and then stuffed it in his pants pocket when the telephone rang again. He didn't even glance at them as they headed out the lobby door and into the street.

"So. Our boy's taken off," Tom said flatly.

"Maybe," Matt shrugged. "We'll find him. Go ahead and radio in a description and get someone to drop into his last known address and any other relatives or friends. Don't let them anyone else talk to him. Just tell 'em to let us know when they find him. Got it?"

Tom nodded and went directly to the radio in the Sheriff's cruiser. Tom was used to taking orders from Matt, as he had worked under him in the Sheriff's Department when Tom had joined as a rookie. They were a good team. Matt was usually calm, direct, and focused. Tom was quick and detail-oriented for such a young man. Neither one appeared concerned that Alejandro Almazan was suddenly absent from his usual work. It was a small county. They'd find him one way or another.

7.

Maude Hill barely touched her lunch, appearing genuinely distressed at the death of Selena Rodriguez and deeply concerned about its effect on the entire Rodriguez family. Every once in a while, she would place her full fork back down on the edge of her china plate and reach for her napkin to dab her eyes and take a sip of water. Jeremy merely toyed with his food, every so often looking off and staring at nothing in particular. Sidney managed to eat the exquisite wild salmon that was delicately broiled and served with a light cream sauce with roasted, peppered Brussels sprouts and new, boiled potatoes. Sidney hoped that she wouldn't appear too heartless if she indulged in consuming every bit of the savory lunch. As usual, she was starving.

"Mother, we're doing everything we can," Jeremy sighed impatiently. "By the way, where's Grace?"

"The nurse is bringing her down. She'll be here shortly." Maude gave her nose a discreet wipe with a tissue.

Sidney was curious to meet with Grace, if only because she was the first person that Maude had directed her to talk to about Joshua Morgan's death, which was the real reason she was there. Sidney didn't feel comfortable around police, even local cops. She had experienced too many close and uncomfortable encounters with law enforcement during her father's downfall. As the conversation lulled and almost as if she were on autopilot, Sidney's mind flashed on the day that one of her own real estate investment clients had complained about hemorrhaging money in a deal of her father's. The complaint had triggered their family's collapse. Sidney had spent weeks going through volumes of documents, signed loan agreements and balance sheets, first for her client's bankrupt development, and then for most of her father's other real estate projects. Slowly, and with dawning horror, she had realized that Adam Dietrich had constructed a giant Ponzi scheme using different companies and entities, some of which he had even placed in her name. As a prominent client of the law firm of Ware, Lyman & Cohen, her father had increased the wealth of many of its partners through the years, but Sidney discovered that it was all built on quicksand. The success of one deal had allowed for the payment of debt-ridden projects that had languished for years without any benefit to hundreds of limited partners. The juggling act was complex. Late at night, deep in the law firm's file room, with documents spread out all over the tables and floor, Sidney had discovered with ever-increasing alarm that her adored father was a thief and a liar.

Sidney suspected that her contact with Matt Dunleavy and Tom Nelson had triggered a resurgence of disturbing memories that she continually struggled to suppress. With her father facing a very long prison sentence, and with absolutely nothing to keep her in the city once her relationship with Paul was over, she had been at the lowest place of her life until the call to Jack McGlynn had saved her. Now she had to get used to an unaccustomed role as a small-town lawyer, helping Jack's extended family of clients as an inexperienced general practitioner. There was a part of her that liked the intimacy of getting to know Jack's clients on a more personal level. It was more rewarding than dealing with surly, over-leveraged real estate investors and money gained or lost in such massive quantities that it was almost meaningless. But she was uncomfortable dealing with distressed people with real-world problems up close and personal, in the easy way that Jack did. Maybe it would come with time, Sidney reflected as she helped herself to a generous salad portion, waiting for the wheelchair to arrive bearing Grace to the table.

A thin and wiry attendant suddenly appeared, wheeling her charge through the dining room door. She handled Grace's wheelchair with ease, and her entry caused no particular notice except to Sidney, who was seeing Grace for the very first time. Sidney was surprised that Grace was such a large woman, not the frail wheelchair-bound invalid that Sidney had supposed. Almost as an afterthought, Maude Hill introduced her daughter.

"Sidney, this is my daughter Gracie. Grace Simon, although she goes by Hill. Grace, Sidney Dietrich works for Jack McGlynn and she's been kind enough to guide us through the legal thickets with the police today. I'm sure you're aware that Carmelo's daughter was found deceased yesterday."

"Yes, Mother. I'd heard. It's a shame."

With deep, dark-hooded eyes, Grace swept the faces of her mother and brother for their reactions, however, both were muted and focused on their meals. Grace's sharp glance settled on Sidney and neither one flinched from their mutual observation. Grace appeared to be very used to being an observer, which was Sidney's natural role as well. In silent contemplation of each other, they finally each suppressed a smile. The meal was completed in relative silence. With Sidney as the outsider, the small family group may have been reluctant to exchange private views of the recent tragedy or they may have just been somewhat emotionally numbed. Sidney decided to breach the uncomfortable quiet.

"Grace," she said softly, but in that already quiet setting, her voice startled everyone. "I wondered if we could have some time together after lunch. I wanted to be able to ask you some questions before the police had their opportunity."

"You can take me for a spin around the garden. We can talk undisturbed." Sidney noticed that Jeremy suddenly looked sharply at his sister. She looked back at him and smiled crookedly. They made an odd pair. Jeremy was tall, slender, and sandy-haired; an attractive and athletic man approaching forty who looked as if working in the winery agreed with him. Grace could have passed for even older than fifty. Corpulent, coarse-featured, and mannish, her name completely failed to describe any of her visible characteristics. Grace's wide face was fringed by casually chopped-off gray hair streaked with thin black strands. Her short, bare nails were devoid of any color and her body was encased in a thick black and white striped Berber kaftan, with a couple of well-worn crocheted afghan blankets, tucked around her knees, under which her damaged legs were hidden. An odd pair, those two, reflected Sidney silently.

Once the plates were cleared, Grace nodded to Sidney that she was ready. Sidney pulled the wheelchair out with surprising ease and turned it without knocking into anything. Grace pointed to the concrete wheelchair ramp just off the patio that met a hardened path, wide enough to accommodate the wheels and smooth enough to navigate. Jeremy and his mother were left together to sip some coffee and scoop fresh strawberry sorbet, something Sidney would have loved to have tasted as well, but Grace was very much in charge here, and strawberries and sorbet were apparently just not enough of a temptation over which to tarry.

The garden was several acres of stunningly beautiful and carefully cultivated landscaping. It was artfully unstudied, but Sidney knew that the exact natural-seeming placement of native grasses, rocks, tulips, and buddleia was carefully planned and quite expensive to achieve.

"Did Carmelo design the garden?" she asked as she pushed Grace along various winding rock-bordered paths.

"Oh, no. That was Mother, entirely. Of course, Carmelo was consulted about plant placement because of sun exposure and access to irrigation, but Mother's the gardening genius."

"Did you know Carmelo's family well, Selena in particular?"

"Well, you see… Sidney, is it? I'm a bit housebound, so I don't tend to get out much. Carmelo isn't in the house except on occasion and I've never even seen any of his family here. I've caught a glimpse of the daughter through my bedroom window from time to time. It faces west, and their cottage is in that direction, but I can't say I've seen her more than a few times getting in or out of a car."

Sidney was starting to get a little hot and tired pushing the wheelchair. She spotted a wrought-iron bench under a weeping willow tree that seemed to offer some decent shade.

"Can we sit here and talk for a bit?" Sidney asked, hoping for an affirmative answer. She pushed the wheelchair to face the bench and gratefully seated herself under the shade tree.

"Your mother has asked me to look into your uncle's death," Sidney said, as Grace's hooded eyes opened in surprise.

"I guess she's uncomfortable with the suicide verdict in his case. Frankly, I don't know what I can do to help. It happened in San Francisco years ago, from what she said. But maybe I can put her mind at ease if she thinks that everything was done properly." Sidney paused to gauge Grace's reaction. Grace sat with her elbows propped on the armrests, her chin resting on her clasped hands. Her thick dark eyebrows were knitted together in thought.

"What exactly does Mother need help with?" Grace queried, somewhat puzzled. "She simply can't accept the fact that her beloved brother committed suicide. There's nothing more to say. You'd be wasting your time."

Sidney was taken aback by Grace's bitter tone. "She doesn't think there was any reason for your uncle to have been so unhappy that he would have killed himself."

Grace snorted loudly and somewhat unattractively. "Did my mother tell you that her brother Joshua was gay?"

"No. She didn't mention that. Do you think that it would have had anything to do with his death?"

"Maybe. Joshua may have been gay or bisexual, I don't know. I think there were men and women in his life and several women who were madly in love with him. I don't think it made for happiness on either part. But in Joshua's case, I'm quite sure that he was deeply in love with one of Jeremy's friends from school, a most decidedly heterosexual boy, who never knew of my uncle's passion for him. His suicide may simply have been a case of unrequited love."

"How do you know about the boy?" Sidney asked. Grace shook her head at the memory and the futility of her uncle's attachment.

"I would visit my uncle in the city with Jeremy. Occasionally

Jeremy's friend would come along. My uncle's personality changed completely around them. Instead of being cold and unfriendly, as he was to me, Joshua would act almost as if he were a giddy schoolgirl whenever Jeremy and his friend showed up for a night in the city or a day of sailing out on the bay. It was embarrassing to watch, it was so obvious."

"Are there any of Joshua's old friends still around? That boy in particular," Sidney asked, inwardly bristling at Grace's callous comments, and struggling to keep her voice light and steady.

Grace nodded, "There might be. Joshua was sixty-four when he blew his brains out. There were a lot of people at the funeral, many of them genuinely grief-stricken. He did have a lot of close women friends: "my fag hags," he called them. Women loved to pose for him. I'll make you a list. You know, they'd probably all still be in San Francisco, if you want to make the trip."

"Thanks, I'm sure I will." Sidney shifted her position. The wrought-iron garden seat was decorative, but not comfortable. "What about Jeremy? Would he be aware of any reasons for your Uncle Joshua's suicide?"

Grace's already unattractive visage became dark with anger. "Jeremy would have told me if he had any thoughts about our uncle's suicide. We're very close. He's already been upset enough by this business with Carmelo's daughter. I would ask you to conduct your own investigation without troubling him. He has enough to worry about just running the winery."

Note to self, Sidney thought: protective of Jeremy. She decided to change her tactics.

"I'm sorry to have upset you. I'm just trying to do the job your mother asked me to do."

With the apology, Grace brightened immediately. "Of course, I understand. Well, we'd better be getting back, or they'll worry that I'll spill all the family's secrets!"

As Sidney pushed the wheelchair up the ramp to the patio, she stopped just short of the open French doors. "Is there any reason that you know of why your mother might suspect that Joshua didn't kill himself? For example, do you know if he had any enemies? Any jealous or rival artists?"

Grace shrugged. "Not that I know of – I think she may be suffering from guilt of some kind, maybe that she didn't understand her brother's unhappiness. I'll give you the names of some of Joshua's women friends, but I think you won't find anything there, either. None of the men in our family had much luck with love, except for my step-father, Hans, and my mother of course. Jeremy oddly enough never did 'fall in love,' madly or in any other way. He's a little standoffish with women. You know that Sheriff, Matt Dunleavy? Well, his wife Sarah had her eyes on Jeremy. I think she thought that she could sink her hooks into Jeremy and marry a rich vineyard owner. But Jeremy ignored her advances, so she finally threw herself at that wine broker. She left the Sheriff in a very bad way. He took it hard. I heard he lost his job over it."

For a brief moment, Sidney felt some compassion for the tall, rangy ex-Sheriff. She knew what it was to be abandoned by someone you loved.

"Well, if you can give me some names of Joshua's close friends, I'll start proving a negative against all evidence to the contrary: Joshua Morgan didn't kill himself."

Grace let out a harsh rasp that Sidney supposed was a laugh. "Come around again tomorrow and I'll have that list for you. And good luck. You'll need it."

After turning Grace over to her caretaker, Sidney tried to find Maude and say good-bye to Jeremy but found that Maude was resting quietly and that Jeremy had returned to the winery. Driving back into Jackson from Quarry Hill, Sidney sighed from the frustration of such a vague and open-ended assignment that really had nothing to do with her legal skills. She knew it was futile to try to prove that Joshua Morgan hadn't killed himself when he had been reportedly found with his head on his kitchen table and a gun in his hand. Maybe she could find a motive, even a broken heart, so that Maude's brother's suicide might make more sense. She already felt strongly attached to Maude and would be happy to do whatever she could to bring her peace of mind. Peace of mind was a rare commodity, Sidney knew, and if she could give a little bit of it to Maude Hill, then that would be a good day's work, no matter how long it took.

8.

Matt and Tom were called to check out Alejandro Almazan's last known address at the Gold Run Trailer Park on the southwest side of Highway 88. The boy was last seen there, just up the road from the Indian casino. The trailer park was known as a trouble spot for drinking, fighting and occasionally, an overdose death or two. Matt remembered that just a couple of months back, two card-playing, hard-drinking friends had ended up with one of them dead after an argument and a knifing, but Bob Grandby had told them that Alejandro was a hardworking kid. Most jobs in restaurants and construction upcountry were still filled by plenty of locals willing to work for minimum wage or less, so workers from Mexico were relatively few. It was only in the low-lying valley vineyards that seasonal Mexican labor came and went. Word had it that Alejandro or "Alex" as he was known, had come to Jackson with an uncle from Michoacan five years before, had enrolled in the local high school and had worked hard as a busboy at the George and on various local construction sites. At Matt's request, the principal at Argonaut High School had been interviewed and vouched that the kid had kept his nose clean. Now, suddenly, Alex's friend or sweetheart Selena was dead, and he'd come up missing from several jobs.

The Sheriff's cruiser nosed into the only driveway available at the trailer park, which was squeezed in between Highway 88 and the rushing spring waters of Sutter Creek. Despite its dubious history, the trailer park mostly housed the working poor of the county, who spent their days logging leased land in the national forest, weed whacking for fire control, or doing the scut work for home building projects. Disability came early for trailer park residents: wrecked knees, ruined backs, diseased lungs from too many pack-years of cigarettes, inflamed livers from a lifetime of alcohol abuse, and grinding poverty all combined to visit a permanent cloud of misery on the inhabitants. The patrolman interviewing Alex's high school principal reported that Alex was still living with his uncle, hoping to earn enough for his own place and a ticket to community college.

Matt and Tom emerged from the cruiser right next to Space No. 23, where they had been told that Alex's uncle lived. An unkempt worn-away dirt path led right up to uneven steps with peeling paint. Behind the trailers lay a junkyard of abandoned cars, the hoods left yawning open following a cursory but futile examination of engine trouble that no one had the money to fix. Refrigerators with their doors ripped from their hinges littered the bank next to the creek, their insides molded and rusting. Here and there, someone had thought to stick a painted duck whirligig out front of a metal trailer for decoration, but Matt thought there was something pathetic about those little wooden wings flailing helplessly in the breeze. Matt noted that there wasn't a wide-body trailer in any of the spaces that did not suffer from rust or roof leaks. Holes were patched with duct tape or in some places, blue tarps known locally as the "county flag" were tied down with baling string. Matt knocked lightly on the screen door that hung slightly askew and was torn in so many places that even the mosquitoes must have sneered. After a few moments, he knocked again, harder. A face appeared at the dusty glass window and the front door squeaked open quickly in response to Tom Nolan's uniform.

"Are you Alex's uncle?" Matt asked the youngish, stocky, dark-skinned man in a too-small wife-beater undershirt. The man nodded, wiping nervously at his black mustache.

"I am Ricardo, Alex's uncle. Is somethin' wrong? Where's Alex?"

"That's what we'd like to know. A friend of his died and we were looking for him to see if he could help us explain what might have happened."

"Ah, Selena. I heard. Is too bad," he shook his head of unkempt black hair. "Nice girl."

"Do you know where Alex is? He didn't show up at his job at the George yesterday."

"No," Ricardo shook his head again. "I work nights – sleep days – I donno where Alex go. He's a big boy now."

"If he were to stay with a friend, who might that be?" Nolan stepped in to complete the questioning. It was obvious this was getting them nowhere. Ricardo shook his head.

"Oh, maybe his frien' Deelan. I donno. Maybe," Ricardo shrugged.

After attempting to get the information of 'Deelan' or Dylan's whereabouts, they left and returned to the cruiser, Alex's uncle fiddling with Tom Nolan's card that listed an emergency contact number. Neither was under any illusion that the uncle would call, even if Alex showed up. Apparently, Alex wanted to make sure he would not be found, and his uncle was either feigning ignorance or he truly had no idea of his nephew's whereabouts.

They needed to get back to Jackson. According to a radio call from Dom Colangelo, the ME's initial report out of Sacramento was ready. The preliminary findings should be reviewed quickly. Tom and Matt drove the twenty minutes back to Jackson to the Sheriff's office. Colangelo was waiting for them in his spacious second-floor office that used to be Matt's. He motioned them to sit down and handed copies of the ME's fax report to each.

"Of course, forensics isn't done with all the fiber and other trace evidence. That'll take another few weeks." Unnecessarily, he read the report out loud.

"The body is of a young, well-nourished female of Hispanic appearance," he began. Much like any autopsy report, the condition of each body part and the weight of every organ was recorded. Everything seemed perfectly routine except for the unnatural cause of death.

"Preliminary cause of death is strangulation with a ligature: a thin gauge wire that was removed post-mortem from around the neck," Dom confirmed what they already suspected. There were no surprises until Dom read, "Upon examination, the uterus and cervix reveal enlargement and softening, consistent with recent vaginal delivery, estimated to have occurred between four to five months previously."

At that point, Dom stopped reading and they all looked at each other. "I think this report says that she must've had a baby, gentlemen: about four or five months ago." There was silence in the room for thirty seconds while the news was processed.

"Why didn't anyone tell us?" Nolan asked. "Someone must've known."

"What happened to the child?" Matt interjected, looking at Tom and Dom, knowing full well that they had no answer. "We'll check at Jackson Memorial. And all the family practitioners and OB-GYN's in and around town. There can't be too many. But before that, let's talk to the family again. They may be holding something back. And it may be the reason why she's dead."

*****

This time, the call to Sidney came from Jeremy Hill directly. More animated than usual, he said that the Sheriffs' deputies had returned to the winery and were questioning the girl's parents. They had asked to resume their questioning of the Hill family members as well, and they all wanted her to be there. It was late afternoon, and Sidney was tired. She was working on a property dispute for one of Jack's clients and she was busy finishing a migraine-inducing Motion for Summary Judgment. She handed the changes to Marjorie as she passed her desk in the reception area that was lined with antique wooden captain's chairs against flowery wallpaper, the stiff leather seats offering only a minimum of comfort. The carpeting, Jack had claimed, was original bordello. He never wanted the office to look modern or upgraded. He was simply delighted that his office was in the upstairs rooms of an old whorehouse, and he kept the red velvet curtains and crimson-splashed oriental carpeting as proof of the original tenants' occupation.

75

"Sorry, Marj. It's the best I can do. Tell Jack that the police – Sheriffs, rather – are out at the winery hounding the Hills again. I should be there. I signed the motion papers, so they just need to be filed at the courthouse by four o'clock."

"Right you are, babe," Marjorie responded. At first resentful, Marjorie now liked Sidney's female presence in the office. Sidney wasn't pushy or demanding, as she had expected, and it was nice to have a confidential ally. The two could smile at Jack's peculiarities while bonding over their shared loyalty.

Troubled by the Sheriffs' deputies' sudden reappearance, Sidney rushed to get into her car on Jackson's Main Street and flew down Highway 88 to the winery. She chewed her lip, wondering why they would return so soon that very afternoon, asking to speak with both the girl's family as well as the Hills. Sidney only hoped that Maude's partiality to Matt Dunleavy, Jeremy's old schoolmate, wouldn't loosen her tongue and cause her to engage in too much speculation. She knew full well that whatever was said to the police could be twisted and negatively interpreted. Sidney's tires churned up a bit more gravel than usual in the sweeping private driveway, as she checked her excessive speed and slid before coming to a complete stop. The Sheriff's cruiser was already parked under the shade of an acacia tree. She took a deep breath before entering the house, not waiting for anyone to respond to her knock. Jeremy was pacing in the hallway just outside Hans Hill's old study.

"They're in there with my mother," he jerked his head in the direction of the office. "She's not well. It's not right." Sidney barged in unannounced and found Matt and Tom in the study with Maude, who looked haggard and deflated. Upon Sidney's arrival, the deputies rose politely, but Maude stayed seated. She looked up at Sidney, guiltily. Sidney suspected that she'd been chatting it up again with Dunleavy and her cheeks flushed with annoyance.

"Oh, hello, dear. The Sheriffs were just letting us know that poor Selena might have had a baby before her death. It just makes everything so much worse, of course. I am so, so sorry for her and for her family."

"We'd like to ask a few questions of your son, Jeremy, if that's okay with you," Tom Nelson asked Mrs. Hill ever-so-politely, even though everyone in the room knew he didn't need her permission.

"I'm sure that would be fine. I think he's waiting for me right outside," Maude waved in that general direction. Sidney scowled.

"Why are you continuing to question the Hill family?" Sidney broke through the constraints of politeness. No one answered.

"Surely, the dead girl's own family might have more relevant information, especially if, as you say, she was pregnant recently," she challenged.

"We'd be happy to question Mr. Hill at the Jackson Sheriff's Office if you'd prefer, Ms. Dietrich," Matt responded flatly in a take-it-or-leave-it tone. Sidney shook her head. Jack had begged her to be as cooperative with law enforcement as possible – saying that in a small county such as this one that cooperation was the key to deflecting law enforcement's interest. Sidney wasn't so sure, and every instinct in her struggled against the urge to tell them to get the hell out and to not come back without a warrant.

"Go ahead," she capitulated uneasily. "But I insist on being present during questioning."

"Sure," Matt nodded. Mrs. Hill sat quietly during the exchange. "Mrs. Hill, thank you for your help. We're finished. Would you mind asking your son to step in?"

Maude nodded and rose to leave the room. Sidney noticed that she seemed more shrunken and stooped than before. The ordeal had clearly exhausted her. Sidney reached for the elderly woman's frail arm and guided her to the door. Jeremy waited just outside.

"May I have a word with Mr. Hill, please?" Without waiting for a reply, Sidney handed Mrs. Hill to the maid and grabbed the short sleeve of Jeremy's arm, steering him into the large living room. They stood together out of earshot of the two Sheriffs' deputies.

"Listen to me. They're about to question you on whether you have any knowledge that the dead girl was pregnant. Do you have any knowledge of that at all? This is a privileged attorney-client conversation." Sidney searched his face, willing him to answer. Jeremy lowered his eyelids.

"If you do, and don't want to answer, you can refuse at this point. But if you answer any questions at all, you must do so truthfully, do you understand me?" Jeremy's face was weathered from constant sun exposure and the lines around his mouth were drawn into a frown. He stared at the herringbone pattern on the hardwood floor.

"I don't know anything about it," Jeremy asserted, and as surely as she knew her own name, Sidney knew he was lying.

*****

For the final time that day, Sidney drove up Highway 88 just as dark settled on the mountains as the sun melted the horizon in a blaze of hot orange and pink. Sidney reflected that she had yearned for privacy when she left San Francisco behind and she now had it in abundance. Jack's old white Victorian farmhouse was enclosed by a picket fence, wrap-around porch, and a much-patched corrugated metal roof. The veranda was her favorite place to sit in the evenings. She could bundle up in the cool weather and sip a glass of local Barbera while swinging gently on the wooden porch swing. Her views were what any realtor would have described as "magnificent" with "end-of-the-road privacy," meaning that there wasn't a living soul around for miles. This part of the Sierra Nevada foothills was a repeating pattern of parallel green ridges and valleys in an accordion formation, rising and falling one after the other. Her farmhouse perched atop a high ridge near Fiddletown, a crumbling relic of a formerly bustling gold mining encampment. She could see the distant twinkle of lights from the sprawling valley suburbs one hundred miles away. When she had first moved in, Jack had pointed out where a couple of hundred miles south over the Blue Mountain in the distance lay the magnificent granite peaks and massive boulders of Yosemite. To the northwest, Sidney could see the snow-covered, jagged crest of the Desolation Wilderness, beyond which lay magnificent glacier-carved Lake Tahoe.

Sidney remembered coming to visit "Uncle Jack" when she was a little girl, driving for hours away from the noise and congestion of San Francisco, emerging from the back seat of her family's car and being immediately struck by the sweeping vistas surrounding her godfather's ranch. Now, she hoped desperately that they could offer her the peace she was seeking. Sipping her glass of rich, full-bodied red wine helped calm her nerves and she allowed her thoughts to wander to the uncomfortable scene earlier that day in Hans Hill's wood-paneled office. Ultimately, Jeremy had been calm, but he had avoided looking directly at either of his questioners. She was troubled by the interview and feeling increasingly uneasy.

"I think she had a boyfriend," Jeremy muttered. "Someone from her high school. I saw him with her a couple of times. He was also Hispanic. I think I remember the boy dropping her off at her house when I was there talking to Carmelo."

Sidney listened on high alert, watching both Jeremy and Matt dance around each other. Matt continued to press.

"Her mother also saw her talking with you. Apparently, you encouraged her to spend last summer taking classes at the National University in Mexico City. They told us you paid for the trip. That might have been about the time she was pregnant," Matt responded pointedly.

"I don't know anything about that. My family and I decided to help Selena with her education. We only spoke a couple of times about her goals and her interests. I wrote the check for tuition and living expenses. Nothing more," Jeremy insisted.

Dunleavy and Tom Nolan had taken turns following up with questions for Jeremy, with Sidney interjecting frequently, trying to get them to back off, and Jeremy taking on an increasingly uncooperative and defensive tone. Finally, Sidney was through with cooperation.

"That's enough. This interview is over. I'm instructing my client not to answer," she stated firmly, without the least idea whether or not she could take such a position. Law school had woefully failed to prepare her in handling interactions with the police.

The questioning had gone badly, from Sidney's point of view, and she was very glad that she and Jack were going to meet first thing in the morning to review the proceedings. She wished that Jack had been there with her. She was too inexperienced, and it looked as if the focus on Jeremy was not going to simply evaporate.

Relaxing on the porch swing, Sidney took another sip of wine and rolled it on her tongue, considering the implications. So, apparently, Jeremy had helped to send the dead girl to Mexico to take some classes and enrich her education. That didn't make him a murderer, nor was there any proof that he knew she had been pregnant. But with rising alarm, Sidney felt that Jeremy knew more than he let on and she knew that Dunleavy and Nolan had felt exactly the same. The interview had ended with an admonishment for Jeremy not to leave town without notifying the Sheriff's Office, and with Sidney escorting Dunleavy and Nolan to the massive front door.

"Ma'am," Dunleavy had nodded at Sidney as they exited the house. No one had ever called her that before, Sidney thought furiously. Now, wrapped up in a patterned throw blanket on her front porch swing, she smiled in spite of herself at the recollection. "Ma'am," she muttered, how totally corny. He had actually tipped his hat to her as he had said it. He might act like a country bumpkin, but there was a quiet assurance in the way Dunleavy handled himself, and the way he commanded the respect of Deputy Nolan, who seemed to defer to him in all things. Sidney resolved to ask Jack about him. As her father had always said, it was best to keep one's friends close and one's enemies even closer.

9.

The Amador County Jail in Jackson was housed in a three-story, nineteenth-century wooden structure perched on top of a hill, with thick-planked porches and carved wooden balconies. The first-floor porch had been built high off the ground to avoid the winter mud that swirled around the rough-hewn planks before the advent of concrete and asphalt. The interior of the building had been remodeled a few years before, and there was a basic, functioning heat and air conditioning system that made inhabiting the building at least bearable for law enforcement, visitors, and inmates alike. The Sheriff's Department housed inmates short-term for court appearances and pretrial detentions, with arrests ranging from shoplifting, DUI, spousal battery, burglary, drug offenses, and on rare occasions, even murder. Those arrested would be booked and sent to appropriate cells, depending on gender, age, and level of offense. Interrogations also took place, although Sheriff's Deputies were reluctant to haul anyone across the county for questioning unless the suspect or witness was particularly uncooperative.

Alejandro Almazan suddenly found himself in this latter category, scared witless and fearing deportation by immigration authorities that he expected would arrive any minute. He was a tall boy, with thick, black slicked-back hair and cheeks still retaining baby fullness. A slight darkening of his upper lip hinted at the need for a razor, but he was proud of this indication of manliness and had no desire to eradicate it. Long jean shorts covered his bony knees when he sat down, due to their habit of sagging below his colorful, striped boxer shorts. Matt always wondered how sagging pants had become popular as a fashion statement since they imitated beltless prison garb and created a comical duck-like walk in their wearers. Matt leaned on the table where Alejandro slumped uneasily, still trying to retain an air of bravado. The room was sterile, with a large, county-issued gray steel table and gray steel chairs. The gray linoleum floor lent the room all the cheerfulness of a mortuary.

"So, Alex, how come you didn't show up for your job? You knew we were looking for you, didn't you?" Matt asked calmly. He had no desire to increase the boy's fear. He had never thought that fear produced anything but witnesses who either spouted lies or clammed up. Tom Nolan listened intently in a corner of the room behind Alex, so as to not distract the flow of questioning. Tom tipped his chair back against the wall, his feet off the floor and arms crossed over his chest. His thinning blonde hair was damp from the heat emanating from overhead lights. The brightness was disconcerting. Earlier, he had placed a hand-held tape recorder on the table and the tiny spinning tape made a slight squeak every few seconds.

"Yeah, I heard. But I didn't know why you were lookin' for me," Alex mumbled, "I didn't do nothin'."

"We just wanted to ask you a few questions about your friend, Selena. When did you hear she was dead?"

Alex shifted in his seat. His dark eyes blinked rapidly, and a look of anguish passed over his features, as if he were about to cry. He pressed his lips together.

"One of my friends from the restaurant – another busboy – he told me. He heard it on the news. I ran outta there. I didn't want to talk to nobody."

"Were you and Selena close?" Matt asked. Alex nodded and swallowed. He pressed his lips together again, so hard that they looked puffy. His leg jiggled nervously under the table.

"Yeah. She was my frien'," Alex said simply.

"When was the last time you saw her?" Matt continued.

"Last week at Sober Grad Night."

A memory immediately struck Matt of a warm, sticky summer evening years before, when he was the Argonaut High School star quarterback and Sarah was a cheerleader with long, straight blonde hair and a short, pleated skirt. They had been dating for a few weeks, but Sober Grad Night at the Italian Picnic Grounds was when she had leaned against an oak tree in the shadows and had first allowed him to explore under her sleeveless top and had pressed her body against the length of his, winding her leg around his knee. Every high school kid in the county who was under twenty-one came for Sober Grad Night, checking in with the adult chaperones who were seated at a long table, the fenced grounds transformed into a gaudy neon-lit carnival, complete with thrill rides and cotton candy. The tradition lived on for new generations of kids from high school and barely out of high school, who roamed freely within the picnic grounds until they could leave at 3:00 a.m., either with bleary-eyed parents forming a mile-long pick-up line, or in their own cars parked in a nearby dirt lot in back of the American Legion Hall. Matt and Sarah had clutched and caressed each other in Matt's beat-up Oldsmobile Cutlass that night until 4:00 a.m., when Sarah's parents arrived, worried and anxious and looking for her. Matt had been sheepish with embarrassment, as Sarah's steely-eyed parents hustled her into their Ford pickup truck and drove off, with Sarah smiling slyly at him from the back seat. The vivid memory touched him with a physical longing he had not felt in a long time. Matt looked at Alex, and realized that despite Alex's background, there was a connection of shared experience between them and that he was no different than any other kid in the county, and really, not that much different than his younger self.

"Did you go there to meet Selena? I mean, did you have a date to meet there?" Matt asked, realizing that Alex's nervousness had increased with Matt's lengthy silence. Alex bit his lip and anxiously flicked his thumb and forefinger together.

"Nah," Alex shook his head. "I knew she'd be there, an' I thought we'd hang out, you know: if I saw her."

"Did you – hang out?"

"Yeah," Alex acknowledged. "I was with some friends, and she was with some friends, and so you know, we hung out."

"Did you ever have an intimate relationship with Selena?" Matt asked, and Alex frowned, completely puzzled.

"I mean, did you ever have sex with her?"

Understanding dawned in Alex's face. He shook his head vehemently.

"No, we never did nothin'. I wanted to, you know, but Selena, she told me she had a boyfrien' and she was gonna get married."

"Did she ever tell you that she was pregnant?"

Alex's eyebrows shot up in genuine surprise. "No, no, nothin' like that."

"Did she tell you who her boyfriend was?" Matt leaned over, just a few inches from Alex's face, intent on getting some useful information, not just a bunch of monosyllabic denials. Alex pressed his lips together again, intent on not divulging too much himself.

"Nah. I dunno. He wasn't at the high school, for sure. I'da known. He coulda been in Mexico when she was there, or at the junior college when she came back. I dunno, she never told me."

Matt sensed that this was the end of anything Alex might be either willing or able to tell them. He drew back, sitting on the edge of the table.

"When was the last time you saw Selena?"

"Sober Grad Night, a coupla weeks ago, like I said. Not since then."

Matt thought he'd try another tack.

"Any idea where Selena might have gotten ahold of a lot of cash?"

Alex's eyes suddenly darted around the room and his cheeks flamed with color.

"No. Nothin' like that."

Matt knew he was lying.

"Okay. It could be Selena came across some cash at some point. Did she ever tell you anything about that?"

Alex mutely shook his head.

"Well, let's say a friend of hers was doing some drug dealing. Nothing too serious. Maybe just selling pot to some kids. He might have asked her to hold onto money for him. Or maybe she was selling drugs herself."

Alex shook his head, staring at the floor. "She never did that."

"How do you know?"

Alex said nothing. He clenched his hands together.

"Alex. We don't care about whether you or Selena were selling drugs. What we care about is catching who killed her. Don't you want to help us?"

Alex pinched his eyes, hanging his head. The tears started to drip from his cheeks, his shoulders shaking. Matt and Tom waited for him to collect himself. After a while, Alex took a deep breath and wiped his face.

"When she came back from Mexico, she needed money. A lot of it. She wanted to leave. Start over somewheres else. I told her about a trimming job. We did it for a week or two. She hated it. But when we left, well, she might have pissed off the owner. Big, fat dude. Mean dude. If he knew she'd ripped him off, well, I don't know what he'd do."

"Kill her?"

"Maybe."

"What's the guy's name?"

"Otis, something."

Matt nodded. "Okay, you can go, but let us know if you remember anything else that might help us find out how she died."

Alex rose abruptly from the metal chair, eager to leave the room. He stepped toward the door, and at the last moment, turned and looked at Matt and Tom, his eyes suddenly filling with tears again.

"I dunno what happened to Selena, okay? But I wanna know who did this to her," he said, his voice breaking. "She was happy the last time I saw her. Real happy, as if all her dreams had come true."

Matt nodded. Alex threw the heavy-framed door open, and strode down the hall, another deputy stepping forward to accompany him to the front office, his overly long jean shorts comically sagging around his skinny rear end. Matt looked at

Tom for his reaction. Tom's chair legs thudded to the floor as he sat upright.

"He knows more about Selena than he's letting on. Maybe this pot grower Otis got revenge if she ripped him off. Or maybe her secret boyfriend was Alex's friend and he doesn't want to get him into trouble," Tom offered.

Matt shook his head. His instincts told him otherwise. He saw Selena, not as she appeared in her tiny school photograph, posed and serene, or how she had looked when he had found her dead, as if she were taking a nap on the ground in the early morning sun, but in the warm spring night a few weeks before, laughing with her friends, her skin reflected by neon lights as Sarah's had been, smiling as she told a besotted Alex Almazan that all of her dreams were coming true. Who was he, the man of her dreams, and why didn't anyone know about him? Where was her baby, if she had one, and why didn't anyone know about that? He felt as if he were in a tunnel, with something dark and heavy pressing down on him. He had no answers. The only thing he could see was Selena, alive and happy on Sober Grad Night and dead barely two weeks later.

"Hey, Matt, you're grinding your teeth," Tom observed. Suddenly, Matt was back in the interrogation room, the bright lights making his eyes blink. He emerged from his near-trance, the scowl lifting from his face, smiling ruefully at what a picture he must make to Tom Nolan, who was such an easygoing guy.

"Yeah, that's me," Matt acknowledged, "I keep my dentist in business these days. Not my bartender anymore."

Tom smiled back, appreciating that Matt's self-deprecating humor would not have been so easily revealed to just anyone. Matt thought for a moment.

"You know, I think the Otis he mentioned is Otis Seaver. Known pot grower and all-around sleazebag. Get a drone over Seaver's property and see if he's just started planting for this season. Not that I really give a shit, but it'll give us probable cause to bring him in for questioning. If Alex is right, and Selena ripped him off, it'll give us motive as well."

*****

Sidney paced in Jack's office, waiting for him to come in from picking up his messages at the receptionist's desk. Her feeling of being completely overwhelmed had intensified overnight and she hadn't slept, even with more than one glass of wine and a Trazodone. She needed to slow down on the drinking and the sleeping pills. It was too easy to knock back a couple of glasses every night when you were all alone.

May was turning into a hot June, something she wasn't used to in San Francisco when the summer fog cooled every day to a brisk 60 degrees. Her usual dress slacks and blazers were too hot, and she had scoured the local stores for something professional to wear, finally giving up and ordering thin, washable outfits online. Sandals kept the rest of her cool, especially when the air conditioning in the old bordello building failed to work properly, as it did on many days. This morning, she had confessed to Marjorie that she had become a huge fan of wash and wear polyester blends.

"I hear 'ya, honey," Marjorie acknowledged. "It's heating up. This summer's gonna be a scorcher."

Still pacing in Jack's office, Sidney decided to sit down. She crossed her bare legs and regarded her sandaled foot, the toes exposed. A lawyer would never wear anything so casual in San Francisco, Sidney reflected. If she had, she might have been mistaken for a paralegal or worse, a secretary, and that would have been a death blow to her career. In Jackson, she was dressed up just wearing a skirt in a town where professional women were very few and far between.

Jack finally strode in, throwing his overflowing briefcase on the worn leather couch, his hand stuffed with little pink message slips, his face shining with perspiration.

"Hey, goddaughter," he hailed her in a way that never ceased to warm her heart.

"Hey, boss."

Jack thumped the pink slips through a spike on his large oak desk, took off his jacket and hung it from a brass-pegged coat stand by the door, loosening his tie as he did so.

"Now, what brings you in here so early in the morning?" he asked, his thick, bushy brows knotting together as his piercing eyes drilled into her.

"The Hill family. Jeremy Hill in particular. And this police investigation," she said simply. "I think that Jeremy is under suspicion of the girl's murder, and I think I'm way in over my head."

"Nonsense," Jack responded, leaning backward into his brown leather swivel chair, clasping his hands behind his head. "I talked to Dom Colangelo. We go way back. I helped him with fundraising for his campaign. He's a complete dolt, but he can be trusted as a straight shooter. If he had something on Jeremy Hill, he'd tell me."

"But Dom Colangelo isn't the one doing the investigating. I've had run-ins with that cowboy Matt Dunleavy and his Boy Scout sidekick, Tom Nolan."

As if deep in thought, Jack rubbed the top of his head, and his thick salt and pepper hair stood straight up. Thank God Marjorie cleaned him up before he ever showed up in court.

"I know Dunleavy. Good man. Great football player. I helped him with his application to Stanford. Had a hard time of it after his wife left him. Maybe he's got a hard-on for Jeremy because of it. There were rumors she was having an affair with him before she ran off with a slick wine buyer from the Valley."

Sidney pondered this information. Was Dunleavy the kind who would bring heat on someone because he had a grudge against him, or because there were real grounds for suspicion? She instinctively felt that it would be the latter, even if the former were true.

"Besides," Jack continued. "They're looking at some Mexican kid from the high school who may have been her boyfriend." Upon making his final point, Jack started reading his pink slips and putting them in order of importance, like a deck of playing cards. She knew she had lost his attention, which was sporadic even in the best of circumstances.

"So, do you want me to recommend that he retain a criminal lawyer to represent him?" Sidney half-hoped for an affirmative answer. Jack shot her a look of disgust.

"Okay," she responded, sighing in defeat, "I'll do my feeble best to keep him off Death Row."

"That's my girl," Jack ended the conversation brightly, picking up the receiver on his phone and punching in numbers with an energy that made Sidney wonder why the little buttons didn't come flying off the keypad.

"Jack, one more thing. Mrs. Hill's daughter, Grace, has given me a couple of names to check out in San Francisco. Maude wants to make sure that there aren't any loose ends from the investigation into her brother Joshua's suicide. I'm setting up a couple of interviews in the city for later this week."

"Sure, sure. That's fine," Jack responded absent-mindedly, waving her off as he waited for his call to be answered. A voice must have come on the other end of the line, because Jack said, "Just a minute, this is Jack McGlynn calling," and then placed his hand over the receiver.

"Hey, Sid," he paused, "Make sure you come back now, okay? Don't get hung up on the bright lights of the City. It's all smoke and mirrors. There's nothing there."

"Don't I know it," Sidney responded quickly, as she left his office. But as she walked toward Marjorie's desk, she reflected on whether that was as true for her as it had been for Jack. The only way to know for sure was if she figured it out for herself.

10.

The drone had been a fruitful effort, even if Dom Colangelo had burst a blood vessel over the cost, Matt reflected. It had taken a couple of days, but the county contracted aerial drone operator had taken photos about a thousand feet up that revealed rows and rows of bushy little plants on about two acres surrounded by chicken wire fencing. A warrant had been obtained for a search of the property and the Sheriff's department descended with vans, dogs and eradication equipment. Matt and Tom waited for Otis Seaver to be arrested and brought into the jail. He was just as fat and ugly as Matt had remembered from prior run-ins and just as loud, demanding to be released because his Constitutional rights had been violated.

"What rights would those be, Otis?" Matt asked as he and Tom entered the interrogation room.

"I have a Constitutional right to grow whatever the hell I want to on my own property! And a right to religious freedom. I use cannabis in my religion."

"Uh, huh. Well, we just have a few questions for you about some young people you may have employed to help you with your religious ceremonies."

Tom laid down photos of Selena and Alex side by side in front of Otis Seaver and waited.

Seaver's beady eyes and flushed jowls bent over the photos, which he handled with thick, dirty fingers.

"Don't know who these Mex's are."

"Right now, we're going over every trailer, every piece of trash and every corner of your property. If there is so much as a partial fingerprint from either one of these two, I'll charge you with obstruction of justice and lying to a police officer. All nice and legal and within your Constitutional rights. Do you get me?"

Otis continued to stare at the photos, eyebrows drawn together.

"Well, what if I say that on second thought, they look like a couple of kids that did some landscaping for me maybe last fall?"

"I'd say that I think you're probably right." Matt drew a chair up to the table just across from Otis. "I don't care about going after you. I just want to know about these two."

"Oh. Are they in trouble? I hope like heck they are."

"Why?"

"Cause these two worked for me for a couple of weeks. Last October. Landscaping. And I paid them, housed them, fed them, took care of 'em and they ripped me off. For a lot of money. My harvesting payroll, if you know what I mean. That beaner and his bitch girlfriend ripped me off."

"What did you do about it, Otis? Did you go after them? Get revenge?"

"Naaah." He shook his head. "Couldn't find 'em. I think they gave me fake names. The girl said she was Maria and the boy said his name was Pedro. Once they took off, none of the other workers knew where to find 'em. They didn't know 'em. Weren't locals. I was pissed off, fer sure. But that was the end of it. Swear to God and on my dead mother's grave."

"And you never saw either one of them again?"

"Nope. Never."

After a long pause, Matt looked at Tom to see if they needed anything else. Tom shook his head. "Don't leave town, Otis. And by the way, all your plants have been seized and the cash hidden under your trailer floorboards has been confiscated. Just a suggestion. Why don't you find another line of work somewhere else?"

"Goddamn you! I'll sue you and your department for…"

"I know. Violating your Constitutional rights. Good luck with that, Otis."

Matt and Tom left the interrogation room after pocketing the photos. In the hallway, Tom turned to Matt, "He's a total scumbag, but I don't see him as a killer. He'd sure scare a couple of kids, but once they took off, I don't see him being smart enough to track them down and kill that girl, do you?"

Matt shook his head. He didn't see it either. A promising lead had turned into a dead end. Time to start over.

11.

The plane engines droned as Matt squirmed in his coach-class seat, his long legs cramped, and his knees bumped against the back of the seat in front of him, its blissfully sleeping occupant tilting as far back as his lever would allow. Matt attempted to distract himself from his physical discomfort and the mental tedium of the long flight by reviewing the status of the dead girl's case, going over every detail to make sure he missed nothing. He closed his eyes and folded his arms across his chest, leaning his head back against the headrest.

It had taken some persuading for Colangelo to approve this trip to Mexico City. Alex Almazan was a dead end, so was Otis Seaver and no new information was likely to be forthcoming. Matt reviewed the chronology of Selena's recent life and focused on her time in Mexico. She must have been pregnant while she was studying there. Someone must have known: a roommate, a teacher, maybe a doctor. She wasn't pregnant anymore when she was killed, so there might have been someone in Mexico who knew something. Maybe she would have been less guarded far away from home. Colangelo had been nervous and prevaricated for quite some time, casting about for other alternatives. He had no jurisdiction in Mexico. It was going too far afield; maybe they should ask for help from the Feds. What if he approved this expenditure and the County Supervisors rejected it? His ass was on the line, and Matt's wasn't. Matt waited him out patiently, pointing out that help from the Feds would take much too long. The trail was growing cold and that they might get some good leads and solve the case quickly, for which Colangelo could take full credit. He finally prevailed and got the approval.

Matt knew he had to leave quickly before Colangelo changed his mind. He retrieved his passport from his home office safe along with a wad of cash, booked the flight to Mexico City for the following day, arranged for the neighbor to feed

Sage and Cloud, his horses, and Bella, his yellow Labrador, and threw some clothes and toiletries in a duffel bag. On the drive to Sacramento, he stopped by Selena's junior college. The administrative staff had been notified of her death and willingly handed her file to him to make copies. Thankfully, Selena's transcript and the details of her courses in Mexico City were in her file, including payment information and a copy of a personal check from Jeremy Hill. Matt noted the name and contact information for the director of the study abroad program in Mexico City. He asked the college's helpful administrative assistant to phone the Sheriff's office. Once he got someone on the line, he asked them to phone ahead and let the Mexico City program director know that he was coming. After thanking the staff for their help, Matt left the junior college campus and headed straight to the Sacramento airport, barely making his flight on time.

The clouds broke through as the plane began its final descent. The city and its suburbs packed more than twenty million people below, a thick haze of smog spreading a gray film over the crowded inhabitants beneath. As they circled their approach, Matt could see the heart of the city with modern, angled skyscrapers clustered together as if creating a steel-ringed fortress of modernity inside a massive circle of poor shantytowns sprawled as far as he could see. Corrugated metals roofs reflected a shimmering patchwork of desperate poverty. As they approached the landing strip, Matt could see a busy snarl of highways crowded with cars. He cleared customs without incident in Mexico City, a Sheriff's Deputy's badge getting him through without luggage inspection. The airport was crowded and hot and he struggled to make his way to the sidewalk. A maze of small, brightly-colored taxicabs swarmed outside, and he looked for one with an official metal license displayed on the dashboard and a meter. After passing over several drivers clamoring for his business, he settled on a small, black, and white sedan with few dents and scrapes. It had the license and meter displayed and the driver and car looked poor enough so that Matt was convinced that its owner made an honest living. He had heard the horror stories of tourists being driven off by armed gangs posing as cab drivers and he didn't want to be their next victim. The driver loaded his duffel in the trunk and knew enough English to ask Matt his destination.

When Matt said the University of Mexico, the driver nodded knowingly and said, "Ah, la UNAM. Sí, Señor, enseguida."

The drive to the University was longer than Matt thought it would be, as it was located on a campus quite remote from the capital. The driver pointed out the location of the old Olympic Village from the Summer Olympics of 1968, the one made memorable by three African American athletes raising clenched fists at the medals ceremony. The fields, amphitheaters, and buildings left over from the Olympics were shockingly neglected, the running tracks covered with weeds, the paint peeling off the buildings, and concrete steps crumbling. It had never occurred to Matt to wonder whatever happened to Olympic venues once the competitions were over, but apparently, they did not fare well in some parts of the world. Not too long after passing by the old Olympic Village, the driver turned into the main campus of the University. Its massive cubed buildings had been relatively well-maintained, helped by brightly-colored tiled murals of a distant precolonial past that loomed over the campus, decorated with feathered serpents and the elaborate headdresses of long-dead Aztec kings. He handed a piece of paper to the driver, who deciphered his handwriting and directed him to the right building. He accepted US dollars with delightedly raised eyebrows and tipped his cap.

"Buena suerte, Señor. Vaya con Diós."

Matt made his way inside the building and past the guards by showing them his US Passport, a relic from his honeymoon in the French wine region with Sarah, as well as his Amador County Sheriff's Office ID.

"Professor Renee Peacock."

"Sí, Señor," the guard responded and lifted the handset of his telephone, announcing Matt's arrival. The faculty was well-protected, Matt reflected, the guards were university security and they were armed. In no more than a minute, a young Mexican woman with a flowing rust-colored skirt approached him, her hair held back with a giant tortoise-shell clip at the base of her neck.

"Officer Dunleavy? I am Professor Peacock's assistant, Leonora Buendia. She is expecting you, if you would come this way, please," she greeted him with perfect, American-accented English. He followed her up the winding stone stairway to the second floor, her sandals clicking on each step. The interior of the faculty building was brightly-lit and spacious, and the stonework mimicked that found in Aztec monuments. Matt admired the architecture as a masterful blend of ancient and modern.

"You must have studied in the States," Matt observed conversationally, as he followed Leonora up the winding stone staircase.

"Why, yes I did. I was an American History major at UCLA," she said. "I am getting my doctorate here at UNAM in Latin American Politics and Economics, studying with Professor Peacock. Her work is highly regarded throughout the Americas."

Although he wasn't there to review anyone's academic credentials, Matt was gratified that the assistant spoke well of her mentor.

"Right in here," Leonora motioned him through a door with a pebbled glass window etched in black with Professor Peacock's name. "I'll be in the adjoining office if I'm needed."

Matt nodded his thanks and knocked lightly against the glass.

"Pase," called a high-lilting female voice from inside. Matt opened the door and let himself into a small office covered with bookcases crammed two or three books deep, stacks of papers on every available surface, and indigenous tapestries hanging from every wall. Matt almost missed seeing Professor Peacock, as her head was bent over her computer keyboard as she poked at the keys with both her index fingers. She raised her head and looked at him directly from behind old-fashioned owl-rimmed glasses. Her hair was blonde mixed with gray, and stray hairs escaped her bun, waving in the stream of air conditioning gusting through the room from a whirring electric fan. An Indian shawl was wrapped around her shoulders and the professor seemed to be otherwise encased in a loose brown handwoven sack with her neck draped with beads and assorted carved stones. Her entire dress proclaimed her affinity for her adopted culture, although her broad, Minnesota farm-wife face seemed oddly inconsistent.

"Professor Peacock? I'm Matthew Dunleavy, Special Deputy with the Amador County Sheriff's Office." Professor Peacock leaned forward from her chair and shook hands, pointing to the empty armchair opposite her computer table. Matt sat down, noting that the Professor never took her blue eyes from his face.

"You're here to discuss Selena's death?" she prompted.

"Not exactly. Yes, she was killed, and in circumstances that leave no doubt that it was murder. I'd like to know anything you can tell us about Selena and the months she was here: her friends, any acquaintances, anything that might help us piece together the months before she died."

She nodded her understanding and then rose, walking slowly to a small table by the window where a pitcher of ice water stood. She poured two glasses and returned, handing one to Matt wordlessly; taking some time in returning to her desk, swiveling her chair toward Matt, and rearranging her shawl. He wondered why she draped herself in so much clothing and yet seemingly needed the fan blasting air throughout the room. Maybe it had something to do with female mid-life problems.

"Selena was very bright with a great deal of potential. Certainly, she was not as accomplished a student as some I've seen in the program, but she made up for it with passion for the subject matter. I find that many Mexican-American students who return to study in Mexico apply themselves very diligently.

But Selena appeared to be distracted and distant. I learned the cause about a month into the program."

"What did you find out?" Matt asked, suspecting that he already knew the answer.

"She was pregnant. I imagine no confidentiality attaches to that disclosure now that she's dead and it may be relevant to your investigation, so I won't withhold anything."

"Thank you," Matt acknowledged. "How did you find out?"

"She came to me asking if I knew a doctor. She hadn't had any prenatal care in the States, and she was approximately four months along. I was the only person she felt she could ask."

"Did you help her?"

"Yes. I gave her the name of a doctor at a woman's clinic close by. The clinic has a good reputation and I felt confident that Selena would receive appropriate care."

"Were her parents notified?"

Professor Peacock shook her head. A few more silver hairs escaped from her bun and waved around her head as if frantically escaping its confines.

"Selena was over eighteen and I had no right to interfere. Of course, I encouraged her to let her family know, but she refused."

"Did she discuss the father?"

"No. Although I did inquire as to her plans, and she said that she was going back to the States to get married. So, I assumed it was someone from home. It was not an unusual situation, Mr. Dunleavy. There was nothing in her demeanor or her disclosure that made me at all fearful for her. I imagined that she would finish the course and return home to get married and have her baby."

Matt suddenly had a feeling that Colangelo would be apoplectic if he came back so totally empty-handed. He sighed.

"Yes, I know, Mr. Dunleavy. It is so very sad when you have a case where a young girl's dreams are so completely shattered."

"Murder always ends someone's dreams," he said.

"Oh, I'm not speaking of the murder, as horrible as that is. I'm talking about her pregnancy. Her dream, you know, was to get married and for the baby to have a father and a permanent home in the United States."

"Why? What happened? Wasn't she still pregnant when she went home?"

"Oh. No, she wasn't. I'm sorry, I thought you knew. She had a miscarriage. Here in Mexico. You could speak with her doctor. Poor Selena. When she left here, her dreams were totally crushed."

Matt breathed in deeply. This was unexpected. He thought of Tom Nolan back in Jackson, interviewing every OB-GYN and GP in the County and then some. He'd better call before wasting any more of Tom's valuable time.

"Thank you, Professor. I appreciate the information. Look, I wonder if you'd be kind enough to contact the doctor in advance of my visit, just so he can be forthcoming."

"She," Professor Peacock corrected. "Doctora Maria Fuentes. I'll have Leonora call and tell her you're on your way. I imagine you won't want to wait until tomorrow."

"No. I'd like to leave tomorrow."

Professor Peacock nodded and smiled, revealing a very youthful expression.

"Americans either love it or hate it here. I gather you're in the latter category."

"No ma'am," Matt lied. "I'm just homesick already." In truth, Matt had always felt uncomfortable the few times he had visited Mexico: the gap between the very rich and the mass of very poor; the class and racial divisions; the rampant political and police corruption; the drug-fueled violence; all these factors gnawed at him and made it a difficult place to enjoy. Back home, he had grown up the poor, part-Indian son of an alcoholic, but here, he was a rich and privileged American, a target either of opportunity or resentment. He couldn't wait to leave. Matt thanked Professor Peacock, and Leonora arranged for his visit to the clinic, volunteering to drive him there. He accepted gratefully.

They left the campus in Leonora's little Volkswagen Beetle, another armed guard waving as they exited the faculty parking lot.

"There seems to be enough security around here to form a small private army," Matt observed. Leonora nodded, negotiating their entry onto the busy highway.

"You must have read about carjackings, kidnappings, and murders becoming more and more common in Mexico, Officer, even here in the capitol. It's the result of narcoterrorism and the endless demand for drugs from the United States."

Matt thought that the rampant corruption of Mexican government officials and the police, many of whom were on the payroll of drug lords, probably had something to do with it as well, but he decided not to argue her point.

"We're here," Leonora said suddenly and exited the highway. Within just a few hundred yards, they pulled into a parking lot in front of a squat, one-story building that had been whitewashed so long ago that the denuded gray cinder blocks showed through more than the paint. The sign "Clínica Infantil" announced the building's purpose as a children's clinic and Leonora squeezed into a tight parking space directly in front.

Shepherding him into the front office, Leonora spoke so quickly that Matt's high school Spanish could not keep up, but he heard "policia" and his name repeated as the well-endowed secretary called and announced their presence. The waiting room was full of dark-skinned women wearing their thick black hair in long braids, their rounded bellies protruding uncomfortably. Many had infants wrapped in baby blankets pressed to their breasts. An astounding number of toddlers played in the middle of the waiting room floor, their mouths either sucking on old, shabby toys or wailing some complaint.

"I'll wait for you here," Leonora told him as he was escorted through the office doors to the examining rooms beyond. Matt was grateful that the many examining room doors were closed, but just to make sure he didn't embarrass anyone, he kept his eyes on the linoleum-tiled floor, its many corners peeling and broken.

"Aquí, Señor, pase porfavor," the receptionist said, calling for his attention. She opened the door to an office and Matt ducked in. A white-coated woman of about forty turned to greet him from her metal swivel chair, her hand outstretched to shake his, which she did surprisingly vigorously. Her dark eyes were lined, but otherwise, her face had a smooth and beautiful olive complexion.

"Hello, Officer, I'm Maria Fuentes. I understand you are here unofficially investigating the death of one of my former patients," she said frowning, whether at him or at the circumstances of his visit, he couldn't tell.

"I'm not really an Officer, ma'am. I'm a Special Deputy for the County of Amador in northern California. I'm here to find out a little more about Selena Rodriguez and her pregnancy because it may be connected to her death. There may have been a jealous boyfriend or even a relative who was upset by her pregnancy."

"Oh, I doubt that," the doctor smiled. "Mexicans love children, as you can see by our waiting room. Even if she was not married, they would always welcome another baby with open arms. Please, sit down. I'm sorry we don't have a more comfortable chair. We run this clinic on a shoestring since we don't charge our patients."

Matt sat as bidden, and the chair, as promised, was uncomfortable. The seat was hard and even though made of metal, he felt as if the whole structure could collapse under him in an instant. The doctor was reviewing a worn manila-folder that had seen use through more than one patient. Her lips pressed together tightly.

"I remember Selena very well. A very pretty young girl, full of life. I saw her three times: the first for an initial patient visit; the second, for signs of miscarriage; and the third, unfortunately, for a procedure following the miscarriage. I remember that she was devastated by the loss of her baby."

Matt pulled out a small spiral notebook from his pocket.

"What were the dates?"

"The first visit was late January right after the winter semester had started for her at UNAM. Her signs of miscarriage began just a month later when she had heavy bleeding and cramping for a number of days before she came to see me. We might have been able to hospitalize her, but she didn't come to me until it was too late. I performed an ultrasound and there was no heartbeat. It was the next day that we scheduled her for a D & C. It's an uncomfortable procedure and the patient does feel some pain. We perform it with a sedative."

"Can a doctor tell the difference between someone who had a living baby and someone who had a miscarriage at four months or five months along?" Matt asked.

"Not necessarily," Dr. Fuentes responded. "Selena's cervix was almost fully dilated. In effect, the baby was stillborn. My procedure essentially eliminated retained products of conception and the possibility of infection."

Matt was relieved that there had been no heavy lunch served on the airplane earlier that day. Although feeling decidedly queasy at the doctor's description, it was tempered by more than a little admiration of what women routinely endured.

"What... uh... happened to the baby?" Matt asked while stumbling a little over the question, feeling fatigued from the long flight, the long day, and the nature of the clinical discussion. Dr. Fuentes closed her file and sighed.

"It's a delicate subject, especially in a Catholic country. Often, there is a funeral service, but Selena didn't want that. She chose cremation. She was not interested in claiming the ashes or having a service of any kind."

"So, there are no remains at all, anywhere?"

Dr. Fuentes shook her head. "No, I'm afraid not. There won't be any way to identify the father with absolute certainty, if that's what you are thinking. I will give you a complete copy of the file. We did type the baby's blood in order to let the mother know if there was an Rh incompatibility problem."

"What do you mean?"

"The father and mother's blood type might have been incompatible, so that there was a high risk of recurring miscarriage if she conceived with the same father. In the States, of course, such an incompatibility can be dealt with rather easily, but in Mexico, unless a patient is under the care of an expensive private practitioner, I'm afraid not."

"So, the father's blood type...?"

"Yes, the father's blood type could have been incompatible with Selena's, and that could have been the cause of miscarriage. But without knowing who the father is, and without tests on the baby, well, we'll never know. I'll get her complete records, but I don't think they'll be of much help." Dr. Fuentes rose with the file in hand. "I'll be just a moment."

While he waited, Matt made a mental note to telephone Tom Nelson and let him know that the trip to Mexico had not been a complete waste. He would head back the next day, file in hand, and be able to deliver both good news and bad. He counted as bad news that there was no baby, alive or otherwise, that could help identify the father. The good news was that they now knew that the boyfriend was not in Mexico. Selena had gone to Mexico pregnant and had returned several months later not pregnant, which must have been news to someone back home. Maybe the pregnancy figured into her killing, maybe not. But Selena certainly took pains to keep it a secret and in Matt's experience, very little good ever came from keeping a secret.

12.

Sidney left her solitary haven in Fiddletown while it was still dark, heading southwest toward San Francisco. For the wealthy that enjoyed their primary residences in San Francisco, Fiddletown would have seemed rustic and quaint in a world where nowhere other than Tahoe or Napa would do for a second home if Tuscany was out of the question. It was a relative point of view, Sidney mused as she sipped her coffee, whether one's place in the world was considered high or low. She felt that the question was particularly pertinent at this point in her life as she struggled to reconcile her view of herself with a new reality. Her father would be living the next decade of his life in prison. She was too young to have established an independent place in the world and was used to enjoying the secure identity of having a successful, wealthy, and respected father. Now, she had one that had been very publicly revealed as a fraud and a cheat, and her world had shattered.

This trip to San Francisco filled her with excitement and anxiety simultaneously. For an hour or so she wound her Subaru down and around the foothills. Pines and cedars receded, replaced by scrub oaks and pastures in the lower-elevation farms and ranches. For miles and miles there was nothing, but the occasional ranch house or wooden shack surrounded by grazing herds of cattle. Then suddenly, storage units, trucking businesses, and landscaping and industrial yards sprang up beside the road.

Traffic increased and slowed as she hit the intersection with Highway 99 just north of Stockton, a straight black asphalt highway bisecting the state vertically as the main artery for long-haul agricultural truckers. The numbers of cars on the freeway increased as she cut through on the crosstown freeway speeding by Stockton's shabby and decaying downtown into the Central Valley beyond, now almost completely filled by suburban sprawl. Rolling hilltops had been razed and crowned with cookie-cutter stucco housing developments that abutted ever-dwindling fields where occasionally, a solitary goat or cow still grazed on withered patches of weedy dirt and junk heaps. Car dealerships, one-level strip malls with an odd assortment of cheap tenants, fast-food outlets, discount stores, and huge big-box retailers filled in every available acre of land previously dedicated to ranching and farming. Red-tailed hawks, seemingly oblivious to these changes, circled small fallow fields next to enormous shopping centers. Sidney didn't know where she fit anymore, except that driving over the massive steel girders of the Bay Bridge suddenly felt like going home. I'll be back in San Francisco in twenty minutes or so, she thought, but I don't belong there anymore. A sick and miserable sense of failure enveloped her, and she struggled to push self-defeating black thoughts from her mind.

After negotiating the Bay Bridge exit onto the Embarcadero Freeway, Sidney drove past the Giants' stadium and what little remained of the old waterfront before massive development gentrified it into extinction. After nosing her car onto Broadway, she headed up the steep hill to Pacific Heights. She tried to focus on her upcoming interview with an extremely wealthy widow, whose dead philanthropist husband's name graced many a gallery at the Museum of Modern Art and the new De Young. Sidney had not forgotten Maude's original purpose in hiring her: she needed to track down any leads or loose ends regarding Maude's dead brother, the artist, Joshua Morgan, with sensitivity and discretion.

Grace had given Sidney the introduction to Uncle Joshua's best lady friend, Patricia Dalton Toomey. With more than his usual glee, Jack had filled her in on Mrs. Toomey's background and reputation. According to Jack, Patricia was the second wife of Al Toomey, who had made a fortune in San Francisco real estate. The salacious part that Jack enjoyed retelling was that Patricia had been Al's first wife's very best friend. Patricia and Al carried on in secret for quite some time until his wife caught on and threw his well-tailored clothes out their Broadway penthouse window. Patricia was persona non grata for quite some time within San Francisco society, but then again, Al himself had never been truly accepted because he was nouveau riche, not to mention Jewish, albeit non-practicing and with an Irish-sounding adopted name. Al eventually married Patricia and they spent an enormous amount of money attempting to buy respectability, including staggeringly generous museum donations.

Grace had told Sidney that her uncle, Joshua Morgan, had been hired to paint Mrs. Toomey's portrait that was destined to hang in some donor's wing or another, during which time she and Joshua became inseparable. As Al's health waned, Joshua became Patricia's main escort. Since everyone knew he was gay and was extremely well-connected through his brother-in-law, Hans Hill, it was accepted without even mildly malicious gossip. He was also charming and wealthy in his own right; not to mention more than acceptably WASP. Besides which, Jack had recounted, warming to his subject, at the time, all of San Francisco was discussing a famous lady author's husband's indiscretion with his male masseuse; with whom he had been caught during his weekly massage in a very compromising position by his furious wife. It was nothing out of the ordinary for San Francisco society for wealthy soon-to-be widows to be escorted by charming and handsome gay men while their husbands lay ill and dying.

As she looked in vain for a parking space right on Broadway, Sidney mentally rehearsed her meeting with Patricia Dalton Toomey. She wanted to investigate what Maude suspected: that although he genuinely enjoyed the company of women, especially wealthy women who could afford having their portraits painted, Joshua Morgan was gay and a serious, committed artist who never showed the least romantic interest in any woman and would never have committed suicide over a love affair with anyone of either sex. It was a pretty tall order and Sidney felt quite unequal to the task.

She finally found a precarious parking place on a side street, with a dangerous downward grade that would doom her car to roll all the way down Pacific Heights and into the Bay should her emergency brake fail. She rested her front tires right into the curb and forcefully set the manual brake. As she emerged awkwardly from the driver's side and tottered up the steep hillside to the top of Broadway, Sidney cursed her high heeled shoes: a pair of attractive, pointed toed pumps in the latest style that she hadn't worn since she left the City. Except for her shoes, she had dressed simply but smartly for the occasion. One look at her usual casual wardrobe from the likes of Mrs. Toomey and she would be condemned as a rube. She didn't want to be at such a disadvantage.

Slightly out of breath, Sidney reached the front door of the Toomey-owned building on Broadway, a massive structure with an elegant façade and art nouveau décor. Every spacious flat contained servants' quarters and the garages were filled with private town cars and waiting chauffeurs. She knew exactly what kind of lifestyle living on the flat part of Broadway entailed, since her father had lived in a very similar building in a very similar way for at least ten years, less than a block away, until his trial and conviction had ended everything for them both. She had steeled herself for it, but try as she might, she couldn't shake the powerful intimations of her past life creeping over her, as chilling as the afternoon fog.

The uniformed doorman inquired politely about her business and confirmed her appointment with a call to Mrs. Toomey from the lobby phone.

"Penthouse," he announced unnecessarily, as he pointed in the direction of the elevator. A separate elevator was designated for the Toomey penthouse and as if she couldn't press the only button herself, the doorman opened the door for her, pressed the "up" button, and closed the door. Once she had traveled slowly up eight stories, the elevator stopped, and the door automatically opened into a large and elegant foyer. She stepped out onto thick patterned carpeting. A young Asian woman dressed in black capris and a white silk pullover greeted her at the elevator door. "I am Mrs. Toomey's assistant, Carol. You are Miss Dietrich?"

"Yes, I'm here to see Mrs. Toomey. Say, doesn't having an elevator door in your hallway make you feel a little, well, vulnerable? I mean, anyone could come up if the doorman's back was turned."

Carol smiled knowingly.

"Robert is not the only security here, I assure you. Plus, there are cameras all over the building."

"Oh," said Sidney, unconvinced. She still thought it was creepy to have an elevator door open up right in your foyer, and creepier still to have someone somewhere watching your every move from hidden cameras.

"Please come into the sitting room," Carol invited her in, and with Sidney following, they took a stroll down the length of the suite of rooms that felt as long as a city block, with vaulted ceilings and breathtaking artwork. Without appearing to gawk too much, Sidney thought she identified a few works by Impressionist masters and several Rodin bronzes lining the wide hallway. About halfway down the length of the building, Carol came to an abrupt stop and grasped a large circular bronze door handle. Sidney thought that she must have been counting doors, keeping track of which one would provide entry to the sitting room. As Carol swung the door open, she motioned for Sidney to step inside while she remained outside, then retreated as Sidney stepped through and closed the door behind her.

Sidney looked around and the jingling of tiny bells drew her attention inward to a room almost entirely done in white. Expansive sofas and armchairs were upholstered in white with the room appointed with white pillows, white drapes, and white ottomans. The only other color in the room was provided by massive gold-framed mirrors and a gilded assortment of glass tables and lamps. The jingling came from the throat of a tiny, long-haired dog that had jumped from a wingback armchair and proceeded to stand its ground and growl at Sidney.

"Waffles!" admonished a disembodied voice. Rising up from the wingback chair and turning to face her, was a woman at least six feet tall, wearing a billowing green-patterned chiffon kaftan with sleeves that trailed like wings as she gestured to Sidney, her hand sporting a ring on every finger and long nails painted bright red. Her silver hair was short and spiked up and her dark eyes were heavily lined with black eyeliner. Black eyebrows were plucked, tweezed, and penciled into an exaggerated dark arch over each dark, expressive eye, leaving Sidney with the impression that she was staring at a raptor.

"Come and sit down, dear," she said with elongated vowels, almost as if she were a vampire murmuring "Cuuuuum and siiit dowan, deah," while gesturing vaguely at any number of white pieces of furniture. Sidney chose a small, cushioned chair in front of the enormous wingback seat from which Mrs. Toomey had risen. As Sidney sat primly, Mrs. Toomey sank back almost lazily and Waffles took his cue to jump into the chiffon folds of her lap and bury his little white body.

"It's been many yeahs since I've seen your fathah," Mrs. Toomey uttered, pulling a cigarette holder from her kaftan. It held a drooping, unlit cigarette and she pursed her bright red lips around it and sucked at air. "I'm trying to quit, deah, but I did love it so. I find I'm cahlmer if I have it in my hand and pretend to smoke."

Sidney was utterly at a loss for words. She had no idea that Mrs. Toomey had known her father and she didn't know what to say about the futility of sucking on an unlit cigarette. Instead, she waited for another opportunity at conversation.

"I understand that you're a lawyah." She paused for dramatic effect, stared at Sidney and sucked on the cigarette holder. "Dahling, whatevah for?"

Again, Sidney was at a loss. No one had ever questioned her choice of career before. It was universally accepted by most people she had known as being a somewhat positive professional choice. Perhaps it had never occurred to Mrs. Toomey to aspire to anything more than to seduce and then marry a wealthy man.

"I guess I have to do something to be able to eat," Sidney shrugged.

The cigarette holder drooped. "Oh, my deah. I am sorry about your fathah. Such a chahming man."

Sidney wanted to straighten her out and tell her that her decision to become a lawyer had nothing whatsoever to do with her father's failing fortunes and prison sentence, but she preferred to avoid that topic entirely.

"Uh, thank you, Mrs. Toomey," Sidney mumbled.

"Pat, dahling," Mrs. Toomey corrected. "Everyone calls me Pat."

"I explained to your assistant, Carol, why I wanted to see you. I represent Mrs. Maude Hill. I'm trying to update information for her regarding the investigation into her brother's death. I'm here to ask you a few questions about the late Joshua Morgan."

"Oh, I know," Pat responded, her unlit cigarette hold waving in Sidney's direction dismissively. "You want to know if we were lovers and if I had his love child."

Pat's red lips sucked at the cigarette holder while her mouth curved into a mocking smile. Was she joking? Sidney tried to ignore the fact that this woman continued to make her feel acutely uncomfortable.

"What Mrs. Hill would like to know, Mrs. Toomey, is whether her brother, your close friend, might ever have had any reason to commit suicide. Were there any relationships that might have caused him grief, or any other reversals in his life – personal or financial?"

Patricia Toomey tilted her head back and stroked her dog, which lay obediently on her lap.

"Do you have any idea who Joshua Morgan was, Miss Dietrich?"

"Not really," Sidney acknowledged.

"Come with me."

Patricia's elegant and statuesque figure rose from the chair and the tiny dog leaped to the floor, running ahead of her to the door. In a couple of steps, she was headed down the hall, expecting Sidney to follow. They passed a few more rooms and Patricia stopped suddenly at a large set of ebony doors that appeared to have been imported from an elegant Parisian apartment. Patricia drew them open and swished through the entrance, her sleeves swaying. Suddenly, she stopped in the middle of a large, open salon with hardwood floors and wood paneling, from which hung a startling number of large, colorful and ornately framed paintings on every wall. Sidney's eyes traveled around the room and immediately recognized Joshua Morgan's bright splashes and forms that made even an ordinary still life arrangement of a table, chair, and some flowers randomly thrown into a vase seem alive with color and texture. California landscapes filled several frames, but the most unusual and arresting original paintings were the portraits of women, or rather, one woman – Patricia Dalton Toomey. She was everywhere, in every pose imaginable: dressed and sitting up, partially dressed and reclining, sprawled on a bed face up and totally nude. There must have easily been a dozen or more intimate portraits and it was obvious that the artist had loved every curve, fold, and smile on the face and body of his model.

"He told me he'd never paint another woman after he had painted me. I didn't believe him, of course, but it turned out to be true. I was the last model he ever painted."

She paused and looked around the room, enjoying all the views of herself.

"If there was ever a woman to whom he might have made physical love, it would have been me. But he didn't. Not once. And believe me, I wouldn't have turned him down. I loved Joshua in every way imaginable."

All of a sudden, Sidney saw the façade drop, the cosmetically altered face fall, and the shoulders slump. The very real pain of her loss and the depth of her love for Joshua Morgan had altered Patricia Dalton Toomey from the inside out like a corrosive acid. Sidney stood silently, and respectfully with eyes averted, pretending to look at a far-off painting until the woman's moment of emotion passed, and the mocking mask settled back over her features.

"So, you see," she shrugged, the cigarette holder lifted to her lips back in place. "If anyone had a motive for suicide, it certainly was not Joshua. Trust me. He was full of life. Besides which, he was mad about a boy, to paraphrase, Noel Coward – or young man, actually. A friend of his nephew's, I think. But he seemed to have that well in hand. We joked about his crush."

"A friend of Jeremy's? Jeremy Hill?" Sidney asked.

"Yes. A thoroughly and stubbornly hetero friend of Jeremy's. Sad, really. Joshua hungered for a straight boy and I hungered for him. That's life, I guess."

"Why did the police conclude that he committed suicide?" Sidney asked. Patricia suddenly stared at her with raptor eyes.

"He never committed suicide," she said angrily.

"But I thought…" Sidney began to explain, but Patricia cut her off.

"I know. Some in his family said he did; the police said he did. He was found in his Russian Hill apartment at his kitchen table with a gun in one hand, shot through the temple. But I can tell you that he did not kill himself."

"I'm sorry Mrs. Toomey, to delve into such a painful subject. Why do you think he didn't kill himself? If not, then what caused his death?"

Patricia looked again around the room at herself in various poses. For every painting of herself, she would have observed Joshua Morgan for hours and hours as he painted her. They would have talked. Shared secrets. She would have missed very little.

"Joshua was totally against all violence. He loved the beauty of the human body, his own in particular. He was very vain. He would never have damaged himself like that. If he had ever killed himself ever, he would have done it with a drug overdose. Besides which he wasn't upset or despondent. I had spoken with him just hours before he died. We were making plans for a sitting the very next day."

"Then what happened?" Sidney asked.

Patricia shrugged in a way that communicated clearly that she didn't care at all whether she was believed or not.

"I think he was murdered."

Patricia Toomey's dramatic announcement made Sidney pause for a moment, wondering whether she was really serious.

"Why do you think that?"

"He was in a hurry when we talked. He said he was expecting someone. He didn't say who – and then, he didn't show up to our appointment. I'm sure he was murdered. I just don't know how, or by whom. And I don't know why. I know you think I'm being ridiculous; that I was just an infatuated old fag hag who couldn't accept what happened. But I'm telling you, Miss Dietrich, that Joshua Morgan was murdered. I know it."

"Did you talk to the police?"

"Of course, I did until I was blue in the face. But he was slumped over the kitchen table in his own apartment with a discharged gun in his hand and a bullet to his brain that matched the ballistics tests for the gun. No other fingerprints or evidence. Easy open and shut case, as they say. Except that I don't believe it. I never will."

Patricia's affected manner was no longer evident. She trembled with genuine anger and grief. Sidney didn't know how to respond. There weren't any words she could think of to offer comfort and she didn't have any information that could be helpful. She walked up to Patricia, who stood rooted in the middle of the room that stood as a memorial to Joshua Morgan while her eyes hungrily viewed what was left of his gifts as a talented artist. But looking at his relics would never be enough. Sidney reached out and gently touched the older woman's sleeve.

"I'm very sorry for the loss of your friend, Patricia. Thank you for letting me come and see you today."

There was no audible response, only a slight shaking of Patricia's head, either in anger or regret, she wasn't really sure. Sidney quietly turned and left the room, walking alone down the lengthy hallway to the elevator, as quickly as she could in her high-heels, hoping that she didn't have to run into Carol the efficient assistant. She wanted to be alone with her thoughts. As the elevator doors closed on the opulent penthouse, Sidney exhaled, unaware that she had been holding her breath until she escaped. She thought that her trip for Maude would be a rather limited errand, except that Patricia Dalton Toomey's dark suspicions turned out to be much more than what she had expected.

13.

"So. Here's the evidence box for Morgan." A young and stunningly beautiful African American woman dressed in a stylish burgundy business suit plunked a heavy cardboard box atop a long gun-metal gray table right in front of where Sidney was seated.

"Thanks, Malena," Sidney said gratefully. "I was worried that there'd be too much red tape if I went through the usual channels. You really helped me in a pinch."

"Hey, that's what ex-law school roommates are for – we get to cut through all that messy tape. I got your back, Sid."

"I know you do. Thanks."

Instead of leaving Sidney alone to sort through the evidence binders, folders, and crime scene photos, Malena sat down opposite her old friend and stared at her intently, beautifully manicured hands folded.

"I don't mean to pry. But how is everything? I know we should've gone out tonight and I could've gotten you all likkered up and pried the truth out of you, but since you're leaving to go back to the boonies this afternoon – well, there's no time. So, let's just catch up right this second. How're things?"

Sidney shifted uncomfortably on the metal chair. She'd just escaped from her exhausting interview with Patricia Dalton Toomey and now, her old roommate's concern was threatening to deplete her even further. Malena wasn't someone she could ever hide her feelings from, not since the first day of Civil Procedure, when they found themselves sitting next to each other in a large theater-style classroom, each dreading being called on at random by their fearsome, bearded professor.

"I didn't read the assignment," Sidney had whispered her confession to Malena, "And if he calls on me, I'm gonna be sick."

The gorgeous young woman with huge gold hoop earrings had stared back and then ducked her head conspiratorially.

"I didn't either. Tell you what. If he calls on either one of us, let's pretend we're gonna barf and rush outta here. Then I can go back to doing what I love: waitressing."

Sidney had to clap her hand over her mouth to suppress her laughter, and thankfully, neither had been called that day, but a mutual bond of fear and panic had built into a deep friendship that went beyond the terrors of law school. Malena and Sidney had kept up their relationship despite their hectic careers, especially Malena's high-profile and meteoric rise within the San Francisco District Attorney's office. Malena had been supportive of Sidney all through the breakup with Paul and had been one of the few friends to have even called her during her father's trial.

"I'm better. You know. Taking it day by day. I never thought I'd be stuck that far out in the sticks. I never thought that I'd be anywhere but here. But I'm getting used to it. And there are things I like about it."

Malena's gold-flecked eyes narrowed. "Like what? C'mon. You don't have to make the best of things with me."

"Well, like really getting to know your clients. Helping real people; not just faceless corporations. Making a difference, I guess. Also, being close to my godfather and having him as a mentor. First-rate guy. First-rate lawyer. It helps."

"What about men? Any out there that aren't wearing cowboy hats and boots?" Sidney smiled and shook her head, thinking about Matt Dunleavy.

"Nope. In fact, I was going to the coffee shop in the morning for breakfast last week and I almost keyed a truck sporting a Confederate flag decal and an old "Buck Ofama" bumper sticker. Can you believe it?"

"Yeah, I can believe it. Don't forget. I grew up in Mississippi."

"I know," Sidney nodded. "I thought you could relate. Pissed me off."

They were both silent, immersed in their own thoughts.

"But not everyone's like that," Sidney assured her friend.

"I'm glad you're in a safe place, Sid. But I sure wish you were back in the City with me. I miss you," Malena reached out her hand and grasped Sidney's in hers.

"I miss you too, Malena," Sidney said sadly, a genuine feeling of loss threatening to cause tears. She swallowed hard and after a few light pleasantries and a strong hug, Malena left for her busy and crowded afternoon court calendar, allowing Sidney to focus on the evidence box and its contents.

Reading through the police reports, investigator's notes, and witness interviews, Sidney had a sinking feeling that everything that could have been done was done in Joshua Morgan's case. The police had been extremely thorough, almost overly so, perhaps owing to the family's prominence and the artist's high-profile reputation. Sidney went through a check-list of the obvious: there had been no forced entry; fingerprints had uncovered no strangers, just known friends and family members; nothing was out of the ordinary, damaged, or destroyed; ballistics had matched the .38 caliber handgun with the bullet; the gun was registered to Morgan as the owner and had been purchased after a break-in years before; there was gun residue on his right hand and family and friends had confirmed that he was right-handed. The cause of death was clear: the decedent had shot himself in the right temple. He had not left a note. An investigation into his finances had revealed that his paintings had been selling well at various art galleries. His agent, gallery owners, friends, and relatives all confirmed that the artist was well-liked – even loved – and that his finances were in great shape. His will left everything to his sister, Maude. Interviews concerning the artist's love life had revealed that he was well-known in town at the more upscale gay bars and clubs where older and well-to-do patrons met willing, beautiful young men for consensual sex. Nothing out of the ordinary for San Francisco or any metropolitan urban area. There was nothing terribly kinky about any of it: no S & M; no unusual sex equipment or drugs were found; nothing to indicate an underground lifestyle. He found pleasure in an assortment of young men, all of whom attested to his generosity and his willingness to help them financially or otherwise if needed. Interviews with Morgan's treating doctor at UCSF uncovered a medical history consistent with a relatively healthy man. Apart from some early heart disease, bronchitis, and such, Morgan had been quite robust for a man in his mid-sixties. His medical records revealed that he had never tested positive for HIV and had survived the AIDS epidemic in the late '70's and '80's unscathed, revealing that he had been quite careful in his relationships. In short, there was absolutely nothing in the evidence box to suggest murder.

There was something that just kept nagging at Sidney and kept her reading and searching long after she should have given up and turned the box back to the D.A.'s clerk. Although absolutely nothing suggested murder, there was also no indication of why Joshua Morgan would have killed himself. No reason at all.

*****

Sidney left the D.A.'s office at the Hall of Justice on Bryant Street and made her way to a day parking lot, where the attendant took $40 in cash and a tip without even a thank you. She hadn't really been aware of the crowds, the congestion, the suffocating press of people, and noise until she returned to the city and relived that experience for one brief day. What had seemed exciting and alluring once now suddenly seemed frantic and pointless. Everyone rushed along littered sidewalks, eyes averted from the ever-present homeless who situated themselves on street corners and under awnings with cardboard begging signs and overflowing shopping carts to which kittens and scraggly mutts were tied with twine around their necks. The smell of urine was overpowering.

Patricia Dalton Toomey's world had offered a glaring contrast to that harsh poverty while illustrating a different sort of personal desperation. As she streamed onto the Bay Bridge with thousands of harried commuters, Sidney reflected that in spite of Mrs. Toomey's endless supply of money, she would not have wanted to be trapped in such a life. Sidney didn't relax leaving the city until she saw the sign announcing that she had crossed into Amador County, just as the valley started to ripple with vast green and gold grasslands where herds of cattle scattered over the landscape. Maybe someday these edges of the foothills would fill with the ever-expanding blight of thousands of identical little stucco houses, but that evil day had not yet arrived. Her spirits lifted as she inhaled a cleaner, purer air, and she eagerly absorbed the sight of thousands of acres of grazing land dotted with black and brown cattle that further along, would unfold into rolling, green hills dotted with oak trees that ascended ever higher as the road wound through thick stands of fragrant cedars and pines.

Arriving home at dusk from her long day of driving to the city and back, Sidney fell asleep to the sound of wind rushing through the valley below her ridge as branches of pine needles swayed and rustled. When she had first moved to Fiddletown, she had been frightened by the unaccustomed noise of nature unmuted by concrete buildings and the competing sounds of people, car-alarms, traffic, and sirens. Often, the howling wind or the pelting rain thundering on her tin roof would startle her awake, making her reach for a sleeping pill. But now she was lulled into a natural, more restful sleep, feeling soothed and protected in her cottage nestled in the woods.

The following morning, Sidney awoke refreshed. The night-time wind that blew so fiercely from the valley had cleared the air. She made coffee and sat out on her front porch overlooking the green, pine-filled valley below, where the roofs of only a few distant homes reflected sunlight to indicate their presence and were otherwise mostly hidden in the thick forests of cedars and pines. Exploring the hills a few months earlier, Sidney had found the adjacent ridgetop off a winding road and had looked back to see if she could find her own house, not trusting completely in the privacy that her small cottage seemingly afforded. She needn't have worried. She could have run around both her house and yard stark naked in broad daylight and not been visible to a single soul. That kind of isolation was frightening to many people, as it had been initially to Sidney. But this glorious morning, where pink-tinged clouds in the eastern sky reflected the sun bursting over the jagged high Sierras and red-tailed hawks circled the valley floor, she wondered whether she would ever again experience the burning ambition and drive that city life nurtured in a million ambitious souls.

Sipping her coffee more quickly as she looked at her watch, Sidney knew that she couldn't put off another trip to Quarry Hill that morning. She was obligated to report that she didn't have any hard evidence to upset the police report and coroner's conclusion. She debated any need to report Patricia's fevered suspicions of murder. It seemed unnecessarily cruel and besides which, what would the point be? After rinsing out her coffee mug and dutifully swallowing a few bites of crunchy cereal, she threw on a pair of serviceable black capris and a loose cranberry-colored top. She slid her feet into black sandals and headed out the dusty gravel driveway to Fiddletown Road, winding down to Plymouth and then over to Jackson. When she had cellphone reception nearing Jackson, she pulled over at the local market and checked with Jack. He told her to go ahead and report to Maude at the winery, with all details, including Patricia's suspicion of murder. According to Jack, it wouldn't be the first shock Maude had ever received concerning that "queer artist brother" of hers. Sidney sighed. Sometimes, Jack was an old dinosaur that would never change.

It was almost ten in the morning when Sidney emerged from her car after reaching the vineyard. Maude was already in the garden out front, and Jeremy stood close to his mother, talking with her in what appeared to be a serious tone. His arms were crossed in front of him and he frowned as if he were scolding her. Sidney walked towards them slowly, hoping to overhear whatever Jeremy was saying to Maude. She thought she heard him say something about "hurting someone close to you," but she couldn't quite make it out. She stepped on gravel and the crunch drew their attention. Jeremy scowled and walked away in the direction of the winery. Maude welcomed her with a gesture that Sidney assumed to be friendly, in spite of the pruning shears clutched in Maude's gloved fist. Sidney returned the greeting with a wave and approached Maude's hunched back as she pulled at an annoying strand of ivy.

"I love ivy," Maude announced. "I know it's an obnoxious vine, but I love it. That's why I planted it to grow up all over these stone walls and give the place an especially ancient look. But it's spreading into my hydrangea beds and I have to cut it back."

"Mrs. Hill, I went to San Francisco and spoke with your brother's closest friend at the time of his death, Patricia Dalton Toomey."

"Oh, yes. That social climber. You know, I liked her husband, although he was so crassly nouveau riche. He was at least a self-made man who had worked hard for everything he had. She, however, was a gold digger who befriended Al's wife and then ended up in Al's bed. Just what she deserved, I might add. He was not what you'd call an attractive man."

"She seemed very fond of your brother."

"Yes, sadly enough for her, she finally found her true love, only with a decidedly homosexual man. That never works out, you know."

"I wouldn't think so," Sidney responded drily. "Here, let me help." She grabbed at the stubborn vine and pulled hard, releasing the tendril from its grasp of the hydrangea bed, and ripping it loose to its origins at the base of the stone wall of the house.

"Good girl!" Maude cried out approvingly.

"Uh, Mrs. Hill, Patricia also had serious reservations about the cause of your brother's death. Quite dramatic speculation, really, but there's no hard evidence to upset the verdict in your brother's case, from what I could find out."

They both advanced on the wayward vine, reeling it in like a fishing line until Maude cut it exactly where she wanted to. It then lay discarded on the path like a dead snake. Mrs. Hill brushed strands of her white hair away from her face and squinted at Sidney.

"Oh, yes, I know. She really is quite the drama queen. I was thinking more of an accidental death, rather than suicide, but Patricia seems off the deep end entirely. I don't know why she seems to think that he was murdered. Well, the police in San Francisco didn't think so."

"And you don't think so, either, apparently."

Mrs. Hill looked squarely at Sidney. "Really, I am just interested to know if there is any possible theory other than suicide. It could have been a tragic accident. I was hoping so, but at my age, it makes little difference. He's gone and that's that. I do appreciate your efforts, but I think the issue is at an end. I can probably count what's left of my life in a matter of months, not years. I feel quite well today, but very soon, I won't, and the end will be here. It's a matter of how I choose to spend the rest of my time. I could believe that my brother was murdered and spend my energy and resources finding out how he came to die, or I can accept his unfortunate death and try to do what I think is important – taking care of the living. You may think I'm cold, Miss Dietrich, but I prefer to think of myself as being quite clear about my priorities. There is nothing to be done for my brother anymore. You've done all you can. And so have I. I'm very grateful to you."

Sidney nodded, puzzled by Maude's reaction. Her sudden acceptance of her brother's death seemed to be too abrupt. Sidney wondered what had happened to change Maude's mind. Something had.

"I understand. I'm sorry that I wasn't able to find out any more."

Maude nodded. "Really, it's quite all right. Thank you for coming out to see me. If you have a little time before Jack needs you, you should go and find Jeremy. He'll give you a personal tour."

With that, Sidney had been given permission to leave Mrs. Hill to her pruning and she wandered off in the direction of the various winery sheds and warehouses, hoping to run into Jeremy. She had dressed for business casual, but her black sandals did not do well crunching over rows of tilled earth and scrambling over raised hardened clumps of dried clay. In a hundred yards or so from the house, she heard voices coming from inside the warehouse. As she approached, she saw a rather haggard-looking Jeremy leaning over the back of his sister Grace's wheelchair while his hands gripped the handles. Whatever it was they were discussing heatedly came to an abrupt halt when Sidney appeared, but not before she heard Jeremy say something in an agitated tone of voice about "Selena." Her sandals crunched on the gravel and Grace's head whipped around to see who was coming.

"Oh, Sidney" Grace said cheerfully. "I take it you're back from San Francisco. How is our good friend Patricia?"

"She's… fine. Thank you for making the introduction. It was a big help," Sidney responded guardedly.

"Not at all," Grace said lightly. Sidney thought that Grace needed a bit more personal attention to her hair and her clothing. Her gray hair was shorn like a boy who had suddenly discovered his mother's scissors. She looked even older due to her dumpy figure lumped underneath knitted afghans, even in the heat. Today she looked particularly unkempt and neglected. Maybe the nurses weren't really doing their job very well.

"I need to get back to work. Would you help Grace get back home safely, Sidney?" Jeremy asked, pushing the wheelchair in Sidney's direction.

"Of course, but I actually came to see you."

Jeremy's pale blue eyes regarded Sidney warily. Then, he shrugged his assent. "Okay. Do you want to take a walk?"

"I'm fine making my way back to the house, Sidney. If you don't think that it will take long, you can catch up to me when you and Jeremy are done," Grace said agreeably. Without waiting for permission, Grace slowly wheeled her chair in the direction of the metal warehouse doors and proceeded to roll away on a narrow cart path toward the house. Jeremy was left with Sidney and he turned to walk toward the huge oak casks containing fermenting wine large enough to have floated Wynken, Blynken, and Nod and their entire families in alcoholic bliss. The warehouse was cool and damp; the air had a sour smell, like vinegar. Sidney had wandered through many a winery in the Napa Valley but had absorbed very little about winemaking. She felt woefully inadequate even to ask Jeremy any intelligent questions. Somehow, she needed to connect with the enigma that was Jeremy for Maude's sake and even more compellingly, to find out if he knew anything at all about Selena's murder. If he did, she could convince Jack to allow her to step aside and let an experienced criminal lawyer handle what was becoming increasingly uncomfortable for her to manage.

"I'm sorry I don't know more about this particular winery, but what kinds of wines do you produce here?"

"Do you really want to know?" Jeremy looked at her carefully. He would have been handsome if his face hadn't looked so drawn. His mouth was framed with deep lines and grooves which had developed where he had habitually furrowed his forehead in a frown. His hair was blonde and thinning, with just a slight bit of gray at the temples. Sidney stepped back and pretended to look around the cavernous metal warehouse.

"Sure. I think winemaking is fascinating," she chirped, sounding phony even to her own ears. Jeremy seemed not to notice. He turned his back and started walking away, expecting that she would follow as he began instructing her, the latest neophyte visitor to his winery.

"We only grow grape varieties that resemble those grown in the Rhone Valley, especially Syrah. We like rich and substantial wines, with flavors of fresh fruit. They age well, but they're fairly drinkable at release, especially our Zinfandel. They don't have to be aged for years. We produce a relatively small number of cases every year so that we can focus on quality. Right now, we have an award-winning Syrah and our first Barbera just won best-of-show at the California State Fair." He spoke almost automatically, without bothering to look at her. His eyes were preoccupied looking at gauges on huge metal vats large enough to resemble corn silos.

"You seem to enjoy the work," Sidney said.

He turned to look at her.

"I guess I do in my own way. I wouldn't actually say I enjoy it. It fully absorbs me, which is a good thing. I don't like to have a lot of empty time on my hands. I tend to brood."

"I like to be busy too. Maybe for the same reason."

They stood watching each other silently. Then Jeremy shook his head.

"Not the same. Similar, perhaps, but not the same. My mother told me about your father's misfortunes. I'm sorry."

"And I'm sorry that this young girl's tragedy has involved your family. It isn't easy dealing with the police."

"The police are the least of my worries," Jeremy said. "My very best crush supervisor is devastated by his daughter's murder and I can't imagine that he, or anyone else touched by her death, will ever fully recover."

"I can't either," Sidney responded readily. "You had to have been deeply affected. After all, she grew up here."

Jeremy looked away, twirling the glass case of a thermometer hanging by a string from a cord immersed in a metal vat.

"We were all affected," Jeremy acknowledged.

"Do you have any idea, Jeremy, any at all – who could have done such a thing, or why?" she asked evenly, not wanting to break the fragile measure of rapport she had established. He stared at her coldly. For a moment, Sidney was acutely aware that she was alone in this vast warehouse with a man she didn't know at all, and of whom she might have reason to be afraid.

"No, counselor. I don't have any idea. Do you have any other questions?"

"No. Let me know if you can think of anything that could help the police with their investigation. But if you do, please call us first."

"It's all I can think about," Jeremy replied with an odd intensity. His slightly mocking look had vanished, and Sidney could have sworn that he was genuinely overcome with emotion.

"Well, let me know if there's anything I can do to help," she said, feeling embarrassed and inadequate. She turned to go, leaving Jeremy standing, staring absently at nothing. That was so lame, Sidney castigated herself silently. Her flimsy sandals prevented her from giving in to an impulse to run away from him as she walked as quickly as she could out of the frigid, sour-smelling warehouse and into the warmth of the morning sun.

14.

"Have a cup of coffee with him. Chat about the case. How's it going, you ask? Is there anything I can do to help? Draw him out, Sid. Bat your pretty lashes," Jack tossed out his final suggestion and Sidney rolled her eyes in disgust.

"No, really," he added, "You should use some of those looks that God gave you to help your clients." Jack continued looking for some important scrap of paper in the utter chaos of his office. Sidney surveyed the mess that surrounded them. A faded life-sized cut-out of John Wayne stood in the corner, an old Western saddle collected dust on top of stacks of law books, fly fishing gear leaned against the far wall, an unoccupied aquarium collected spiderwebs among collections of old bottles, a bow and arrow, an antique flintlock rifle, and an assortment of weathered cowboy hats cluttered the credenza. Jack McGlynn was not what you'd call tidy.

"How do I bill for my time batting my eyelashes?" Sidney asked sweetly.

"Oh, come on, be creative: 'Conference with law enforcement agent re: criminal investigation and assistance re: same.' Get it? I'll pay for the time AND the coffee," Jack directed. Sidney walked up to his desk, rifled through the papers stacked on the corner and drew out a copy of a message slip.

"Is this the number you're looking for, Uncle Jack?" she asked innocently, handing the slip out to him as if proffering candy.

"You hid that number from me, you little minx!" Jack roared and Sidney retreated, laughing. She shut the door behind her and grinned, giving Marjorie a high-five as she fairly skipped down to hall to her own office. Teasing Jack took the sting out of what she knew she had to do next: call Matt Dunleavy and invite him to have a cup of coffee.

She settled in behind her desk and checked her computer for e-mails, stopping mid-scan and staring blankly at the screen. The thought of calling Dunleavy was acutely embarrassing, such an obvious and transparent move. He would interpret it as a fishing expedition, and he would be right. But with Jack breathing down her neck, she had no choice. She had failed to elicit anything out of Jeremy Hill, she had failed in her snooping for Maude, and she didn't have enough information about the girl's murder to head off trouble if trouble was brewing. She resolved to be braver.

"Marjorie," she pressed the button on the intercom phone. "Could you get the number from the card I gave you for Sheriff Matt Dunleavy? I need to set up a morning coffee appointment with him."

"You betcha," Marjorie chirped back over the intercom. "He's a handsome devil, dontcha think? Kinda dreamy with that thick, dark hair. Nice, broad shoulders."

"No, I don't think," Sidney contradicted sourly.

"Sure ya don't," Marjorie responded and having had the last word, quickly clicked off.

*****

Matt dumped an armload of hay into Sage's feeding bin and watched as his soft muzzle buried into the fragrant alfalfa and pulled a tasty morsel to chew. Matt reached over the rail and scratched Sage's forehead. He then went over to the next stall and watched the little black and white Paint mare lift a hay flake the size of her head out of her feeding bin with bared teeth and shake it over the stall floor. Cloud always preferred having breakfast on her stall mat. He felt badly that he wasn't riding her very often, but she was a bit petite for his large frame. He wondered if he should sell her, but dismissed the thought, recalling that Sage would miss having her around.

"Your mama went off and left you," he reminded the Paint. "I'm your only hope."

She looked at him with rounded, black eyes and shook her head as if in agreement, although he knew she was just shaking more hay loose. Sarah and Matt used to ride the horses together, but Matt had always known she was just doing it to please him. She was afraid of horses in general and of her little Paint mare in particular. After Sarah left, getting up to feed the horses, fill up their water buckets, and close them in their stalls at night when the weather turned ugly was one of the only things he could do other than drink. He remembered one winter night stumbling in Sage's dark stall and slumping down into the pine shavings where he woke up stiff and sore the next morning, Sage looking at him steadily as Cloud poked her head in to gaze at the bizarre sight of their human curled into a corner underneath the automatic waterer. Matt knew that they just wanted to be fed, of course, but their silent gazes had made Matt feel as if they were judging him for his stupidity. He had quit drinking that day. He had responsibilities and animals that depended on him, even if he didn't care about himself. He went back to Sage's stall for one last forehead scratch.

"Since my horse likes me, I must be okay," he affirmed, brushing off stray hay stalks from Sage's ears. "So, what am I supposed to talk to her about, boy?" Sage's ears twitched. Matt remembered the dispatcher's call with Sidney Dietrich's message the previous afternoon: "Jeremy Hill's lawyer wants to have coffee at Rosie's tomorrow morning. She says 8:00 a.m. would be okay, but earlier is fine, too."

Matt greeted the dispatcher's message with stunned silence. Then, after a moment, he responded with assent, "No, tell her eight is okay. I have some barn chores to do in the morning." So, the early morning coffee meeting was set up and now Matt was delaying. He'd rather stay at the barn mucking out stalls and digging more fence posts than play cat and mouse games with the Hill family lawyer, even if she wasn't hard to look at. No point dragging it out, he thought to himself and left both horses munching contentedly. He slid the heavy metal barn doors together and walked to his white Dodge RAM 2500. He started the engine and put his dark aviator Ray Bans on to cut the glare of the morning sun. He was glad he wasn't drinking anymore on a morning like this, when the combination of bright sunshine and a meeting with a female attorney was enough to guarantee a headache, much less with a hangover.

Thirty minutes later, Matt parked on Jackson's Main Street and walked into Rosie's. From the booth farthest away from the door, Sidney could see him scanning the crowded tables for her, cowboy hat in hand, dark corduroy jacket rolled up at the cuffs and the oversize silver belt buckle completing the western ensemble. She knew without even looking that he would most certainly be wearing cowboy boots. He seemed right at home at Rosie's, where most of the ham and eggs crowd in the early morning were local ranchers and farmers, either similarly clad in western garb or in overalls and well-worn work boots. No one bothered to remove any baseball caps or cowboy hats while eating. She lifted her hand slightly to wave to attract his attention. He nodded when he saw her and threaded his way easily through the tables to the corner booth she had claimed earlier when the place wasn't so busy. The waitress's resentment that Sidney had occupied a booth for a quarter of an hour without ordering seemed to vanish as Matt slid on the opposite side and looked expectantly for his order to be taken. After his ham and cheese scramble with home fries and wheat toast was duly noted, he turned his attention to Sidney.

"Thanks for coming," she said, nervously shifting a bit and taking a sip of ice water.

"No problem," he responded.

"I just wanted to know how you were doing in your investigation and whether there was anything I could do to be of assistance," she said blandly.

Matt continued his gaze. Sidney's face looked a bit pinched and pale. Under his stare, she brushed aside a lock of honey-colored hair from her forehead. The girl could use more fresh air, he thought. She took another sip of ice water, nervously blotting the table where sweat dripping off the glass had left a soggy ring. She would have been a lousy poker player, he thought, as she took another sip of water. She was so obviously uncomfortable, he wondered why she would have called and asked him to coffee; unless, of course, it hadn't been her idea. He had plenty of time to observe her, and he took his time. She shifted in her seat, still averting her eyes, picking at the sleeve of her cotton pullover.

"If you're worried, you should know that I'm not here to charm you into making some indiscrete disclosures," Sidney blurted suddenly, startling them both.

"Of course not," Matt nodded in agreement. He waited. It was an interrogation technique he had always found to be effective. Most people were uncomfortable with silence and ended up talking too much.

"We're here to help," Sidney offered the bait as casually as possible. "I understand that you've hit a dead end in your investigation, and I was wondering if there was anything that I could do to facilitate communication with the Hill family or any of their employees."

Matt smiled and ran his hand through his thick, dark hair. Really, Sidney thought, the man was maddeningly slow on the uptake. Why didn't he just tell her where things stood, so she could sympathize with the lack of results and walk away?

"Well, ma'am, I really appreciate that. But the truth is we're not at a dead end. As a matter of fact, I was going to ask your client Jeremy down to the station to answer a few more questions. Would you like to make it easier for him and for us and just bring him in this afternoon?"

Sidney stared. His answer surprised her. "Why? He's already answered all of your questions."

"Oh, that's right. Let's see: he told us that he hadn't really known the dead girl, and then it seems he sponsored her on a trip to Mexico, and now we have a witness who saw them talking together a while back, and she seemed really upset, as if she were crying."

"Who's your witness?"

Matt smiled, genuinely amused. He waited for a moment while their waitress brought his ham and eggs and poured more coffee. "Now, you know I don't have to tell you that," he responded flatly, liberally salting everything on his plate. "Not yet, anyway."

"Do you consider him a suspect?" Sidney asked uneasily, watching Matt shake more salt per square inch of egg product than she's ever seen before. "You don't have any real evidence."

"As they say, the investigation is ongoing. He's more what you'd call a person of interest. He may have more information than he's letting on. Once we get the entire forensic report, we'll have something more to go on. They're looking through microscopes at everything from fingernail scrapings to fiber analysis. If I were you, I'd figure out what my client knows. Now, before he needs to go down to the station this afternoon. I tell you what you can do. You can ask him to come voluntarily so that we don't have to go get him and upset Mrs. Hill."

Sidney picked up her coffee cup, looking at Matt curiously. Matt chewed quietly, discomfited by her stare. "You went to high school together, you and Jeremy, didn't you?"

Matt nodded, swallowing a piece of wheat toast.

"Did you like each other?" Sidney asked. Matt placed a slice of half-eaten toast back down on his plate.

"What are you saying, Ms. Dietrich: that I've hated Jeremy since high school, so I have it in for him now?"

Sidney shrugged, "Just wondering if you weren't maybe a wee bit prejudiced where it comes to Jeremy Hill or his family."

Matt stared directly into Sidney's eyes. They were hazel and flecked with amber. Her hair shone with thin streaks of gold and copper under the fluorescent lights. He was thinking carefully about what to say. How could he explain what it was like to grow up, the part-Indian son of the town drunk, alongside the handsome, fair-haired boy of one of the county's richest and most prominent families?

"Frankly, I've never been a huge fan of Jeremy's. He's reckless. Things have always been too easy for him. But you'd be wrong if you think that I'd let anything I feel personally interfere with my job."

"I wasn't saying that... Mr.... Sheriff..." Sidney stuttered.

"Matt. Just call me Matt. I'm not the Sheriff anymore."

"Matt," Sidney repeated firmly. "I'm just saying that in a small community like this where everyone knows everyone else that there are certain preconceived ideas people have about each other that may prevent someone from seeing other possibilities."

"Like what?"

"Like, for example, that the dead girl had a boyfriend who was insanely jealous and killed her after arguing about her interest in another man."

"Okay," Matt seemed to concede her point. He pushed his plate aside and folded his hands on the table. "We've actually considered that kind of scenario. Let's say there's another possibility. Let's say that the very young daughter of the Mexican vineyard foreman catches the eye of the wealthy winery owner. Because of her age and the predictable disapproval of his family and hers, they have a secret affair. She gets pregnant and leaves the country, where she suffers a miscarriage. When she returns, the relationship ends badly, and she threatens to make their affair public. He is seen having an emotional argument with the girl just a few days before her death. He kills her to keep his reputation and position intact as primary heir to a considerable fortune. That's a fairly interesting scenario don't you think?"

"And entirely lacking in any evidence," Sidney contradicted flatly.

Matt called the waitress over for the check. He took out a twenty-dollar bill and left it on the table. Feeling as if the conversation had taken a rather tense turn, he rose and nodded to Sidney. "We'll see. Thanks for the breakfast."

"Thanks for meeting me. I appreciate the information. Are you still insisting on seeing Jeremy this afternoon?"

"Three o'clock. If that's convenient for you."

"I'll be there. Jeremy will be with me."

"Fine. See you then, Ms. Dietrich." Matt was done with any pleasantries. He didn't like people from cities, and he didn't like highly-strung professional women. They were edgy and unhappy, and they made him nervous. Sidney Dietrich in particular, made him feel uncomfortable and unsettled. He obviously had that effect on her. Anyway, he didn't really care whether it was his fault or hers: the less contact he had with her the better.

Sidney watched as Matt said hello to a couple of farmers in bib overalls and feed caps. She conjured every negative thought she could about the scene, mentally calling as many names as she could muster: hillbilly cop, rube, know-nothing redneck. Sidney's mental stone-throwing stopped when Matt smiled as the waitress handed him his change. It wasn't cheesy or fake. It was a warm, engaging smile that reached his eyes as he leaned on the counter and thanked the waitress, leaving a generous tip in the counter jar. He walked easily out of Rosie's without looking back and Sidney didn't know whether to be relieved or offended. She decided that if she were honest with herself, she felt offended. He didn't like her, that much was clear. Her father once told her that if she was well-liked, she wasn't doing her job as a lawyer. She didn't want to believe that was true. But she found herself time and again in situations in which she had to be a cautious adversary and watch her back with everyone with whom she came into contact. She felt that way now and she closed her eyes and rubbed her temples with her fingertips in an effort to ward away another headache.

"How'd it go?"

Sidney startled at Jack McGlynn's sudden appearance. He slid into the chair Matt had just vacated and searched her face. Sidney snorted, "Well, that's the last time I take your advice. He wants Jeremy Hill front and center at the Sheriff's Office this afternoon. Someone saw him and the dead girl arguing. I feel it in my bones that he's now the prime suspect."

"No shit?"

Sidney sipped ice water. "No shit, Jack. I mean it. You'd better start calling some of your high-priced defense lawyer friends from the big city, or this local cop is going to make mincemeat out of our client this afternoon."

Jack waved the waitress away, "No need to take any orders here, darlin'. We're packing up. C'mon, Sid. Let's take a ride down to the vineyard. I'll cancel whatever I've got going today. We'd better have a chat with young Jeremy Hill. Before the next round of police questioning."

Jack had already charged out of Rosie's and was headed around the corner to the Court Street parking lot. Sidney trotted to catch up as Jack dug into each pocket to find the keys to his ancient steel-gray Mercedes sedan. Sidney waited as he unlocked her door and settled in behind the wheel. The back seat was piled high with a mess of files and stacks of paper, just like the office. Jack backed onto Main Street in front of a red Toyota pickup that screeched to a stop as Jack's car swerved and headed south on Main Street. Sidney buckled her seatbelt tighter than usual. Jack's poor driving habits were legendary.

"C'mon, honey. No one's going to run into me. That's why I drive this old tank made of solid German steel. Scares everybody else shitless."

Sidney shook her head and smiled. No one could simultaneously both scare and amuse her quite like Jack McGlynn.

15.

"So... fill me in. What do you think of Jeremy's connection to the dead girl?"

Sidney frowned. Jack was driving way too fast. It made her almost too nervous to think. It was a brilliant early summer's day. The oak trees were sprouting bright but thorny green leaves that would turn old, yellow, and brittle in the fall. She had a faint headache already from the sun's brightness. Maybe she was too tired to care, but she said the first thing that popped into her head.

"He's a cold fish. It's hard to believe that he's obsessed enough to commit murder, Jack. He's way too self-controlled. I guess I just don't see the passion. He's so calculating. You should see him calibrating temperatures and degrees of fermentation. That's the Jeremy I see; not someone getting carried away to the point of murder."

"Do you find him attractive? Not to you personally, I mean. I'm just thinking ahead, wondering if a jury would ever find the guy sympathetic."

What an odd question, Sidney thought. Attractive and sympathetic were two entirely separate things. No, she had never found him attractive. His kind of slender, pale, blonde, northern European looks had never attracted her. As a subconscious contrast, an image of Matt Dunleavy popped into her head, and then her feelings followed: she had felt acutely uncomfortable when he had stared at her underneath frowning dark brows earlier that morning. His brown hair was the color of mahogany and almost black, but his eyes were warmer and more expressive than Jeremy's icy blue ones. From Dunleavy's tan, she concluded that he spent too much time outdoors and his hands were workmanlike, strong and capable. She suddenly remembered with distaste the pasty, soft, white hands of neophyte lawyers at her old firm, looking as if they hardly even ventured from underneath fluorescent lights. She had been attracted to Paul the minute she almost collided with him while running in the Marina one windy San Francisco day. He was tanned and fit and caught her eye. It was only later when she knew he spent every waking moment working out, honing his muscles at the gym and on the running trails in the Presidio that his physical appeal started to evaporate. Narcissistically dedicated to developing the perfect bedroom physique, Paul would position his chair at their favorite outdoor lunchtime café for maximum sun exposure, so he could maintain his even tan, even in winter. In hindsight, there was nothing appealing about Paul's self-absorption and constantly wandering eye. Even though she had been devastated when he had moved on to someone else, she had to admit that there was a part of her that was relieved. She was working on nurturing that small part and wondered what kind of idiot she was to have endured the pain he had caused her.

"Is he the kind that a young girl might fall for? I sure as hell can't tell," Jack interjected, and Sidney shook off her day-dreaming in order to answer.

"Oh, Jeremy Hill? Sure. A young girl might find Jeremy good looking in an older-man kind of way. Plus, he's rich. That couldn't hurt his attractiveness, but I find it hard to believe that a thirty-five-year-old heir to a winery fortune would mix himself up with the teenage daughter of one of his workers. I don't get it. He must have had his pick of available, more age-appropriate women. What could the police have found out to make Jeremy a suspect?"

Jack pondered the question. "And if he is a suspect, why the hell would he kill a kid like that? I mean, so if there was an affair, and if it went sour, or he tired of her... I mean, what's the motive? Even if someone saw them together, so what? What does that prove? Jesus, if someone suspected me of murder every time I talked to someone or got into an argument, I might be locked up for life. You've gotta have evidence, for Chrissake!"

Jack's sour humor was making his driving even more erratic than usual. Sidney didn't take her eyes off the road. It occurred to her that she might have to grab the steering wheel at any second to save both their lives. They careened around the curve that led to the winery, across the highway from its ugly stepsister, the gravel quarry. The juxtaposition of the elegant winery and the raw terraced layers of exposed red dirt, gray shale, and granite cliffs just across the road had always looked odd to Sidney; even when she had no connection to the area. According to Jack, the Hill family apparently owned them both and the business of quarrying was just as busy and as profitable as the business of raising and crushing grapes to make award-winning wines. The quarry was crisscrossed with huge metal scaffolds and machinery with conveyor belts that carried pulverized rock in various stages and sizes of decomposition from one huge pile to be deposited onto other huge piles. As they drove past at Jack's frantic pace, Sidney examined what she could see of the quarry from the road. No one appeared to be operating the machines, although she was sure that some human presence was required at least to push buttons to make the conveyors stop and go. They were like the skeletons of giant metal creatures with a life of their own, dropping tons of gravel from a great height onto piles from which dust rose in an unceasing gray cloud. Seemingly for effect, several vultures circled above the quarry, putting the finishing touches on a raw and ugly picture. Sidney grabbed her door handle as Jack swerved into the private driveway leading to the house.

"Damn. I hope we're here ahead of the fuzz. I didn't have time to call and warn Maudey."

Gripping onto the door handle, Sidney smiled at Jack's word for the police, so reminiscent of the sixties.

"They're here already," Sidney exclaimed when she saw the Sheriff's car parked to the side of the gravel driveway. Jack slammed on the brakes and skidded to a stop. They both jumped out as quickly as they could and rushed to the front door. Jack pounded on the huge knocker both to announce their arrival and purposefully interrupt anything that could be going on inside. The door handle gave way and he stuck his head in, calling "hello" at the top of his lungs. Sidney looked at her godfather admiringly. The former combat Marine veteran never lacked for guts in any situation.

"Oh, Jack," Maude's distressed voice called from the end of the entry hall. "Jack, come in, come in."

Maude's face was drawn with worry and her bony hands appeared to claw at the air in front of her as she tottered in their direction as quickly as she could move at her age. She reached for Jack's arm and clamped both hands around his shirtsleeve, the ropy blue veins bulging as she gripped to keep from falling. Sidney moved quickly to her opposite side and lifted her under her other arm.

"Jack," Maude breathed rapidly. "They're talking to Jeremy and I don't think it's good. I told him not to say anything until his lawyer could be here. I'm so afraid, Jack."

"They have to leave the house if you tell them to, Maude, if they don't have a warrant."

"That's just it, Jack, they do have a warrant, to search Jeremy's apartment and anywhere else in the house they want. They're doing that now and then they said they were going to take him to the station for questioning. What's happening, Jack? Why are they taking my boy? What's he done?" Maude pleaded. She would have fallen if they hadn't been supporting her on either side.

"Where are they?" Jack almost growled with anger.

"In Hans's study. There." She pointed to the door at the end of the hall.

"Sidney, stay with Maudey, right here. I'll go in." Jack opened the door and Sidney could see all three men inside turning suddenly to stare. She saw Matt Dunleavy, one hip resting on a polished desk corner, his arms crossed over his chest. Jeremy sat in a leather covered armchair in front of Matt and the young deputy stood over Jeremy, his hands on his hips, looking grim.

"Gentlemen! The warrant, please!" Jack announced as he closed the door behind him.

At first, Sidney was resentful that she had literally been shut out of the room, but she led Maude into the nearest parlor, her weight sagging against her arm. She would have fallen if Sidney hadn't held her up. Sidney led the distressed elderly woman to a comfortable armchair. Maude sank into it and glanced up at Sidney, her look of gratitude making speech unnecessary. She cleared her throat and shook her head, wisps of white hair escaping from her bun.

"I never thought anything like this could happen to us. Not even when my brother killed himself. He was so talented. Look, my dear, look at those paintings. See those incredibly deep colors and the life in those forms? What kind of recognition would he have had if only had he lived!"

Sidney saw her opportunity to keep her client distracted. Surely, that had been Jack's intention when he had shut her out – to protect Mrs. Hill.

"Were you very close to your brother?"

"As much as we could be living very different lives. But we were close. He was devoted to Jeremy, you know. Jeremy spent time sailing with his uncle and visiting his studio in San Francisco."

"Patricia mentioned that your brother was in love with one of Jeremy's friends at one time. Do you know who that might have been?"

"That makes no sense," Maude snapped suddenly. "Jeremy's friends weren't homosexual, and his uncle was decades older. I hardly think that even my brother would have gone looking for partners among his nephew's friends."

"Yes, it sounded odd to me too," Sidney acknowledged. "Were Jeremy and his uncle close?"

"Yes, yes they were. My brother took Jeremy to San Francisco sailing with him often, and then they would spend time together in the city. There is a very lively arts scene there. You know, my brother studied with Richard Diebenkorn. We have a piece or two of his around here somewhere." Maude waved her hand, puzzled by knowing the paintings were around but confused as to where exactly they might be.

"Many of Diebenkorn's paintings are in museums now," Sidney prompted. "They must be very valuable."

"So my insurance company tells me. But let me tell you, Miss Dietrich, my brother's paintings are every bit as good. I don't know why Joshua never received the attention he should have gotten in his lifetime. Maybe that's why he chose to kill himself. I guess I'll never know."

"Mrs. Hill, even though I don't particularly have an eye for it, I took Art History in college. It seemed to me that many artists don't get the recognition they deserve in their lifetimes. But very few commit suicide. They seem driven to create, and recognition is secondary, I imagine. Besides, many become successful eventually, if they stick with it long enough."

"Yes, yes, that's true. Joshua never did seem to care overly about public recognition. Our parents had left him enough so that he was comfortable, and then Hans always helped him in one way or another, so he was never exactly starving. And his paintings eventually sold and sold quite well. Really, I just don't understand why my brother chose to kill himself, and now this. My own son being questioned by the police! For murder! Oh, it's too much. Just too much. I sometimes wish my time on earth were over already."

Maude slumped back in the chair closing her eyes, her breath shallow and fast. Sidney discretely touched the bony wrist and felt for a pulse, which fluttered rapidly. Mrs. Hill was pale and cool, but her forehead was damp. Not good. She got up and half ran through the dining room to the kitchen, hoping to find help. She pushed open the swinging door and called out, "Can anyone please help Mrs. Hill? A glass of cold water please?"

Grace wheeled around from the far end of the kitchen near the breakfast nook and pushed her wheelchair over to Sidney. Her black and gray hair stood up in the back as if she had been napping against a chair and had just woken up. "What's wrong? Where's Mother?"

"She's outside of the study. She's not well."

Grace called out, "Betty! Betty! We need you in the hall! It's Mother!"

A heavyset nurse in uniform pushed open the kitchen door, heard the summons and looked expectantly at Sidney. "Where's Mrs. Hill?"

"I'll show you," Sidney pushed past her and ran back down the hall, the nurse in close pursuit. They all reached Mrs. Hill's chair at the same time. Maude's eyes were still closed, and she looked deathly pale. The nurse pulled out a stethoscope from her uniform pocket and placed it gently on Mrs. Hill's rapidly rising and falling chest.

"She's hyperventilating and her pulse is erratic. At her age, I don't want to take any chances. I'm calling for an ambulance."

"I agree," Grace seconded, as she wheeled her chair next to her mother and leaned over to reach for her hand. Grace's bare arms were heavy and round, Sidney noticed. She probably weighed more than twice her mother's weight. The afghan blanket that usually shrouded Grace fell to the floor and Sidney bent to pick it up. She was practically at Grace's feet and under her bulky form as Grace leaned forward to clasp her mother's arms, trying to prop her up. Grace saw Sidney and let go of one of her mother's arms in order to pull the colorful blanket back over her knees.

"Thank you," she said gruffly. Sidney stood up supporting one side of Mrs. Hill while Grace struggled one-handed with the blanket while grabbing her mother's other arm. As Mrs. Hill seemed to slump farther over on Grace's side, Sidney had the urge to yell at Grace to forget the damned blanket and help her mother, but the nurse returned just in time and caught Mrs. Hill under her arm.

"The ambulance will be here in just a few minutes," she said calmly.

"I'd better let Jack and the Sheriff's deputies know," Sidney said, after hesitating for a split second as to whether she should interrupt them to announce the imminent arrival of an ambulance at the front door. She strode quickly down the hall to the study and opened the door without knocking. Jack stood behind a leather wingback chair where Jeremy slumped. Matt's knee touched the side of the chair's arm as he leaned into his interrogation from his perch on the corner of the massive desk. Intimidation tactics, Sidney thought, alarmed by the scene. Jack cut Matt off in mid-sentence.

"That's it, Sheriff. Arrest him, charge him. But I'm not going to allow this continued fishing expedition. You have no evidence and you know it." Jack paused and looked at Sidney, detecting the urgency in her face. "What is it, Sid?"

"It's Mrs. Hill. There's an ambulance on the way. She's fine... I think... she's just fainted." It wasn't entirely accurate, Sidney knew, but it had the desired effect. All four men jumped up and followed her out of the door, Jeremy keeping up a quick pace with her down the hall. They reached Mrs. Hill's still form on the chaise lounge just inside the front doors that were propped open while waiting for the ambulance's arrival. Jeremy knelt by his mother while Grace held her hand on her other side. Betty spoke to them both in a reassuring tone while Jack, Matt, and Tom Nelson stood on the porch outside. The ambulance arrived with sirens blaring and tires crunching gravel, pulling up right in front. Before anyone had said a word about what was going on, the stretcher had popped out of the back doors and hit the ground with legs extended. Two dark blue-uniformed paramedics, one young female with an up-twisted ponytail and another equally young cherub-cheeked male yanked the stretcher up the front steps and through the doorway. Everyone stepped out of the way while they expertly checked Mrs. Hill's pulse and heart rate and strapped on an oxygen mask to help her breathing. She was bundled up and lifted onto the stretcher in a matter of seconds while Betty answered their few clipped questions.

"We're headed to Jackson Memorial ER. Anyone who wants to can follow by car."

"That's ok, Jeremy," Jack said. "We'll stay behind for a bit to finish with the police and then check on your mother at the hospital later. You two go on." Jeremy nodded his understanding.

"I'll take Grace, Jack," Jeremy said in a strained voice. "Maybe you can give us a hand getting Grace's contraption in the car."

Jack, Matt, and the young Sheriff's deputy were all eager for something to do and they followed Jeremy as he wheeled Grace's heavy wheelchair down a side ramp to one side of the front stone steps. Sidney watched the ambulance doors shut Maude's stretcher inside. Red flashing lights were again turned on and the ambulance crunched gravel and spewed dust as it sped out of the driveway. Jeremy strained to push Grace's chair up onto the paved sidewalk that bordered the gravel drive and Jack reached to help him push her chair towards a large forest-green van with a blue disabled license plate. Jeremy opened the passenger door, positioned the chair alongside, and with practiced moves, Grace grabbed a handle attached to the inside roof, pulling herself out of the chair and sliding onto the front seat. Jeremy collapsed the chair and opened the back-cargo gate with an electronic button. Matt and Jack took the folded wheelchair from him, and with the deputy's help, slid it on its side into the cargo area in the back of the van.

Matt found the button and the door closed just as Jeremy started the van and rolled forward, peeling out of the driveway as quickly as he could, spraying more gravel in his wake. The ambulance sirens screamed in the distance. For a moment, they stood and watched as the van sped after the ambulance. Matt, Jack, and Deputy Tom Nelson turned away simultaneously and walked back towards the front steps of the house, where Sidney waited with her arms crossed. She didn't think for a minute that this particular disruption would interrupt Matt's determination to conduct a search.

"You want to show me that warrant again, Matt? I'd like to take a good close look," Jack said as they reached the steps.

"Sure, Jack, take your time," Matt replied politely as he took the folded warrant out of his back pocket. "Don't mind us. We're going to get the evidence bag out of the cruiser and trot on upstairs to Jeremy's apartment. You're welcome to wait around downstairs, so's not to get in the way of a police search. We'll let you know when we're done."

Dunleavy and Nelson retrieved their shiny aluminum case from the back of the Sheriff's cruiser and Nelson carried it back up the front steps and into the hallway with Dunleavy alongside. As the pair walked up the massive winding staircase to the second floor, Jack and Sidney looked at each other. Jack shook his head in disgust. There wasn't a damned thing either one of them could do.

*****

The oleander hedge provided another perfect screen from which Billy watched as the ambulance sped away, leaving the fancy lawyers and the Sheriffs' deputies behind. For a heart-pounding minute, he thought that they'd all be leaving, and the bastard would get away with it. He almost broke through the hedge and started waving his hands to attract their attention. But there was no need. The deputies went around the side of the house closest to him and looked up the winding outside staircase where he had seen Selena come and go so many nights. They and the lawyers then walked back inside the house. He knew they would search. He knew what they would find. Slowly, he backed out of the bushes and unseen by anyone, crept back to his trailer. Cause for celebration, Billy, he said to himself. There was a six pack in the refrigerator, and his mouth salivated at the thought.

16.

Jeremy was arrested at the hospital after Matt and Tom found a bundle of Selena's letters stuffed in a shoebox on the top shelf of Jeremy's closet. Matt found stacks of the same childish, looped scrawl in multicolor gel pens, on lined school paper torn out of spiral notebooks. They were crammed into envelopes decorated with hearts and drawings of disembodied kissing lips, all signed with a large, flowery capital "S." He scanned just a few of them, touched by their simple declarations of love. They seemed to be all that remained of the obviously besotted young girl. Carefully, Tom pulled out a camera chip from one of the envelopes and held it out for Matt's inspection between thumb and forefinger-encased latex gloves. Matt nodded approvingly, guessing that it would contain a treasure trove of digital images, probably of Selena. Of Jeremy too, he hoped.

Matt called in the find to Dom Colangelo, quietly explaining Maude's sudden illness and the results of the search. He was careful to do so outside of Jack and Sidney's hearing, on the outside deck, using Tom Nelson's cellphone.

"We don't know how this is going to play out, Dom. I wouldn't say just yet that a suspect has been arrested. Maybe just say that a person of interest was brought in for further questioning. Love letters might establish a romantic involvement and the fact of his lying to the police, but not murder," Matt warned, despite his hunch that Colangelo would probably ignore the advice and jump to announce an arrest to get the County's grousing supervisors off his back.

"Not for now, at least," Colangelo responded. "Forensics just issued a report on the ligature used to strangle the girl: an 8-gauge wire – exactly the type used to string grape vines at Quarry Hill Winery, by the way. We've tracked down their wholesale distributor and we can probably match the manufacturer to the exact piece used to strangle the victim."

Matt rubbed his eyes, fighting off both fatigue and his growing annoyance with Dom Colangelo's impulsive conclusions. "And it's likely common enough that it's used by every other grower in the County – not to mention the hundreds of people in and out of wineries that have access to 8 gauge wire every day. Nothing linking Jeremy Hill, Dom."

"We'll see," Colangelo said darkly, and abruptly ended the call. Matt sighed and turned back into the apartment, where Tom was systematically searching through dresser drawers with latex gloves.

Jack and Sidney waited impatiently outside of Jeremy's rooms, observing the search from afar to make sure that it didn't extend to any areas not specifically described in the warrant. Jeremy's apartment took some time to comb through and they waited for a couple of hours while Matt and Tom went systematically through all the cabinets, drawers, and closets. Jack was on his cellphone almost the entire time, checking in with various clients and former constituents, so it was left to Sidney to assume a posture of vigilant monitoring, watching both Matt and Tom, but mostly Matt. He moved methodically, searching with focused and silent care. Sidney wondered what it felt like to sift through all of the artifacts of someone else's life, from their dental floss to their pile of bills. The search was so thorough and professional that Sidney felt invisible. There was no banter or commentary between Matt and Tom; not even one snide remark concerning a figure so prominent in their world, whose privileged life was about to become a complete train wreck. Sidney had anticipated some sign of satisfaction from Matt, but if he was privately gloating, it was indiscernible.

Sidney had considerable time to observe that Jeremy's private apartment had been designed and outfitted with a separate kitchen, breakfast nook, living room with rock-wall fireplace, office, and spacious bathroom complete with Jacuzzi tub. Nothing but the finest brushed bronze fixtures, plantation shuttered windows, Italian tile, and thick pile carpeting. Quite the crib, she thought. She watched as Matt stepped out of the sliding glass doors onto the deck. He looked over the railing, grasping the top rail with both hands and leaning over quite far. Odd, thought Sidney. Was he inspecting for wood rot? She sighed, looking sideways at Jack, yakking on his phone. What had already been a long morning was stretching into a long afternoon and Sidney was starving, staring longingly at the refrigerator door in Jeremy's kitchenette. She would have killed for some pita chips.

Matt scanned the perimeter of the property from the deck. He spotted the caretaker's cottage and then looked as far over the deck as possible. The winding wrought iron stairway hugged the back of the house and allowed for outside access to Jeremy's second-floor apartment. He noted that there was no gate and no lock, allowing for accessible entry all the way up the twisting stairway to the deck. That's where she must have come into the house to spend time with him, Matt thought. Not through the front, rear, or even side entries; she would have been seen by Maude, Grace, her nurse, or the household staff. Matt went back through the French doors into the living area. Tom Nelson walked out from the bathroom, a thin smile on his face. He was holding up a hairbrush for Matt to see. Even from a few feet of distance, Matt saw long black strands snarled in the bristles. Matt nodded, and Tom carefully bagged the hairbrush. It would likely yield the evidence they sought.

Within a few minutes, a forensics team from Sacramento arrived to brush for prints and take over any dusting or swabbing. Matt had called ahead, and he briefed them when they arrived. Sidney was too far away to overhear, but she assumed that things were going well from an investigative point of view, but disastrously for her client. Matt and Tom stepped into the interior hallway to get out of the forensics team's way. Jack spun around and quickly clicked off his cellphone. Sidney looked at Matt expectantly.

"Okay. We're done here. You can stay or go, Jack. They're going to brush all over looking for prints and it'll take a while."

"I'd like to see that," Jack jerked his head in the direction of the shoebox stuffed with letters that Matt had handed over to the forensics team.

"You'll be able to examine it all after we've logged them into evidence, but I'm afraid it doesn't look good for your boy, Jack. My guess is that after the parents confirm their daughter's handwriting the letters will prove your client a liar. The D.A.'ll make them available to you, you know that. As soon as we're done with our examination."

Jack nodded. There wasn't anything else they could do. He knew that Matt had shared more information than any city investigator ever would have and had shown no animosity in doing so.

"I'll get him to turn himself in," Jack said flatly. Matt nodded, anticipating that charges would be drawn up within a day or two and that the D.A. would soon be dealing with Jeremy Hill's defense team.

"That won't be necessary. I've already called. Deputies'll pick him up at the hospital. Judge won't be around over the weekend, so my guess is that there won't be a hearing until Monday at the earliest. I don't know if the judge'll be inclined to set bail pending an arraignment. Your client's a liar and has the means to skip the country. I think they'll keep him in jail as long as possible."

"Do you really think he killed that girl?" Jack asked exasperated by what was taking place completely out of his control.

Matt shook his head. "Not up to me. I just dig up the facts and turn over evidence. The rest is out of my hands."

"I don't think you've got the whole story," Sidney interjected.

Matt turned to her, his gloved hands still holding the shoebox, "Maybe we don't. Maybe there are other plausible explanations for why she was found strangled to death. So why would he lie about an affair that was obviously going to be discovered? That one's going to be a tough one to get around, Miss Dietrich."

"People lie for a lot of reasons – maybe it was to protect her because she was so young – maybe it was because he knew if he admitted an affair, he'd be the prime suspect. Maybe it was because her parents didn't know about their relationship, nor did his own mother, and he wanted to protect them. There could be a million reasons."

"Well. You can work 'em all into your defense, counselor if it comes to that. Excuse us." Matt was followed by his young deputy and they brushed past Jack and Sidney and descended the stairs, exiting by the open front door. Sidney watched from the top of the landing as the Sheriff's cruiser left the driveway.

"Now what?" she turned to Jack. "This doesn't feel right."

"Let's call our client," Jack responded firmly. "He's at the hospital and we can reach him before they get there to arrest him. I'll tell him to keep his trap shut and not say a word until we can see him. Let's go," Jack barked. "My goddamn cellphone's out of battery. We'll charge up in the car and call on the way."

*****

They weren't allowed to see their client while he was being booked. As Jack had instructed, Jeremy asked for his lawyers immediately, but they made them wait until the following day. Jack and Sidney parted ways at the jail, as there was nothing either of them could do until morning. Sidney drove home in a daze. More than once, she swung her headlights wide as she twisted her car around the turns on Fiddletown Road, crossing the double yellow lines. Jesus, she thought: straighten up. You're going to kill yourself. With a deep exhale of relief, she turned into her driveway and drove the narrow gravel drive up the hill to the house. She pulled up and parked in front of the farmhouse porch. Grabbing her shoulder bag, she dragged herself up the front porch stairs and reached the darkened door, fumbling with her keys.

The house was dark and more than a little bit spooky. The wind had picked up from the valley and rushed through the trees, shaking leaves and swaying branches. Sidney's heart was pounding as she let herself in the front door and only started to slow down when she flipped on the lights, locking the door behind her. She exhaled softly with relief as she looked around the familiar surroundings in the wood-paneled entry. The carved wooden hat rack held Jack's jumbled fishing, hiking, and assorted baseball caps on jutting pegs; many of which he had collected through years of congressional campaigning and had worn proudly emblazoned with decals from myriad manufacturers of farm machinery. Even though Jack had told her to clear out "all of my junk" from the house when she had moved in, she couldn't bring herself to do it. His hats greeting her return every day gave her a sense of security and signaled his presence, as though she were not completely alone.

She dumped her jacket, purse, and keys onto the cedar chest in the front hall and hauled herself up the stairs to her bedroom. She didn't even bother splashing her face with water or brushing her teeth. She stripped off her clothes in a heap on the floor and pulled on flannel pajamas. Her head hit the pillow and as she snuggled down into her cold sheets, she wondered if Matt Dunleavy had anyone to come home to, or if he was just as much alone in the world as she. "Maybe I should get a dog," she muttered, as she drifted off to sleep.

*****

Jeremy Hill was ushered into the interview room dressed in an orange jumpsuit with big, black letters spelling "ACJ" on his back and chest. Amador County Jail, Sidney spelled out to herself silently. What a comedown for him, Sidney thought, and if he was charged and convicted of murder, that would be the end of his life, his career, and his enviable position as the scion of a wealthy family. Poor Maude, she thought, as Jeremy sat wearily down at the table facing them, his face unshaven, hair slightly greasy and unkempt. Still, he was Maude's beloved son. Sidney knew all too well that every jail or prison inmate had at least one person on the outside whose heart had been ripped into a thousand pieces.

Her thoughts shifted to her father and the last time she'd seen him several weeks before at the Federal Penitentiary in Livermore. Adam Dietrich was dressed incongruously in drab gray prison garb as he entered the visiting area, waving at his daughter jauntily, as if they were meeting at an airport. His smile beamed across the crowded visiting room, embracing her before they even reached one another. Sidney had had to wait for an hour until other visitors left and made way for new family members before they called her father in to visit. Lined up before security scans with other anxious or expectant family members, Sidney had been screened and every inch of her clothing searched from her purse to her shoes, which she removed so they could be examined for contraband. The cookies she had brought in a colorful Christmas tin were confiscated at the security gate almost immediately, and she let them go reluctantly. She had so carefully made the dough according to cookbook instructions in her new country house, courtesy of Uncle Jack, in the bright yellow kitchen decorated with flowered chintz curtains. She had baked them in her under-used oven, staring through the slotted glass oven door every minute or so to ensure that they would not burn. As her father's thin form approached with open arms, she had nothing to give him but a hug. She closed her eyes, hiding her face in his shoulder, breathing in his pungent pipe tobacco smell. Their murmured greeting was interrupted by a guard who instructed them to be seated at a nearby metal table across from each other. Her father had lost weight, even since his sentencing hearing, Sidney noticed. Without his private barber to cut, shape, and color his hair every month, Adam's dark hair was growing with light gray roots. His beltless khakis hung from his hips, even with his stiff cotton prison shirt tucked in. He held her hand and looked into her face, but within moments, pleasantries gave way to her father's anger and irritation with his lawyers. They were too damned slow on the appeal, he complained, bankrupting him in the meantime. It was hard for him to call from prison and they never took his calls. His friends had stopped writing, and no one had visited in ages. He was in prison, rotting away, forgotten by everyone, he fumed. Sidney's presence alone should have been proof enough that what he said wasn't true, but he was in no mood to be forgiving of anyone, even her.

"It's been months since you've come, Sid. Why can't you visit more often?" he complained.

Sidney was stunned. Instead, she calmly explained.

"I lost my job, Dad. I was fired, remember? I've had to leave the city. I'm a pariah. I moved a hundred miles from nowhere so that I could work for Uncle Jack. No one else would hire me. I've started over in a place that seems like it's a million miles from here." She thought that would be enough, but her father rarely spared a thought for anyone but himself.

"Jack," her father spat out bitterly, shifting to another target for his anger. "I asked him to help me appeal to the President for a pardon. You know he's got connections from all those years in Congress. But he just said that pardons were for the innocent who were wrongly convicted, not for the guilty. Can you imagine that? My own daughter's godfather refused to help me."

Sidney sighed, "I don't think he meant to hurt you, Daddy. He has helped. He's been helping me get back on my feet." She wanted to point out that Jack was right. Her father's guilt had been determined in a unanimous jury verdict. In Jack's book, that didn't qualify Adam Dietrich for a pardon. It might not have been a diplomatic answer, but her father's old friend was being honest about his own principles. Her father's strained face was pale, and his shoulders slumped.

"I know that, sweetheart. I'm grateful to him for helping you. It's just hard for me to be here day after day, not being able to do a thing for myself or even know what's going on. The legal bills alone are killing me."

Sidney burned to ask him why he would spend every last dime of their family's dwindling assets on filing appeal after frivolous appeal, ignoring her advice to serve his sentence hoping for early release rather than expending fruitless energy burning through money trying to overturn a conviction rendered in an air-tight case. But she didn't. She was his daughter, not his lawyer, and he had already ignored her advice in both capacities.

Jack's voice broke into her thoughts and brought her suddenly back to awareness. Her memories of the Livermore visit with her father were so vivid that she was almost surprised to find herself sitting in the Amador County Jail, across from a nervous, perspiring Jeremy Hill, who asked for a cigarette.

"Sure, Jeremy. Next time I come. I quit smoking, y'know, and Sid here, well, I hope she never started. We don't have any cigarettes. Right, Sid?"

"If you tell me what kind you smoke, I can always buy a pack for the next time we see you," Sidney assured their client. Jeremy nodded, rubbing his eyes.

"It's okay. I don't really smoke anyway. Make sure my mother's okay, will you Jack? And postpone telling her where I am. It'll just upset her. We'll get this straightened out. I'll be out in no time, right?"

"Well, Jeremy, it depends on what evidence they have and what kind of case they can build against you."

Jeremy leaned over the table, his blue eyes wide with fright as he struggled to keep his voice calm. "I didn't kill her," he said emphatically, volunteering the answer to a question that defense attorneys rarely ever ask their clients. "We were involved, okay? Selena was young and beautiful. Full of life. You should have heard her laugh. She was amazing – bright, talented – she could have done anything. I would have helped her. I did help her. But we knew that her parents would never approve of us – I'm so much older. I'm not Hispanic, not Catholic – there were so many reasons. And my family – well, you can imagine. So, we saw each other in secret for months. I didn't know she was pregnant until she called me from Mexico. I wanted to keep the child and marry her, but she wouldn't hear of it. We argued over the phone and she hung up. By the time she came back, there was no baby." He paused, shaking his head, rubbing his eyes at the memory.

"She told me she'd had an abortion. I was angry. Really angry. I had a hard time forgiving her. And then she was dead." He sat hunched over with his head in his hands, rocking softly back and forth in his chair. The sobs escaped. "I couldn't forgive her, but I loved her. I never would have hurt her."

Sidney was stunned. Jeremy had just blurted out the strongest motive she had ever heard for murder.

"Why did you lie to the police?" Sidney asked quickly, trying to seize this moment of openness before Jeremy shut them out again.

He looked up from his hands, his eyes red-rimmed. "Because I knew they'd suspect me. I was her lover. I was the one closest to her, and she'd been pregnant – with my child. My child. And Selena had an abortion! I couldn't admit to the affair. They'd think I killed her because of the baby, or because I was jealous that she didn't want to be with me anymore. Any reason to convict me. I'm not exactly a popular guy in this county. Ask Matt Dunleavy. He thought I was having an affair with his wife. He tried to beat the crap out of me."

"And were you?" asked Sidney, giving into her voyeuristic interest in Jeremy's conflicts with Matt.

"No! It was some other guy – a marketing guy from the wine distributorship. But he suspected me. He's hated me since high school. Ask him. They're just looking for reasons to convict me of this murder."

Sidney sat back in the steel chair, arms crossed, considering Jeremy's story. She remained unconvinced of Jeremy's persecution theory. Matt didn't seem the devious, vengeful type and with the compelling circumstantial case against Jeremy growing ever stronger, he didn't need to be. She leaned forward again.

"They'll go where the evidence leads them, Jeremy, unless you can tell us something that might help."

"So, what did happen? You said she came back from Mexico, without the baby," Jack asked. Jeremy nodded. Jack continued to prod. "So, she comes back. She's living in the caretaker's cottage with her parents. Did she come to see you?" Jeremy nodded again. Jack and Sidney waited for more.

"She came up to see me – maybe a day or so after she got back from Mexico. She climbed up the staircase outside my deck. That's how she always got in. We argued about the baby. She said she didn't want it – that it would ruin her life – I yelled at her that she was stupid and selfish – she didn't have a right to get rid of our baby. I was so angry that I... I might have struck her. But I only slapped her face. Once. I swear it. She left after that. It was the last time I ever saw her."

The room was silent. Sidney looked at the glass window above Jeremy's head. It was reinforced with chicken wire and steel bars. Jesus, she thought to herself. He had the opportunity to kill her. He had the only motive to kill her. How were they going to defend this guy? She glanced at Jack. His jaw had tightened as he looked at Jeremy. His fingers gripping the pen were white-knuckled as he jotted down notes on a yellow legal pad. Sidney wondered if he was going through a mental checklist of reasons to keep his client off Death Row – diminished capacity, voluntary manslaughter – anything to keep him from a first-degree murder conviction.

"Okay. You haven't made this easy for us, son. You lied to the police and that's going to affect your credibility. The jury'll wonder if you're lying then or lying now."

Jeremy nodded as Jack continued. "We'll try our best. I assume that your mother will want us to make every effort on your behalf. I'll have to advise her as to what we face."

Jack stood up and motioned the guard through the glass window of the interview room door that they were ready. After reapplying handcuffs, the deputy escorted Jeremy out.

"Jesus Christ," Jack muttered, as their client left the interview room without so much as a glance back. "Sid, you're going to have to dig around. I need your help. I know you're not an investigator, but we're in deep shit here. I'll talk to the D.A. – Rich Rodoni is an old friend of mine. Assuming they're going to charge him and arraign him, Rich'll turn over their list of witnesses and evidence pretty quickly. We've got to be all over it. Interview everyone they've talked to – find anyone else who knows anything about the dead girl and Jeremy. Figure out any other plausible motive – jealous old boyfriend – protective father – yeah, yeah, I know," Jack responded to Sidney's blistering look at his mention of the dead girl's father.

"Look, if her father knew about the affair, it gives us another possible motive. You can't be chickenshit about this. This is a potential death penalty case. You got the rich white man, poor Mexican girl angle and if the D.A. doesn't charge first degree, you'll have the Mexican-American Legal Defense Council tearing the D.A. a new one. No holds barred, Sid. Pull out all the stops. Maudey Hill's money might just help save her son. I'll call Francis X. Mahoney, Jr. or one of my other top-notch friends in the criminal defense bar to associate in as co-counsel. It's the way of the world, Sid. Money buys the best legal defense. You know that, or ought to."

Yes, she knew it. In spite of the fact that her father had been sentenced to prison, his high-priced lawyers had encouraged his cooperation in unraveling the complex fraud and had bought him a place in a Club Fed in Livermore, Minimum to Medium security, not doing hard time. Ten years and he might be out in seven.

"Francis X. Mahoney, are you serious?" Sidney asked, shaking her head.

"I know. Your father's lead defense lawyer. Yes, I'm serious. Who do you think helped get him for your father, anyway? Just because Adam Dietrich was guilty didn't mean he shouldn't have the best damned criminal defense lawyer in Northern California! C'mon, now, buck up, Sid. Let's get ready for a fight." Her godfather put his arm around her shoulders and squeezed her tight. She smiled in spite of herself.

"Thanks for the pep talk."

"You're welcome, sweetheart. Now get your butt back to the office and get to work. There'll be a lot of late nights and weekends around here in the next several months. We need to be ready and Jeremy is counting on you. I'm counting on you. More importantly, Maudey Hill is counting on you to help her no-good, scoundrel, likely murderer of a son. Let's go."

They signed out of the jail's interview area and exited to the front parking lot. Like every other building in town, the Jail's red brick exterior and covered porches were relics from prosperous gold-mining days. To Sidney, it looked like a set piece from The Wild, Wild West. Jack's office was just blocks from the jail and they parked in the alley in the back of the building, next to an ancient wooden barn around which the town had sprung up. Whatever its current uses, the locked and abandoned barn no longer housed livestock, even though a few cattle still grazed on creekside pastures within city limits. As they mounted the stairs together, Jack stopped, gripping the railing.

"I've got some calls to make. Sid, just as soon as you can, get ahold of the autopsy report, police investigative reports, interviews, and forensic reports. Comb through 'em. I'll work at getting the great Francis X. Mahoney Jr. as co-counsel with Maude's authorization. You'll be Mahoney's right hand. You'll know everything about the D.A.'s case against Jeremy." He paused, shaking his head. "God help the poor bastard."

As Sidney followed Jack up the stairs to their offices, she reflected that Jeremy Hill might be a lot of things, but he was definitely not poor and as far as she knew, not a bastard. Whether any god was even the slightest bit interested in helping him, however, remained to be seen.

17.

Jack saw Maude in the hospital the day following Jeremy's arrest. He found Grace in her wheelchair sitting vigilantly by her mother's side. Maude was sleeping when Grace saw Jack duck his head inside the doorway. Grace motioned that they should talk outside, and Jack backed up into the hospital corridor, waiting until Grace could maneuver the chair around her mother's hospital bed. She slowly pulled the door closed to her mother's private room. Grace looked down the hall at the visiting area and noticed a couple of empty armchairs available. She motioned Jack to follow her and they sat facing each other. What an odd-looking woman, Jack thought to himself. It wasn't the wheelchair – those were common enough – it was how little effort Grace made to ever look presentable, even in public. Her graying hair was chopped at odd angles. She had lost all semblance of any shape and simply looked like a big sack of flour covered in a faded print house dress, her bosom sloping into a large soft mound around which was tucked the ever-present afghan blankets. Her face hadn't seen any make-up in decades, and he doubted that she had ever attempted to delay the onset of wrinkles with any lotion or feminine skin products. Grace's complete lack of any attractive quality had always faintly repelled Jack and he had avoided contact with her whenever he had socialized or conducted any business with Maude and Hans. She also smelled faintly of unwashed body, especially in close quarters, such as they found themselves in the visiting area of the hospital.

"I'm sorry, but I need to speak to your mother urgently, Grace."

"It's about Jeremy, isn't it? The police haven't released him."

"That's right. I've talked to District Attorney Rodoni. They'll be charging Jeremy with murder any day now and I have to know from your mother that I can do whatever is necessary for his defense. I want to bring in a very prominent criminal defense attorney, Grace, and it won't be cheap." Grace's face crumpled, and her eyes filled with tears.

"Jeremy," was all that she could whisper in her anguish. "He's innocent, Jack. He never would have harmed that girl."

"I believe you, Grace. I don't think he murdered her either, but Jeremy's the only obvious suspect and there isn't another theory that we've got to work with, so far." Grace mopped tears that ran down her lined cheeks and her nose reddened from blowing into a tissue she pulled from a pocket of her shapeless dress.

"Look," Jack said, "I know this is hard, but I have to get your mother's okay to proceed."

"Do whatever you need to do, Jack. I have Mother's power of attorney. I'm authorizing you to proceed with Jeremy's defense. Hire anyone you need, do whatever it takes to clear him. I'll take care of Mother."

"Okay," Jack nodded. "I'll send Sidney around to get your signature authorizing us to represent your brother and outlining our fee agreement. I don't want you or your mother talking to anyone about this case without me or someone working with me present. Is that understood?"

"Absolutely," Grace nodded.

"And, oh, ah… about the girl's family. It's a little awkward that they're living on your property."

"I know. Actually, they've left. We didn't ask them to, of course. But right after they arrested Jeremy, Carmelo and his wife and the younger children just packed up a trailer and left. We don't even know where they are."

"I'm sure the police do. They can't have gotten very far, not when there's a trial pending."

"I feel so sorry for them," Grace said, with great emotion, the tears flowing again. "What a horrible situation."

Jack could think of nothing to say but, "How's your mother doing?"

"Better. Exhausted, but her doctors say she can go home, perhaps as early as tomorrow."

"Grace, I'm going to send Sidney by whenever your mother's in the clear and can go back home. She'll need to go over every detail of the days just before the girl's death with your mother, with you, and with each and every one of your employees. We can't overlook anything."

Grace nodded. "Just let me know if there's anything else I can do. Anything at all."

Jack nodded, patting Grace's rough hand.

"We'll need all the help we can get. I won't lie to you, Grace. This is going to be really tough on you and your mother, not to mention Jeremy. But I promise you, we'll do everything we can to help your brother."

Grace thanked Jack and wheeled back to her mother's room, leaving Jack to exhale softly with relief, grateful that it wasn't he that would have to deliver the news to the frail and sickly Maude Hill that her son would soon be on trial for murder.

*****

Within days of Jeremy Hill's very public arraignment on charges including first and second-degree murder, as well as the lesser included charge of voluntary manslaughter, the D.A. delivered four moving boxes containing copies of police reports, medical examiner's report, forensic reports, and test results, along with potential witness interviews. The boxes were dumped in Sidney's office. Jack made good on his promise to bring in Francis X. Mahoney, Jr. as co-counsel. The noted criminal defense lawyer betrayed no objection to Jack's announcement that Adam Dietrich's daughter would serve as his research attorney for trial preparation. Maude Hill was paying the team's legal fees, and Maude Hill wanted Sidney to stay on the case.

"He's not going to hold your father against you," Jack tossed the comment Sidney's way as he rushed to pack his old battered black court briefcase.

"I hope not."

"You graduated from a top-tier law school and you have great big-firm experience. He should count himself lucky to have you."

Sidney wasn't so sure. "I hope you're right."

"Sure, I'm right. Now, get to work. I've got to get to court." He waved his hand in her direction of her office and bolted from his in his usual hurried fashion, papers from stacks on his desk fluttering to the floor behind him.

Unable to stall any longer, Sidney looked over the boxes of court documents and evidence stacked knee-high on her office floor. Sighing, she bent over and lifted the topmost box, heaving it through her door and down the hallway to the small conference room, dropping it with a thud onto the polished antique conference table. Fifteen minutes later, Sidney had lugged all the boxes out of her office and into the conference room, taking all the lids off for a second look at each to see which one to tackle first.

She pulled out the black trial binders that Marjorie had pulled together, flipping through the complaint, indictment, and other criminal procedural court filings. At first, she reviewed carefully and cautiously, daunted by her inexperience in criminal matters. But then, the familiar routine of reviewing each slip of paper, scanning every last item, and committing it to memory reasserted itself and took over. She jotted notes on a yellow legal pad, immersed in the minutiae of the case. For years, she had digested evidence for litigation in far fewer compelling cases, digesting engineering and soils reports for real estate development and professional liability claims, poring over blurry snapshots of chimney and window cracks when houses settled and broke apart. Millions and millions of dollars of clients' insurance money had been at stake and for Sidney, hundreds if not thousands of hours of drudgery that in hindsight had all been just a huge yawn.

Soon, she forgot her own awareness of her inexperience, striking "criminal case" from her mind and substituting it with her own disciplined framework, classifying everything that had been produced by the D.A.'s office. The organization of the case suggested itself: the formal pleadings and indictment, police reports and witness statements, interviews and finally, crime scene photographs and physical evidence. This last part was hard to take, especially the photographs in brilliant color, reflecting the girl's slim, motionless body in the mid-morning light. The ligature mark on the girl's smooth skin looked like a thin, crimson ribbon around her neck, and her bluish tongue protruded through pale lips as if she had just licked a popsicle; her eyes slightly open. Sidney forced herself to take in every detail of the girl's face. It was hard to know how death had altered her features because even then, she was heartbreakingly beautiful. The girl had carefully made herself up with thinly dark-penciled eyebrows, eyeliner, and thick mascara. Her cheeks were puffy and childlike under her blush. Loose strands of long black hair looked as if they should be brushed off her forehead, which glistened with dampness. Every conceivable angle had been photographed of the body and immediate surroundings. She had been carefully arranged so that she appeared posed with her hands folded, her feet that were lined together and her clothes that were neatly arranged. Tiny blue-purple wildflowers were threaded through her fingers. Her killer or killers had taken great care to display the body just so. Like a lover, Sidney sighed while she stacked the photographs together, laying them face down on the table, thinking of Jeremy.

She picked up several photographs of the grassy areas surrounding the body. Footprints in the mud were marked off with measuring tape. The tread designs appeared common enough and might have come from any one of hundreds of pairs of ordinary work boots. As hard as she stared and wished for some small scintilla of significance to reveal itself, there was nothing in these pictures but carefully staged and unreal horror. Sidney returned the photographs to the tan clasped envelope from which they came. She hoped that she would never have to look at them again.

After sorting through the final box, Sidney pulled out the girl's autopsy report. The M.E. was from the Sacramento County Coroner's Office and the report was signed and dated by R.J. Richey, M.D. Details seemed straightforward. Death was caused within a matter of minutes by strangulation using an 8-gauge wire still embedded in the skin. Time of death was fixed at between 4:00 p.m. and 10:00 p.m. the evening before the body was discovered due to the temperature and lividity of the body and taking into account exposure to the chill night air that had hovered between 38 and 42 degrees Fahrenheit. The report described organs of the body, how much they weighed and that there was nothing abnormal in their appearance. As Sidney had expected, the girl's uterus showed signs of a recent near-term or full-term pregnancy.

Sidney carefully put the report back down on top of the table. She stared with her lips firmly pressed together at the conference room wall where a massive early California landscape hung, complete with cowboys, cattle, and sunset streaking across a brilliant sky. An idea had pressed itself into her mind and had refused to dissipate. Pushing the conference room chair away from the table, Sidney suddenly stood up and walked quickly from the room towards Marjorie's desk in the foyer.

"Hey, Marjorie – would you call the Sacramento County Coroner's Office please and let them know that I'd like a few minutes of the M.E.'s time – it's a Dr. Richey. Let them know I'm already on my way, okay?"

Marjorie looked up from her computer screen and shrugged. "Sure. What if Dr. Richey isn't in today or can't see you?"

"Just let me know if the doctor is there today or not, okay? Call me in the car. It takes an hour to get there and I don't want to get there close to quitting time for coroners, whenever that is."

"Can do. Have a nice trip. Enjoy the coroner's office," Marjorie shouted after her, but Sidney barely heard Marjorie's sarcasm as she rushed out the door to her parking space in the alleyway behind the office.

The drive to Sacramento was long but uneventful. Marjorie called to let Sidney know that the doctor was in. Sidney's impatience was revealed in uncharacteristic tailgating along the pokey old two-lane Jackson highway that meandered past fields with grazing cows, goats, and the occasional donkey. An overloaded hay truck slowed traffic down for at least twenty minutes. At long last, the truck turned left into the Rancho Murieta Equestrian Center's white picket gates, rumbling past several covered arenas in which well-dressed equestriennes balanced expertly astride cantering horses. Sidney pressed on the gas pedal.

Within another half an hour, Sidney was pulling into the parking lot of a two-story glass and concrete office building. A small street sign displayed the five-pointed star bearing the Sacramento County Sheriff's Department seal. Small lettering underneath identified the County Coroner's Office. The building looked brand-new and utilitarian in the extreme. As she entered the lobby, Sidney thought drily that the county apparently had spared every expense in attempting to soften what was doubtless a chilling place for almost every visitor. She walked up to the plexiglass window that insulated the receptionist from the outside world. A thin, petite Asian woman of indeterminate age looked up sharply as Sidney leaned against the counter to better speak through the small, circular hole cut out of the middle of the pane of thick plexiglass.

"Don't lean on the counter, please," the woman pointed at the sign facing the lower part of the counter. Sidney backed up.

"Makes it hard to talk to you from this distance," Sidney muttered. The woman cupped her ear and leaned towards the hole.

"What do you need?"

Sidney stepped forward again, avoiding the leaning. "Dr. Richey, please."

"You have appointment?"

Sidney pushed her card up against the window facing the woman. "No. But I've come a long way to speak to him if he has a minute."

"She. Dr. Richey a she – Regina Richey. Wait here. I'll check."

After she left, Sidney was left alone with framed black and white portraits of coroners past and photographs of street and river scenes of old Sacramento. She was alone in the waiting room until the front doors opened behind her and an older well-dressed African American woman entered the lobby, leaning on a cane. On her other side, a young boy wearing sagging pants almost to his knees held up by a belt strapped around his thighs and a red hoodie held on to her other arm and helped to support her. Her bewildered face was tear-stained as she wailed in Sidney's direction, "My baby. I'm here to claim my baby."

"I'm sorry, Ma'am, but the receptionist is coming right back. She'll be able to help you." Sidney willed the receptionist to return. There was something so frightening in the elderly woman's crumpled grief that Sidney was compelled to flee the place herself. Come on. Come on, she repeated silently. Suddenly, the "Staff Only" door on Sidney's right opened up and a red-haired, middle-aged woman in a white lab coat stitched with Dr. Richey over her left pocket emerged and said, "Miss Dietrich?" Relieved, Sidney stepped over and extended her hand. "I'm Sidney Dietrich, Dr. Richey."

"Your office called to give me a heads-up about your visit. Follow me to my office, Miss Dietrich."

Sidney quickly followed the doctor down a wide, white-tiled corridor and into a small, book-laden, and paper strewn office with stacks of file folders piled high on every surface. The doctor sat down in her swivel chair and motioned Sidney to do the same in the only available metal guest chair.

"Usually we meet defense counsel in the deposition room or in the courtroom. This is an unusual visit. But since our office is entirely independent from the Sheriff's office, and since we serve the public, I'll be happy to answer any questions that I will doubtless be required to answer in court. However, let me warn you that I can't draw any opinions or conclusions regarding guilt or innocence of any party and that this conversation is not privileged."

"Understood. And I wouldn't ask you about guilt or innocence. I'm not here about that. I just wanted to ask you about something in your autopsy report of the victim, Ms. Rodriguez. I have it here." Sidney pulled out a copy of the report from her satchel. "It's of a factual nature. I won't be asking about your opinion."

"Okay," Dr. Richey agreed as Sidney handed her the document. "But if I'm ever asked if I've discussed the case with a member of the defense team, I'll have to testify truthfully." Sidney nodded her agreement.

"You noted that the victim bore signs of a recent near-term or full-term pregnancy. Is there any difference in the physical signs of an abortion, a miscarriage, or the delivery of a live baby?"

Dr. Richey paused. "The signs of an early miscarriage are the same for an early induced abortion – the uterus does not expand fully, and the cervix appears essentially as before. With a fetus that dies in utero at greater than 22 weeks or during delivery, that is a stillbirth, and the signs of such are identical to that of a live birth."

"So, just to recap, doctor, can you tell from the condition of the victim whether she had a miscarriage, an abortion, or a live birth?"

Dr. Richey furrowed her brow and took a moment to consider the question. It was already as if she were testifying at trial. Sidney made a mental note that Dr. Richey would make a great witness for either side in the case.

"Spontaneous miscarriages usually occur quite early on, so it is doubtful that this woman sustained a miscarriage. The condition of her uterus was consistent with either a stillbirth after 22 weeks or the full-term or near-term delivery of a live-born infant. An abortion after 22 weeks would be unlikely. It could be quite difficult to get, depending on where she was when it happened. If it happened."

Sidney looked down at her notes. "I'm sorry, doctor, if I'm failing to understand you. From the condition of the body, can you tell for a certainty what happened to the baby?"

"No. I can't tell. I'm sorry. As I said, there is no difference in the condition of the uterus with a live birth or a stillbirth. Usually, there's no question as to which occurred. Frankly, I've never been asked that question before. The least likely scenario is an abortion, given the estimated age of the fetus. The two likeliest possibilities are a live birth or a stillbirth. Does that answer your question, Miss Dietrich?"

"Yes, I think so, Dr. Richey. Thank you for your time. I can find my own way out." Sidney stood up from her metal chair and extended her hand. There was no doubt Dr. Richey was puzzled by the questions but felt that she was in no position to turn the tables and satisfy her own curiosity by asking Sidney questions in return.

"Thanks again," Sidney turned and said as she left Dr. Richey's tiny office. The lobby was empty when she pushed open the glass door and breathed in fresh, outdoor air. She closed her eyes and breathed in deeply, her face upturned to the afternoon sun. She felt the same way she did on the occasions when she had to visit her father in prison. It was an almost out of body experience, with everyone acting as if the situation were perfectly normal and mundane, while Sidney's chest constricted with the effort to appear calm. She looked sharply to her right across the parking lot in response to a harsh, sobbing sound, and saw the elderly woman who had followed her into the lobby waiting area being gently supported to a long, older blue sedan by the young boy with sagging pants and angled baseball cap, who lovingly helped her into the passenger seat. The sobbing was muffled by the car door closing, but her tear-stained face turned towards the building's entrance as if unable to part with the place where her loved one still remained. Her baby could be forty, but he or she was still her baby, just as Jeremy Hill was still Maude's baby, even though he was a thirty-five-year-old man in jail accused of murder. Sidney was unsure where this train of thought would lead her or what it had to do with the case against Jeremy, but the thought struck her as she watched the grief-stricken mother as she was driven away: could a young, Hispanic girl really have aborted her own baby, especially late in her pregnancy? Suddenly, Sidney knew as deeply as she knew anything, that Selena's baby could not have been unloved and unwanted. It went against every primal and biological instinct, imperative, and cultural norm. There was something about this case that no one was seeing, she was sure of it. Her every instinct told her it was about Selena's pregnancy, but not as everyone else had understood it, not even Jeremy.

As Sidney drove away from the coroner's office, the details of the case, the reports, witness statements, and crime scene photographs replayed in her mind to the point that she barely saw the turnoff to the Jackson highway that crossed over rarely-used railroad tracks.

"Selena," she muttered, as she pointed the car down the long stretch of rural road. "What the hell happened to you? What the hell happened to your baby?"

18.

A florid fat man's girth arrived in the conference room well in advance of the rest of him. Francis X. Mahoney, Jr. sweated profusely despite wearing loose cargo pants and an oversized short-sleeved tropical shirt. He mopped his forehead and stuffed his wrinkled linen handkerchief back in his hip pocket while surveying Jack's western-themed conference room piled high with boxes, black trial binders, assorted yellow legal pads, and pens. Sidney felt shrunken into insignificance with Mahoney's appearance and he did nothing to reverse that feeling, failing to acknowledge her as she sat quietly at the far side of the large, polished table.

Mahoney was followed by a very thin, well-dressed young man in Harry Potter owlish glasses carrying an expensive retro leather briefcase. He looked up from his iPhone to remark to no one in particular, "How can there possibly be absolutely no cellphone service?" Mahoney ignored the rhetorical question and finally looked right at Sidney under heavy, black brows.

"Adam Dietrich's daughter, right?"

"Sidney. Dietrich."

Mahoney chose a leather side chair, leaving his thinner assistant to sit down in the plushest high-backed chair, presumably because his boss could not sit down within the confines of any chair with arms. Sidney wondered if the man always flew first class for the extra seat room.

"So. Give me background. I want a succinct chronology of events, witnesses, and facts relevant to the case so far. Begin." Mahoney leaned back and closed his eyes, placing his meaty hands with thick fingers laced over his chest, as if he were about to take a nap. Sidney didn't know where to begin, but the owlish assistant, who had not introduced himself, stared at her intently with yellow legal pad and pen poised at the ready. She cleared her throat and started at the beginning, with her first visit to Maude Hill and then the discovery of Selena's body, through the search of Jeremy Hill's apartment, and the discovery of Selena's letters and fingerprints all over every surface. Finally, she revealed the prosecution's statement from the Mexican doctor who had performed a D&C post-miscarriage and the damning admission that Jeremy Hill was very likely the father. In interviews of the Sheriff's investigators, he had admitted to an ugly argument that was also witnessed by a winery worker, presumably over the termination of Selena's pregnancy. The assumption was that Selena had told Jeremy that she had had an abortion in Mexico to break all ties with Jeremy irrevocably. As Sidney spoke, she brought out witness statements, crime scene photographs, and her own notes of Jeremy's emphatic assertions of innocence.

"So. There is no direct physical evidence tying our client with this murder. The circumstantial evidence to date includes one witnessed fierce argument, love letters, strands of her hair on hairbrushes in his apartment, and her fingerprints in said apartment. Correct? No DNA on the body or elsewhere."

Sidney nodded.

"And the alleged motive is that our client flew into a rage upon learning that his true love aborted the product of their passion without his knowledge or consent and thus, he strangled her to death, then drove her body in the victim's own car, and dumped her on a remote mountainside. Correct?"

"That's what the prosecution is likely to argue, yes."

"What do you think is wrong with that theory, Ms. Dietrich? Sounds as if our client had both motive and opportunity."

Sidney's instinct told her the theory was wrong. Jeremy was angry with Selena, but she believed him when he said that he loved her and would never have harmed her, whatever the circumstances, much less killed her. But given Mahoney's questioning, she knew she had to come up with a more rational and legally sound explanation. She paused, looking down at the crime scene photographs.

"I think we can drive a truck through the holes in that case. If Jeremy was going to kill her, he would have done it in his apartment, when he flew into a rage, and she would have fought for her life. There are no wounds or injuries suggesting such a struggle. There is no DNA under her fingernails and no signs of struggle in the apartment. Why? Because she wasn't killed there, and Jeremy wasn't the killer. So, where she was killed and by whom is still a mystery. And it doesn't make any sense that Jeremy would have transported her dead body in Selena's little car and then dumped both the car and the body forty miles up the road. How did he get back to the vineyard? Why doesn't anyone remember that he was missing for the three or more hours it would probably have taken him to accomplish all of this?" Sidney stopped and looked up, unsure where she should go from there.

"Go on," Mahoney commanded, with eyes still closed. His assistant scribbled like mad.

"Okay. Her car was found dumped way upcountry. How did it get there? Was the murderer in the car with her? Or, did she have an accident or a car breakdown and then became the victim of some vicious opportunist whom she flagged down for help on the highway? The only physical evidence found at the crime scene were the flowers in the victim's hands and the drag marks from the victim's feet in between prints of ordinary work boots. No such boots were found belonging to Jeremy Hill in the search of his apartment, his car, or the warehouse where he works. Nothing ties him to this murder."

Mahoney looked as if he was asleep, but then his head started to nod up and down on top of his large chin roll. His eyes suddenly flew open and pierced Sidney with a predatory look under bushy black brows.

"Good," he said. "A criminal defense is all about holes in the prosecution's theory. I like yours. Anything else?"

"Just one thing. Apparently, Selena told Jeremy that she'd had an abortion, but the coroner said that she couldn't tell one way or another. There's no certainty that Selena had an abortion or whether she had a live birth or even a stillbirth."

"Your point?" Mahoney asked curtly.

Sidney shrugged. She was working solely on instinct now, "I think it's highly unlikely that a young, Hispanic girl, who finds herself pregnant by her lover, a very wealthy man, would actually feel desperate enough to terminate her pregnancy. Why would she? These days, thousands of unwed teenage girls give birth in California every year. Many of them are being raised by loving, extended families. Many of them give up their babies for adoption. I'm not convinced that Selena terminated her pregnancy. I'd like to follow up on that possibility."

"Why? How does that affect the murder case? Our client was told that the victim terminated the pregnancy. That gives him motive to kill her. What difference does it make to our defense how the pregnancy actually ended?"

Sidney shrugged uncomfortably. "It changes life for the families that are grieving the loss of their daughter. For the family, it would make a huge difference if Selena had a miscarriage or stillbirth versus an abortion. It may give them some comfort to find out what really happened."

Mahoney dismissed Sidney with a brush of the back of his hand through the air in front of his face.

"That is not our goal here, Ms. Dietrich. Our sole purpose is to keep our client from years and years of solitary confinement on Death Row at San Quentin State Prison. His personal and familial happiness is of no concern to us."

Sidney vehemently disagreed but kept her feelings firmly in check for the moment.

"How would you like for me to proceed with assisting you on this case, Mr. Mahoney?"

"Well I suggest, Ms. Dietrich, that you leave no stone unturned regarding every piece of unexplained physical evidence that could help us create further holes. Please return to the investigators' reports, witness statements, and forensic findings. Even something as banal as flakes of dog dander can give us an alternative theory that will be a sufficient hook with which to hang reasonable doubt. Keep at it."

As suddenly as he had sat down, Mahoney slammed his hands on the conference table top and tipped forward as his assistant scrambled to pull the chair out from under him so that he could push his massive frame and stand up. Sidney realized the meeting was over and that she had been dismissed. Mahoney left the conference room with his assistant hurriedly gathering up his notes, shoving them in his briefcase, and turning his back to Sidney so that he could scramble to keep up with Mahoney's lumbering exit. Sidney stood up and exhaled deeply, stretching her back. Jack McGlynn's voice carried up the stairs as the door closed behind Mahoney and his assistant.

"Pompous ass!" Jack growled and appeared at the top of the red-carpeted stairs in front of the conference room door. Sidney smiled her agreement.

"You must have done okay, Sid, in your first command performance before His Majesty Mahoney. Otherwise, I would have gotten an earful and you would have gotten fired, which frankly, would have been a blessing for both of us. As it is now, your usual stellar performance condemns you to further enlightening interactions with Francis X, and deprives me of your time."

Sidney shook her head. "I don't know. I floundered a bit. I'm not sure I even remember what I said, I was so nervous. But thanks. One thing I wanted to ask you, though. You may think I'm nuts, but in your capacity as Maude Hill's family lawyer, do you think that I could pursue a hunch that Selena didn't terminate her pregnancy? I know this sounds crazy, but I was thinking last night that there might be more possibilities than miscarriage, abortion, or stillbirth." Sidney had unfurled three fingers to emphasize the possibilities.

Jack frowned, pulling his bushy black brows together, "What do you mean?"

Sidney took a breath. "What if the baby is alive?"

Jack stared at her. "What makes you think so?"

Sidney shrugged. "I know this is lame. I don't have any actual evidence. Just a hunch. Something just tells me that

Selena wouldn't have ended her pregnancy; especially if she was that far along."

"Sid, you know Maude Hill means the world to me. There isn't anything I wouldn't do for her. But don't get her hopes up. Don't say a word. Don't say anything to Maude or Jeremy, and don't say another word about it to His Majesty Mahoney. Bill your time to our 'overhead account' and if we find evidence that Maude had or has a grandchild, then we'll bill every single minute you spent running down this lead and the Hill family will be thrilled to pay for it. If not, we'll eat the time. But go ahead. Look into it. For Maude."

Sidney looked at her godfather gratefully and said, "Thanks, Uncle Jack." He had more heart than a head for business, but she wouldn't have had it any other way.

*****

Sidney brought a couple of portable file boxes home with her to study. She'd stopped by the Pinecrest Market on the way home. The tiny general store only had four aisles, but they were crammed full of every necessary item that local customers or skiers in transit might need. The last aisle was lined with a solid wall of freezers and Sidney stood in front of one of them while she mulled over her choices. She hated to cook and had no aversion to consuming serial low-calorie frozen dinners. As she pondered her limited choices in the freezer, she was startled to hear a voice behind her.

"Fresh is better, Ms. Dietrich, and worth the trouble."

She turned around and looked up at Matt Dunleavy. He looked as if he'd just showered and shaved. A thick fringe of dark hair hung over his forehead, slightly damp. He ran his fingers through it. Sidney's cheeks flushed and she pursed her lips nervously.

"Oh, hi. You surprised me. I was just going home and needed to pick up a few things."

"Sure. Four minutes in the microwave?" he responded, his eyebrows rising quizzically.

"I'm a lousy cook. This is a lot safer." She smiled faintly and looked down. Matt had changed into a fresh plaid flannel shirt, jeans, and leather boots. Sidney had no avenue for escape, standing facing Matt in the narrow aisle, her back to the freezer case. He looked as if he were undecided whether to pursue a conversation or turn around and leave. After an awkward moment, he made up his mind.

"Well, look, I was just picking up a few things for a beef stew and wondered if you'd like to join me. I do like to cook, and I like company."

Sidney stood and stared, suddenly speechless, but Matt seemingly failed to notice. He had put his plastic basket full of vegetables on the floor and had pulled a little spiral notebook and a pen from his front shirt pocket. He was busily scribbling.

"These are directions. I don't live far away from you at all. It's just off Fiddletown Road, just below you."

"How do you know where I live?"

"It's Jack's upcountry ranch, right? Everyone knows where that is. He used to host an annual barbeque for the whole county when he was still in Congress."

"Oh. Right."

"I'll see you around six thirty, okay? You'll want to catch the sunset."

Sidney nodded and turned back to look at the freezer offerings without seeing anything in front of her other than her reflection in the frosted glass. "Jeez, Sidney," she muttered under her breath, and then mocked herself, repeating, "Oh. Right. You idiot."

She kicked herself mentally for having failed to say one intelligible thing to Dunleavy. After a minute, she looked carefully down the end of the aisle and then around the corner at the check-out stand. He was gone and she breathed in relief. She barely remembered checking out, paying for her items, and driving home in a daze. Why was she so nervous? And wasn't it a dangerous, galloping conflict of interest to be having dinner with Dunleavy? He would be testifying for the prosecution in court. But if neither of them talked about the case and never disclosed that they had shared a quick dinner, where was the harm? Oh, man, Sidney. Slippery slope. What a reckless but rather exciting thing to do. She had been intrigued by Dunleavy since the very first, even if she had strong feelings of antipathy at times. It would be interesting to explore those feelings further. The decision was made.

She drove into the long, graveled driveway, where at its end, her house stood empty. Within a few minutes, she had showered and dried her hair, trying to figure out what to wear. She didn't want to appear as if she was trying too hard, so she picked out a fresh pair of jeans and a light green, scoop-necked pullover. With a light jacket and half boots pulled on, she was ready. She lifted a just-purchased bottle of red wine she'd picked out at the market. It was expensive, and she hoped it would be good.

The drive on the back-country Fiddletown Road seemed to take forever. As the road wound down in elevation in between two ridges, the sun began to dip behind the westernmost ridge, darkening the sweep of canyon below. A scraggly wire fence stretched along the edge of the road, with no shoulder acting as a buffer between Sidney's car and a precipitous five-hundred-foot drop below.

"Jesus," Sidney cursed as she crept around hairpin turns for a half-hour until she passed the Big Trees Market and then bore right at the "Y." Dunleavy's directions continued past a black water tank and then she was supposed to keep a look out for a huge oak tree and a split-rail fence with "Dunleavy" carved on a polished slab of wood. Sidney slowed and turned left into the gravel drive that was lined for a quarter mile with split-rail fencing. A couple of acres of green pasture rolled by and two horses lifted their heads with curiosity as she drove past them and then past a green-trimmed wooden barn with a corrugated green metal roof. The two-story house came into view in a stand of pine trees with a wide, wrap-around porch and split cedar planks. Two tall, river-rock chimneys stood framing either end of the house. Nice place, she thought, surprised. She pulled her car behind a white pickup and a yellow Labrador jumped off the porch, wagging its tail so hard that its entire body moved back and forth. Sidney was greeted with wet dog breath and a lick on her hand as she opened the car door and reached to pet the beautiful golden head.

"Hi, sweetheart," she whispered as she stroked the dog's neck and back. The leather collar sported tags that said "Bella."

"Bella, come!" Matt called from the porch, where he stood, wiping his hands with a dishtowel. He was dressed the same as he had been in the market, but his hair was combed back off his forehead. "Sorry. She's a real attention hog."

Bella wagged her tail back up the front porch steps and shoved her head against Matt's leg, waiting for a pat on the head. Matt's hand dropped down reflexively and stroked Bella as he looked out at Sidney. She climbed up on the first step and held out a bottle of wine.

"I hope this goes with what you're cooking," she said. He held his hand out.

"Welcome," he said, and pulled her up the next two steps to stand beside him. He took the bottle out of the gift bag and looked at the label. "Nice," he assured her. "It will go perfectly."

Sidney walked through the front door into an expansive and open living area, with the kitchen set against the far wall and framed with wooden counters and inset tile surfaces. The vaulted ceiling and rough-hewn wood beams gave the living space a wide-open feeling. The floors were custom built with wide cedar planks and the picture window frames were a warm reddish fir. Matt had built a fire in the natural rock fireplace and the long, polished wood dining table was simply set for two places. Matt took the bottle of wine into the kitchen and pulled out a counter chair for Sidney to sit in and watch as he finished dinner.

"Can I help?" she asked.

"Almost done," he said as he stirred a cast-iron pot. "You can help me start on the wine." Matt removed the cork and poured two generous glasses, handing one to Sidney. He turned his attention back to the stove.

"So, what brought you from the big city all the way out here?" he asked, taking a taste from a wooden spoon, glancing at Sidney.

"My godfather... Jack... offered me a job," she said, "And you? I take it you grew up around here." She sipped her wine.

"I did. But I went away to college."

"Oh? Where?"

"Stanford. On a football scholarship. But when I graduated, there wasn't a big demand for Comparative Literature majors with career-ending knee injuries, so I came back here."

"How'd you end up in law enforcement?"

"Well, my dad was a mean drunk and he used to beat up on my mom. I grew up hating bullies in general and him in particular. I had a bunch of relatives living in trailer parks who'd beat on each other or end up stabbing each other. I thought I could help if I moved back. So, I spent time at the Police Academy and joined the Sheriff's Department."

"It looks as if things worked out well for you. This is a beautiful place."

Matt laughed. "My law enforcement career didn't help me get this place, I assure you. Gambling did. Ironic, isn't it? Gambling is illegal everywhere in California except for Indian casinos. My mom's Aunt Loretta was tribal chief for the Mi-Wuk. We're tribal members, so when Aunt Loretta decided that our fortunes would best be served with Indian gaming, well, she got funding and built the casino and everything in it – the hotel, restaurants, RV park, gas station – I'm just a lucky beneficiary of twenty years of her hard work for our tribe. But enough about me. How'd you get dragged out of the city? San Francisco, wasn't it? Jack must have really done some persuading to get you to come all the way out here."

Sidney didn't answer right away. Matt took a couple of plates out of the cupboard and lifted out a tray from the oven with a steaming hot bread loaf. He piled a goodly amount of stew on the plates, with a side of bread, and carried them over to the table. Sidney carried their wine glasses and Matt placed a plate of stew in front of her. She sat down and waited until he sat as well.

"Try the stew first. Let me know if it needs anything – salt or pepper?"

Sidney took a small bite and was pleasantly surprised by the flavor. It was delicious. The guy could cook.

"It's wonderful. I'm not kidding."

Matt smiled at her praise. "You're not much of a food critic. I know you now – you'd heat up something frozen in the microwave and call it dinner."

"Yeah, but I mean it. Actually, I love food. But I hate to cook, especially just for myself. This is great."

Sidney happily ate and then took another couple of sips of wine. Warmth spread throughout her body and she relaxed. She noticed that Matt did not even touch his wine glass.

"In answer to your question, it was a combination of a bunch of lousy things that made me run away to Uncle Jack's. Family problems. Relationship break-up. Last year sucked, frankly. I was lucky to have somewhere to go and someone to take me in."

Matt nodded in understanding. He poured a bit more wine into Sidney's glass.

"Yeah, I hear you. I went through a tough time a few years ago – bad breakup. Too much drinking. I quit the Department. Felt really sorry for myself."

"Was it a girlfriend?" Sidney asked delicately, knowing the answer. Matt shook his head.

"Wife. Now ex-wife. That's who named the dog Bella, after the *Twilight* vampire series character. I was going to change the name when she left, but the dumb dog wouldn't come when I called her anything else."

Sidney laughed. Matt smiled back.

"That's the first time I think I've ever heard you laugh."

"Yeah, well you didn't have anything really funny to say in your role as murder investigator."

"True," he acknowledged. "And you were totally intense and lawyerly and in my grill every second. You didn't exactly make it easy on me."

Sidney nodded in agreement. "Not my job."

"Clearly not."

"Well, don't hold it against me," she smiled. "There are a few people in this world who think I'm pretty fun to be around sometimes, really."

"Yeah, me too. Hard to believe."

Sidney stared at Matt appraisingly. "Not too hard to believe," she said. "Why did you invite me here?"

"Impulse. There you were, all alone and pathetic, looking at frozen food options at the market and suddenly, I thought I wanted to have dinner with this girl. She may be too serious and a real pain in my rear, but I don't think I've met anyone as interesting in my entire life."

Matt leaned over and kissed Sidney so gently on the lips that she felt only a brief flutter, and then he was up clearing the plates away to the kitchen. She sat stunned, watching his back as he rinsed the plates and put them into the dishwasher.

"Come on," he said, turning around and drying his hands. "Let's take the fifty-cent tour."

He grabbed a jacket and held Sidney's out to her. She shrugged it on and followed him out the front door, Bella's tail wagging eagerly ahead of them in anticipation of a walk. She wasn't disappointed. Matt walked Sidney all over the property, showing her the barn and the horses, talking about his plans to put in a garden one day, showing her the ridgetop views of the canyon as the light faded and dimmed to dark. He pointed out the first star of the evening. They sat on the front porch in two wide Adirondack chairs and looked up into the sky.

"I'll bet all the girls love this tour," Sidney commented.

"I'd like you to think I was in great demand, but the truth is, you're the first girl I've invited up here since my break-up. This place is special to me. I wouldn't ask just anyone up here."

Sidney turned away, pretending to look out over the darkening sky. There was something so direct and honest about what Matt said that it disarmed her; penetrating all her snarky and sarcastic little defenses.

"Well," she finally said, "It's really beautiful. Your wife must have been nuts to leave it behind."

"She was a country girl who chafed at still living here her whole life, even though she had a great job at the winery. When a slick city-guy smooth-talked her she just dropped me like a hot rock and bolted with him. I didn't react well, as I expect you've heard. I thought she was having an affair with Jeremy Hill, but I was wrong – about which guy, not about the affair."

"Do you know how it ended up? After your divorce?"

"Don't know. Don't care. She got a settlement, but I kept the dog, the horses, and the house. I could let some money go, but those other things, I could never replace. Especially the dog," he laughed. Bella sidled up to him as if she recognized that he was talking about her, and she let him know with a shove of her wet nose under the palm of his hand, exactly what was expected of him. He didn't disappoint. She was blissful as he stroked her behind her silky ears.

"I want a dog," Sidney said suddenly, although she had never had any such inclination in her entire life that she could remember, other than when she came home alone the night before.

"You can have anything in this life that you want, Sidney Dietrich. Don't let anyone ever let you think that you can't."

"That's what Jack keeps saying."

"Believe it."

Sidney was silent, and after a while, she got up regretfully, letting Matt know that she had an early morning appointment in Sacramento. Matt thanked her for a great evening and walked her to her car. He opened the door and she slid into the front seat, pressing a button for the window to come down so that they could say their goodbyes. Matt leaned into the open window and kissed Sidney again on the lips, a little firmer than he had before.

Sidney kissed him back and then retreated into her car. He stepped back and she started the engine, driving slowly down the gravel drive, glancing back in the rear-view mirror at the dark figure standing there watching her leave with the dog at his side.

When Sidney slipped into her bed that night, she felt that the cold, dark emptiness of her house had dissipated; replaced by a feeling of security and well-being she only remotely remembered having felt before. Her last thought before she fell asleep was the gentle, soft touch of Matt's lips and the comforting sound of his voice saying her name.

19.

Sidney reflected that she and Matt had not once discussed anything having to do with the case. It would have been highly inappropriate had they done so, but if they had, she wondered whether their interaction would have been half as pleasant. But the evening had been so very entirely pleasant, that she went over every detail in her mind on yet another long drive to Sacramento.

This time, she was going farther west than Sacramento to the 2,000-acre flat expanse of UC Davis, to keep her 10:00 a.m. appointment with renowned plant biologist, Dr. David Benedict. Equally renowned attorney, Francis X. Mahoney, Jr. had suggested the visit and his assistant had hurriedly made arrangements when Sidney reported to Francis X. that the rather cursory forensic studies had not actually included a study of any samples collected from the dead girl's tires or the underside of her car. Sidney thought it was pretty clear that the car had been driven some distance and dumped by the side of the highway, and Francis X. was insistent that all samples should be studied, thoroughly tested and documented in order to build a plausible case for a scenario other than the one that had been constructed to convict their client. Sidney had sent various samples to Dr. Benedict by courier after having requested them from the D.A.'s office. She had not said a word to Matt last night other than the fact of an early morning appointment. Although she was acting within the scope of attorney confidentiality, on some emotional level she was personally uncomfortable withholding information from Matt, as if she had some guilty little secret.

There were several highway exits off of I-80 for UC Davis and she chose the one that went right through downtown. The streets were lined with one-story buildings containing coffee shops, bicycle repair shops, sports and backpack outfitters, bookstores, restaurants of all ethnic varieties, and ubiquitous bagel purveyors. It was a little like Berkeley, Sidney decided –

only smaller, less congested, and not as scruffy. Maybe more like Palo Alto before the dot com boom. Musing about Palo Alto made Sidney think of Matt – one of the least likely persons she would have guessed had attended Stanford. She wondered if he'd been happy there. It was likely that he had felt comfortable on the football field, but she wondered what his friendships and social life had been like. Coming from a remote, rural community and being part-Indian could not have been easy. Matt was quite a complex puzzle, she mused.

She stopped by an information booth and asked for directions to the Plant Reproductive Biology Building and followed directions to Hutchison Drive, just north of Aggie Stadium. Sidney parked at the first visitor parking area she could find. It was a short walk to the Seed Biotechnology Center, a modern brick, concrete, and glass cube set in an oasis of green grass and flowering shrubs. Sidney stopped and checked the building directory and located the elevator to the second-floor offices. She walked down the wide corridor until she found office number 256, stopped, checked the name on the door, and knocked softly. There was no response. She waited a moment and then rapped louder. When there was no response on the third attempt, she tried the doorknob and slowly opened the door just a crack so she could see if there was anyone in. A thin man in a broad-brimmed safari hat sat at a large corner desk surrounded by stacks of files and papers, with his chair leaning back, feet on the desk encased in hiking boots, eyes closed with earbuds in his ears, listening to music. He was sharp-featured and waxy pale, and for a moment, Sidney wondered whether he was asleep or dead, until suddenly, his feet swung to the floor and his heavy-lidded eyes shot open, staring at her.

"Ten on the dot," he said, delightedly. "My electronic alarm told me the time and I was going to wait for you, but here you are. Right on time. You can't know how much I wish that my undergraduate students possessed your punctuality."

"Dr. Benedict?" Sidney asked.

"Well, yes. That's the name on the door!" he replied brightly, motioning for her to come in. "Ms. Dietrich, I presume."

Sidney nodded and sat in the chair that Dr. Benedict pointed to, taking her notebook and pen out of her satchel.

"I've done some defense forensic work for Mr. Mahoney before. I issued a report and never had to testify. I don't believe that my results were favorable to his client. But I was so handsomely paid that I am willing to consider doing it again – the report I mean. There are some findings that I think may be of interest to you." Dr. Benedict shuffled through his desk and pulled out several labeled baggies containing the various samples that Sidney had couriered to him for analysis. Dr. Benedict pulled a leaf out of the top of his desk and laid all the baggies out in a row. He looked like a pot dealer, Sidney thought wryly.

"Now. Your instructions were to analyze these samples in order to determine their identity and origins, correct? They all came from the interior and exterior of the victim's car, correct?"

Sidney nodded.

"And may I ask exactly where the car was found?"

"Off of Highway 88 headed northeast to Tahoe at about the 6,000-foot elevation level. The car was in a ditch on the east side of the highway."

"Ah, interesting. Here is a map. Do you think you can point to the exact location?" Dr. Benedict unfolded a Tahoe-area highway map and Sidney traced Highway 88 from its junction with Highway 89 all the way southwest to a point almost off the physical map to within a mile or two of Cook's Station where she thought the car had been found.

"Interesting," Dr. Benedict repeated, pushing the wide brim of his safari hat back off his pale forehead, exposing a sparse array of blonde, bristly hairs.

"Why?"

"Because the samples from the tire treads are mostly dirt packed in layers, like sedimentary layers at the bottom of a lake that has dried. Even though, as you can see, the thickest of these is probably far less than a quarter inch, they provide a view of where these tires have been." He held out a baggie filled with red dirt and tiny pieces of gravel, with tiny stalks of dead grass.

"You see… and I would request a larger sample in order to be certain… I dissected the sample from the inside out – older material to more recent material. The more recent outside material corresponds with the elevation in which the car was found – the upper mid-range of the Sierra Nevada Mountains. There is the very typical red surface dirt and minute particles of several types of common pine needles. However, the older material deeper inside the tire tread is generally called loam which comes from quite a different elevation. This is borne out by the samples taken from the underside of the car. Accounting for the exact time of year when you indicated the crime took place and assuming a relatively limited range for this automobile to have traveled within a day, I believe I have a guess as to where this vehicle was before it was found abandoned in the higher elevation."

Dr. Benedict excitedly opened another, more unfamiliar type of map in front of Sidney.

"This is a very detailed map of the native plants found in various parts of California within a one-hundred-mile radius of this campus. A few generations of plant biology students have completed this over time as part of their field work. It is invaluable for mapping the locations of native and foreign plant species and for purposes of conservation. Have you ever heard of vernal pools?"

Sidney shook her head. "I'm sorry, Dr. Benedict. I majored in Political Science, which as you know, isn't like science at all."

Dr. Benedict's eyes crinkled as he smiled.

"Yes, well, I will launch into a mini-seminar courtesy of Mr. Mahoney's handsome hourly compensation." He took the map over to a large white board and placed four magnets at each corner so that they could survey its entirety. "So, this is a paper map of a survey that has been ongoing for a couple of decades.

Of course, it's all computerized now, but I still like keeping track of my students' research in this aerial view of the San Joaquin Valley and the foothill counties that border it. California Fish and Game, the Federal Government, native plant organizations, and others are all committed to our research," he said, surveying the map, which contained literally thousands of tiny colored dots; some isolated and others in clusters that seemed to spread over large areas.

"Which is what, exactly?"

"Well, we collect data and try to determine areas where native plants grow in the wild so that we can protect threatened species."

"Like with animals, except – with plants?"

"Exactly," Dr. Benedict said, nodding his head. "There are laws to protect threatened species of plants. Many species are rare, and they are threatened by development. There are plants in and around the Central Valley and Sierra Foothills that are unique and found nowhere else in the world."

"Did you find anything in the crime scene samples?"

Dr. Benedict nodded and his eyes widened with excitement. "You have to understand that several species of exceedingly rare plants thrive only in the unique habitat that is a seasonal vernal pool. A vernal pool will form only in areas where clay soils harden into layers that restrict water percolation into the soil, such as in low lying areas in the Central Valley. Rain water during the winter fills these depressions in the soil and they stay there until the water evaporates in the summer."

"So, are you telling me that vernal pools are only found in low lying areas and not at high elevations?" Sidney asked, puzzled.

"Precisely. Much of the material identified in these samples did not originate at high elevations. Some recent layers did, but older layers, as well as the large samples from the wheel well and undercarriage of the car, reveals a much different picture."

"Which is?"

"Certain rare plants are only found at vernal pools where they germinate under water during the early spring and then flower around the edges of the drying pools. In addition, vernal pools are isolated from one another. Note the clusters of different colored dots at the border of Sacramento County and western Amador County. Vernal pools are frequently isolated from one another so that different species evolved in unique localized areas."

"Dr. Benedict, are you telling me that you can tell exactly where the victim's car was in this case, based on these samples?"

The scientist nodded enthusiastically.

"Absolutely. Without a doubt. Of course, I can't tell you what she was doing there or why she was there, but I can tell you with certainty that at the very least, her car was there."

"Go on, please."

Dr. Benedict approached the map and picked up a colored pin from the chalk tray below the whiteboard.

"Okay. Our studies reveal that the soils in and around the town of Ione in western Amador County are quite acidic, with a pH level below 4. Are you with me so far?"

Sidney nodded.

"Eriogonum Apricum is an endangered and very rare plant, commonly known as Ione Buckwheat. The plant survives and thrives under extreme conditions at several vernal pools just outside the town of Ione, on barren outcrops among the chaparral, just at the elevation of 295 feet. The large clay mud sample contained bits of flowers and leaves from the car's wheel well and undercarriage, as if the car had driven on and over these plants. Which upsets me, of course, as it's a violation of several environmental laws designed to protect this fragile habitat."

"Uh, yes, I'm sorry about that."

"Well, never mind. You didn't drive it there. The point is that the calyx or outer whorl of flower parts can be seen here and here. It's white with reddish midribs. See?" Dr. Morgan held up bagged samples of dried mud and dirt and pointed out the tiny pressed and dried bits of material he was discussing. Sidney's heart started to beat faster.

"I see. I can't believe this. Would you swear to it?"

Dr. Benedict nodded. "Of course. My analysis is sound, I assure you. But that's not all."

Sidney didn't know if she could take much more. Science was never her strongest subject. She waited expectantly.

"These flowers. The ones found intertwined in the victim's fingers. They're Downingia Bicornta, commonly known as Doublehorn Calicoflower, for reasons that will be apparent. See this dark blue-purple corolla tube?"

Sidney nodded, and Dr. Benedict continued.

"These flowers are a dark blue-purple with a central white field with yellow-green spots. Stunning flowers, really, and very rare. See these two nipple-like projections? That's why they're sometimes called two-horned Downingia, because of these. They're also only found in vernal pool habitat. So, my educated opinion is that your victim, or at least her car, was physically present at possibly one of two vernal pool locations near Ione just before or at the time of her death, given the condition of the plant fragments and the fact that they captured within a layer in the tire treads just before the most recent, outermost layer."

"Not in the high Sierras?"

"No. Definitely not. Not until the car's last trip. The pine needle fragments were from the most recent, thinnest, outermost layer. They're from high-elevation northern foxtail pines that begin growing above 6,000 feet, which correlates to the elevation that you identified was where the victim's car was found."

"Her body was also found at around 7,000 feet."

"She was transported there, certainly. It was her last stop. Either she drove herself if she was still alive, or perhaps she was transported there when she was already dead."

Sidney leaned back against a desk, her arms folded, trying to process everything she was hearing.

"Dr. Benedict, can you tell me exactly where these vernal pools are?"

"I'll do one better. I can enter the coordinates and the computer will print out a detailed map of these two specific pools. Although, they're probably dried by now and the flowers will have long since ceased blooming. Pity."

"That's okay."

Sidney waited patiently for the process to complete. She could barely keep herself from snatching the printout as it came through and took it from Dr. Benedict's fingers as soon as she could do so politely. After thanking him profusely, Sidney turned to make her escape.

"Shall I send my report and a bill to Mr. Mahoney?"

"Yes, yes, please do so," Sidney encouraged the scientist emphatically, as she made her way out of his office door. "Please keep the samples, especially if we need further analysis. And thank you!"

Dr. Benedict had already returned to his office chair and was just tipping his chair back, feet on the desk with his earplugs inserted, as she made her exit.

"You're welcome," he muttered, his eyes closing. Suddenly, the chair dropped to the floor and the startled eyes flew open. Dr. Benedict stared at Sidney and motioned her back inside the office.

"One more thing. There were some fiber samples in one of the evidence bags taken from the clothing on the body. Fibers aren't my area of expertise, so I invited one of my colleagues from Textiles over to take a look in the lab. Funny thing."

"What is it, Dr. Benedict?" Sidney asked; her hand on the doorjamb.

"Well, the girl's clothes had the usual cheap cotton and polyester and latex. Nothing unusual, except for one thing. My colleague identified an animal's hair strands that are commonly used in South American textiles."

"What animal?"

"Alpaca. Damndest thing. Just a few strands, mind you. But you should know about them. Might be helpful."

Sidney was eager to leave but took a quick moment to consider.

"The victim in the case was Mexican-American and the area can get chilly in the winter. The strands were probably from a scarf or sweater belonging to the dead girl if they were found inside her car."

"No doubt," Dr. Benedict responded, "Just thought I'd mention it."

Sidney relayed her thanks again and closed the office door.

As she drove back on the Jackson Highway towards Ione, Sidney mulled over the entire conversation with Dr. Benedict, chewing the inside of her lip as she did so. Instead of going back to the office, she decided to pull over to the side of the road and punched in a number on her cellphone.

"Matt? Are you home?"

Matt's voice sounded low and warm when he answered. "Need dinner again tonight? I'll cook again if you like, now that I know what a sucker you are for a home-cooked meal."

Sidney laughed, "Yeah, I'm always pretty hard up for food. And I've gotta say, Dunleavy, you make a hell of a stew."

"Where are you now?"

"I'm pulled over on Highway 16 wondering how long it would take you to get to Ione. Are you still interested in figuring out who killed that poor girl?"

"Sure. But my official work is winding up. I heard that they've got a suspect and he'll be on trial soon," he said drily.

"Yeah, right. That would be my client. But what I really need is for someone with an open mind to come with me on a wild goose chase over some fields and mud-puddles nearby. Just in case there's evidence pertinent to the case to be found."

"What evidence?" Matt asked.

"This may be nuts, but I think the actual crime scene might just be around here. Near Ione, I mean. I can't tell you any more than that."

193

Sidney waited for Matt to respond.

"Look, it'll take me a few minutes to wrap up here and then about 30 minutes to drive down the hill and find you in Ione. Can you find a café on Main Street called Clark's Corner? Have some coffee and wait for me."

"Okay. Can you bring one of those crime scene cameras and some evidence bags, too? Just in case."

"You're pushing your luck, Miss Dietrich. If by chance we find anything, I can always call someone to collect evidence."

"Well, okay. See you at Clark's Corner. Make it as soon as you can."

20.

Sidney pulled back on the highway when the call ended. She passed several miles where the old Boyette Ranch occupied thousands of rolling acres of grasslands on both sides of the highway. The hills were dotted with several hundred black and brown grazing cattle. She took the left-hand turn to Ione on Route 124 and after a few deserted miles bordered by dry manzanita, sage, and chaparral, a gas station appeared, then a Quik-Stop convenience store, a sandwich shop, and a Tastee-Freeze. Sidney followed a small sign and turned right on Main Street. Every town in the county seemed to have a Main Street.

Ione was smaller than Jackson and even more off the beaten path. It was located just a couple hundred feet above sea level and was flat, dry, and hot most of the year. It had acted as a central supply junction during the Gold Rush and now boasted a small golf course community. Jack had told her when she first moved upcountry that because of Ione's Mule Creek State Prison, many Ione inhabitants worked at the prison as guards or were families of prisoners who moved up from the Valley so that they could be closer to their incarcerated loved ones. The café wasn't hard to find. It hugged a corner of the small three-block downtown, across from the hundred-year-old Ione Hotel and tiny public library. Ione looked like the town that time forgot, even more so than historic Jackson. The old wood-framed and brick buildings were generally run down and neglected, but the café looked like an upscale bistro. Unfortunately, it was a one of a kind establishment in the heart of a place greatly overlooked and largely ignored.

Sidney parked the car and gladly took refuge inside the café, ordering a latte and a scone. Happily, she munched and sipped milky foam while she waited for Matt. She looked around. It was the middle of the afternoon on a weekday. A couple of older women were enjoying a companionable visit at a table for two by the window and a table of elderly, obviously retired men sat unhurried, commenting on the news of the day, mostly having to do with upcoming city council elections. Sidney again felt like an outsider and was careful to not get caught eavesdropping. These were not her people; not her kind. She was more at home in San Francisco, New York, or D.C. Yet, there was something comforting about overhearing the surrounding muted conversations among a different community of people sharing ordinary thoughts and ideas about details of lives that would have been very similar in rural Texas, or Arkansas, or Iowa. She heard the men commenting on the lack of winter rains and the skyrocketing cost of cattle feed, pronounced "caddlefeed." Then, Matt walked in freshly showered with his dark brown hair combed back. A light plaid shirt was tucked into the waistband of his jeans and his belt was tooled leather with a large, silver belt buckle. His leather work boots trod heavily over the wooden floors as he approached her table. Sidney was acutely aware that her heart started to beat a little faster and she gripped her coffee cup a little more firmly.

"Hey," Matt ducked down and kissed her cheek, which Sidney was afraid had blushed bright red.

"Hey yourself," she smiled back as he pulled a chair out next to her.

"So, what's up?"

"Do you want some coffee first? You might need it."

"Sure," Matt responded and got up again to saunter over to the counter, where he grabbed an empty cup from a tall stack and served himself from a large percolator. He dug in his pocket and pulled out a couple of dollar bills, leaving them on the counter. Matt slid back onto the chair and leaned on the table to listen attentively.

Sidney took a breath. "So, what if I had a new theory about where the girl was killed? I can't tell you how I know, not yet, and I can't say anything about who was driving, or who was in the car, or who killed the girl. All I'm saying is that the investigation could be more complete." Sidney paused to gauge Matt's reaction. He was listening attentively.

"What if the car was in a very specific location in Ione before it was dumped upcountry? The girl might have been killed beforehand. There might be physical evidence at a crime scene other than where the body was found."

"And it might point to a different suspect?"

"Maybe. I don't know. It just wouldn't be right if we didn't look."

"We?" Matt asked, putting his cup on the table, his eyebrows arched questioningly.

"Well, I'm not a cop and before I go looking, I'd rather have you with me so whatever procedures need to be followed, are followed correctly. I don't want to stumble over evidence and be accused of planting it in order to get my client off."

"Okay. But we're not picking and choosing. If we find something, I'm calling Tom Nelson in, no matter what it is. If we find graffiti that says, 'Jeremy Hill was here,' we turn it over, deal?"

Sidney suppressed a smile.

"Deal." She grew quite serious. "I'm going out on a limb, here, I know. Calling you – well, I could get fired. But honestly, what I really care about is figuring out what happened to that girl, not just spinning a defense. The trial hasn't started yet. The investigation is ongoing, as they say. Help me look into this, please."

Matt put down his coffee cup.

"Okay, Sid. Where are we going?"

*****

The first vernal pool was a dried hole surrounded by parched grasses and dead flowers. Foxtails clung to Sidney's shoelaces and the cuffs of her jeans. There was no path leading to the pool. The dried excrement of long-absent, grazing cattle created a minefield that both Sidney and Matt stepped around carefully as they scanned the ground for tire marks. The sun was high and hot, illuminating and heating the air around them so it

197

shimmered on the horizon. Matt was convinced that nothing had ever crossed this endless, open field but cattle and the occasional rabbit or coyote. They stood at the edge of the cracked clay depression. Sidney knelt and picked at dried stalks.

"I'm no botanist, so this looks like ordinary, dead wildflowers to me. An expert could tell us if they're the same kind that was found in the dead girl's fingers. You saw her. What do you think?"

Matt bent his head as Sidney knelt and pointed at the ground. He leaned on his knees and pushed his hat back on his head. He shrugged.

"The reason I think it might be the place is because there are only two locations for these flowers."

"It might be, Sidney. But then again maybe not."

"Let's try the other dried out mud hole. You game?"

"Sure."

They walked back to the car and saw a white, black, and gold Sheriff's cruiser parked behind Sidney's Subaru. The deputy in light short-sleeved, tan shirt and dark green trousers wore a felt-brimmed hat. His face was shaded, but Matt recognized him immediately.

"Hey, Nelson. Don't you have anything better to do than check out cars parked off the highway?"

Tom Nelson laughed and put down his hand-held speakerphone.

"I got a call out for Ms. Dietrich. Her office called to say she was late coming back from Sac and might be lost. Thought her car was broken down and she might need some help. I was cruising near Ione anyway when I got the call."

"Well that's the kind of service you just don't get in the big city. Thank you, Deputy Nelson," Sidney said, feeling awkward.

"No problem. Everything okay?"

Matt stood next to Tom and the Sheriff's cruiser. He looked briefly at Sidney and then back to the deputy, whose quizzical look revealed his wondering as to what they were doing together.

"Ms. Dietrich here's got a wild idea that maybe the vic in the Hill case was actually killed around here, maybe at a mud hole not far from here. In case there's actually any evidence we come up with other than pollywogs, d'ya want to tag along?"

"Sure," Nelson agreed. "I'll call it in, so they don't panic and send out the SWAT after me."

Sidney flushed red and glared at Matt. He quickly took her arm and propelled her to the driver's side of her car.

"Look, if there is anything there, you want it captured and recorded. Right? No chain of evidence problems that way. Okay?"

"Okay," Sidney responded uncertainly, still mulling over whether she'd placed her client in more danger of a conviction with Nelson on the scene.

"This only works, Sidney, if you trust me. Frankly, I'm not totally convinced that Jeremy Hill is guilty, either, and if there's evidence that can corroborate his story, I can at least save the D.A. from making a horse's ass out of himself. You with me?"

Sidney nodded her assent as Tom Nelson hung up from radioing in his location and his next move.

"Lead the way," he said.

"I've got a map. You drive and I'll tell you which way."

Matt got in the driver's side while Sidney unfolded the map Dr. Benedict had given her. They drove down Highway 88 past the turnoff to Ione.

"At the bottom of the hill turn right on the Buena Vista Road towards Lake Camanche."

Matt slowed, glancing in the rear-view mirror to see the gleaming white and gold Sheriff's car following them. They signaled right and turned down a narrow country road that was in acute need of asphalt resurfacing about twenty years before and continued east for a couple of miles past sagebrush and chaparral growing in scruffy clumps over a terrain of dry limestone. Matt squinted at the road ahead.

"How far, Sid?"

"Slow down here and in about 100 yards, pull off on the right-hand side."

Both cars executed the maneuver in tandem. Matt and Sidney stopped in front of a chained and padlocked gate, with a corroded metal sign warning that trespassers would be prosecuted to the full extent of the law.

"Whaddya know," Matt exclaimed. "All this belongs to cousins of mine – the Buena Vista Band of Mi-Wuks. Big plans for another casino, until the recession hit. Now it's just a thousand acres of nothing. We can climb over that gate. I'm a relative, so we're not trespassing."

"Implied consent," Sidney muttered the legal theory reflexively and climbed out. She shut the door behind her, clicking it locked with a shrill beep of her key.

"All set for a cross-country stroll, Deputy?" Matt called out at Tom Nelson, who had already secured the cruiser and was following just a few yards behind them. They all climbed over and Matt started down a narrow dirt trail leading them south of the gate. Sidney jogged quickly and caught up with Matt.

"Do you know where we're going?"

"My cousins and I grew up rounding cattle here. I'm pretty sure I know every dried-up mud hole around."

"Vernal pool," Sidney corrected.

They hiked in silence for about fifteen minutes, Matt leading the way, then Sidney, then Tom Nelson, whose wary blue eyes swept all around them in every direction. They approached a wind-swept hill already turning brown from the early summer sun and heat. Suddenly, a huge bird flushed out of the tall grasses and took flight, leaving Sidney's heart beating wildly in its wake.

"Great Blue Heron. You don't see them out here unless they're near water," Matt called back to her. Sidney breathed in deeply. Her eyes scanned the horizon. In the distance, she spotted an abandoned shack that may have been used as a barn or cattle shelter. As they climbed, they reached the crest of the hill and looked over into a small and shallow valley that was still partially covered with an inch or two of scummy water. Green grasses grew all around the edges of the pond and drooping wildflowers just past their first bloom scattered yellow and purple patches of color nearby. The grasses were almost knee deep and they approached carefully, not wanting to disturb the area. Matt turned back to Tom and Sidney.

"I'm going to take the right side of the pool and you go left, Tom. We'll circle around. We're looking for any signs of tire tracks or human presence here." Tom nodded and headed off to the left. Matt headed right and Sidney stayed at the top of the crest looking out at the valley with her hand shading her eyes. She followed the fence line with her eyes farther to the south until she spotted an open gate swinging on its hinges slightly in the breeze. She could see a faint and narrow trail coming at them due north from the gate and her eyes followed until she saw where the trail and Matt's receding form would intersect. Suddenly, she realized that she was looking at a mirror image from where they had just come, except that instead of a dirt footpath, narrow parallel tracks threaded north to the pool, directly opposite their trail, like the intersecting arms of a cross. Sidney could see the tracks from her vantage point, but neither Matt nor Tom could at their lower elevation, obscured by tall grass. Sidney shouted and bounded down the hill, running towards Matt over knots of grasses and low, tangled brush, trying not to lose sight of the tracks as she reached the far edge of the fetid pool. Most of the edges were slicked over with thick, green algae. Matt stood with his hands on his hips, watching her approach.

"There are tracks over there," Sidney said breathlessly, pointing to the right. "From here I can't see exactly where they end up by the pool, but we're within twenty yards or so."

Matt nodded and turned. Sidney followed and they made their way in the direction that Sidney had pointed. Matt stopped ten feet before the edge of the pool and surveyed the area.

"I think the pool must have been at least a couple of feet wider a month ago, before the heat began evaporating the water."

"Good call, Dietrich. You should have been a detective."

"Nah," Sidney snorted. "It's just common sense. You can see the water level was higher recently. The mud is still moist around these edges."

Matt walked slowly and deliberately around the pool, in a circle approximately ten feet out from the edge. Sidney looked across the pond and saw Tom Nelson carefully walking the opposite perimeter. Sidney struck out into the brush on her right, intent upon finding the parallel tracks that she could see so clearly from above but that were now hidden from sight by knee-high reeds. She just hoped that she wouldn't step on a snake and made sure she walked firmly, almost stomping with each step to make sure that whatever slithered nearby would get the hell out of the way. She broke through the brush and stepped on a dirt trail that threaded its way south to the gate she had spotted from the knoll.

"Stop right there, Matt," she called out and walked between the tracks on the parallel grass strip down the middle towards the pool, scanning the dirt for any signs of tire tread. The weather had been mild the last four or five weeks and the mud that had previously saturated the surface of the trails had captured clear tire tread marks now preserved in crusty tracks. She looked up to catch Matt's eyes and waved, pointing to the ground so that he could see she had found something. He turned around and shouted for Tom Nelson, who quickened his pace. Sidney walked between the parallel tire marks tiptoeing heel to toe, tracing their path to the pool. She stopped about ten yards from where Matt and Tom stood waiting.

"Okay. Tire treads are coming from that far gate and presumably back out again. The car must have stopped somewhere between us," she said, gesturing at the distance between them.

"I'm going back to the cruiser for my camera, Matt. Don't touch or stand on anything, Ms. Dietrich," the deputy instructed and hurried away in the opposite direction. In spite of the warning, Sidney continued a slow creep towards Matt.

"The car had to have stopped somewhere in front of you, Matt, and then maybe done a three-point turn to go back."

"If it is a car. Just one car and not more."

"I only see one type of tread mark, even going back over the first track in the opposite direction."

Matt nodded. They stood just a few feet apart, waiting for Tom Nelson's return. Nelson arrived within fifteen minutes and began taking photographs of the pool. He then approached Matt and walked slowly on the grass strip in the middle of the tracks towards Sidney.

"This is where the car stopped and then backed up into the brush to turn around," Tom said as he snapped digital photographs of the terrain. He squatted to take snapshots of the tire treads in the areas around the pool. Sidney squinted into the sun, shading her eyes to survey whether there was any sign of distinctive two-horned purple flowers.

"Hey, I see some boot prints!" Sidney called out, excitedly. The soles of large work boots had made definite imprints in the gray clay mud that had dried and fixed them as if they had stepped in plaster. For the next several minutes, Tom was busy photographing tread marks and boot prints. Matt moved aside, out of the way, and leaned over to search the dried grass around the boot prints.

"Tom, you got an evidence bag with you and some tweezers?" Matt asked.

"Sure," Tom replied, pulling a baggie and tweezers out of the camera bag slung around his shoulder. "What've you got?"

Matt crouched in the grass and rose up again, tweezers aloft. He looked straight at Sidney.

"Dried-up purple petals," he said. "Lots of 'em."

21.

"So. Without consulting me you went into a cow pasture with a special Sheriff's deputy to collect physical evidence of what could be the crime scene. Why?" Francis X. Mahoney's bulk filled Jack McGlynn's office. Sidney sat in a small side chair and Jack sat scowling at his desk, his leather armchair tipped back.

"I know it's not what I should have done," Sidney admitted.

"That's right. So why did you?" Francis X.'s face was redder than usual.

Sidney looked at her godfather. His black, bushy eyebrows shot up in a quizzical look. Jack might defend her, ultimately. But for now, she was on her own.

"I wanted to develop an alternate theory of the case. That the victim was killed away from where the body was found and dumped by someone other than our client. So, I went looking for new evidence. We had just heard from the lab that the tire tracks matched the victim's car. We submitted the dried flower petals to UC Davis. They're a match for the same type as the ones found entwined around the victim's fingers."

"And if you had found anything that incriminated our client?"

"I'm pretty sure that everything that incriminates our client is already in the D.A.'s hands," Sidney responded drily, thinking of the boxes of physical evidence collected from Jeremy's apartment. "I felt that anything I could find could only help our defense."

"Nice sentiment, Ms. Dietrich. But whatever you found could have dug our client's grave even deeper. Sometimes it's better to leave well enough alone, especially when a case is entirely circumstantial."

"I don't believe that."

"Why not?"

"Because whatever else Jeremy Hill might be, I don't believe that he killed that girl. Do you?"

"It's my job to defend him. Not to make poorly reasoned guesses as to his guilt or innocence."

Suddenly, the intercom light on Jack's phone lit up and Marjorie's raspy voice came through.

"Mr. McGlynn, could you come into the conference room, please? Just for a minute?"

"Sure. Excuse me."

Francis X. Mahoney stood silently by the window, his massive frame blocking out most of the light, while Sidney examined her nails. They were bitten down and ragged. She was certain she would be fired. Again. It was one of the longest minutes she'd ever endured.

Jack returned. "I've just been on a brief conference call with our client, Jeremy Hill, and his mother, Maude, who is, after all, paying the bills around here. I explained what happened and what Sidney found. I also explained how I thought it might be helpful for the defense of the case."

"And?" Xavier demanded, clearly angered.

Jack walked around his desk and sat down. He looked at Sidney and winked. Then, he gestured to his leather guest chair for Xavier to sit down. Jack tipped his chair back and tented his fingertips together thoughtfully.

"For the first time since their nightmare began, they believe that there's a ray of hope for Jeremy. I explained that we can build another theory that someone else killed Selena at that little mud puddle in Ione and transported the body in the victim's car upcountry. There's very little unaccounted time for Jeremy in that time frame. He was working at the winery during most of it. For Jeremy to have killed her almost requires him to have killed her at the winery. But if she was killed south of Ione... well. It's a long drive down to Ione and an even longer one doubling back north all the way upcountry. He would have had to have been missing for at least three or four hours to accomplish it. There's no window of time that long that's unaccounted for. It's just not logistically possible."

Xavier nodded, his face darkening.

"This isn't about the alternate theory, Jack. It's plausible. Still in its infancy with too many holes, but plausible. This is about my team. Either Ms. Dietrich takes complete direction from me and doesn't make a single move without consulting me, or you can find yourself another trial lawyer."

Sidney decided to speak up. She had nothing to lose.

"Mr. Mahoney. I know that I'm just an associate working on the case. But I don't think that Jeremy Hill killed that girl. I don't understand why you don't seem to care either way."

"Very sentimental of you, Ms. Dietrich," Francis X.'s tone dripped sarcasm. "But you're paid to be objective. Perhaps questions of guilt or innocence are too deeply troubling to you, and thus, overly distracting, considering your background."

Sidney's cheeks turned scarlet, as if she'd been slapped. The sneering reference could only have been about her father.

"Give us a minute, Sid," Jack scowled.

Sidney left her chair and exited Jack's office, closing the door behind her. She gripped her fists, realizing that she was shaking.

"Fat fucking bastard," she muttered.

"Uh, oh," Marjorie clucked as Sidney approached her desk.

"Tell Jack I'll be a minute." Sidney went down the front steps and out to her car. She leaned the seat way back and closed her eyes, certain that the discussion she'd been asked to leave centered on her termination. She breathed in deeply, trying to slow her heart rate. Maybe she could insert her keys into the ignition and drive until she couldn't drive any farther. Maybe she'd stop in San Luis Obispo or Santa Barbara. Stay for a couple of days on the coast. Breathe in the chilly coastal fog. Then, regretfully, she thought of her excitement as she had followed her intuition, first to the morgue, then to UC Davis. Then the pure adrenaline rush when she discovered the trail and the tracks, running downhill heedlessly to Matt. Matt. Sidney placed her head in her hands and rubbed her forehead and temples. Damn, she thought. Of all the unlikely people to like. And now this. What would he think of her if she just disappeared? Why should she care?

Suddenly, a sharp rap on the passenger side window snapped her to attention. Marjorie was tapping her long, lacquered fingernails. Sidney punched the electric window down.

"What? Have you got my last paycheck?"

"No way, honey. You'll be runnin' the joint when Jack retires."

"What the hell, Marjorie?"

Marjorie looked very pleased with herself, as she leaned into the car window, her creased cleavage revealed by a low-cut, wildly patterned top.

"That fat old gasbag just got the boot. Swear to God. Comin' in here from the big city – tryin' to push everyone around with his fat, old, sweaty self. Got what was comin' to him, 'ya ask me."

Sidney's eyebrows shot up in surprise.

"Did Jack fire him?"

"Nah. Mrs. Hill told him to take a hike, right after he called her. Tough old bird, that one. Doesn't put up with any shenanigans."

Relief flooded Sidney's core and her eyes filled with tears.

"C'mon back in, honey. Jack needs you."

Sidney nodded, extricating herself from the front seat, locking the car behind her. She took another deep breath and followed Marjorie up the staircase, wondering how many pairs of stiletto heels Marjorie must own, since every day Marjorie managed to reveal yet another pair.

Marjorie nodded towards Jack's office. "Go on."

The door was cracked open and he was on the phone. Sidney stood waiting for Jack to notice her, and when he did, he waved her in, motioning to the chair she had vacated a short time before. He waved a couple of sheets of fax paper at her and she leaned over to take them from his fingers. The D.A. had produced the preliminary lab reports from the vernal pool and studies from Tom Nelson's photographs. The tire tracks matched Selena's red Honda. The thistles from underneath her car matched similar thistles from the edges of the pool and most significantly to Sidney, the boot prints, although common, matched the boot prints where the body was found. Jack pointed to the fax pages in Sidney's hands.

"I'm getting an independent analysis of everything from the upcountry scene and comparing it to everything at the vernal pool. We'll use your Dr. Benedict for the plants and flowers," he whispered with his hand clamped over the receiver. "I want you to go over every witness statement, everyone with any connection to either Selena or Jeremy, and figure out where everyone was and what they were doing within twelve hours either way of when she died. Then, we've got to find ourselves a new head trial lawyer."

Sidney nodded her understanding and started to get up from her chair.

"And Sid. Francis Xavier was my choice. He did a pretty decent job in your father's case. But your father was guilty, sadly enough and damned lucky that Xavier got him as short a sentence as possible under the circumstances. This is a different situation that may call for a different approach. I'm working on it now. So, you go do what we've got to do to help the next defense lawyer we hire save Jeremy's bacon. Okay? Just go do it like my life depended on it and just keep me in the loop."

With that, Sidney knew she was dismissed. She had been so tense the last few days that she hardly noticed her own exhaustion, but now she yawned outside the conference room door and rubbed her eyes. Her mind was a complete blank and she knew that what she needed now was sleep. Across the lobby, Marjorie was packing up her purse and shutting down her computer.

"Go home, Ms. Sidney. Start again fresh in the a-m. See 'ya."

"I'm heading out right after you," Sidney promised. She gathered up her trial notebooks from the conference room table, replete with summaries of evidence and witness statements, and headed for the rear alley parking lot. Unceremoniously, she dumped the binders in the back seat and crawled into the driver's side, not looking forward to the thirty- minute drive up windy upcountry roads. As she drove, she kept alert by going over the timeline in her mind. The body was found within ten or so hours of the girl's death and her abandoned car a few hours earlier. Witnesses placed her at the winery just the day before. Somehow, her car ended up at least an hour's drive from the winery in the high country, but it had been at the vernal pool near Ione where she was presumably killed. Why not just leave the body at the vernal pool? Why take it in the victim's car all the way into the mountains? Sidney firmly gripped the steering wheel, her mind racing.

"To deflect attention," she muttered out loud. "Create a false scenario. Girl is killed. Her body dumped in the high country – maybe by a hitchhiker. Has nothing to do with the winery and people she knows. A random stranger killing a young girl."

Sidney mulled over the stranger theory. She'd looked it up and the statistics placed random killings by strangers at a fairly low probability. So maybe it was Jeremy. She turned over the possibility in her mind, remembering the apartment where Jeremy and Selena had spent time together and the childish letters he had kept as mementos. It didn't feel right. He could have been enraged; smacked her around, even. But grabbing a wire to strangle her from behind? No way. Every time she went over the possibilities in her mind, she came up with the same answer: Jeremy didn't do it. But if not Jeremy, then who? Who else could have a motive?

Sidney finally pulled into her gravel drive as the sun lit up the evening sky with streaks of orange. She dragged the binders out of the car with her and stomped up the front steps of the porch. Sleep was her only goal. Sidney barged her way through the screen door, using her hip to prop it open, fumbling with her keys and the doorknob. Once in, she threw her purse and binders on the dining room table. Upstairs, Sidney stripped everything off to her underwear and dove under the covers, pulling the comforter up around her chin. She was asleep within minutes, the outside racket created by thousands of chirping crickets notwithstanding.

*****

Sidney awoke with the sun's streaming rays through the slatted blinds creating a pattern of light and dark bars on her bed and floor. Someone was insistently knocking on her front door. The rapping grew louder and more urgent. She jumped out of bed barefoot on the knotted cotton throw rug and threw a glance at her bedside alarm clock whose fluorescent arms shamelessly announced 9:00 a.m. at a perfect right angle.

"Christ!" she exclaimed, hopping about while she pulled sweatpants over her underwear. "Just a minute!" she hollered, hoping that she could be heard from upstairs. Sidney scampered down the front steps but stopped cautiously at the front door and peered through the peephole. Urban habits disappeared slowly, like locking her car doors in the driveway even though the nearest human was a mile away. She drew back, horrified by the sight of Matt Dunleavy, leaning on the side of the porch as he waited, his white cowboy hat pushed back off his forehead.

"Shit," she said under her breath, turning to the ornate Victorian mirror in the hallway as she wiped the mascara smudges from under her eyes. Her hair stuck out everywhere, and she used her fingers to shape it into some semblance of order. She unlocked the sliding bolt and opened the door. Dunleavy shot her an amused glance from under his Stetson.

"Sorry," he said, taking his hat off and appraising her disheveled appearance. "Your office called me when you didn't answer your cell or the house phone. I volunteered to make a house call."

Sidney's mind flashed back to the night before, when she deliberately turned her cellphone off and unplugged her landline. She had wanted a good night's sleep and had eliminated all potential interruptions.

"Oops," she said guiltily. "Sorry. Slept in. Didn't know it would send out a 911. How about some coffee?"

Matt nodded.

"You need to be a little careful, Ms. Sidney Dietrich. No kidding. You're tippy-toeing around a murder investigation and if your boy didn't do it, someone else did, and he's still out there. And that someone else might think derailing you and your investigation would be in his best interests."

Sidney stifled a huge yawn. She had slept for ten hours but still felt riddled with fatigue.

"Sorry. Big day yesterday. Thought I'd gotten fired."

"So I heard. Marjorie filled me in when she sent out the APB on you. Thought you might have pulled a runner."

"Me? No. I've run as far as I can run. I thought about it, but there's nowhere else to go." Sidney fiddled with the brown Melitta filter and poured, rather than measured, a hefty amount of Peet's coffee grounds. When she was through filling the coffeemaker with water, she punched the "on" button and pulled out a couple of mugs.

"Besides, I'd like to see this case through."

Matt took a seat at the kitchen counter, placed his Stetson on a stool and rubbed his forehead. Sidney got a matching china creamer and sugar bowl and placed them ceremoniously in front of Matt.

"I put a lot of my stuff into storage when I left San Francisco, but I brought these with me. They belonged to my mother."

"Pretty," Matt commented, admiring the rose painted floral pattern. "My mother liked delicate things like this, too." He toyed with the sugar bowl. "Are you planning on bringing the rest of your things here, or haven't you made up your mind yet?" Matt asked. Sidney looked at Matt squarely. The silence hung heavily between them.

"I don't know. I've always been a big planner. You know –
college then law school, then a brilliant career, then maybe a
family. I've always been pretty driven," she shrugged. "Right
now, I can't see anything ahead. It's really strange. Since I left
the city, I don't see anything clearly at all."

"Maybe it's a better way, living right now. Not making big
plans."

"I don't know if it's better or not. I just know that's where I
am," Sidney said quietly, her hands grasping her coffee mug.
"Maybe I'll get a dog, like Bella."

Matt laughed. "Sure, that'd simplify things. You know,
you're very unexpected."

"You have no idea," Sidney smiled back.

"I'd like to. I'd like to get to know you better. I hope you
stick around."

"Like I said. I've got nowhere else to go, at the moment."

"Just be careful." Matt reached for Sidney's cellphone lying
dormant on the counter. "You know the only thing that these
things are good for way the hell out here is emergency service.
They'll actually connect if you call 911. Remember that."

"Good to know." Sidney punched her phone to life and drew
back, aghast. "Crap. I've got a court appearance at eleven."

"Well, I'll let you get to it. Call me when you come up for
air, okay? I can cook up a little halibut in olive oil, with basil
and heirloom tomatoes, with white wine and bake it in
parchment."

Sidney snorted. "You're kidding. If you can do that, I swear
I'd marry you."

"Be careful what you promise," Matt said, swiveling off of
his breakfast counter stool and heading out the front door. "Call
if you need anything."

Sidney barely heard Matt close the front door before she
bolted upstairs to the shower. If she was even thirty seconds late,
she was in for an embarrassing public tongue lashing by Judge
Duggan, who brooked no nonsense in his courtroom. As she
closed her eyes and let the stream of warm water wash over her

face, her thoughts lingered on Matt and his concern for her safety. Nice, she thought. Needlessly overprotective, but nice.

*****

Jeremy Hill was released on bail pending trial but was essentially under house arrest. Sidney left her interview with him until last, having re-interviewed everyone who had had anything to do with either Jeremy or Selena in the weeks before her death. She was building a snapshot of Selena's last 24 hours of life as well as Jeremy's every movement. The Hill family had set up a picnic table with a couple of chairs in a cool corner of the winery warehouse and the workers came to see her one by one. The workers were cooperative but wary, not wanting to get their boss into trouble. They had already been interviewed by Matt Dunleavy and Tom Nelson and had signed witness statements. Sidney went over these line by line to pinpoint any unaccounted time or holes in potential testimony. Knowing that she was the attorney for their boss helped somewhat. Every one of them was supportive of Jeremy as a decent boss and a stand-up guy.

"He paid the hospital bill when my kid was born," a 19-year old local boy with a shaved head named Brandon said. "I don't know what my girlfriend and I would have done without his help."

Everyone had vouched for Jeremy in more ways than one.

"But you didn't see him every minute of the day, did you, Brandon?" Sidney asked, anticipating what Brandon would be hammered with on cross-examination.

"No. But he was here. When the boss is around, everyone knows. When the boss isn't around, everyone knows," he shrugged. "Like I said, he was around."

She worked her way through the day to the last of the witnesses.

"He was here that day, all day. No way he disappeared. We would have seen him leave and I'll tell you, lady, he never left," repeated Hank emphatically. He was a local who had worked at the winery on a seasonal basis for years. He was a solid, middle-aged farm-hand and would make a reliable witness. Sidney was about to snap her notebook shut when Hank burst out excitedly.

"Hey, if you're looking for suspicious characters, you should check out the junkman next door. What a creeper. I just thought about it now. Caught him in some bushes not long ago. Looking at her. Looking at the girl." Hank said.

"What creeper?"

"If you go up Gold Mine Road, it goes along the edge of the vineyard. There's a dirt driveway. Go up it and wait for the dogs to stop tryin' to tear you to pieces. Billy will come out. Indian. Long black hair. Scars up and down his arms. He's a gimp. Ask him if he was spying around here. You'll find out."

Sidney made a note in her book. Look up Billy, "the creeper." Maybe Matt knew something about him. After several hours, Sidney was done with the winery workers. Each one of them saw Jeremy for at least several minutes or longer throughout the day Selena died, but none of them was with him continuously for hours at a time. It wasn't that kind of work. Jeremy would be in and out of the vineyards and the warehouses, the tasting room, the back office, and the main house throughout the day. It was a nightmare to piece it all together. There were too many witnesses and too many gaps. Sidney thought she would need a stopwatch and an Excel spreadsheet to figure it out.

She sat on a steel chair in a corner of the dim, dark warehouse, thumbing through the yellow legal pad full of her scribbled notes. She leaned back in the chair, the cold steel back pressing against her thin white blouse while she closed her eyes. Her head hurt. She could see the interior of Jeremy's apartment and the traces of Selena's presence everywhere, from the long strands of black hair casually left in a hairbrush to the box full of multi-colored, curlicue handwriting. The crime scene photos jumped into her brain and she squeezed her eyelids harder. Someone did this to her, but who? The carefully arranged pose, the flowers wound around her fingers, the hair neatly coiffed around her shoulders. Suddenly, Sidney's eyes flew open. The hair. It was too perfectly draped around her head. Who would brush a dead girl's hair? How weird. Her heart beat faster. Somewhere in the recesses of memory, something she couldn't get her mind around seized her with the certainty that she knew enough to know who, only it was vague and disturbing, as if she were trying to remember the jumbled fragments of a dream while wide awake.

"Damn," she breathed. The moment was gone. Her mind was blank. It will come, she thought. Just let it happen. Sidney glanced at her watch. Maybe she could catch Jeremy or Maude at home and pester them yet again. There could have been some overlooked detail in the timeline that someone could remember if prodded sufficiently. She only needed to figure out how. But first, she needed to find the creeper.

22.

Matt glanced at his watch. Sidney had called Theresa's Restaurant to say that she was delayed for their dinner date, but she was now about twenty minutes late. Matt swirled his Calistoga and cranberry over his melting ice cubes and pondered the state of his love life. He knew that women were drawn to him. It was clear every time he stepped out to have a drink at Hootenanny's, Jackson's only sports bar. He used to order a solitary Jack over ice, and before long, unaccompanied women would be casting their heavily mascaraed eyes at him and pulling skimpy tops down to reveal even more exposed skin. He ignored them, even the ones who insisted on occupying empty stools next to him. As a matter of long habit, he still wore his wedding ring for a year after the divorce. So that was a real conversation-stopper, especially when he fingered it none too subtly as he lifted his drink to take a sip. He would also keep his eyes glued to the screens all around him, either on the Giants, the 49'ers, or Stanford Cardinals depending on the season. After a while, they usually gave up and shifted their attentions to someone more promising.

What Matt first found attractive about Sidney is that she had never issued any come-hither messages. She was wary and suspicious from the start and more than a tad defensive. She didn't seem to make more than a minimum effort with her appearance and her singular focus on her work was as off-putting as his cold-shouldering every interested woman at every bar. It took effort to break through Sidney's intensely serious demeanor and he was surprised that he even wanted to make the attempt. But he did. There was no artifice there. The woman wouldn't even know how to play games. If she was late, there must have been a compelling reason. He was sure that she would not make him wait simply to engage his interest.

He looked around Theresa's old-style Italian restaurant and the many museum-quality artifacts from gold-mining days that were mixed in with ancient sepia family photos and memorabilia from the last one hundred years. He had been coming here with his mother since he was born. Matt remembered when his mother, Peggy, had been called upon frequently to help with restaurant cleaning on Mondays after busy weekends. Matt would accompany her after school, and they could always count on a good, home-cooked Italian dinner as part of her pay. It was the kind of place that didn't need any designer decorations to look old-fashioned and Italian because it was the genuine article and always had been. A yellowed newspaper clipping of Matt suited up at a Stanford football game hung in a frame among local school sports photos that lined the old brick walls. The huge open fireplace lined with quartz and serpentine rocks lay dormant and dark. It was hard to imagine explaining to a newcomer like Sidney how every place in the county held memories for him and having her understand not only his attachment, but the occasional pain that attachment caused him.

Sidney rushed breathlessly into the front door as strands of her hair blew around her face in the draft. Pressing forward into the restaurant, she cast her eyes over the tables looking for Matt. He saw her from the back of one of the many separate rooms that used to house and feed miners when the place was a boardinghouse. She looked anxious, so he lifted his arm so that she could more easily spot him in a cozy but dimly lit back corner. The effect was immediate, and a sweet smile lit up her face. Matt's heart quickened a little as their eyes connected and he realized that the smile was for him. It had been a long time since he had felt anything like a crush, but he realized with a pang of vulnerability how strongly he was drawn to this thin, intense young woman with the large hazel eyes and fine features who made her way to his table.

"I am so sorry. I'm still not used to how long it takes to get from point A to point B around here. I was at the winery, then talking to the Hills, and then I had to drive all the way home to shower and change into something decent, then come back down here. Thank you for waiting," she exhaled gratefully, sitting down quickly, arranging her print dress and smoothing her hair. He had never seen her look so feminine. It was quite a transformation.

"I would have waited all night if I knew you were going to show up looking like that," Matt said with a smile. Sidney visibly blushed in the candlelight.

"Yeah, well. It's a pretty infrequent event."

"So how are things at the Hill manse now that Jeremy's home pending trial?"

"I think they're feeling more hopeful," Sidney said carefully. "I spoke with Maude, Jeremy, and Grace, as well as most of the winery workers there at the time of Selena's disappearance. All over again."

"Still working on that alternate theory for trial?"

"Yup," she nodded, her fingers reaching for the pickled carrot sticks and black olives that had shown up on the table. "Maybe you can help me with that. There's a guy named Billy. One of the workers called him a creeper. Always spying on Selena."

Matt nodded. "I know Billy. He's harmless. Had a few drunk and disorderly calls involving him, but nothing worse than that. If you want to talk to him, I'd rather go with you. As a friend."

Sidney nodded, relieved. She didn't want to interview a drunk and disorderly creeper by herself.

"Drink?" he asked, raising his hand to signal their waitress.

"I'd love one. A glass of the local red, whatever they're pouring."

"The Cooper's Barbera. It's the best."

Sidney watched while Matt ordered. It felt so good to be in Matt's quiet and competent presence. She exhaled, relaxing immediately. The meal progressed pleasantly, with Matt ordering the veal parmesan and Sidney the house special roast chicken. They exchanged tastes of each other's dinners as they praised their savory selections. When coffee came, Matt decided to probe a bit further.

"So, you were a virtual runaway from city life. You mentioned it was personal and professional. Sounds like a double whammy."

"Yep. It was. Maybe you know that my father is in federal prison for the next many years. Real estate fraud."

"I heard," Matt said solemnly. "And your mother?"

"My mother died suddenly a couple of years before his conviction. I used to think that her death was the worst thing that could have ever happened. But even though it's been really hard to be without her, it might have been a blessing. Had she lived, my father's prison term would have caused her unimaginable suffering. And that would have been the worst part for me."

They were both silent momentarily, contemplating their wine glasses.

"And your job?" Matt asked.

Sidney's pressed her lips together and frowned.

"My father's case didn't exactly lend luster to my legal career. He had been my law firm's most important client for years. So, when the fraud was discovered, they didn't take it well. I was pretty quickly canned."

"And the personal? Did you break someone's heart? Sorry to ask all these questions. Just have to know what I'm dealing with here."

Sidney smiled ruefully. "Not really. Just the opposite. My intended latched himself to another more viable prospect. She was taller, blonder, and from a very good, very prominent family without felony convictions. I'm sure his parents were happier with how things turned out. They deeply disliked me, I guess you could say. Boy, did I feel it. I was not the fulfillment of their fondest hopes for their son, the crown prince of San Francisco. Unfortunately, my father's prison term rather blinded them to my better qualities," she laughed softly, shrugging off the palpable hurt. "I'm sorry if I sound just a wee bit bitter. I'm getting over it."

"And your plans now?" he encouraged.

"Day to day. I used to be quite the planner. Like I said, I had my whole life laid out in a detailed schematic of when exactly I'd make partner and when I'd get married. Not anymore. And you?"

"If you're in the county for ten minutes, someone will tell you that my wife ran off with a wine distributor, but not before I made an ass out of myself accusing Jeremy Hill. I've been an idiot more times than I can count. I don't really blame my wife. Being married to a cop is no picnic. She didn't like the long hours and the worry. I was glad when she went to work at the winery. It gave her something to do and meeting new people was a social outlet. A little too social, as it turned out. Sorry if I sound just a wee bit bitter, too, and like you, I'm getting over it."

Sidney raised her water glass since the table had been cleared of everything but the coffee. "Here's to getting over it. Sooner rather than later. Cheers." She touched her glass to Matt's with a clink and he smiled in agreement.

"So, without giving away any attorney-client secrets or trial strategy, I gather you've been pretty involved in the case. Especially now that your head trial lawyer has returned to the big city. There must be a lot riding on your shoulders."

"Oh, you heard about that, did you? The good news is I'm still employed, but the bad news is I'm still employed. This murder trial is making me a nervous wreck."

"It'll start soon, and I'll be sitting at the prosecutor's table while you'll be sitting at the defense table. Kinda puts a damper on our budding friendship. At least temporarily," Matt said reluctantly, not wanting to ruin the moment by talking shop. Sidney nodded.

"Well, I've been going back over old ground and I've tried everything I could today to flush out anything we'd overlooked. I intimated to everyone I talked to that we knew far more than we do, just to see if there were any interesting reactions."

"Be careful, Sid," Matt cautioned. "Someone murdered that girl, and if it wasn't Jeremy, then you could be putting a murderer's back up against a wall. Any suspicions?"

"It's really weird. It's like there's something I know that I just can't figure out. It's just not coming to me. The way Selena was found is just so personal. It's like someone arranged her body just so and made her look peaceful and pretty with those flowers wound around her fingers. It couldn't have been random, like a crazed, full-moon serial killer or a hitchhiker. It had to have been planned."

Matt nodded. "Makes sense."

Sidney warmed to her subject.

"Hypothetically, okay, she has a passenger in thick-treaded work boots. They drive to the vernal pool in Ione. Let's assume she's killed there and then her body is driven an hour upcountry and not just randomly dumped, but carefully laid out. Her hair looks freshly brushed. Who would do that?"

Matt shrugged. "Possibly your serial killer with the same MO repeating some murderous pattern. Or, someone who knew her, or loved her."

"Exactly," Sidney's eyes brightened. "But if not Jeremy, then who?"

"I hope we nail the bastard, whoever it is."

"Me too," Sidney said wistfully. "She was still a child, Matt." Sidney touched Matt's hand and the softness of her fingers and her voice surprised him. He caught her hand and upturned her palm, leaning over to kiss it. The gesture was so gentle and sincere that Sidney's eyes welled with tears. Matt saw her wipe a tear away with her other hand and frowned with concern.

"I'm sorry. You surprised me. It's been a long time. I really like you, Matt. It scares me."

He nodded. "Me too. We can take as long a time getting to know one another as we want to, Sidney. There's no rush. No timetable. It's good enough as we are. Besides which, we'd both be in big trouble if we got carried away right now."

She nodded. The restaurant was quiet as country-early diners had long since eaten their fill of multiple courses and had wandered back home to bed. Matt paid the check and they rose to leave.

"Thank you. My treat next time, after the trial," Sidney said.

"I'm counting on it," Matt replied as he walked her to her car. The parking lot was dark and deserted. They could hear the creek rushing by behind them and nearby cattle clanging their bells as they settled down for the night. Matt kissed her gently on her lips and Sidney responded, molding her mouth to his and reaching around his neck with her arms to pull herself closer to him. After a long minute or two, Sidney forced herself away from the embrace and unlocked the driver's door with a click of her electronic key. Rushing into something she would later regret was a complication she just didn't need right now. Better to be careful and slow.

"Goodnight, Matt. Thank you for dinner. It was really wonderful."

He smiled as her politeness created a screen between them, knowing full well that she needed a little distance from what had just transpired. No rush, he admonished himself, although every instinct was clamoring for the exact opposite. He watched as her taillights receded from the parking lot and down the street. Concern for her safety suddenly chilled him in the cool evening air. Damn, he thought to himself. Stay safe. His thoughts were a heartfelt plea in the dark to a cold and uncaring universe where solitary young women could fall into harm's way in an instant and the light of their lives could be snuffed out forever.

*****

Matt agreed to meet Sidney at Quarry Hill the next day to visit Billy Vega, the alleged creeper. He arrived in his own truck and not the Sheriff's cruiser, as this was not an official call. Sidney's car was already parked at the winery tasting room. Memories of Sarah filled Matt's thoughts. He was suddenly aware that they hurt just a little bit less. Sidney walked through the heavy oak doors of the tasting room, wearing jeans, a t-shirt, and a smile for Matt. Easy boy, Matt cautioned, feeling his heart flutter a little bit. Sidney walked right up to Matt and gave him a kiss on his cheek.

"So, are you ready to protect me from this creeper?"

"No problem," Matt nodded. "We can take my truck. I know the way."

Sidney hopped in and buckled up. It had been a long time since she had been in a man's car, except for Jack's. Matt's smelled like a combination of dog, horse, and Old Spice. Manly. They headed down the long driveway and turned right at the stone gate, cruising for just under a minute along the highway before turning right again on a side road abutting the vineyard. Long rows of oleander bushes separated the vineyard from the neighboring property.

"Jesus. What a dump," Sidney muttered. The mailbox hung upside down by a wire, having long ago been knocked off its weathered post. Up a rutted, dirt driveway, chickens pecked at dried weeds. Old cars lay wherever they were abandoned; hoods yawning open and rusted parts littering the bedraggled landscape. To call the place a junkyard would have been too flattering. Trash heaps were half-burned, clotheslines lay defeated on the ground, and the crazed barking of territorial pit bulls filled the air.

"Who the hell is this guy, Matt?"

Matt stopped a good hundred feet from the rusted manufactured house with its patched tin roof covered with a blue tarp.

"He's not allowed to have firearms. But we need to be careful. Wait until he comes out and recognizes me." He turned off the ignition. "Billy Vega was in my high school class. Wild kid. Mostly Indian but born even on the wrong side of those tracks. He's not Jackson Mi-Wuk. His kin come from the Ione Band and they've never been able to get their tribe federally recognized. So, no gaming casinos. Nothing but just the dirt patch you're looking at, where everyone but Billy has lived and died for generations. He's the last of his kind."

Sidney didn't know what to say. She'd never even seen anyone so clearly Indian before and had never thought of how California Native Americans were faring in modern times. Not well at all by the looks of it. She watched the broken screen door open a crack and half of a face peeked out. Matt got out of the pick-up and stood by the truck's open door, his hand waving a greeting.

"Hey, Billy," he called out. The pit bulls threw themselves in a frenzy against a weak chain-link fence. Sidney was seized with the urge to lock the truck's doors, but she waited to see what Matt would do. Slowly, the screen door opened on squeaky hinges and a tall, whip-thin man stepped out onto the sagging porch. His skin was mahogany dark, and his long black hair was parted in the middle, hanging loose around his bony shoulders. He scowled under black eyebrows.

"Matt," he shouted, "I don't want no trouble. I checked in with my P.O. already. I'm clean, man." Matt approached with his hands out in front, palms up.

"Not here about that, Billy. I know you're good."

"Who's in the truck with you?" Billy asked suspiciously. Matt turned around.

"Come on out, Sidney. It's okay." He turned back and said, "It's Jack McGlynn's god-daughter, Billy. She works with him. You remember Jack, don't you? He was your trial lawyer."

Billy nodded. "He's okay," he said. "What you here about, Matt?"

Matt and Sidney walked up the rocky hill together until they reached the front porch. Sidney had a good look at Billy. His face was a pockmarked mess and down both arms snaked the largest, ugliest scars she had ever seen. They looked as if angry cords of red rope had embedded themselves just under his skin.

"Do you know anything about what's been going on next door, Billy?"

Billy nodded. "Selena's dead. That bastard killed her. But was arrested, right?"

"Did you know Selena, Billy?" Matt asked.

"Sure," he shrugged. "Seen her around. Lived next door," he said, jerking his head in the direction of the adjoining vineyard.

"Well, someone saw you hanging around. Maybe watching her."

Billy spit on the weathered porch in disgust. "Fucking liar. Never did. Just watched people come and go. No harm in that, is there?"

"No, there isn't. But if you saw anything that could help us find her killer, let us know. You know how to reach me."

"You already did. You arrested him, didn't you? That fucker, Jeremy Hill."

Matt nodded, hands on his hips. "You don't like the Hills, do you, Billy?"

Billy spit again. "The old man tried to run me offa here. My property. Been in my family longer than his. Tried to force me out for another vineyard. Fuck him. And his son killed Selena. An innocent girl. Fuck 'em all. I hope he gets the chair. The needle would be too good for 'im."

"Okay. Thanks, Billy. Take it easy."

"Always do, bro."

Matt turned back to the truck, holding Sidney's arm.

"Is that it?" Sidney whispered under her breath. Matt nodded and walked Sidney to her side, securing her in, and shutting the door before getting in his own side. He waved to the frightening scarecrow figure on the front porch and backed out of the dirt driveway. Once he faced the highway, Matt pulled over and turned to Sidney.

"Billy hasn't been right in the head since he crashed his motorcycle a few years ago. He was torn to shreds. Brain damage. He's gotten into trouble with alcohol and weed, but nothing worse. No violence. I've known him all his life and he'd never hurt that girl."

"Just like that? Because you think you know him?" Sidney responded, her irritation barely concealed.

"Sidney, it wouldn't be right to build your alternative theory of the case on Billy."

"But what about the part where he's a creeper, watching her?" she argued. "Maybe he was a peeping Tom, and she found him, and then things turned ugly?"

Matt shook his head and started up the engine, pulling back on the road. "It's too easy to pin it on Billy. He's a creepy, ugly Indian, but he wouldn't hurt a fly. Trust me."

Sidney sighed, shaking her head in frustration. Matt dropped her off in the winery parking lot and leaned out of the window with a smile. "See you soon, Sid. Take care. Call me if you need anything else."

With mixed feelings, she watched his truck roll down the driveway and turned to her own car. Her trust and her patience were increasingly in short supply. Time was running out.

*****

Sidney unfolded the detailed spreadsheet on the conference room table that she had carefully taped together. End to end the sheets of paper were probably five feet long. They listed every known witness's schedule in fifteen-minute increments throughout the 24 hours before Selena's death. Unaccounted for blocks of time were highlighted in yellow. Sidney stared at the yellow markings as if trying to see a pattern. The winery workers clocked in and out with time cards. Of course, one of them could have stealthily escaped observation, lured Selena into giving him a ride in her car and then strangled her at the vernal pool. Highly unlikely. They worked in teams under supervision. Unless there had been a mass conspiracy, the workers could be exonerated, more or less. That left strangers, friends, acquaintances; basically, the rest of the universe under suspicion.

"Damn," she breathed. "Where is it?" Either there was someone of whom they were unaware, or there was a time slot filled with a plausible alibi that was not accurate. Sidney sighed and pushed her chair away from the table. She closed her eyes and visualized the vernal pool as it must have been a few months earlier. Near Ione. Why would Selena be going near Ione? What was in or around Ione? Nothing came to mind. She sighed. She could have had a new boyfriend, but if she were trying to be discrete because of her stormy relationship with Jeremy, then who would know about it? An old boyfriend might know, she thought. Especially one that was still in love with her. She looked closely at the grids corresponding to Alejandro Almazan's whereabouts. He had reportedly not seen Selena for at least two weeks prior to her death. That didn't sound right, especially for a boy who had such strong feelings for her. Sidney decided to visit the St. George Hotel restaurant in Volcano, where Alex worked as a busboy. She told Marjorie where she was going as she grabbed her keys and notebook from her desk and headed down the red-carpeted lobby stairs.

The drive to Volcano took about twenty minutes from Jackson, up Highway 88 to Pine Grove and then a left-hand turn down a steep, windy road that bottomed out by the creek. The village sign boasted 105 permanent residents, but the number was crossed out and chalk marks noted 102 inhabitants. Sidney wondered at the loss of three citizens. She continued to drive slowly down Main Street past the original rock, brick, and lumber shanties that thankfully, no one had bothered to tear down, creating one of the area's most original gold mining towns.

Sidney parked her Subaru in front of the new Post Office building just down the street from the St. George Hotel. It was quiet in the early afternoon. A couple of stout locals in overalls graced the front of the General Store drinking beer and exchanging local gossip on the hand-carved wooden bench set out hospitably on the rocky sidewalk. Sidney watched her step as the rocks set into the sidewalk were three-dimensional and created numerous opportunities for self-injury. She made her way gingerly to the front steps of the George. The double glass-etched doors had ancient brass doorknobs set almost at knee level. People must have been quite a bit shorter one hundred and fifty years ago, Sidney thought as she bent to turn the doorknob to the restaurant. It was locked. Dinner would be served in about four hours, she noted from reading the descriptions of savory entrée selections from the posted menu. Sidney had not stopped for lunch and she was suddenly starving. She looked around and walked to the right of the front porch that wrapped all the way around to the back of a lush and well-tended garden bordering the creek. The garden was dotted with tables and chairs set out on a flagstone patio for outdoor dining. The back door was open, and Sidney stepped past the ancient screen door into a hot and busy kitchen. Sous chefs were busily chopping vegetables and the smell of sautéed garlic filled the air. No one even glanced her way. She stood in the doorway and looked around for anyone who was young, male, and Hispanic who could have been Alex Almazan. His back was to her and his hands were submerged in suds as he cleaned a sink full of gleaming metal pots and pans. She walked through the kitchen unnoticed and stood by the side of the sink so as not to alarm him.

"Alex," Sidney said softly. He jumped anyway and turned to her with wide, frightened eyes.

"Who are you?" he asked.

"I'm an attorney – a lawyer. My clients are the Hill family that employed Selena's father. I know you were her good friend. Do you have a minute to talk to me?"

His dark eyes narrowed. "Jeremy Hill killed her."

"How do you know?" Sidney asked.

"He didn't want to let her go. It was over. She broke up with him and he killed her."

"I want you to know that there isn't any direct proof of that, Alex. So, I'm asking again, is there something you know that you didn't mention to the police?"

"Like what?" he demanded.

"Like, maybe you saw her shortly before her death. Maybe you know who else she was seeing at the time she died. There may be another suspect."

"Not for me," he shrugged, his dark features set in a look of harsh resentment.

"Was she seeing someone else? You for instance?"

"No lady. Like I told the cops, I hadn't seen her for about two weeks before she died. I don't know nothin'.""

"But she was seeing someone, wasn't she? You heard about it, didn't you?"

Alex shook his head, staring at the sink full of suds. Tears welled up in his eyes and spilled over on his cheeks. "No. It was nothin' like that. You didn' know her. She had plans. Dreams and plans. She was goin' to college – nothin' could slow her down. She was outta here, believe me."

"Was there anyone who would want her dead – anyone that you could think of who might have wanted to end her dreams and plans?"

"No. No one 'cept Jeremy Hill."

With sinking feelings, Sidney examined the cast-down face of the young man with a wispy, dark mustache who suppressed a sob and turned his attention to the pots and pans with fierce determination. Damn, Sidney thought. He would be a great witness for the prosecution.

"Okay, thanks Alex. I'm sorry to bother you. I'm tucking my business card in your front pocket, in case you can think of anything else. Call me if you do, okay?"

Alex never raised his eyes even to look at her directly. He ignored the business card she placed in his shirt pocket and started scrubbing away again as if he could remove his personal pain along with the encrusted grease stains. Disheartened, Sidney stepped back through the screen door and into the garden that was beautifully bordered by carefully tended red azaleas and pink rhododendron. Back to the office, she thought, retrieving her car from the Post Office parking lot. Another dead end and a chilling realization that if Selena really wanted to leave her past behind her, there was no one who could have been more motivated to try and prevent that from taking place than Jeremy Hill.

*****

"All right. Jeremy did it or didn't do it," Jack McGlynn spoke to an audience of one as Sidney listened intently. They were back in the conference room the day following Sidney's visit to Volcano, when she admitted to Jack that despite the physical evidence of the crime scene and the fact that eyewitness testimony could place Jeremy at the winery for almost the entire time involved, there was no real evidence that could exonerate Jeremy and no hard evidence to support an alternative theory. She gave him a thumbnail sketch of her visit to see Billy Vega with Matt and how Matt had insisted that was a dead end.

"Casting reasonable doubt on a circumstantial case was what got O.J. off with the right jury, right? We need to do the same."

"I'd feel better if we could find the real killer," Sidney interjected with frustration.

"So would I. Justice served and all. But that's a job for the police. And they think they've found the killer – our client. So that's not going to help us here. So, let's focus. Jeremy didn't do it because some person or persons unknown kidnapped Selena in her car, drove to Ione to a cow pasture with a mud puddle, killed her, and then drove her body all the way to the high country to divert attention away from themselves and hide the crime scene. Right?" Sidney nodded. "Then they laid her out near a well-traveled highway overlook so that she could be found. Sounds psychopathic and personal to me, but I'm no expert. That's why we hire experts, and one will testify all about motives that could not have anything to do with our client, or that will have everything to do with person or persons unknown. So far so good, right?"

Sidney watched Jack scrawl little illegible diagrams on the whiteboard with black felt marker. "Of course, the grieving family could make for a perfect alternate theory of the crime. Father enraged by discovering that his daughter had gotten pregnant. He strangles her in a type of Hispanic honor killing."

Sidney made a face of obvious distaste with that theory. Jack ignored her and continued.

"Then we have a parade of self-interested winery workers whose jobs depend entirely upon the noblesse oblige of the Hill family to testify that Jeremy Hill was at the winery every single minute of every day and could not possibly have escaped for long enough to commit said heinous crime."

Again, Sidney nodded.

"Last but not least, we have Billy Vega, a neighboring peeping Tom who was obviously besotted with the victim. For now, we defer to Matt's knowledge of that suspect and put him on the back burner. But we can always pull him out if we feel like we're going down in flames." Jack paused to view his handiwork.

"Of course, if our client did murder his young girlfriend," Jack continued to think out loud, "We have several defenses, including insanity and diminished capacity, especially if we can argue she had a back-alley abortion to get rid of Jeremy Hill's love child."

Sidney made another face. No one used the term "love child" anymore.

"Uh, don't think that'll fly either," she responded.

"Okay. But our job is to convince our client of the best defense that will likely result in either acquittal or a very reduced sentence. Your thoughts?"

Sidney had nothing logical to add, so she went with her gut.

"I think I'd recommend the plausible alternate theory involving person or persons unknown. Otherwise, you're forcing the jury to pick between Jeremy and some other known or likely candidate – her father, for instance, or Billy Vega. Then you're making it a contest between Jeremy and someone else who will be called to testify. What if they're totally believable and sympathetic? Jeremy could lose that contest. No, I think our best argument is that there is no direct evidence that Jeremy did it and that there are many other possible suspects that the police overlooked. The conclusion should be that the D.A. failed to carry his burden of proof beyond a reasonable doubt. That's really what I think, and if we're convinced, there's a chance the jury'll be convinced. A jury will accept that although he was devastated by Selena's news of an abortion, Jeremy still loved Selena and would never have harmed her. But we have to risk putting him on the stand and have the jury hear it from his own lips. That's the only way they'll be convinced of his innocence."

Jack looked up at the white ceiling momentarily and then nodded. "I agree. Trying to pin it on any other specific individual, especially the grieving family would backfire at this point. So, we go with person or persons unknown and reasonable doubt."

"It sounds like you're trying this thing, Jack. Are you?" Sidney asked, surprised.

"Well, so far, we have no other takers that aren't known alcoholics or are otherwise in trouble with the State Bar, and thus, somewhat unreliable. I guess the Hill family could do worse than you and me, kid. And if we lose and he's convicted, then we'll find someone else to appeal on the basis of the incompetence of trial counsel," Jack declared.

Sidney smiled and shook her head. Jack was a piece of work and regardless of his self-deprecation, Sidney knew that if she or anyone else she knew were in deep shit trouble, she wouldn't want anyone but Jack McGlynn coming to her aid. She was sure that the Hill family felt the exact same way.

"Besides," Sidney said. "We do have home-town advantage over anyone from the outside, right?"

"Right. Like I said, they could do worse than you and me. Pretrial arguments start in two weeks, Missy. Clear the decks. It's going to be a bumpy ride."

With that extremely mixed metaphor, Jack strode purposefully from the conference room to his office, leaving Sidney staring at the boxes of binders and papers for which she would solely be responsible for organizing and preparing for each witness as they rebutted the prosecution's evidence and presented their own. She was looking at night after night of late work hours and total unavailability to any other endeavor. Sidney shook her head. It was going to be a long time before she could reciprocate Matt's invitation to dinner. From now on, the case owned her.

23.

It had been some time since Jack had been first chair on a criminal trial and never for the defense on a murder case. The stakes could not have been higher. Try as he might to inform his client that he would be better served with another expert criminal defense attorney and that the judge might be amenable to postponing the trial so that new counsel could be brought up to speed, Jeremy declined to listen to Jack's earnest and sage advice with astounding indifference. Jack burst out with a stream of profanities when back in the privacy of his own office, after a particularly irritating exchange with Jeremy, who seemed not to listen and especially seemed not to care.

"It's effing suicide by lawyer," Jack fumed. "My God, I was a prosecutor way, way back and a defense attorney for a few years thereafter, but Jesus, Sid, it's been almost twenty years since I tried a serious criminal case. But at least the clients I defended gave a shit what happened to them."

Sidney couldn't help but agree. She was shocked by Jeremy's flat affect and almost hostile indifference to his fate.

"I don't think he cares. There's no fight in him."

Jack's dark eyes blazed. "Even guilty men fight like hell for their freedom – just look at your father."

Sidney's looked away; a mere mention of her father at any time was unpleasant. She practiced compartmentalizing so that she could seal off that reality and keep it at a distance.

"What if he doesn't seem to care throughout the trial? How is that likely to impact the jury?"

Jack sighed and kicked his loafers off as he dipped his leather chair back and hoisted his feet on his desk in one practiced move.

"You heard. I tried to tell him to look serious but concerned at every single juror throughout voir dire and focus on proving his innocence. No laughter, no banter, no chit chat. His emotions have to show through just enough so that the jury can feel his pain at the loss of the woman he loved, and he has to testify with conviction. They need to hear from him that he did not kill that girl and I don't know whether he's up to it."

"Would you consider putting Maude on the stand? And Grace, too? Plus, character witnesses to Jeremy's hard work and devotion to the winery. Especially the workers who saw him the day before Selena's body was discovered. Maude can talk about her son being a caring employer and an exemplary son. Grace can talk about her brother's kindness to the poor and dispossessed…"

"All right," Jack growled. "I get it. He's going to be portrayed as St. Francis of Assisi. Maybe his dog can testify that he gives him daily treats."

"No. Seriously. That kind of family and friends' testimony can be very effective in setting the stage for Jeremy's own testimony regarding his innocence, if we put him on the stand. I swear my father didn't get the life sentence he deserved simply because he had an army of friends and even some former clients testify to his decency. We get all that positive testimony in when we put Maude and Grace on the stand to say that they saw Jeremy off and on the entire day before Selena's body was found and that they never saw him leave the property."

"Yeah, but the D.A. will rip holes in everything they say because he'll cross with questions that will elicit testimony that they didn't see him all day long and that they can't account for every minute of the day or night."

"We know that. But the jury will sympathize with a frail old woman and a crippled older sister in a wheelchair being reduced to tears by our ruthless and hard-hearted D.A. No joke. It's important," Sidney's voice rose with urgency.

"They don't say "crippled" anymore, young lady," Jack interjected, but then paused to consider Sidney's advice. "You really are quite Machiavellian at heart."

Sidney heard it as a compliment and smiled.

They never counted on Jeremy's reaction to their plan to call Maude and Grace to testify on his behalf. He was livid. Under court order not to leave the Hill estate, Jeremy was housebound and waiting for his trial to begin was clearly fraying his last nerve. He paced the expansive living room at Quarry Hill as Maude and Grace watched his temper reach the boiling point. He turned and confronted Jack and Sidney, seated on the brocade patterned rolled arm couch.

"Leave my mother and sister out of this," he said, practically snarling as he rose and turned his back to them all, staring out of the window.

"Jeremy!" his mother snapped. "Jack is perfectly right. Grace and I will testify. It's the only thing we can do to try and help you. That's settled. We have nothing else to discuss. Sidney, dear, when would you like to meet with Grace and me? I imagine you'll need quite a bit of time with each of us? We can meet here. I can give Hans's old office over to you and your team, Jack. Whatever you need from us, please don't hesitate."

"Thank you, Maude. We'll start Monday. This being Friday, we'll have some work to do over the weekend and then Sidney and I will be here on Monday. Sid will meet with you and Grace, and I'll be sequestered with Jeremy. Does that sound like a plan?"

There was no audible response from anyone, but mother and daughter turned to Jack and nodded their assent. There wasn't much else that could be said.

*****

The weekend work schedule was interrupted only by the occasional need to eat, take bathroom breaks, find a couch on which to sleep briefly and fitfully, and change clothes. Jack, Sidney, and Marjorie lived at the office round the clock. Hardbound blue criminal procedure volumes littered the conference room. Sidney pounded out jury instructions, pretrial motions, and trial briefs on her desktop computer, returning to Marjorie's desk to pick up drafts spitting endlessly out from the printer. Jack sketched out the order of rebuttal witnesses to the D.A.'s list and questions on cross-examination in his black scrawl on yellow legal pads. Marjorie poured coffee, took notes, made phone calls, brought in take-out, and once, woke Sidney up after she fell asleep at the conference room table.

Come Monday, Jack drove with Sidney to Quarry Hill to meet with Jeremy as well as with his mother and sister. Sidney felt so exhausted by the reams of pleadings she had churned out over the weekend that she hadn't given much thought to her preparation of Maude and Grace. She knew that the character witnesses were a minor part of the case, but critical to establishing that Jeremy was a kind and attentive son of an elderly and noble lady in the community and a devoted brother to his much older and tragically disabled sister. If that could get across to the jury, they would then find a much more receptive audience for their alternate theories of the case. One small hesitation to convict might lead to an acquittal or a hung jury and a mistrial that the D.A. would be hard-pressed to justify spending limited county resources re-trying.

It was a brilliantly blue late summer day. The spring grasses had long ago dried and had carpeted the hills in yellow gold. The cattle huddled around concrete water troughs and swished their tails languidly to fend off swarms of flies. Red-tailed hawks perched on fence posts preening before launching into the morning air, skimming over the fields in search of rodent prey. Jack talked non-stop during the twenty-minute drive to Quarry Hill about the trial. Pretrial motions were to begin on Wednesday, the jury selection would begin on Thursday and trial would begin the following Monday. Judge Kelso was known for keeping his trials under a tight rein and any foot-dragging or delays would most certainly result in a tongue-lashing at minimum and possible monetary fines. Jack was telling Sidney what questions he wanted her to prepare both Maude and Grace to respond to and to make sure that she covered yet again the details of what they remembered about the events leading up to learning of Selena's disappearance and murder. Sidney suppressed a yawn. It was getting hard to focus.

"I'll be about three hours or so with Jeremy. Take up to an hour with Maude, but don't exhaust her. Keep it light. With Grace, the wheelchair alone will be sympathetic, and her protectiveness will make her compelling. She's always been close to Jeremy. She can talk about him in terms that we'll never get from him directly."

Sidney nodded. That had been her plan exactly, but because the instructions had come from Jack, she wasn't the least resentful at their repetition. He could tell her to open the door before trying to walk through it and she wouldn't have considered him patronizing. They parked under the shade of a madrone tree after reaching the end of the half-mile-long private gravel drive that had covered the car in a fine dust. The summer heat hit them like an open oven door as they emerged from air-conditioned comfort. The short walk to the stone steps in the blinding sunshine made Sidney yearn for the cooling Bay Area fog. Jack and Sidney both were each laden with thick trial binders and briefcases full of notes and legal pads that Marjorie had prepared like a conscientious mother prepared school lunches for her brood. Sidney had lost hope that the office would become less paper-dependent and more reliant on laptops and iPads, but Jack claimed to be an old dog incapable of adapting to any new tricks. They were separated at the front door by a maid and led to separate interview areas.

Sidney was quietly thrilled to be shown into Hans Hill's former office, with its heavy dark wood and leather furnishings, Remington bronzes, and antique guns recalling a different era of the old, golden West. She had wanted to take a closer look at the family's mementos and now she had her chance. Before Grace arrived in her wheelchair, she had a moment to peruse the silver-framed family photographs. A faded color photograph was lodged in the back recess of the walnut credenza behind the massive and ornately carved desk. Maude, Hans, a teenaged Grace, and toddler Jeremy posed for the camera. She picked it up and admired the thin, tanned and blonde radiance that was Maude in her late forties. Her hair was short and curled, smoothly tucked behind her ears. She wore a sleeveless but collared, red shirt open at the neck and her athletic tautness was revealed in sculpted arms and a tiny waist. Grace had her arms intertwined with her mother's. She was darker and thicker-set than her graceful mother, wearing her hair long and straight over a peasant blouse. No smile lightened her heavy features. She looked every bit the resentful, dour teenager. Jeremy was a two-foot towheaded version of his current self, but a smile reached his crinkled blue eyes with a look that spelled mischievous delight with his entire world. Hans Hill was tall, Nordic, and well-muscled in his late forties, wearing a plaid cowboy shirt and string tie. His rugged, tanned features were shaded under a white Stetson decorated with a leather and silver-studded hat band. A huge hand rested possessively or protectively on Jeremy's suntanned little shoulder and his face reflected the unexpected joy he found in his family so late in his life. He looked like Gary Cooper, Sidney thought admiringly.

Behind the family portrait, Sidney found and examined a small and tarnished silver frame with a color photograph of Grace and Jeremy taken perhaps twenty years after the large family photo. If only we could see in the future, Sidney mused, some of us would lose the courage to go on. Jeremy's serious, frowning face looked down on the top of Grace's short haircut as he stood behind her wheelchair. His hand grasped hers as she sat looking off in the distance, her vision of herself altered beyond imagining. Her legs were covered in a colored afghan, similar to the one she used now to tuck her legs into her chair and cover their metal-encased and shrunken shapes. Jeremy looked haunted by what his recklessness had done to his sister, but his protective posture affirmed his dedication to her. A chill tickled down Sidney's spine observing tangible evidence of the pain so evident in them both, trapped forever in the consequences of one reckless act. She turned, surprised by the noise behind her as the door opened and Grace maneuvered her chair through the doorway.

"I'm sorry, Ms. Dietrich, but my mother isn't feeling well today. So, you just have me to contend with," she burst out with a jocularity inappropriate to the situation. Grace positioned herself in front of the massive desk, as if she expected Sidney to sit in her step-father's old leather chair. Instead, Sidney drew up a wingback tapestry side chair so that she could sit closer opposite Grace. Their knees almost touched. Sidney felt a pang of pity that even with the withering heat outside, Grace still hid her legs under blankets from embarrassment at their exposure.

Sidney started her preparation with where Grace's testimony fit in with the trial and what effect she hoped that Grace would have with the jury. Grace nodded her understanding. After forty minutes of questions involving Grace's relationship with her brother and her generous and warm assessment of his character, Sidney pulled out her binder from her satchel and quietly reviewed the timeline she had so carefully filled in half-hour increments before, during and after the crime. Grace waited quietly but intently for Sidney to continue. An ornate Victorian clock loudly ticked off the seconds.

"So, Grace, when did you leave the house the day before Selena's body was found... for your physical therapy appointment, right?"

"Right."

"And were you alone?"

"Yes."

"And what time was that?"

Grace paused, as if searching her memory, eager to be fully cooperative. "My appointment was at 2:00 that afternoon. It takes me about thirty minutes to get there. So, I probably left right after lunch, say around 1:30."

Sidney perused her timeline, flipping through her printouts. "Your mother's nurse said that she only served Maude lunch that day. Did you and your mother have lunch together?"

Grace tried to stifle a yawn as if she were already overdue for a nap.

"Sometimes I have lunch with my mother and sometimes I take it in my room, depending on how sociable I feel. I frankly can't remember whether I had lunch with my mother that day."

"But you remember being home all day until you left for your therapy appointment, right?"

Grace nodded.

"And do you remember seeing Jeremy that day at any time?"

"Sure. I saw him at breakfast around 8:00 a.m. as usual, but I remember that day because he was expecting a shipment of special oak barrels that was already a week late. Fermentation was just at the optimum time. I clearly remember that he was annoyed that pouring the fermented wine into the oak barrels was being held up. Then I'm sure I saw him throughout the day, as he came and went to and from his office."

"If you did, okay – but I want you to be sure. I want you to think through every second of that day. If you had so much of a one-second glimpse of Jeremy at any point in the day, I want you to be able to testify to it under oath, okay? We'll go over this in excruciating detail when it's your turn at the trial, so I want you to reconstruct the day. Every minute of it. You may have seen or noticed something important that would help in Jeremy's defense."

"Of course," Grace responded earnestly. "I would do everything I could to help my brother, you know that, don't you?"

"Of course," Sidney nodded absent-mindedly, already focused on the next questions. "So, you saw him at breakfast, and I think you already said that was around 8:00 a.m., right? And then you saw him on and off. How many times, and where, and when? Do you remember?"

Grace furrowed her brow and stared down at her knees. Her large hands gripped the wheelchair's arms as if she were forcing the memories to surface in her mind. She shook her head. Sidney suddenly realized that she had probably worn Grace down to a frazzle.

"Never mind. We'll come back to that tomorrow when I return to talk to your mother. Could you sketch out your day exactly, on paper? Like every hour from 8:00 a.m. on? I can go over it with you tomorrow." She paused. "You're not sure if you had lunch in your room. Then you left the house at around 1:30 p.m. for your therapy appointment. Did you see either Selena or Jeremy? You might have come across one or both of them as you left. You did drive yourself, right?"

Grace nodded. "My van has hand-controls and my wheelchair isn't too heavy. I also have an electric platform and a ramp so that I can load and unload it easily by myself."

"Can you get out of your car and access the rear of your van where the wheelchair is? How do you manage?"

"Well, if it's important I can describe it to you," Grace responded, indicating clearly that she didn't find this line of questioning relevant in the least. "I have braces on my legs and metal crutches that help me get out of the driver's side and maneuver to the rear of the van."

"Oh. Thanks for indulging me." Sidney paused and flipped through her other notes. "That's probably all – oh, except for one more thing. Do you harbor any resentment towards Jeremy for the car accident that left you disabled?"

Grace's eyes narrowed and her lips pressed together.

"I don't see why that's any business of yours."

"Saving your brother from the death penalty is my business. You're a character witness. Anything that has bearing on his character or yours is bound to come up. The prosecution may ask you about the accident just to show that he was reckless and almost killed you."

"I don't see how Jeremy's mistake twenty years ago could have anything to do with that young woman's death. But in answer to your question, no. It was an unfortunate accident. I harbor no resentment whatsoever."

Sidney nodded. "Sorry, I had to ask. I want you to be prepared in case the prosecutor brings it up."

"Understood," Grace responded curtly.

"Thanks for your time today," Sidney rose from her chair and extended her hand to Grace, who fumbled her right hand from under the cover of her blanket and reached out to grasp Sidney's hand in a strong grip. As she did so, the blanket dislodged.

"Oh, I'm sorry," Sidney said, reaching down in front of the chair to tuck the loose edges back behind Grace's leg braces.

"Don't worry about it. I'll manage," Grace said impatiently.

Sidney rose again, grabbed her files and satchel and exited ahead of Grace, hoping to diminish her embarrassment as Grace awkwardly rearranged herself. As Sidney walked down the long hallway towards the center of the house, she reflected on Grace's equanimity in the face of such a devastating accident. Sidney wasn't sure that she could forgive, much less forget, the harm that even a beloved brother had caused when in a moment of drunken recklessness, he ruined his sister's legs and her life. She knew that she struggled with forgiving her own father's perfidy and wished that someday she could be capable of such spiritual generosity. Still, she wondered whether Grace was truly as forgiving as she allowed everyone to believe. Family bonds were always complicated, Sidney thought, and the Hill family's was especially entangled.

Sidney quickly found Jack as he wrapped up his preparation of Jeremy. She only had a moment to observe Jeremy as he shook Jack's hand goodbye from a seated position, as if he didn't even have the energy to rise from his chair. His face was downcast but resigned, as if he realized that he was a man condemned, no matter the outcome of the trial against him.

*****

Marjorie abruptly opened the conference room door. Her short skirt and leopard print sleeveless top matched her leopard-print stiletto heels. Sidney blinked with startled appreciation.

"I know," she laughed, shaking her curled dark hair. "They're something, right?"

Sidney smiled, grateful to have been distracted and amused simultaneously. "What's up?"

"Your client, Mrs. Hill, is now well enough to meet with you. Feel like another drive out to where the other half lives?"

Sidney sighed. "No. But I'll go." She looked around the piles of boxes and mounds of paperwork spread out all over the conference table. "It's not like I've got anything better to do."

"Sarcasm," announced Marjorie, "Does not become you."

Sidney dragged herself to her car and stepped back when she opened the door to allow the blistering heat to escape. "Like a frickin' oven," she muttered to no one in particular. The spring rains had turned everything Irish green. But nothing had prepared Sidney for consecutive summer days with temperatures over 100 and a sun that was a nuclear fireball singeing everything under its relentless eye. She drove the half-hour to Quarry Hill with the air conditioning blasting through every vent that she could point in the direction of her face, feeling slightly sick. Her stomach churned acid and there was a metallic taste in her mouth. She guessed it was from too much of Marjorie's canned coffee grounds diluted by white powder and several packs of sugar. Never again, Sidney promised, struggling to focus on the road and on her preparation of Maude Hill. Other than prompting her to go over the timeline and allowing her to wax nostalgic over her wonderful son, Sidney wasn't quite sure what else she could accomplish. She felt more than a bit resentful of the time she was spending on this trip; time that she could ill afford. Jack was expecting a finished draft of their trial brief that afternoon and she was less than happy with her efforts.

She stopped at the only red light on the highway on a wind-swept intersection overlooking the craggy valleys of the lower foothills. The scrub oaks dotted golden grasslands that shimmered in the heat as cattle sought shade desperately wherever they could find it. The springtime creeks had dried, exposing rivers of rock clusters. Small windmills pumped iron-tinged water into concrete tubs to relieve the exhausted animals' thirst. Sidney used the thirty seconds to scan her face in the rearview mirror, wiping smudged mascara from under her eye and smoothing her hair. She was suddenly startled by loud honking from the car behind her as she noticed that the light had turned green. A big, black Chevy truck roared its disapproval past her. She read the hostile bumper sticker: "Flatlanders suck" and mentally cursed back a hearty "Fuck you," as she stepped on the gas and accelerated forward. Whether it was the adrenaline pumping through her or just a sudden insight, Sidney' mind suddenly sharpened on a clear and almost tangible memory of the vernal pool site. She couldn't piece together with complete certainty whether Selena had been killed there or who had murdered her, but the reason why Selena's dead body hadn't been left there instantly became crystal-clear. That odd location must point directly to someone. Sidney could fathom no other logical reason. The moment of clarity was replaced with another frustrating puzzle. If the vernal pool outside Ione pointed to the murderer, the question of who still remained, flooding Sidney with anxiety. She felt no closer to knowing the answer to a question everyone else seemed to be ignoring, as if Jeremy were the only possible answer.

She pulled off the highway at a well-marked turn-out. Dust clouded around the windows as she pulled to a stop and yanked her cellphone free of her purse, dialing Matt's home number. It rang and rang and then Matt's deep voice came on the recorded message, announcing to no one in particular, "You know what to do." After the beep, Sidney paused, thinking she should hang up, but then, she stuttered.

"Uh, hi, Matt. It's Sidney. I'm on my way to Quarry Hill to talk to Maude, and I thought… well… did you guys go through everyone on parole or otherwise any and all shady characters in the general Ione vicinity? I'm sure you did, but just wondering… uh, well, since the vernal pool site it's been on my mind: why there? Then, why was the body found way the hell up the highway? Why go through the trouble? I've gone over it and over it… I don't know… but I've got a feeling that there's something about the vernal pool we're missing…Something about that particular location." She paused, unsure of what else to say and embarrassed about rambling. "Well… I'm obviously obsessed. Sorry. Hope to see you sometime this century." She cut off the transmission, noting that it was less than a minute long, but feeling that it trailed on much for much longer.

Sidney pulled back on the highway. Within a few minutes, she turned onto Jackson Valley Road, winding through the parched hills to the winery. The wrought iron gates yawned open and Sidney drove up the meandering private driveway to the stone manor house, wondering how many more times she would be compelled to make this trip. Maude's nurse met her at the front door and beckoned her to come in.

"Her mind is sharp this morning, but she tires easily. No more than thirty minutes, please."

Sidney nodded. "That should be enough."

As she followed Maude's nurse through the wide, carpeted corridor, Sidney passed the cavernous drawing room with its oddly bright, impressionistic paintings that immediately drew her attention. She was always eager to see Joshua Morgan's riveting portraits and expressive landscapes even in passing. His suicide was inexplicable still. Maybe a broken heart; maybe not. Maybe he just tired of living or was ill and sick of the pain. She had never been able to give Maude a satisfactory answer to explain her beloved brother's death and she regretted deeply her inadequacy to the task.

Maude's nurse stood aside at a wide doorway to usher Sidney into a sun-swept bedroom. An enormous four-poster bed dominated the room with swirling mahogany carvings that were reminiscent of European royalty. Thick tapestry hangings depicting medieval hunting scenes hung from every wall. Maude's delicate and shrunken form huddled in a wheelchair. She looked up as Sidney walked in and Sidney had a difficult time not revealing her dismay. Maude had aged suddenly and terribly. Her deeply furrowed skin was tinged with gray and her hands gripping the arms of her wheelchair looked like raven claws. She beckoned with an outstretched finger and patted the upholstered chair next to her.

"Come here, dear. Let's look at you." Maude's voice trembled, thin and reedy. Sidney wondered if it was a mistake to call her at trial.

"I know I look at death's door, dear; it's all over your face. But don't worry. I can summon the energy this one last time. For Jeremy. What do you need for me to do?"

Sidney sat close to Maude's chair and spoke into her ear in a low and soft voice. Very clearly, she explained what she hoped that Maude would be able to convey to a jury: that this loving son, generous employer, model citizen and leader in the community would never, ever have been capable of murdering the young woman he loved; that Maude had seen Jeremy throughout the day and that as far as she knew, he never left the property.

"It's true," Maude nodded, closing her eyes. "It's all true."

"Well, then, that's how it's going to come across to a jury."

Maude's hooded eyelids fluttered open.

"But I can't say I saw him every minute of every day just before that poor girl's body was found. Don't you think the prosecutor will make mincemeat of me?"

Sidney shook her head. "They'd be idiots to treat you with anything other than kid gloves."

"Well, I don't mind a little battering," Maude smiled bravely. "I can bear up."

Sidney touched the mottled, dry rice paper hand lined with blue veins. "We could only hope they'd be that clueless. If they battered you at all on cross, the jury will be furious, and they'll be on your side. You'll be terrific either way."

Sidney patted Maude's bony knee encased in a colorful throw blanket. "I should probably get back to the office. We have a lot of work yet to do. The trial starts next Monday, but I don't think you'll be called until the end of the week after the prosecution rests. We'll talk one more time before then." Sidney stood up to say her goodbyes. She wondered silently if Maude would be well enough by then to testify. Maude hung on to Sidney's hand.

"He's innocent. I hope you know that."

"I believe it, and Jack will do everything he can to prove it."

Maude sighed and released Sidney's fingers. "You give an old woman hope."

Maude's nurse summoned Sidney to the door. "That's it for today, I'm afraid."

"Thanks, we're good," Sidney responded with a farewell smile to Maude. If she only felt as confident as she appeared. At worst, a guilty verdict would make a liar of her, she knew, but it actually might kill Maude, who had done absolutely nothing to deserve it. Not for the first time recently did Sidney reflect on life's unfairness.

As she walked to her car, she suddenly remembered that sitting in her former office on the 10th floor at Ware, Lyman & Cohen she would frequently scribble lists of everything for which she should be grateful. Her lists included things like: not starving in Somalia, not living in a refugee tent in Syria, not being married in India at age 9, not being sold by traffickers in Cambodia, or not being abandoned as an infant in China. She wondered what people must have thought when they discovered list after list stuffed in her old desk drawers, reminders that she had no real right to be miserable working in the exalted halls of a prestigious San Francisco law firm; except for the fact that she had in fact been deeply, profoundly miserable for all those five years. At least, she sighed, as she slid into the driver's seat of her car, tossing her file folder on the passenger seat, she hadn't made one of those reminder lists since arriving at Jack's office. She hadn't needed to. And that was something of a pleasant surprise.

25.

For what she fervently hoped was the last time, Sidney drove slowly down the private road leading away from the house, careful to avoid kicking up too much powdery gravel dust. The winery and tasting room had not welcomed any visitors since Jeremy's arrest, and the public road was closed. She quickly glanced at her watch to gauge how long it might take her to get back to the office to the waiting trial brief. Just as she turned onto the highway, she spotted a large, forest-green van with a blue disabled license plate partially obscured among oleander bushes at the closed public entrance to the winery. She didn't see Grace sitting in her wheelchair until she slowed just past the van. Grace was waving frantically, signaling to Sidney to pull over and stop. Reluctantly, Sidney did so, hoping that she could take care of Grace's problem with just a phone call and be on her way. Sidney got out of the car and walked back to the front of the van where Grace sat patiently waiting.

"Thank goodness you're here, Sidney. I was just on my way to my physical therapy appointment and the stupid van died on me. I had to pull over. I hate cars. I don't know anything about them," Grace exhaled breathlessly. Sidney stood in front of her, looking down at her rough-cut gray hair and her flushed, broad face. Even in the heat, Grace was bundled in a blanket.

"Uh, I have my cellphone in the car… I can call a tow truck," Sidney offered.

"Oh, no. That will take far too long… I'll miss my appointment. Would you be a dear and give me a lift to my physical therapist's office? It's just a mile or two down the road. It will just take you a few minutes out of your way."

"Sure," Sidney responded, trying to keep the reluctance out of her voice. "But your chair might not fit in the back of my car."

"Nonsense," Grace cackled. "It folds up to fit in the back of practically any car. Great design. I'll sit in the back seat where there's more leg room. It will be fine. I'll call a tow truck from the therapist's. Someone will bring me back, so you won't be further inconvenienced."

"It's not an inconvenience, really, Grace. I'm happy to take you," Sidney assured her, suddenly ashamed of her previous hesitation. "No big deal."

"Thank you. Thank you. You don't know how grateful I am. They won't take me if I'm even a minute late," Grace shook her head at the unreasonableness of it all as she pushed her wheelchair alongside Sidney's Subaru. Sidney popped open the hatch and the back door. Grace expertly positioned herself so that she could lift from her chair laterally into the back seat behind the driver's side by pulling on the hanging strap and dragging herself inside. She swiveled and lifted her legs one by one so that she sat facing forward. After a few awkward tries, Sidney figured out how to collapse the wheelchair and slid it sideways into the rear and closed the hatch.

"Okay," Sidney said as she slid behind the wheel and closed the door, "Where to?"

*****

Matt came in from his morning barn chores and saw the red light blinking on his answering machine. He punched the play button and listened to Sidney's long-winded questions. He stood with a half-smile on his face, his hands resting on his hips as he followed the meandering message to its conclusion. He shook his head. She never gave up on an idea, that girl. He rewound the message and played it back. Something about Sidney's suspicions concerning a connection to the vernal pool troubled him. As the remainder of the message trailed off yet again, Matt walked over to his desk, pulling out a green and white topo map with thin whorls and lines drawn into the perfect squares that covered the entire county in a checkerboard of latitudes and longitudes. It had been a necessary tool in his days as Sheriff and he carried it over to the dining room table with Bella following, sensing his tension. Absentmindedly, he ruffled her ears and she moved her head under his fingers for more. He sat down, tracing the highway southwest with his finger until he squinted at the area of the vernal pool. It wasn't on the map, but he knew exactly where it was, just north of Lake Camanche near Ione. Memories of the lake crowded his mind as a summer playground with waterskiing, camping, and drinking copious amounts of beer while floating on huge rubber inner tubes without benefit of sunscreen, with predictable consequences. On the north end was Camanche Village, where beer, ice, cigarettes, and barely edible snack foods were available for packing coolers to overflowing and then heading out to the lake's shore.

He remembered that the village had a small grocery store, a real estate office, a gardening supply, and landscape nursery, gas station, and medical offices. Nothing more. For the life of him, he couldn't imagine any connection between the lake and nearby village and the vernal pool just a mile away to anything or anyone in the case. Maybe there was a migrant worker that had worked at the winery who lived by the shore in one of the cheap manufactured houses. He shook his head; they had carefully checked the records of every itinerant worker that had passed through the vineyard, the house, and the winery for the year before Selena's death. Nothing had shown up among the workers, seasonal or permanent, other the usual arrests for domestic disputes and a couple of DUI's.

Reluctantly, Matt rolled up the map and shoved it back in his desk drawer. When he next saw Sidney, it would be in the courtroom after he had been called as a witness to describe finding Selena's body off a little-traveled stretch of Highway 88 way upcountry in the still-frozen springtime. The vernal pool was a detail, nothing more. The beaten-up red Honda belonging to Selena Rodriguez had been driven there, by Selena or someone else. It had been parked for long enough to impress worn tire tread in the mud near the pool and someone with common enough work boots had walked around. Not Selena. Not just someone. The killer. Then, with Selena alive, or already dead, the Honda had been driven almost an hour up the highway.

The body had been pulled and dragged to where Matt and Glenn Lucas had found her at Maiden's Grave. If the vernal pool was where she had been killed, then the drive all the way up to snow country was a diversion. In his gut, Matt was sure that Sidney was right about that, but from what or from whom was the question. It certainly didn't rule out Jeremy as the killer. If he strangled Selena, he could have done it almost anywhere, including at the vernal pool with no one the wiser.

Matt sighed and pushed his chair away from the desk. The vernal pool was close enough to Quarry Hill. Jeremy had both motive and opportunity. It was an example of Occam's Razor: the case involving Jeremy concerned the simplest hypothesis requiring the fewest assumptions. Matt believed that the trial would only confirm that theory, despite Sidney's and Jack's best efforts to create enough doubt to derail a guilty verdict. He hoped that beyond the verdict that there would be a way for him to deepen his connection with Sidney; if she could ever get over their being on opposite sides at the trial.

"Wouldn't you know it, girl. Just my luck," Matt said, ruffling Bella's ears. "Well, we'll see, won't we?" Bella gazed at him with limpid and adoring brown eyes, leaning in as his fingers scratched behind her ear. They were both startled when the phone jangled loudly. Matt picked up the receiver mounted on the kitchen wall on the third annoying ring. For a moment, he thought it might be Sidney until a gruff voice barked a question.

"Hey, Matt. Do 'ya know where the hell Sidney is? Is she with you?"

"Hey, Jack. No. She's not with me. She left a message on my machine earlier today... I don't know when. I never set the answering machine for date and time, so it could have been anytime. Isn't she with you?"

"That's the point. She's supposed to be with me, here, at the office. She went down to the winery and no one's seen her since. She's about three hours overdue. I called Maude. She told me that Sid left there hours ago."

Cold fear gripped Matt's chest tightly. He breathed in deeply to try to keep calm so he could think. Think. Think. Where could she be?

"She called my house... on her way to Quarry Hill. If she left hours ago, did you check with the Highway Patrol?"

"No... this is my second call to track her down. Frankly, I was sure she must be with you."

"Okay. Just stay there, Jack, in case she calls or comes into the office. Don't go anywhere. I'm going to put in a call to the CHP and Jackson PD, as well as the Sheriff's Department. We'll have a dozen cruisers on the lookout for her car. Just sit tight. I'll call in when I know something. Even if I don't, I'll check in with you, just in case. You call in if she shows up, okay?"

"Got it," Jack responded. "Matt. Find her. Please."

"Will do," Matt assured him with a confidence he didn't feel. He hurriedly made his other calls, describing Sidney and her car, and her last known location until he had finished with every law enforcement agency he could reach. As he hung up, he glanced at his watch and then looked outside. It would be dark soon. They might have an hour or so left of daylight. Bella sensed the excitement and waited panting expectantly at the front door. Matt was going to lock her in the dog run out back before leaving, when he suddenly changed his mind. He grabbed her long retractable leash and snapped in on her collar.

"C'mon, girl."

They hurried to the truck and jumped in the front seat. Matt took his key ring and opened the locked box between the front seats, drawing out his holstered .45, checking the magazine and sliding it with a firm click into the wood grain handle. He lay the re-holstered weapon beside him on the seat and put the truck into drive, spinning the tires on the gravel, kicking up a trail of dust as he careened out to the road. Matt gunned the engine as they wound their way towards Highway 88 and then turned onto Fiddletown Road headed toward Sidney's house. The twists and turns on the narrow asphalt road practically lifted the squealing tires as Matt sped as fast as possible, keeping to the center line as much as he could. He hoped no other car was headed their way this time of the evening. Luck held, and within twenty roller-coaster minutes, he was swinging up into Sidney's steep driveway, coming to a hard stop at the front porch.

Matt bounded up the steps, knocking frantically to confirm what he already knew. Her car wasn't there, and neither was she. He tried the door handle. It was locked. Good girl, he thought. He went back to the truck and let Bella out. She trotted delightedly after Matt as they circled to the back of the yellow-painted clapboard house. Matt tried the back door and then stepped back to survey the windows. The second-floor bedroom window was open about four inches for relief from the stifling heat. Matt looked around to see how he could leverage his way in and spotted a small, covered eave jutting out from the corner of the house, about six feet from ground level. Matt climbed the corner gutter pipe and lifted his entire body weight onto the eave, swinging his legs up over the roof. Standing up with his full height on the tar-paper shingles, he could just reach the second-floor deck. He tested the gutter pipe to see if it would hold, and satisfied, he clambered up the side of the house and grasped the balcony railing, lifting himself awkwardly, and then stepping over and onto the balcony. From there, he could just lean into the partly-open window and jimmy it fully open to allow him enough space to crawl through.

Sidney's bedroom was in disarray, with the bed sheets messy and unmade and clothes dropped randomly on the floor. Matt shook his head. The Sidney he knew was so controlled and organized that it was a relief to see that at least one part of her life wasn't totally buttoned down. He looked around the second bedroom that served as her office and without any consideration as to privacy or attorney-client privilege, quickly perused boxes of documents, files, trial notebooks, and three-ring evidence binders strewn around the room. Nothing stood out. He walked over to Sidney's desk, where her laptop was closed. Next to it was a three-ring binder opened to witness statements and timelines. He flipped through the pages before and after the page where the binder was open, scanning the contents. Matt deferred caution in favor of his growing fear for Sidney's sudden absence. If he was wrong, then he could be apologetic and sheepish, and hope that she would forgive him. Until then, he would press forward, brushing aside hesitation.

As Matt flipped through binder pages laid out in spreadsheets with sections highlighted in yellow, one word suddenly caught his eye. He flipped back, staring at the page, running his finger down the various lists of witnesses and timelines. And then he saw it: Lake Camanche. Grace Hill's physical therapy appointment was in Camanche Village the day before Selena's body was found, one mile from the vernal pool. A cold chill ran through him and he dropped the binder on the floor, scattering the pages. Matt suddenly bolted down the hall and rushed down the flight of steps to the first floor. He opened the front door and let Bella in, who was wagging her tail expectantly. Matt looked around for a telephone. Please, please, let her have a landline. Please. He spotted an old seventies' Princess phone on the kitchen counter and dialed Quarry Hill Winery. A recorded voice inviting visitors to tastings responded and Matt slammed the receiver down. He called Jack's office and Jack answered on the first ring.

"Look, I want to know if Grace Hill is home. Right now. Don't say why. Just say you're confirming that she's home in case you have to call her for trial tomorrow. Then call me right back, here, at Sidney's house… your house."

"Right," Jack hung up. Matt waited several agonizing minutes. The telephone rang with a soft purring sound. Matt picked up.

"She's there. Maude and Grace are in the dining room having dinner."

"Tell them I have some news about the case. Tell them all to stay put. I'll be there in about 30 minutes."

"Matt," Jack snapped, "Where is she?"

"I don't know. I'll call you when I do."

*****

Sidney opened her eyes into the pitch blackness and closed them as the pain pounding in her brain radiated to the back of her skull down the back of her neck, throbbing unmercifully. One word resonated so loudly in her brain it was if she could actually hear it. Alpaca. Damned alpaca. Grace's goddamned blankets. Made of alpaca. That was the animal the UC botanist had told her about when they discussed fibers found in the red Honda. I should have known, she groaned, but the pain was so intense that she could feel nothing else as the pain had replaced every other sensation in her body. She turned to test whether her head was still attached to her shoulders and felt the crunch of gravel beneath her skull.

Sidney breathed in deeply and performed a mental inventory, struggling to ignore the pain. She could move her head, even if it felt as if a giant troll was trying to rip it off her shoulders with even the slightest movement. Her bare arms prickled with the pain of their weight on gravel. Why did they hurt so much? Oh, she blinked, they were underneath her back and she was laying with the full weight of her upper body on them. Her hands? That must be the painful lump underneath her lower spine. She tried to extend her fingers, but she couldn't feel them at all. They were cramped into fists and wouldn't come apart when she pulled. Then she tried to move her legs. No go. Her ankles felt fused together. She felt as if a hand was muffling her mouth and stuck her tongue between dry and cracked lips to taste adhesive tape. Then she remembered the feeling of cold steel against the base of her skull, jammed painfully hard to startle her into quiet submission. She searched her mind to remember every detail of what had happened to her.

She remembered driving down the private road, away from the house. She had turned onto the highway, but just past the closed entrance leading to the winery tasting room, she had seen Grace's van; half-hidden in the oleander bushes by the winery gates, as if broken down in an inconvenient place. She remembered being waved over by Grace, who had been sitting in her wheelchair by the rear of the van. Sidney's head continued to throb as she pictured herself pulling over, talking to Grace, folding the wheelchair and loading it in her car, while Grace slid her bulky form into her back seat. Grace had asked her to move her van even further off the road. Sidney had complied, nosing it deeper into the oleander because, as Grace said, she didn't want her van to be hit by accident. She remembered getting back into her car with Grace in the back seat, driving down the highway toward Camanche Village. Grace had told her to turn left off the highway so that they could take a shortcut, and naively, Sidney had done so. How stupid, she upbraided herself. Then, she remembered a painful jab of cold steel against the base of her skull and Grace's grating voice.

"Listen carefully. Pull over by that fencing on the side of the road. Don't make a sound or I'll blow your head off," Grace spat out venomously behind her. Sidney froze – her mind racing, her heart pumping. She remembered gripping the steering wheel tightly, wondering if she suddenly lurched off the road whether Grace could still get a shot off that wouldn't splinter her skull.

"Stop. Here. Now get out of the car," Grace ordered.

Sidney got out slowly. She was completely exposed in a familiar dry, weed-covered field adjacent to a remote one-lane country road. She looked around, wondering if she bolted into a run how far she could get before Grace got her first shot off. Grace had simultaneously opened the back door, never taking her eyes from Sidney's face while she nimbly swung her legs out, standing over Sidney as they faced each other. Grace was much taller than she had looked, hunched over in her wheelchair.

"Actually, I can walk," Grace announced the obvious.

"Actually, I can see."

"No one else knows. No one else has ever guessed," Grace crowed triumphantly.

"You killed Selena," Sidney said flatly.

Grace didn't answer. She motioned with her head.

"Walk," she said. "Don't worry. I'll follow. If you try to run, I will shoot you, and I'm an excellent shot."

I'll bet you are, Sidney thought. Walking ahead of Grace, she immediately recognized her surroundings as they hiked past the dried-out vernal pool. She looked farther up the trail, to the top of the hill where an old wooden shack stood that once might have been used as a cattle or sheep barn. She remembered having seen it on the hillside when she had explored the pool with Matt and Tom Nelson. It took another fifteen minutes of slow plodding to reach the shack.

"Step through the door," Grace motioned with her head at the shack's wooden door, hanging awkwardly from rusted hinges. Sidney stepped through. The packed dirt floor was as hard as concrete, and cobwebs hung from the beams. The glass windows were so dirty that nothing outside was visible. Sidney turned around to face Grace just as Grace delivered a heavy blow to the side of her head.

Lying trussed and gagged on the floor of the shack Sidney looked through cracks between the old wooden slats and tried to think. Grace was going to kill her, no doubt about it. But why had she not done so already? Because she needed her to die somewhere else; somewhere more convenient to her purposes. If she killed her in the shack, her body, or physical evidence of the killing, would be too easy to find. Plus, Grace would be stuck transporting her body elsewhere. Their simultaneous absence from Quarry Hill would not go unnoticed. She guessed that Grace was probably busy setting up her alibi right now. Sidney closed her eyes against the throbbing in her head. She was suddenly, overwhelmingly sleepy. A concussion would do that to you, she thought. Grace must be waiting for a better time to come back and finish the deed later or even somewhere else. Sidney opened her eyes and turned her head slightly to see through the cracks in the bottom of the shack's wooden slats. It was almost dusk, she guessed. The light was softer and fainter. Maybe Grace would come back at night. Maybe sooner. Well, this is a stupid way to die, she reflected; at the hands of some deranged woman who fooled everyone into thinking she was cheerfully, harmlessly disabled. But she had already succeeded once with Selena, and Sidney knew she had to use every resource at her disposal to avoid becoming another victim.

Sidney struggled to sit up, to try and loosen the tape around her wrists and ankles, to flip around so that she could kneel with her hands behind her back. Even though the temperature was cooling rapidly, Sidney's entire body was drenched in sweat from her efforts. She rocked back on her heels, her hands still tied behind her back, unable to stand because her ankles were crossed and tightly taped together. She was so exhausted trying to breathe through her nostrils with her mouth taped shut, her chest heaving as she grimaced, pulling and twisting against the restraints that she didn't hear the footsteps outside until Grace was through the door, looking down on her, the gun pointed at her head.

26.

Matt bounded up the front steps at Quarry Hill and lifted the heavy knocker, slamming it loudly several times.

"All right! All right!" a piercing voice shrilled from the other side of the door that opened a crack.

"Special deputy, Sheriff's Office," Matt snapped, his impatience rising. "Open the door!" A middle-aged woman in crisp nursing whites opened the heavy front door and peered at him suspiciously.

"Who are you?" Matt demanded stepping into the foyer. "Are you Maude's nurse?"

"Yes, young man. I'm the night nurse. And may I remind you that there is a very elderly and sick lady who can't be disturbed. Keep your voice down," she ordered.

"Look. This is an emergency. Where is Grace?"

"Somewhere in the house. I don't know. I'm not in charge of her whereabouts. Dinner was over a half-hour ago."

"Where is Maude... Mrs. Hill?"

"In her bedroom, getting ready for bed. She tires easily."

"What's going on here, Dunleavy?" Jeremy's haggard face appeared from the shadows of the hallway.

"Sidney is missing. Do you know where your sister is?"

"Why?"

"Where's your sister, Jeremy," Matt's voice rasped gruffly.

Jeremy stared at the pattern in the Persian carpet. He looked older and thinner than Matt had ever seen him.

"She left right after dinner. She said she was going to bed, but I saw her leave from Dad's study. She's an adult. She may have had plans with a friend. She doesn't tell me everything."

"No. I bet she doesn't. But I bet you know a lot more than you let on."

"What do you mean?" Jeremy asked cautiously.

"I don't have time for this, Jeremy. Do you have any idea where Grace would go?"

"No. I don't."

"Great."

Matt paced in the hallway. Jeremy stood frozen, pale, and helpless.

"Bring me something of Grace's like her clothes or a blanket. Something she's worn or slept in recently. Bring it to me in a plastic bag – unused, like a garbage bag that's new. Now, Jeremy." Jeremy stared at Matt for a split second and then turned wordlessly, walking away.

Matt waited in the hallway, alone. The cavernous house was dark, lifeless, and cold. Matt thought of Sidney's serious, pinched face and her deep almost green hazel eyes that pierced him whenever she looked at him with suspicion or mistrust. He had to find her.

Jeremy came back with a white plastic kitchen bag and held it out to Matt.

"You know I'm responsible for ruining my sister's life, don't you? I crippled Grace. I'm responsible for what she does."

Matt nodded to acknowledge that he had heard him while he sealed a huge patterned nightgown in plastic.

"I'm guilty of a lot of things – I've made a lot of mistakes. But I didn't kill Selena, Matt. Whatever Grace has done, she's done for me – and because of me."

Matt stared at Jeremy, his old high school adversary, the golden boy who had everything in the world going his way, now looking shrunken and weak.

"I don't have time for this, Jeremy." Matt opened the huge wooden door and went out into the dark. He placed the plastic bag in the bed of the truck and slid into the cab next to Bella, who was waiting patiently in the passenger seat.

Matt's training had taught him that killers repeated old patterns. Sidney was convinced that Selena had been killed at the vernal pool and then was transported upcountry. How the killer could have navigated the back roads and highways of the county alone had always troubled Matt about Sidney's theory. It still pointed to Jeremy, or maybe Jeremy aided and abetted by his sister. Thinking that Selena's killer might have taken Sidney to a familiar place, he drove directly to the vernal pool in Ione.

Matt pulled over by the rutted entrance and got out, holding Bella firmly by her leash. He lifted the plastic bag out of the truck bed and pulled out Grace's voluminous cotton nightgown, holding it up to Bella's nose. Bella sniffed, rooting around in the heavy folds with her nose and wagged her tail in appreciation. Matt tossed the bag and blanket back into the truck bed. He grabbed a flashlight from the cab and made sure his weapon's safety was disengaged. Matt searched the ground with the flashlight while Bella sniffed the gravel turnout near the trail where he, Tom Nelson, and Sidney had hiked to the vernal pool.

The moon was half full, giving an eerie whitish glow to the straw-colored hills all around, as if they were blanketed in snow. Matt picked up the trail and hiked in as hurriedly and as silently as possible, with Bella straining on her leash leading the way. Within a few minutes, Matt and Bella had the old wooden shack in their sights, and Bella began to whine and strain against the leash. Matt stopped briefly to unclip it.

"Go find," Matt ordered Bella, who bounded away straight at the shack. Matt un-holstered his weapon and followed stealthily, turning off the flashlight. The moon illuminated the shack, reflecting silver light from the dirty-paned windows and broken, jagged glass. It stood eerie and silent on top of a knoll just fifty yards or so from the depression where the vernal pool lay exposed with its deep dried-up mud cracks. Bella turned her golden head and barked at Matt, then dove into the open door of the shack just as Matt raced in to follow.

Matt turned on the flashlight, sweeping the tiny shack's interior with light. Nothing. But Bella's excitement was palpable. She sniffed and sniffed the dirt floor, concentrating her barks in the middle of the room. Matt knelt and tried to push Bella away. Fresh scuff marks and imprints marked the dirt and gravel, concentrated in that one area. The rest of the shack appeared undisturbed, except for old beer cans crumpled and tossed into a corner. The fear rose up in Matt's chest and threatened to explode into panic, but he stood up, closed his eyes and thought. He could visualize Sidney alive, thrashing around on the floor in a futile attempt to free herself, and then being led out of the shack back into the night. She walked out, alive, he was sure of it. There were footprints, but no drag marks anywhere. He reviewed the timeline in his head, of Sidney calling and leaving a message, driving to Quarry Hill, somehow being intercepted and then left here for hours, until her abductor could return to deal with her. It must have just happened. He was only twenty or thirty minutes behind Grace. Grace. He shook his head at the improbability of the thought that Grace was both Selena's killer and Sidney's abductor. What the hell, he cursed silently, desperately searching his mind for what to do next.

Where would they go? All the way back upcountry to where Selena had been found? Unlikely. They could be stopped at any point on the hour-long drive. It was too dangerous for Grace to attempt that trip with a live victim. Matt tried to visualize the drive from the shack. To the southwest lay Lake Camanche and unfamiliar, one-stop agricultural towns all the way to the Central Valley. In the other direction, the highway wound past Quarry Hill towards Jackson and then upcountry. They could only be going in one car, Sidney's or Grace's. So where was the other car? Matt and Bella hurried back to the truck and jumped in. He radioed the Sheriff's Department.

"I want an APB out for a green van with disabled license plates. Registered to someone in the Hill family: Jeremy, Maude, or Grace. We're looking for that van or Sidney Dietrich's silver Subaru Outback all up and down the highway, between Lake Camanche and Cook's Station. Watch for any vehicle meeting those descriptions either en route or parked off the highway."

"Roger that."

"And radio the vehicles to CHP, Jackson PD, CDF, and anyone else in the area. Circulate drivers' license photos of Grace Hill and Sidney Dietrich with vehicle descriptions. Sidney Dietrich is a possible kidnapping victim and her kidnapper may be Grace Hill. Armed and dangerous. Got that?"

"Got it, Matt."

Once he had disconnected, Matt grasped the leather-covered steering wheel with both hands. He closed his eyes again. There was a decision to be made and he risked Sidney's life if he guessed wrong. Up the highway or down the highway? The shack and the vernal pool just beyond it were south of the winery. North, he thought; they would go in the opposite direction from where they were headed before. He hoped his hunch was right. He knew he didn't have any time to lose.

*****

Still blindfolded, Sidney stumbled, trying to feel her way. They had stopped somewhere unfamiliar and Grace had forced Sidney out of the car to walk ahead of her. There wasn't much of a path and what was there was rocky and uneven. She could see nothing, not even a sliver of light. Her hands were still tied so tightly that the lack of circulation had numbed all of her fingers. Every once in a while, Grace would shove the muzzle of the gun painfully between her shoulder blades. Grace had forced her to walk from the shack to her car, and then had her lay down in the cramped, rear cargo space with her bound hands aching underneath her body. Sidney estimated that they drove for less than ten minutes, which meant that wherever she was now, this is where it would end.

"I did a stupid thing not getting rid of the body," Grace mumbled, but loudly enough for Sidney to hear her. "I was paying my brother's lover my respects, out of concern for him. I didn't want him to be hurt by her body being found all nasty and decomposed. So, I made it easy for them, right off the highway at a public rest stop and made her pretty and presentable. As pretty as that cheap little slut could be."

Sidney said nothing; her mouth still taped shut, her head pounding. Grace must have brushed Selena's hair, she thought suddenly, her mind still trying to sort through the pieces of the puzzle. With piercing clarity, Sidney suddenly remembered

Joshua Morgan's touching mother-daughter portrait hanging in the Hill family's front hall: the child Grace brushing Maude's hair, now juxtaposed with an image of the vengeful brute that child had become as she brushed her victim's dark hair. Something had bothered her about that painting, Sidney thought, a feeling that hadn't quite reached her conscious mind. As a result, she had never focused on Grace. Sidney trembled, from fear and from cold. She forced her mind to focus, desperately searching for a way, any way that she could try to escape and stay alive. But without being able to see and with her hands bound behind her back, she was trapped.

"Move," Grace ordered, shoving the gun viciously against Sidney's spine. Sidney stumbled again, almost falling to her knees. Grace's voice was shrill.

"That's right. I tricked Selena into driving me the exact same way I fooled you. You both were too polite not to drive right by me and too blind to see me the way I really am. I've been able to walk for years, but no one knew, not even Jeremy. I never let him know. I never wanted him relieved of the guilt. I wanted him to suffer the way he had made me suffer. I wanted to be a daily reminder of exactly how much pain he had caused me," she spat out bitterly. "I went through years of physical therapy, with my spine and my legs crushed and no hope. Torture, that's what it was. They tortured me. But then I started working on my own, away from everyone, and I got so I could stand up and then, take a few steps and then walk. I didn't want anyone to know, so I kept up the pretense, and it came in very handy, believe me."

Behind her back, Grace laughed, snorting in mirthful appreciation of her own cleverness. She's insane, Sidney thought. Totally insane. The fear like bile crept into Sidney's mouth and nausea hit her so hard she almost vomited. She wanted to cry and whimper from her own terror, but she didn't want Grace to have the satisfaction. She turned her mind to her predicament and forced her feelings to turn to stone. I hate her, she thought. She will not kill me. I will not die this way. Keep your mind open, she ordered herself: look for any way out. Try and get away, no matter what.

"Stop!" Grace ordered. "I need for you to lie down right here."

Sidney stood still. She didn't bend. She didn't try to get down. It would be the end of her if she did. I'd rather die on my feet, she thought.

"Lie down!" Grace repeated. Sidney shook her head. Her blindfold kept her from knowing if Grace was about to shoot her or not.

"You stubborn bitch!" Grace shouted. Sidney stood still, her hands tied behind her back. Suddenly she felt Grace's fingers fumbling with the blindfold and then the tape was ripped from her mouth, leaving her lips bleeding and burning.

"You want to see where you're going to die, do you?"

Sidney looked around, her eyes blinking. The moon illuminated the jagged peaks and valleys of the Hill quarry and shone against the metal conveyor belts that transported tons of broken rock high up in the sky so that it could be dropped into huge piles. Suddenly, Sidney felt flooded with hope: if she could see, she might be able to get away. Play for time, she thought.

"Why kill Selena, Grace? What did she ever do to you?" Sidney demanded with a bravado she did not feel, her lips stinging. She stood facing Grace's bulky form, trying to stall. Grace's fury turned to malevolent pride.

"She was never going to let Jeremy go. That bitch had already gotten pregnant once and given birth to a half-Mexican bastard. She was going to keep her claws into Jeremy until he married her, and her wetback kids were going to inherit everything. I couldn't stand it."

"But Jeremy was the one who wanted to marry Selena, not the other way around. Selena was leaving – leaving Jeremy behind. She broke up with him – she was no threat to you."

"That's what she said. But I didn't believe her. Lying bitch. And my mother. She's so weak and addled she would have given anything for a grandchild, even one that was the child of a Mexican migrant."

"The child died."

"No," Grace shook her head, a strange smile stretching her lips, barely discernible in the dark. "Selena begged for her life, telling me that I couldn't kill her because she was the mother of Jeremy's child. She said the baby was alive. I don't think she lied about that. But she was wrong. She assumed that I would care. But she gave me an even better reason for killing her. And now I'm going to kill you. You couldn't leave well enough alone, could you?"

"Grace, how can you let your brother be tried for Selena's murder? He could get the death penalty."

Grace shrugged her broad shoulders and twisted her mouth, making her face even more ugly in the dim light.

"I won't let it get that far. Jack is going to get him off."

"You hate your brother," Sidney stated flatly, trying to stall again, as she glanced quickly at her surroundings.

"No!" Grace contradicted immediately. "I've done everything for him. I've protected him. I've given my life for him! I've killed for him."

"Selena."

"Not just Selena. Even before Selena. And then there's you. Now, get down."

Sidney looked down. There was nothing but gravel at her feet.

"Not there. Behind you."

Sidney turned and looked, and a chill went through her body. She stood right in front of a still and quiet gravel conveyor belt on a steel framed ramp heading straight up into the darkness. She couldn't see where it ended, except that whatever was conveyed on the belt at the end would be dropped hundreds of feet into the blackness of the yawning gravel pit. She stood at the edge of the pit, blinking back tears. There was nowhere to run.

*****

Matt forced himself to travel slowly up Highway 88. His high beams were trained on as much of the right side of the shoulder as possible without going off the highway altogether. Cars honked and drivers waved fists, both coming and going, not just from the high beams, but from the fact that he was halfway off the road traveling ten miles under the speed limit. Cars passed him recklessly, ignoring the double yellow lines. He squinted into the deepening darkness, searching for driveways or bushes on both sides of the highway in which either a green van or Sidney's car might be hidden. As he drove slowly past Quarry Hill Winery, a light glinted from a thicket of oleander on the side of the stacked stone pillar entrance to the closed winery road. Matt pulled directly across the road and shone his brights. A reflection of glass and chrome headlights glinted back. He pulled over and jumped out of the truck, his lights flashing. Charging across the highway and into the screen of oleander, Matt pulled branches and leaves apart to find Grace's empty green van. He touched the hood. It was cold. He rushed back to the truck and grabbed his hand-held radio.

"I've found the van. It's been abandoned for hours. Keep looking for Sidney Dietrich's silver Subaru Outback. They're traveling in the Subaru. Got it?"

"Got it, Matt. Everyone in the tri-county area is on it – they're all out looking."

"Okay."

Matt clicked off. He sat for a moment, visualizing every trail, turn-off, dead-end public and private road from the winery to Jackson. He wracked his brain – where would they go? Somewhere remote, somewhere they wouldn't be spotted, somewhere Grace could fire a gun or strangle her victim and dispose of the body. He looked up the highway at the reflection of the rising moon. Up ahead, about two hundred yards, Matt saw the outline of crisscrossed conveyor belts and the black outlines of huge excavators with prehistoric-looking buckets and steel teeth like dinosaurs frozen in the darkness. The Hill quarry.

Matt stepped on the gas and the diesel engine roared the truck up the highway. A sharp turn right swiveled the truck right up to the padlocked quarry gates. Matt got out, telling Bella to stay. He listened in the dark. Nothing. He could see very little of the huge quarry. It would take too much time to search an area a half-mile long and a half-mile wide, with pits hundreds of feet deep and cliffs hundreds of feet high. I'll need a helicopter to illuminate the pits from above, he thought. Just as Matt was circling back to the truck to order up a life-flight emergency helicopter with searchlights from the small Jackson airport, he glimpsed a light glinting from the far edge of the quarry. He looked and looked again, squinting into the darkness. The light flashed again. Matt blinked his eyes, willing himself to see more clearly. A cloud drifted past the moon and as if on cue, he could see the quarry pits and gravel mounds more clearly. He climbed over the steel gates and hurriedly hiked uphill, struggling to stay in the deep ruts carved out by heavy gravel trucks. The flashlight flickered again a hundred yards out. Matt gauged his speed over a hundred yards over difficult terrain uphill in the dark. Too far; too long, he thought. Minutes, precious minutes could be lost. He broke into a trot, stumbling as his ankles twisted on clods of dirt and rocks, his heart pounding as he picked up speed, trying to cover as much ground as quickly and quietly as he could.

Up ahead, Sidney tried to keep Grace talking as she measured her options. Her back was to the conveyor belt that went up at a precipitous angle over the yawning pit below. Even if she could avoid being shot on the spot and her body being dumped onto the conveyor belt, she still stood at the very edge of the carved-out pit with her hands bound. Grace could easily just push her off the edge. She would land on the gravel mound below. Even if she were alive after the fall, Grace could bury her body under a ton of rock. There were few options.

"Grace, you couldn't have done this alone. How did you get back from dumping the body and the car so far upcountry? Did Jeremy help you?"

"No, that coward. He was never capable of taking care of his own problems," Grace snorted. Sidney watched the gun barrel that was pointed at her chest wave in front of her as Grace reacted with disdain. "I did it by myself. I killed her at the pool and drove the body in her car up the mountains. I left her there and then drove her car back down the highway close to the ranger station where it would be found. The ranger station is just a half-mile from the Shell station where a county transit van picks up and takes passengers all the way down the highway to Ione. All I did was sit down and wait at the bus shelter. I had a hat, a shawl and a white wig and no one could recognize me, believe me. The bus came along and took me all the way past Jackson to another bus stop just a mile from the winery. I walked back, got in my van and drove myself and my wheelchair to my physical therapy appointment. No one keeps track of me that closely. I was gone for three hours and no one suspected a thing." Grace was boasting now, puffed up with pride at her own cleverness. Sidney knew her time was short. There was very little that she could ask her to draw things out. It was now or never.

"What did you mean when you said you've killed for Jeremy before?"

Grace started to laugh, a long, cackling eruption from the base of her throat. No horror movie that Sidney had ever seen could possibly have duplicated the maniacal laughter of the truly insane. It was chilling.

"Everyone thought that Uncle Joshua committed suicide. Mother wondered and doubted, but no one ever really suspected a thing. You couldn't even figure it out. I did it. I did it alone."

Sidney recoiled. The outburst was entirely unexpected.

"Why in God's name would you do such a thing?" Sidney whispered, stunned.

"My mother never, ever knew what Uncle Joshua – her brilliant artist brother – did to Jeremy. But I knew. Jeremy told me that Uncle Joshua's sailing partner had fondled him and kept trying to do it again and again, every time they were alone together. Well, I took care of that problem, didn't I? Just like I'm going to take care of you." Grace steadied her hand, pointing the barrel right at Sidney's chest.

"But why would you kill Joshua for something his sailing partner did to Jeremy?" Sidney asked, genuinely mystified. "Joshua didn't do anything."

"Yes, he did. I trusted Joshua to take care of Jeremy. But he didn't. He was negligent. Jeremy was molested by Joshua's best friend. That made Joshua responsible and I told him so right before I forced him to hold the gun to his head."

"How? How did you get him to do it, Grace?"

"It was easy. He let me, his beloved niece, into his apartment without even a question. I had on latex gloves and my gun was trained on him the entire time. I told Joshua to find his own gun and sit at the kitchen table. Then I told him to pick his gun up and put it against his temple. The barrel of my gun was against the back of his head. I only helped him to pull the trigger. Just a few pounds of pressure. It wasn't murder. It was justice."

Sidney was frozen; her mind a daze. If she didn't try to escape now, she knew she would die. Don't think, Sid. Act. Suddenly, she ducked and threw herself bodily right at Grace's stocky middle. Her right shoulder slammed into Grace's solar plexus, just underneath the gun barrel, knocking the wind out of her. They both went down with a heavy thud, Sidney rolling off of Grace's corpulent body chest-first into the gravel with her hands still tied behind her back. As Grace's right arm flailed upward, she got off an ear-splitting shot just over Sidney's head. The dark became Sidney's friend as both women scrambled to get to their feet. Sidney lunged away from the edge of the pit but tripped and started sliding down a steep embankment. Grace recovered the flashlight, shining it wildly in every direction, searching for her victim, the gun still gripped in her right hand. Sidney grimaced from the intense pain of rolling over and over on gravel and rock. She kept sliding and rolling further away from her pursuer, landing face-first on the top of the gravel mound. Cringing with pain, she forcibly flipped over onto her knees and struggled to get upright. She couldn't see anything around her. The moonlight didn't penetrate that deeply into some of the pits and Sidney was as disoriented as if she had fallen to the bottom of a well.

Somewhere above her, Grace was desperately searching for her. Sidney could hear the crunching gravel and saw the intermittent frenzied light beams flashing all around her. The light suddenly caught her eyes directly, blinding her. Sidney fell back on her knees again to make herself less of a target and rolled away, as one of Grace's bullets hit and sparked on the rocks close by. She scrambled upright again and ran as fast as she could in the dark with her hands still bound and her knees and elbows bruised and burning. Within ten yards, she tripped and fell again, rolling downhill out of control for another few yards to where her head struck a boulder with blinding pain.

Darkness descended. Sidney never heard Matt yelling at Grace to drop the gun, never saw Grace's startled face, never saw Matt take the shot when Grace leveled her gun in the direction of his voice and never saw Matt's bullets hit his target twice in her chest. Sidney never saw Grace's body fall backward into the yawning pit a hundred feet below, rolling and landing within a couple of feet of where Sidney lay unconscious and still.

27.

"You missed all the excitement," Sidney heard Jack's baritone voice as her eyelids fluttered. She struggled to stay conscious, but it was hard. She wanted to sleep.

"Morphine," Jack informed her. "For the pain you would otherwise be feeling from several broken ribs, a ton of bruises, and a slightly cracked skull."

Sidney struggled to open her eyes. Jack sat by her side right next to her on her hospital bed.

"Grace," she whispered.

"Yes, we know. By the way, you'll have to be interviewed by the D.A. and the judge if we're going to get the case dismissed against Jeremy. In a week or so, you'll need to have your deposition taken. Until then, you'll need to rest."

"Rest," Sidney agreed, her eyes fluttering closed again.

"By the way, Matt Dunleavy was your knight in shining armor. He shot Grace to keep her from killing you."

"Grace. Dead?"

"That's right. And a lot of people around here are feeling pretty foolish right about now. Even me. The only person who can hold their head up in this town after this fiasco is my young partner, Sidney Dietrich."

Jack's words echoed in Sidney's brain, but she was having difficulty understanding.

"Partner?"

"That's right. It won't take you seven years to make partner around here, Sid. We make brilliant young lawyers partners immediately, especially if they're willing to lay down their lives for their clients. But Sid," whispered Jack softly, next to her ear, "Please, please don't do it again. You're my only goddaughter – and I want some grand-godchildren someday. So, promise you won't scare me like that ever, ever again."

"Promise," Sidney whispered back, seeking Jack's hand with her bandaged one. She closed her eyes and fell asleep again, exhausted by the effort. She hadn't noticed Matt standing on the far side of her hospital room, leaning in the doorway, looking as if he hadn't slept in several nights; his shoulders sagging with relief when Sidney surfaced to consciousness, even momentarily.

*****

Before the week was up, Sidney gave her deposition in her hospital room. Her memory was still fuzzy, and her head hurt like blazes. The neurologist, Dr. Peterson, monitored the proceedings and insisted on taking a break every ten minutes. Sidney went over every detail that she could remember, from the time she realized that Grace might be implicated by her timeline and the vernal pool's proximity to Grace's physical therapist's office in Lake Camanche to her hours in the shack when she was bound, blindfolded and gagged, to her terrifying escape in the quarry at night, until she was knocked unconscious. She told them about Grace's disclosure of the logistics surrounding Selena's murder, how Jeremy was never implicated at all, and how, surprisingly, Grace had confessed to Joshua Morgan's death and finally, her belief that Selena and Jeremy's baby was alive.

Jack, Judge Kelso, and D.A. Rich Rodoni were uncharacteristically quiet throughout and the court reporter could barely contain her visible shock at every new revelation.

"That will be all, ladies and gentlemen. I hope you have everything you need for now because my patient is exhausted and needs to rest. If you have any other questions, they'll have to wait," Dr. Peterson ordered.

Jack looked at the judge and the D.A. They looked back, nodding in agreement.

"I think we have enough to close this case," the D.A. announced.

The judge agreed.

"Let's adjourn for today. We'll dismiss the indictments tomorrow on the record and let the jury go home." As they were leaving, Jack leaned over and kissed Sidney's bandaged forehead.

"Great job, Sid."

Sidney grabbed his hand and looked up at Jack pleadingly.

"Maude?" she asked, using one word to describe a multitude of questions and concerns pertaining to Maude Hill: Grace's death, Jeremy's exoneration, and news of a possible grandchild that still might or might not be in Mexico.

"Trust me, Sid. I'll take it from here."

Sidney closed her eyes and sank into oblivion. She was not used to letting go but she had no choice. Everything in her world was now officially out of her hands. The only thing she could do was sleep. And sleep she did.

Epilogue

The day Sidney returned to her office, the local sign designer was etching "McGlynn & Dietrich" into the glass on the front door and stenciling the same name change on the signpost to the building itself, with "Attorneys at Law" underneath. Marjorie squealed with joy at the sight of Sidney, still thin from hospital food and a bit weak, still troubled by occasional vertigo and piercing headaches. She led her into her office with a firm grip on her elbow, as if Sidney had forgotten which office was hers in the intervening few weeks. Phone messages from well-wishers around the county were piled high, as were any number of Hallmark cards wishing her to Get Well and Get Better Soon. As she sorted through it all with increasing surprise that so many people seemed to care, Jack strode in with great excitement and plopped down in Sidney's only client chair.

"Well, it's about damned time you got back. So. Do you want to find out what's been going on in your case in your absence?"

Sidney nodded. Jack was looking supremely pleased.

"Matt Dunleavy was instrumental in recovering Jeremy's baby. He volunteered to fly down to Mexico City and confront the doctor at the clinic. She broke down immediately, admitting that the baby had been born early, and that she had lied because Selena had given the baby to her to raise. Until Matt's visit, she hadn't known anything about the father, and ever since then, she's been torn by guilt. She was more than willing to give the baby back in exchange for not being charged with kidnapping and thrown into a Mexican jail. She signed the consular papers and Matt brought the baby back."

Sidney's eyes grew big. "Alone?"

"No, thank God. Maude had one of her nurses fly with him to take care of the baby if Matt was successful in persuading the doctor to do the right thing. That baby screamed bloody murder throughout the entire flight, so it's a good thing."

"How's Maude taking Grace's death?"

"Philosophically, I'd say. She knew Grace wasn't right ever since the car accident. She doesn't blame Matt for her death; she's just deeply relieved that Grace didn't go through with her plan to kill you. She said to tell you she's sorry she cut your investigation into Joshua's death short, but Jeremy had warned her that if you pursued it, someone close to her could be hurt, and she was afraid it might be Jeremy. By the way, Jeremy's a changed man since he learned he's a father. You should have seen his face when Matt got out of the car with the nurse and the baby. He and Maudey both cried buckets. I think that baby's giving them both a new lease on life. Jeremy's getting plenty of help and Selena's family has moved back into their old cottage so they can be close to the baby. They're overjoyed. Everyone is."

"Is the baby a boy or a girl?" Sidney asked.

"A boy. And you'll never guess what his name is."

Sidney waited for a heartbeat.

"Jack. Jack Hill. Ain't life grand? I've got a goddaughter and now, I have a godson."

Sidney smiled delightedly and then looked around at her desk and her flowers.

"Are there any other... messages? From anyone else?"

Jack McGlynn looked at his god-daughter.

"Only a million. Every day. Begging me to have you call him the minute you showed up. Matt Dunleavy's driving me crazy, so you'd better call him before he calls me again. I swear. You'd think that guy was in love."

Sidney's eyes suddenly filled with tears. Jack looked horrified as Sidney started sobbing.

"I haven't heard from him. I haven't seen him. I didn't think..."

"Oh, for God's sake, Sid. The man's been crazy busy winding things up in this case, flying to Mexico and back, and then waiting for you to recover. He's not the kind that'll shove himself forward for you to notice him. Half of Marjorie's post-it messages are from him. Call him, for God's sake, and then get back to work."

Jack feigned irritation and stomped out of Sidney's office. Sidney looked through a stack of hitherto unnoticed post-it notes and smiled broadly as she sorted through message after message from Matt. She stared at the phone for thirty seconds, breathed in deeply, picked up the receiver and dialed Matt's number. Two rings, and then she heard his voice answer.

"Hey, it's me," she said. "I owe you a dinner. Remember?"

*****

Billy sat on his sagging front porch stoop. In the weeks before, he had watched the trail of Sheriff's cars travel in and out of the Hill place with lights spinning. In his heart of hearts, he was glad that trouble had visited that family, for what they had done to him. He could never prove it, but he knew his motorcycle crash was no accident. The old bag in the wheelchair had screamed at him more than once to stop the noise from his Harley, whenever she traveled the road adjacent to his property in her green van. Just to shove it in her face, he had revved that hog's engine as loud as he could while popping wheelies up his dirt drive. Except for that night a few years ago, when he'd come back from shooting pool. It was dark and he gunned his engine to hit 70 up the road, just to wake the old bitch up. He didn't know what hit him. He never remembered what happened, but he had been airlifted out by emergency crews to the hospital in Sacramento, where they had saved his life, but left him with angry red welts and scars all over his body. He'd never been right in the head after that. It took a year or more for him to walk. He'd tried gimping his way up and down his road to gain strength in his legs, even though the pain was a bitch. That's when he'd found it. A line of 8-gauge wire tied around an acacia tree. He'd picked it up and stretched it across the road to a tree on the other side, right where they told him his crash had taken place. He never knew what had happened the night that Selena had disappeared. But he could guess.

He knew now that the crone in the wheelchair had waved her down that night. Through his camouflage screen of dense oleander, he had seen Selena stumble away from the main house. He remembered that the sky had darkened as thick clouds threatened rain. Over the days and months, he had watched for her whenever he knew that she was home. So young. So beautiful. He could get lost watching her, forgetting his own torn and scarred body in the pleasure of the curve of her cheek, the flounce of her dark hair, and the sound of her laugh. He didn't deserve her, of course. No one did. Especially not him. Pale-faced Jeremy. Near the house, he had heard the raised voices, the harsh, guttural accusations, and the girl's plaintive cries. He saw her run to reach her battered red Honda. She had popped open the trunk and thrown a backpack into the void, slamming it shut as quickly as she could. She had jerked the driver's door open to slide across the worn seat, breathing hard. Spatters of rain had hit the windshield, turning into muddy rivulets dripping down the dirty glass. Cold drops had traced down Billy's pockmarked cheeks like tears, but he hadn't cared. He'd seen her through her car window gripping the steering wheel tightly as she leaned her forehead against the worn leather cover. He had burned with the urge to break through his hiding place to help her. But he couldn't reveal himself. Not ever. The car had lurched forward, crunching gravel as the windshield wipers slapped muddy smears into coffee-colored arcs.

The little red car had rolled farther down the driveway until the tail-lights flashed as her tires bit into wet gravel. Why was she stopping? He strained to see. Just then, he had heard voices that startled him coming from the other side of the hedge near the vineyard rows. He didn't want to get caught again. The humiliation of past encounters while watching her burned his cheeks red in the cold air. He had turned away and abruptly ducked through the bushes as she stopped in the road. It never occurred to him that she would not come back. The last thing he remembered was seeing her brake lights as she stopped on the road. It was the last he ever saw of her.

Billy took another sip of Rolling Rock. He promised himself he'd watch her son grow and keep him safe, even if he had failed his mother. Everyone else might want to forget what had happened. But he never would. His chest felt crushed with a pain that would never go away. Tears rolled down his pockmarked cheeks. "Selena," he whispered. "Selena."